BLOOMING AFTER THE BLAZE
Three Years on The Run

Library of Congress cataloging-in-publication data has been applied for

BLOOMING AFTER THE BLAZE, Three Years on the Run

ISBN: 979-8-9918618-9-2 hardback

ISBN: 979-8-9918618-8-5 paperback

ISBN: 979-8-9918618-7-8 kindle

Cover Art done by Jamie Lee Carrie

THE BANKSIA FLOWER

This book is dedicated to my beautiful children.

For Kristi M, Lee & Kimberly M, Riyaz & Alaa. For the family I've lost, and for those who still choose to remain in my life.

~And to the reader. Don't ever forget how magnificent you truly are.

A NOTE FROM THE AUTHOR

There are species of plants that only exist because of severe trauma. Plants whose seeds must experience the extreme heat of fire before they will germinate.

PYROGENIC OBLIGATE FLOWERING is the fire adapted trait that is defined by an ability to flower only after a fire event, such as a forest fire.

There is a high variation in the length of time between when a fire occurs and when pyrogenic flowering is triggered, and it is species specific. Some flowering does not occur until up to a year post fire, whereas in extreme cases, flowers can emerge just hours after. Some seeds have been known to lay dormant for up to one hundred years waiting for a fire to cross their path, signaling them to open and sprout in the freshly burned-clean dirt.

Precise physiological triggers for pyrogenic flowering have not been heavily studied, but from what is known, some suggest, stimuli of pyrogenic flowering, such as their surroundings/environment, soil, sun, etc. influence the rate or time of bloom.

*WIKIPEDIA, GOOGLE

Maybe some people are like this species of plant. Just maybe some of us can only reach our full potential and become our truest beautiful form after a catastrophic event...or two; or many.

I'm not sure, but what I do know is that I feel a kinship with these special blooms. I understand the process. I'm sure I would not be where I am today without so much tragedy, or things that were simply out of my control.

Cheers to the resilient ones of any species.

PROLOGUE

My name is Jamie. The names in this story have been changed, but I am choosing to keep my own.

The year is 2020. I'm currently sitting Indian-style on my floor in a small flat in Giza, Egypt.

To my left is a double bed covered in an old, well-used plaid blanket. The window at the end of the room is open with traditional wooden shutters propped back to let in the evening breeze, and my hand-washed laundry is hanging on a line I've managed to string just inside the frame. I have simple and sparse furnishings, which is common for the area.

Two antique chairs sit against the main wall, which I imagine have been reupholstered countless times. At present, they are rocking a 1980's vibe with dark, rich floral fabric in shades of blue and burgundy. The only other furnishing being a small round plastic table, an end table, and a rather large armoire.

I can hear the neighborhood. Voices of children playing just five stories below in the alleyway, where they live in a makeshift outdoor home with their parents. Horns from traffic are sounding almost on cue every few minutes. Tuk-tuks and a wide variety of automobiles and motorbikes are trying to make their way home.

The smell of Egypt is so strong. I could be led blindfolded into this country, not having a clue before arriving where I was going, but after two minutes in the thick of a neighborhood at dinner time, I would know exactly where I was. The scents are all their own.

The heavy smell of cardamom that laces the coffee lingers in the air all hours of the day and in every single crevice of this country. Mixed with shisha, it wafts up from cafes and food stalls below.

Egyptian men sit in those shops and relax after their long workday, or for breaks and meals in between. You can walk along any street and find them young and old, in business suits or traditional Egyptian attire, having a cigarette or smoking shisha, drinking their coffee or tea, and playing backgammon or dominoes. It is how they end their day and start their day, and I suspect it's how they stay connected to one another.

Most times, I find myself sharing the road with a camel or a horse-drawn carriage. Vegetable and fruit stands are set up a few yards from one another down each and every street. Fresh bread is baked all through the day by the area bakers, and their goods are on display from 5 a.m. until 12 p.m., three hundred sixty-five days of the year.

There is always music playing. Old style, more of a soulful opera sound, and the newer, funky dance genre that is definitely the most unique that I've ever encountered. The best way to describe it would be snake charmer meets 1970's disco—loud, thumping base included. It feels like I have my own theme song as I walk around any town here.

These people are proud of their country and do everything with passion and consistency. It's felt in every single pizza, shawarma, or cup of coffee they make. The food is a wide variety of local cheese, meats, pasta, and bread. Recipes and methods of cooking that have been passed down for hundreds, if not thousands, of years. There is no lack of culture here, and the wonderful smell of their traditional food is traveling into my window as I write, and it is absolutely intoxicating.

To my right is a small kitchen, just big enough to hold a small stainless-steel sink and table with a portable gas stovetop. It's where I cook all of my meals. I barely have space to turn around in there, and so my refrigerator must sit in my living room. My bathroom is just inside the apartment door, and I do enjoy hot water, which is not always the case here.

This is what my home in Egypt consists of, and it's honestly all I want and all that I need.

Egyptians are a bit guarded by nature. The atmosphere feels as if they are stuck in the 1950s. If it were not for cell phones and the newer model automobiles, it would be impossible to tell exactly what year it is.

Many things that are deemed acceptable here would not be accepted in most other cultures. For instance, some coffee shops are *just for men*. I mean, I could go in them with a man and sit, but definitely not alone. The same gender rules apply at the local gyms.

Just one of the many things that still has me shaking my head—even after six months.

English is not commonly spoken here except inside of the tourist areas. Even there, it's a hit-and-miss. They are only loaded with enough English to get the point across, and that's enough for them. They even take pride in their Arabic language.

For a girl such as myself, who at some point started walking around narrating my own life every minute of every day, it is proving difficult to adequately describe the true feeling of this country. So, I will explain in more depth as I go and let you create a picture for yourself.

I have a story. A story I feel I must tell. I hope it reaches people who can learn from it or—at the very least—can relate.

This is a story of how, at fifty-one years of age, damaged, alone and on the run from the law, I ended up traveling the world and living abroad. It's a story of mistakes as well as healing. It is a tale of survival, acceptance, new balance, and learning to find and live with my own truth—past and present.

I am better at writing fiction, and I wish I could be satisfied investing my time and energy into work resembling old timeless classics. Like Jane Eyre or Pride and Prejudice. One of those great literary masterpieces with lovable characters and a wonderful happy ending. I'd rather write a trashy romance novel or a beautiful love story with a hero who saves the day. But if I do that, I know I'll never get relief or stop writing my own story in my head.

Day after day, year after year, I add content, rephrase, and retell my life's story that never gets put down onto paper; only retold over and over in my own mind. I know this is what I need to do and now I want to do it.

It's not a work of fiction, and I won't get the usual thrill I get from writing a made-up story from my imagination. The excitement of being able to change the outcome or mold a tale or character will be lost to me, while I relay to you this very real one. It's my story.

I am confident it will calm my mind to finally reveal it all. Hopefully it will have a result like nothing else that I've tried.

CHAPTER 1

I was born in the United States of America, in Dallas, Texas, in 1968, to blue-collar parents, whose marriage was already in trouble. I was the birth that sent the relationship over the edge.

My brother Ricky was born four years before me. My sister Kelle followed two years later. Both being the pride and joy of my father. Two years after her, I was born. I was the surprise child that my father was not ready for and never really could accept. I'm not saying he didn't try a few key times in my life, but we never had a connection.

It was always strained and awkward between him and me. No matter how hard either of us tried to bridge the gap or form a relationship—we just never could. I always fell short of my father's expectations, and I looked and behaved too much like my mother for him to ever get comfortable with me. It isn't anyone's fault, really. We were just too different.

My mother, Charlotte, was a beautiful woman. She was the kind of person who had a solution for everything and could take over a room in a matter of minutes. She was strong. She was magnetic. People were always drawn to her. She was a cheerleader and the homecoming queen of our town. She wore the confidence and pride that came with those accomplishments in her personality and deep into her soul the rest of her life. Even now.

She stood 5'6 with a perfect hourglass figure, the kind Marilyn Monroe sported. Green eyes, shoulder-length brown hair, and enough sex appeal for ten women. Even as a little girl, I watched men fall all over her and women get jealous. The women adored her as well; they just didn't want their husbands to look at her the way all men did. They saw her as competition even when she was not interested in competing. Men definitely sensed the strength she had and just couldn't help being attracted.

But Charlotte's beauty was not all she had to offer. My mom was, and still is, one of the most talented artists I have ever known.

She excelled at everything she set her mind to. She was a painter of anything she could see or conjure in her head. Her oil paintings were outstanding; she was once on the local news as a featured artist.

As a kid, I was in awe as I watched on our television while she sat there in her 1970's tan polyester dress suite being interviewed, and showing off her latest work.

It was a copy of the old master's picture, "The Hay Wain," an oil painting that hung in my grandparent's home for years. My grandfather used to sit and smoke his pipe and stare at that painting. The placement on the wall across from the couch was intentional on his part.

He wanted to be able to admire her work whenever he chose to with ease, which he did often. He was her biggest fan and most difficult critic, and he adored that painting.

He used to say that with that work, my mother had achieved what most artists spend their lives trying to accomplish. He considered it perfect. It really is flawless.

Charlotte was a perfectionist, to say the least. She spent so much of her life getting better at everything. Long after she had mastered any particular talent, she would surprise all of us with yet another one. With more knowledge and just as much flair and perfection at whatever she made her new interest.

Whether she was painting, writing poetry or short stories, sewing, starting and running a company, baking, or planning and building a house from the foundation to the dry wall, she excelled. She failed at nothing.

Oh, and to hear her sing! She could sing better than most professional singers. She sounded like Patsy Cline, or a female version of Elvis. Strong and clean with just a touch of soul and rasp. To this day, she still has that gift.

Another wasted talent that she did not dare to dream of or pursue. Instead choosing to marry for love and raise her three children.

Yes, my mom was the whole package. It was beautiful the way she would just decide to do a thing and then accomplish it. Grandfather used to call her a jack-of-all-trades and master of none. He said this jokingly because he was more than proud of her abilities and considered her a master in more than one category.

Like so many people that have known my mother, I am envious of all of the talents and skills she possesses.

With that said, I have to say that it was also pretty difficult to grow up around that level of achievement, for obvious reasons.

I did not inherit her abilities, and although I was constantly trying to mimic her and all that she did, I failed miserably, but I never stopped trying. I can still hear her telling me words of wisdom whenever I take on something new. Especially painting. She would say,

"Paint what you see, not what you think you see." A sentence that still echoes in my mind when I'm holding a paintbrush or pencil.

I realize now that I wouldn't trade her for another. I made great use of her abilities—all of them. More times than I can count, she sat up late to help me with school art projects, writing assignments, or gifts for friends, family, or teachers.

She made curtains for my first apartment and taught me how to use the sewing machine so that I could make my own after I was married.

She sewed many Halloween costumes for us when we were growing up and for my children after they were born. She made baptism gowns, wedding gowns, baby blankets, and quilts. As well as China dolls and Christmas ornaments for our tree. There was, and is nothing she couldn't and wouldn't do for us. If we were happy, she was happier. I feel lucky to have had that kind of talent to look up to and experience.

I don't remember much about my father, Gary. Shortly after I was born, my mother and he got a divorce. I don't have anything bad or positive to say about him. He was a man small in stature, but strong in personality. When he was young, he was handsome and worked hard. I inherited his smile and dimples, as well as his olive complexion. My brother and sister were wild about him, and they were all very close.

My mother and he just couldn't get along.

Two very strong personalities with different ideas of what life should be and what they should strive for. Like so many marriages in that time period, they cut their losses and walked away absolutely hating each other. To this day, they just don't have nice things to say about one another or their time together.

Sometimes, I suppose, pain is just too great to ever reconcile or forgive enough to put behind you. This was the case with them.

The last I heard; he'd sold all of his used car lots, retired successfully with his wife of the last forty-or-so years, and bought some property and land where he built a grand house to live out his life— *and that is that*.

My mother did get remarried. She married my stepfather when I was just a little girl. I would have to asked her exactly when; I was too small to remember. I only know that he was always there. All memories from my childhood include Wess. I don't recall any time in my life that he wasn't around.

He was handsome, and he was a hard worker. An ex-navy man turned long-haul truck driver who was gone for weeks at a time. Which seemed to suit them and their marriage just fine since my mother was extremely independent and best when left to her own devices.

I suppose my childhood days passed like everyone else's. I have fond memories of frequent camping and fishing trips on the weekends when he was home. We would load up the truck and go to the Galveston coast, or Padre Island. Most summers were spent at the lake every weekend. Others were spent at different speedways or racing tracks. Wess was a hobby drag racer. A very good one. Our living room walls were adorned with several of his trophies.

Holidays were always a huge deal for my mom and were celebrated pretty extravagantly. Thanksgiving, Christmas, Easter, Halloween, the fourth of July, and birthdays were all days of the year that we really just spent the rest of the year preparing for and looking forward to.

At the end of one holiday, she would often be discussing plans and a menu for the next. If there was a reason to celebrate or get together with all of her sisters and the rest of that side of the family, we did. Even now, when I think back, so many of the things in my life are correlated or remembered in conjunction with a holiday. Like,

"Oh yeah, I remember that, because that was the year I got a bicycle from Santa Clause." Or, "That was the year it snowed on Easter."

My mother spent countless hours of planning and cash to ensure that she was creating great memories for us. I can still remember and actually smell our home at Christmas time if I linger for a few minutes on a certain memory.

The real tree that she always had to have. The way she spent days decorating it. It always looked like a tree from the front cover of Better Homes and Gardens magazine. Packages were wrapped to perfection with foil wrapping and homemade velvet bows. She sat for hours wrapping our gifts and making them special and beautiful. Anyone who received a gift from her would absolutely hate opening and destroying the wrapping! They were just too lovely to take for granted.

The weeks before December 25th were spent in the kitchen making Christmas cookies, candies, pies, chocolate fudge, and treats. She took pride in her baking, and that time of the year was a perfect occasion to showcase her gift and knowledge of all things sweet and delicious. It was a truly wonderful part of my childhood.

If it were not for some unforeseen, life-altering events, it would have been pretty perfect, I suppose. But it's life, and we are all just kind of at the universe's mercy when it comes to luck.

Some things just go beyond the consequences of our own actions. Some things just happen, with no rhyme, reason, or way to make sense of them, and sometimes we're just the casualties of someone else's internal war or wrong choice.

Events that can happen in a split second that we are left to deal with however we can at that moment, with no real way to ever understand it.

Often, we aren't equipped to face things at the time in our lives that they *actually* happen, and so we spend years damaged by what we can never quite get a handle on or heal from. We are only humans, and some things are impossible to understand or compartmentalize.

We are given a life. It's not a good or bad life to begin with; it is just a life; a beginning. It's what we do with it and how we juggle and adjust to things that happen to us—and around us—that influence it and make it what it becomes.

With my family, we were never the greatest in our decision-making skills. I would insert an *LOL* here if I were writing this on my phone—a behavior I've adopted when things are a little too real or painful to write or think about.

I'm not laughing though, and the very parts of my story that need to be told are the sections of my life that are the most painful; parts I have not addressed. All of the stories I will tell you are events that have had a huge impact on how many of the later things came about. I must try and include all of it.

A few of those unexpected events define my childhood. For me, they don't just define my childhood but had such an impact that they molded who I am as an adult. Fleeting moments in history really, but events that I would spend most of my young adult life trying to make sense of, or even now, trying in vain to sort through.

Things that overshadow anything good in most instances. Happenings that are still quite difficult to see past, or in many cases, are still very raw.

When thinking about writing my story, I had to realize and come to grips with the fact that, at fifty-one years old, I would have to relive some of the most hurtful and confusing times in my life. The last forty years, I've chosen not to address or even discuss some pretty serious stuff.

That ends now.

CHAPTER 2

My family lived on a quiet, middle-class street in the suburbs. It was beautiful, really. The road made a Y, splitting off into two directions that ended at the same main road.

Cute a-frame houses with manicured lawns and huge trees that created shade in the hot summer. A perfect place for birds to dwell. I can still hear them and the locus in my mind. They were a constant buzz in and around our homes, and our area always smelled of honeysuckle and magnolias. Everybody knew everybody.

We had aunts, great aunts, and uncles that lived on our street. At the end of our side, the last house on the block was where my Mimi and Pawpaw lived—my biological father's parents.

The two giant magnolia trees were in their front yard and loaned their fragrance to the whole area. My favorite playmate, Misty, lived just past the Y. She is my cousin and my only lifelong friend.

A train track ran right behind and along our road. After many years of living there, I stopped hearing that train; even though it was so loud, it vibrated the glass in the windows as it made its way through our area multiple times throughout the day and night. When we did finally move, I couldn't sleep. I was too used to hearing that train. I still love the sound of trains making their way down a track; it calms me.

There was an abundance of kids on our block. The children of our generation were the ones who had to be home when the street lights came on and were watched by all of the adults in the neighborhood—relation or not—living within a mile or two. If one of us misbehaved, by the time we got home, our parents already knew the details of what we'd done, and we were in for it! It was a wonderful time to be a kid. We didn't really worry about abduction, robberies, drugs, or molestations.

Not to say that they weren't happening at the time; it just wasn't a constant concern as it is now. It was not common enough for us to be made aware of.

It was simple summer days of chasing the ice cream truck down the road, riding our bicycles, and playing in sprinklers. We collected glass Coca-Cola bottles and turned them in the local grocery store for change to get some candy or soda. We left our homes when the sun came up and returned only for lunch, and again just before the sun set.

As children, we didn't want to be inside. After school and weekends, you could be sure that we were outdoors. Summer nights were spent playing freeze tag or catching fireflies. We all gathered at the house that had the brightest gas lamp in the yard, and that happened to be our house. The place where everyone chose to hang out and play.

My family, and extended family, owned homes all around us, and made sure we were never hungry. These were older generation southern women who spent their days shelling peas or making homemade cornbread and beans. We got fed all day, every day.

It felt like a safe environment. They all had the mentality that it took a village to raise a child, and it seemed to work. We knew how to act, and our respect for our elders was unwavering.

Every now and then, I needed a babysitter. Whether it was because my mom needed to work and Wess was gone, or on rare occasions, they would go out together. My usual babysitter was Nina.

Nina was my biological father Gary's cousin. My Mimi's niece. She was about nine years older than my brother and was very close to us. Throughout my life as a child, she lived in our house. I adored her. She was so beautiful with her big, almond-shaped, bright blue eyes and her thick, almost black waist-length hair. She was like an extra mom, really. She taught me how to bake cookies and treated me so sweet. She even let me brush and play with her hair. I do not ever remember her not being around in my younger years.

Nina was lesbian. During a time that it was not in any way accepted and was, in fact, actually treated as a perversion. We lived in the Bible Belt of Texas during a time that these things were just not acknowledged, and definitely not tolerated. If it was discussed, it was behind closed doors.

If it was a member of your family who professed to have these feelings, they were either disowned or put into a mental ward. Sometimes, they had self-professed homosexuals taken to jail on trumped-up charges, or even kidnapped and taken to a religious "camp" in some crazy effort to pray the gay out of them.

I was a little girl. I had no idea what gay meant. I only knew that I loved Nina, and she was kind to me.

Anyway, she became a point of contention in our family after my mom married Wess. He was not okay with her being around.

The folks in my neighborhood would sit around and talk about how awful and irresponsible it was of momma to have her around us. I heard those discussions.

They had no problem talking about it around me because they knew I didn't understand. Looking back, it just seems so ridiculous to me that they acted as if we could *catch homosexuality,* and even now it breaks my heart to talk about the bigotry. What she must have gone through at that time in history had to have been soul-crushing.

Nina was a warrior. From what I understand, she'd even gotten engaged to be married to a man at one point, to appease her parents. She called it off later to choose living in truth over the lie. With all of the awful complications that entailed. I admire her greatly for that. She was so damn strong.

Later, Nina was my sunshine in an otherwise scary world of constant change and confusion. She was my friend, caregiver, and protector. One of the few consistencies I can remember in my life. I trusted her like no other person throughout my teen years, but for that period of time, she was pushed out of our lives by persons that just didn't understand her lifestyle or know her. They were afraid of what they didn't know. So, she went away. One day, she was simply gone.

I went years that I thought she'd left on her own and just didn't love me enough to come back. I didn't find out until much later what it was about.

When she left, I had no one to confide in. I had no one to trust. It would be something that would have immediate ramifications in my little life.

After she was gone, my caregivers changed to two teenage girls who lived in a house right in the middle of our block, almost directly across from our house.

Their house was always in disrepair; the lawn never mowed, and trash never taken out. Their house smelled of weed, dog and cat urine, and, on good days, incense.

They would often throw loud parties in their backyard, with their ten-foot weatherbeaten fence to keep out prying eyes.

Patsy and Peggy. They were the hippies of the street. With their bellbottom jeans and long hair, and rock and roll music. Their brother Matt played the drums, and you could hear him beating on those things all over the neighborhood, at all hours of the day and night. He was about nineteen years old, I think, and the girls were just a bit younger. Peggy being the youngest, prettiest, and definitely the sweetest. I'm not entirely sure where their mom was because I never saw her.

I don't know how old I was when it first happened. I have a polaroid picture of me somewhere, taken in their house, on their mom's bed, and I appear to be about four or five years old. I was wearing my favorite sundress. It was white cotton fabric with little yellow daisies and black and yellow bumblebees. It's odd to me that that picture was taken the actual day my world changed.

All of these years later, I can still smell that house.

The day was like any other day. I was told to walk across the street to stay with them so that my momma could go to work. I did as I was told. I walked the short distance to their house with my sundress on and new sandals on my feet.

When I walked into the house that day, it was different. I immediately knew something was off. Even as a little girl, my sixth sense kicked in, and after I knocked on the screen door and was told to come in, I stood there—hesitant. By all appearances, there was nothing that should have made me feel like that. But everything in me told me to run back home. I didn't; I couldn't. I walked in and then just stood there, right inside the doorway.

The curtains were all drawn closed. I remember the dogs were not there to greet me. It was quiet—no music, no television, no dogs barking. Just complete darkness and silence. My eyes had to adjust. When they did, I saw Patsy coming from the kitchen. She instructed me to go with her because she was cooking. I shyly followed.

Peggy was nowhere around. She was the one I knew and trusted. She was the only one I really ever talked to. I realized later that she was not in the house at all.

Patsy grabbed my hand and took me to the dining area.

She was standing at an old avocado green stove, stirring something in a large pot, wearing tiny hip-hugger shorts, a striped tank top, and no bra. Her almost waist-length hair was tangled and stringy, and she looked un-kept; dirty.

Not one single detail of those few hours on that day has left my memory in almost fifty years. Because—you see—I have a photographic memory.

What that means for me is, that if I observe something of interest for any amount of time, I can recall it later as if I am looking at a picture. Not mundane things that are meaningless, but anything I deem important, like, or commit to my memory. If it's a passage in a book that I find interesting, I can recall which side, where on the page, and position in the book. I am not a savant; I can't remember page numbers or details to that extent, just whatever I commit to my picture memory.

At the grocery store, if I get something from a shelf, I will always remember which isle, which row, and how far down, right or left side, etc. It's handy; I count on it a lot in my life. It's also awful.

Long after I want to forget certain things, my photographic memory will still recall them. It's like randomly watching the most horrific parts of a horror film over and over with no way to stop it. I suspect it's why my dreams to this day are so vivid.

I've never been able to turn it off. I have no control over it; it's just part of me. Sometimes it is a good part, and sometimes I consider it horrible. It's my very own personal torture device, installed in my brain and part of my make-up as a human. My *special* gift was at its all-time best that day; I've never been able to shed one detail.

I sat in the dark kitchen on an old chair with silver legs and vinyl seats. A sparkling Formica table in front of me—the kind of table and chairs old diners used to have in the 1950's. It was covered in random stuff. Old newspapers, a sugar bowl, miscellaneous condiments, and used cutlery. Stains and crumbs were everywhere. It was sticky.

My feet were dangling and swinging nervously. The kitchen sink was full of dishes, with flies buzzing around them. Patsy placed a cup of grape Kool-aid in front of me. Even now, I can't stand the smell or flavor of grape kool-aid. Then she leaves the kitchen.

I sat there, drinking my juice, looking around. I heard a male voice coming from the living room. Her brother Matt was home. It had only been a few minutes since she left the kitchen when she called out for me to come into the other room. I hopped down and went.

She was lying on the couch, wearing her tank top, but nothing else. Her knees were up, legs spread. I immediately looked down at the ground. My face flushed hot with embarrassment. I started walking backwards to go back to the kitchen. Matt comes from the hallway and takes me by the arm. He scoops me up, and in one swift move, I am plopped down at the end of the couch that isn't occupied, at Patsy's feet.

I'm unsure and uncomfortable as to where I should direct my eyes, so I watch Matt. He goes to the chair just diagonal from the couch, sits down, unzips his trousers, and pulls out his penis. He starts stroking it slowly and looks directly at me, with a grin on his face.

Tears welled up in my eyes, and spilled over. In my peripheral vision, I could see Patsy moving her hand and arm, but I refused to look up and see exactly what she was doing. I know that no matter what it is, it can't be good.

In an uncharacteristic voice, honey sweet, she says to me,

"We have kittens in the bedroom. If you do what I tell you to do, you can go play with them."

I said nothing. Matt was still stroking himself, but with much more vigor.

She leaned forward, grabbed my shoulders, and pulled me close to her. I was pulling back, but it was no use. She had both of my shoulders and pushed me down to a laying position, on top of her, with my face centered above her nether region, between her legs.

The kindness from a few minutes earlier was gone as she angrily told me what to do through gritted teeth.

I was confused, crying, and scared. Matt moved from the chair and was seated behind me. I don't know when that happened; all I know is that there was no escape. I was trapped. Snot was stringing from my nose, and tears were dripping down onto her mound of pubic hair a few inches from my face.

I don't know how long I was made to please her. It felt like forever. I was coughing and gagging; I don't know how I managed to keep from vomiting. I felt Matt put his hands on my legs and bottom.

My panties remained on but were pushed aside so that his rough fingers could explore my little shaking body.

I was in a trance until I heard a car door slam outside. In seconds, I was left, laying alone on the couch. They'd both run from the room. The front door knob rattled, I heard the key insert into the lock, and the door swung open. In walked Peggy.

I'm sure I looked exactly how I felt, because she threw her purse and bags down and rushed over to comfort me. On her face was one of the strangest looks I have ever witnessed on any person's face. It was a mixture of love, fear, hate, and questions. All wrapped into one.

As I sat up, she sat down beside me. She put her arm around me and pulled me tight. She did *not*, however, ask me what was wrong. She only asked if I was okay.

Patsy, who was clothed once again, leaned against the door frame, watching. Observing intently, listening to hear what I would say. I couldn't immediately look at her, but when I finally did, I saw a look exchanged between the two girls that gives me chills to this day. A look of knowing, and pleading. With that look, it is perfectly clear to me now that I was not their first victim.

Peggy picked me up and took me to her mother's room. There was indeed a box of kittens.

At some point that day, pictures with a Polaroid were taken. Many pictures, but only one was given to me to take home. I gave it to my momma and never said a word.

Even as a child, I knew that if I said something, she would have no one to watch me so that she could go to work. I didn't want to be the source of a problem. I wasn't sure she would believe me and that maybe she would tell them what I said instead of just not making me go there anymore. Really, looking back, I didn't want anyone to know what I'd done. I was ashamed.

What I thought should be obvious to the whole world wasn't. The change in me was immediate. No one questioned why, all of a sudden, I cried and screamed when I had to walk across the street to be watched. Not one soul ever wondered why I started sneaking out of my house late at night, in my pajamas, to walk down the street to my Mimi and Pawpaw's in the dark and sometimes rain or cold. All hours of the night, I walked the long block and knocked on their door. They would let me in, give me juice, and sometimes let me stay the night. Only to return me the next morning. Why didn't anyone ever ask me why I did that?

I started having nightmares, and then bedwetting became a common occurrence. It was a problem that persisted well into my preteen years.

The abuse continued. I don't know how long it lasted, but it's one of the things that blurs my memory of anything else. I don't remember any school, birthdays, or even holidays during that time. I only remember the hell I was living through and the secret I was keeping.

Eventually we moved from that neighborhood, and it finally stopped. The damage was already done. The seed of guilt was planted, and I was used to not having any control whatsoever in my life.

After a while, I just accepted it. Each time, I did what I was told so that I could get it behind me and move on. Each time was worse. The secret ate me up from the inside as a little girl. When people looked at me, I felt they knew what I was doing. I felt alone, and I felt bad. I stopped trusting adults around me and stopped talking. I blamed myself. Somehow, I felt it was my own fault.

That would become a consistent theme in my life. My childhood and teen years were littered with secrets. I got to where I excelled at carrying guilt and shame that was never mine to carry. It became my superpower of sorts. Those years were a precursor. A training time for me to learn techniques to endure and conceal many other things that were in my future that would be much worse.

CHAPTER 3
The New Normal

I feel the need to record the date today. It is March 11th, 2020. It's a beautiful day in Giza. I am on the rooftop of the hostel where I'm staying. I am sitting here, literally a stone's throw away from the great pyramids. At a glance, and if I didn't know any better, it looks like any other day has looked before. It is anything but. We are in the midst of a global pandemic.

I just came back to Giza after two weeks of splitting my time between the cities of Luxor and Hurghada. Two cities that are now infected with the deadly Corona virus. Sixty-nine new infected in Cairo and one death in the span of a few days. The whole world has basically shut down to try and contain this virus. My flight plans are now suspended for an indefinite period of time.

I am prevented from returning to what I now consider my home country, Indonesia, or anywhere honestly. All flights coming or going to any country have been grounded on this side of the world. The news tells the story of America and their panic. This country, as well as all surrounding ones, are just as scared. Many people I know are now quarantined and unsure of their future. I'm concerned for them.

As I write this, it occurs to me that I have not held in my arms anyone that I completely love or that loves me in many years. Not even my own beloved children. This realization is saddening to my soul. I'm sure it's magnified by the fact I am sick. Very sick.

It started when I broke a tooth in Luxor and had to have two separate oral surgeries to extract the remaining tooth and contain the infection. A few days later, I came down with a very high fever. Antibiotics and fever reducers have not helped this in over three weeks. I have a persistent cough; my throats raw, and I can't eat. My natural inclination is to use my common sense.

I just left two very touristy areas. Generally, I don't do what tourists do, but this time I did. I was unsafe in almost every possible way I could have been.

From exploring with tour groups to taking night trains and public transportation. Now I'm faced with the very real possibility of having contracted COVID-19.

"Would you like a cup of tea?" Mohamed asks.

I am wearing his coat. It's unusually cold outside here on the edge of the Sahara for this time of year, and I didn't pack accordingly. He looks at me, waiting for my answer. His face is gentle, showing concern. His eyes are dark brown with a playful spark and some unknown source of strength. I'm sure he hasn't had an effortless life here in Egypt.

He is still patiently waiting for my reply.

"Yes, please." I tell him.

He's not a big man, standing about 5'5, I am guessing. However, he has been gifted with an overabundance of personality. He's been my constant companion since I arrived here. He owns the hostel where I am staying. We know each other, as well as two people can with the language barrier. He is warm and generous and funny. He seems naive to the ways of the world and wears his sweetness like a fifteen-year-old boy. He has professed his love for me, and I'm confused as to why all of my friendships with men end in this predicament.

He comes back with my tea.

As I sit with fever, shivering, sipping my cup of calm, I cannot help but wonder about a few things.

Firstly, I am here alone. People are dying. We aren't even close to containing this. Will I remember today ten years from now if I do survive? Will my family and children survive this? Can I successfully commit to memory the smell in the air? And, mostly, I wonder if it will ever return to the way it was just a few short weeks ago when this is all over.

The sun is setting in its usual glorious fashion. Going down as the great fluorescent orange ball, leaving streaks of yellow and crimson across the sky. Casting a beautiful pink blanket on the whole city, desert, and pyramids. Giving the impression that the buildings are being lit up with neon lighting somehow.

Now that it has completed its nightly ritual, it has disappeared, leaving it dark.

There is no light in the desert, and no people are allowed on the street after the sun is gone. The normal traffic filled streets are virtually empty. There are no busloads of tourists every day converging on the ancient ruins and pyramids. No camels, no horses, mules, tuk-tuks, or cars. The music that usually fills the air twenty-four hours a day, seven days a week, has gone silent. Although there is still the call to prayer five times a day, they have closed the mosques to try and instill social distancing. The sand has taken over, and it fills the air in a thick, smoggy haze over everything.

The pyramids—what I can see of them— are clouded and blurred from real view. When I look down onto the street and happen to spot a human, they are wearing what looks to be "fall-out" gear, just exactly like the video game or a futuristic movie based on the fall of civilization.

It is unreal. It's a weird dream. The only thing clear is the bright north star in the sky, and it makes my mind recall, vividly, the biblical story of how they used the star to find their way.

Everything has changed, seemingly overnight. Nothing is the same. Except for that amazing star. There are no airplanes dotting the airspace, no light pollution, and no dogs barking. The lack of light is blinding. The silence is deafening. No movie, horror story, or book could ever do this scenario justice. I find myself overly grateful for that star.

This is the new face of panic and fear for the human race.

I am sure I join the rest of the world when I say I am frightened.

CHAPTER 4

My mother had a brother. His name was Michael Vance. We called him Vance. My grandparents had him extremely late in life, and he was the only boy out of five children. My aunts and grandparents fell in love with him the second he was born. My grandfather really acted as if the sun rose and set in his son and didn't hide it. They spent countless hours together.

They played tennis, chess, and talked. Some of their chess matches lasted days. They were both such skilled players; they would often play all day and then go to bed and pick up their chess match the next morning where they'd left off. I think they were closer than any father and son I have ever encountered. Maybe because he was born when my grandparents were old enough to truly understand what a blessing any child is, and for them, especially a son.

Possibly because my grandfather was able to pass on so much of his knowledge, and he had so much knowledge to pass on.

Vance always asked questions and was eager to learn everything my grandfather was willing to teach him. Whatever the reason, everyone worshiped Vance. Including my siblings and I.

There were periods of his life he lived with us. He joined us on our vacations and spent most weekends and summers at our house. He was two years older than my brother, six years older than me. He and Ricky were extremely close. We all were.

He was a handsome young man with broad shoulders, a little waist, sandy blonde hair, and blue eyes. He had fair skin and a full mouth that always seemed to hint at a smile. He was quick to laugh. He had a very affectionate nature, and his sisters all doted on him, and he loved them. He was their baby brother in every sense of the word, and he knew it.

For Ricky, Kelle, and me, he was just part of our family. We all viewed him and treated him like another sibling. He never felt or acted like an uncle; he acted like our brother. What I mean is, he did all of the normal horrible stuff to me as a kid that brothers do. As well as some pretty great stuff. I have some of the fondest memories of my childhood because of him.

We used to wait for my parents to leave the house, and we would all play this game called "house climbing." The rules of the game were fairly simple; we had to climb around the whole interior edge of the house without touching the floor. We had a starting point, and we just climbed along the walls or furniture, swung on doorknobs, cabinet doors, or whatever else it took to make it all of the way around each room until one of us made it back to the starting point. It was so much fun! We broke countless lamps and pictures, though. I am not sure we ever told my momma about that game.

The thing I looked forward to the most was the "imaginary trips" he took me on. He would blindfold me and walk me around the house, backyard, and garage. He told me things like,

"Duck, we are going into a cave," or "I have to carry you over quick sand.".

Those trips took me all over the place in my imagination. Mountaintops, rivers, or stairs leading to temples. We encountered wild animals, like tigers and bears, or giant spiders and dragons. I'm not sure how long those little imaginary excursions lasted, but it seemed like hours. They were the most fun of anything else I experienced as a kid. I begged him every single day for those.

Vance was similar to my grandfather in that he was extremely smart. They were both geniuses. So, many things he did as a kid were science experiment type of stuff.

I remember one time he made a huge kite. Did I say huge? I mean massive! He started building the frame in my grandparent's double-car garage, and it covered the whole floor. This caught the attention of my grandfather, and the next thing I knew, they were *both* building a monster kite! Wooden frame and bed sheets. My grandfather kept telling Vance that it would break when the sheet caught the wind, but he still continued to help him.

He was correct. It flew and broke from the first big gust of wind that grabbed it, just like he said it would.

I remember my grandpa, pipe in hand, laughing his soundless laugh with his mouth open, showing his toothless gums. Even though the kite broke, he relished the time he spent with his son making it. He considered it time well spent. They were always involved in one of Vance's crazy projects.

One time, my otherwise very intelligent uncle decided to make a homemade bomb. Yes, a *bomb*. So, he enlisted my brother to help him, knowing my grandpa would disapprove.

They succeeded in making a pipe bomb. But, when Ricky went to light it, he didn't get away from it quick enough, and it blew up in his face. It singed all of his eyebrows completely off and burned his face pretty badly.

Looking back, it seems like Ricky and Vance were constantly in the hospital over their wild ideas.

There was the time they decided to rob a beehive for honey and didn't cover themselves properly. Ricky ended up in the emergency room with a huge face, eyes swollen shut, and almost went into anaphylactic shock.

Then there was the time they cornered a skunk; Vance got bitten and spent weeks getting rabies shots.

Vance broke his leg after deciding to take his telescope onto the roof of the elementary school across from their house and spent two months in a cast. I think it was the only two months in that boy's life that the whole family didn't worry about what he was up to. It was pretty constant with those two.

Sometimes, when they got really bored with all of the normal stuff, they would tell me to run after them. If I could keep up, they would take me along with them. I was a phenomenal runner and always kept up, so they started a new game.

They took me to different spots around our neighborhood, or within a few miles, and put me somewhere they felt I couldn't get down from—or out of. Way up on a carport or tree. Sometimes they locked my legs Indian-style around a post or pole or zip-tied my arms together around a sign or post, then took off running. I had to figure out how to get out of the situation and catch up to them. I got excellent at this! Though sometimes I couldn't get down and I would sit up there for hours, usually crying, until I figured it out. What choice did I have?

They nicknamed me Little Houdini.

On Thanksgiving one year, they tied me between two chairs, facing each other, shoved a sock in my mouth, and left. They assumed I would get out of it like I always did. I was in a back bedroom with the lights off, and that time, I couldn't get myself untied. They ended up forgetting about me, and I cried myself to sleep. I actually missed our holiday dinner. When my mom finally noticed I was missing and found me, she was so mad!

Growing up with Vance and Ricky was an adventure. Even with all of the bad episodes they put me through, I loved both of them very much.

At some point, Vance became different. He came around less and less, and I overheard my momma on the phone discussing him with my grandfather. He was concerned that Vance was using drugs. He was sixteen, had stopped going to school, and had started sneaking out of the house at night. Sometimes he stayed gone all night. My grandparents at up and waited and worried until he returned. His whole disposition changed. He became mean and hateful to everyone. He started getting into trouble with the police and became unpredictable. It was a horrible time for my whole family. He had four sisters who worshiped him, and it really did affect all of us.

No matter what happened in those few years, no matter how much he changed or what he did that was out of character, none of us were prepared for what happened.

I was twelve years old when Vance was murdered. He was shot in cold blood by his best friend in the alley behind my grandparent's home. My stepfather Wess had to identify the body of the young man he had essentially helped raise. Vance was barely nineteen years old. It was my first loss from death, and it was tough.

The pain I felt when I heard made me physically ill. For my mom, it was like losing a son instead of a brother. I was in a fog for weeks; we all were. At my age, death was not something I had faced and never really considered. The finality of it hit me in stages for years to come. I know that my grandparents and momma never got over it.

What we understand now about his senseless death still brings no closure. We know that Vance had decided to get himself clean. He had told my grandfather he needed help. He'd gotten involved with a family in the neighborhood that had close ties with organized crime. His best friend and he both got their drugs from them to sell and use. When he decided to cooperate with the police and the family discovered that he might implicate them, they paid his best friend to kill him.

I am sure there is more to it than that. I'm sure his best friend was just as scared of them as he was. He was caught, tried for murder, and served only seven years. Seven years for taking our beloved Vance from us. Even now, it's impossible to wrap my head around.

As painful as that was, and before we could catch our breath from one tragedy, another followed.

My mom had a good friend named Winnie. She had a son and a daughter. My sister Kelle was best friends with her daughter, Rene. They'd been friends for years. We all spent most of our off-time together. Weekends we all went out to eat or hung at Winnie's house and cooked out. Museums, parks, theme parks, and the state fair. We did pretty much everything together. I got really close to Stephen, her son.

He was my age. Tall, copper skin, green eyes, and athletic. He was the sweetest and most shy boy I knew. I was only nine or so when we met, so after a few years, our families joked about how we would be married someday. I don't remember feeling that way about him, but he was a great childhood friend. Especially since I was not good at interacting with kids my age.

We spent days playing basketball or taking walks. He liked to hear me read books to him, play poker, or we would watch television together. I loved Stephen.

It was a Saturday. We were supposed to be at their home early that day to go to the lake. We were all going to spend the day together. Momma and I had overslept and were trying to get out the door when we got the call.

Stephen had been playing basketball in the mobile home park where they lived. The ball rolled under one of the trailers, and he'd gone to retrieve it. There was an uncovered electric line that he accidentally touched when reaching to get the ball, and he was electrocuted. We met them at the hospital.

He was on life support for some time after the accident. We spent weeks at the hospital in the ICU ward. Taking turns reading to him or holding his very swollen hands.

He was above average in life, standing about 6 ft., but after the accident, he was so swollen he looked like a man twice his normal size. Even at my age, I knew he was gone before the doctors told us there was no brain activity. I would sit there, hold his hand, beg him to wake up, and cry. Losing Vance had taught me the finality and pain of death, and I was scared of it.

Eventually, he was taken off of life support, and a second person we adored was taken from us. It was devastating for me. I just couldn't get over his passing. Weeks of crying, going to see the school counselor, and nightmares.

I still carry guilt over that. Had I been there, I would have been the one to go get that ball. I was always the smallest person playing, and that particular task was left to me in most cases. A fact my mother still recounts when we discuss Stephen.

It was a rough year. One that showed me that there is no promise of a person's lifespan. Stephen was thirteen. Vance was nineteen. I always think of the phrase "only the good die young" when I think of those two. They were both gentle, transparent, and lovely souls that made that part of my life beautiful. I will never forget or stop loving either of them. It was a difficult lesson to learn so early in my life. I think of both of them often and will always miss them. I am grateful to have known and loved them.

It begs the question—Why are we not always living our lives as if we are about to lose our loved ones at any moment?

CHAPTER 5

It seems that once we moved from the neighborhood— away from my abusers— we never stopped. We just kept moving.

The most formattable years of my life, we were in constant upheaval. We moved to apartments, rent houses, mobile homes, and to different states. Some years we attended multiple schools, which made it difficult to build friendships or develop normal relationships. Other than seeing kids in school or around whatever neighborhood we were temporarily calling ours, I spent no real bonding time with anyone.

Sometimes we relocated for Wess's job, sometimes for my mom's. Other times I'm sure it was for financial reasons because there were a few times in between the old and the new places that we stayed with my grandparents. My mom's parents. We were very close to them.

My grandmother and grandfather Lee were always a safe place for me. I adored their house. It was consistent. Except for the occasional new furniture or paint, it looked and smelled exactly the same the whole entire time they lived there.

It was classically elegant, simple, and clean. There were no extra trinkets or anything out of place. My grandfather was extremely obsessive-compulsive and wouldn't tolerate anything untidy. He took comfort in having things stay neat and unchanged. So did I. Their house always smelled of cherry pipe tobacco and coffee.

Most homes were that way from the 1950s to the 1970s. Simple, clean, homey, and never overdecorated. What made theirs unique was my mother's oil paintings in ornate frames that hung in almost every room. From the first picture that she'd painted in high school of a rose and oil lamp, to ones she'd done on velvet of grapes and flowers that hung above the sofa, to the hay-wain. They kept them all.

I loved that house. It felt like home to me. I truly enjoyed visiting my grandparents. They were the most normal and reliable people in my life, to this day.

Eventually, our family ended up settling in the Dallas suburbs, into a three-bedroom apartment when I was ten years old. We lived there longer than any other place that I remember. I was able to establish some real friendships and I attended the same school for a few years. This was where we were living when we lost Vance and Stephen, and it was the only place we ever lived that felt like home.

As a child, and well into my teen years, I always kept the same personality. I was a book lover and didn't like crowds of people. I liked other kids but didn't really know how to act around them. I was expected to act our age, and with my secrets and knowledge beyond theirs, I didn't know how. I always felt outside of the social circle. Which didn't bother me; I enjoyed being alone. I didn't understand people my age. I spent most of my time in my room reading or doing homework, listening to music, drawing elaborate costumes from old movies, or going to my cousin Misty's.

It's safe to say that I have always been a bit socially awkward. Recently, speaking to Misty about it, she said that I enjoy being social, but from the outside. She said I was always happy observing people from a distance but didn't like to be included. I guess she is correct. I'm still this way.

It never once escaped my attention that I was nothing like anyone around me and had absolutely nothing in common with them. Not quirky or emo, but more reserved and unsure of where I was supposed to fit in, or if I was actually supposed to fit in at all. So, I found my adventures in books and learned anything I could get my hands on. Other than having to wake up early, I really enjoyed school.

I recall so many nights in my room, with a flashlight under my covers, reading a book until the sun came up. It made it next to impossible the next day to get up on time. I was still a good student who made high grades. It came naturally for me because I loved to study.

Misty and I were inseparable those years. We attended the same middle school. We spent weekends together, and I went on summer vacation with her family. Nina was her aunt, so they felt like immediate family, and I loved them as such. She was the only functional girl relationship I had then, and we have remained friends. She was always my escape when I needed one, and I never had to pretend to be anyone other than who I was. But I still kept her at arm's length. I kept her just close enough to be best friends, but not too close so that she wouldn't question anything.

I know now, that if there would have been anyone who was safe to tell what had started going on, it should have been her. I just didn't know that at the time.

My brother and sister were always running in and out of our house, going to parties or concerts, or whatever great adventures they were involved in. They'd both stopped attending school, choosing to drop out and speed onto adulthood instead. Whatever I imagined they were doing was probably better than what they were *actually* doing. They were the *cool kids*. The ones everyone knew and everyone wanted to be like.

They enjoyed free reign at that time because my mom was always working at her hair salon, and Wess spent so much time on the road.

Because my family was busy with their own lives and I was too young to have one, it left me alone most of the time. Time at that point ticked by, the way time does with no way to mark it, until another one of life's little perverted curveballs knocked me on my butt.

I remember wondering if that is what God had in store for me the rest of my life. Always having to get accustomed to people with corroded hearts and screwed up moral compasses.

Like I said, I was home a lot by myself, and eventually, so was Wess. In between his cross-country trips, he was home for extended periods of time.

I was twelve and developing like every young lady does. His affection started to change for me, and I started to feel uncomfortable around him. I didn't like being alone with him. Something I couldn't put my finger on at first, but definitely something I needed to keep constant awareness about.

His touching, when my mother wasn't around, became more frequent and sexual in nature. Accidentally brushing my breast or my bottom with his hand. It was unnerving. I would wake with him sitting on the edge of my bed, sometimes kissing my face and neck.

He also began to limit my ability to leave the apartment when he was home. If I asked to go to a friend's house or to the mall or a movie, the answer was always *no*.

When I think back to those years, there are two things I remember the most. The first being what was going on with my stepfather.

Pay attention to the next thing, because the person I am about to introduce to you will be a recurring character in my life. The only person who is still around from my childhood who is not related to me.

I was around fourteen years old. I came in from school one day, and there was a boy standing in our dining room, in between our kitchen and Ricky's room. He was standing there, hands in his jean pockets. Wearing a t-shirt and navy windbreaker. He looked to be about my age, but he was friends with my brother and sister, so I assumed he was much older. I found out later that he was just two months older than me.

I threw my books down on a chair and headed to the kitchen to grab a drink or after-school snack. Ricky said,

"This is my baby sister, Jamie."

I looked at him while I stood there with my glass of tea; our eyes locked, but—for the life of me—I couldn't speak. I tried to say hi, but I couldn't make my mouth and brain work together to manage it. The only time that had ever happened. I just stood there in my awkwardness. Staring into that stranger's eyes, wordless and struggling. My odd reaction had him blushing and smiling. He looked down at his shoes. He too was speechless.

As they got ready to run out the door, he looked up with a grin and a giggle and said, "Hello, and good-bye."

He waved as he walked away. Trailing behind Ricky and Kelle, he turned around at the door and said,

"I'm Jack, by the way!"

And then they left.

Now, listen. I have been analyzing that day for about thirty-eight years, and I still have no clear answer as to why, from the first time I met him, and every time that I've been in close proximity of this guy, I can't speak. He has jokingly said that he thought I was deaf mute the whole time he knew me as a kid, and it is a painful, somewhat embarrassed laugh that escapes my mouth right now as I think about it.

It didn't matter how many times I saw him; it still ended with me red-faced, nervously standing there, struggling to form words.

I have come to a couple of plausible explanations for this. The first one being the old blanket term, *love at first sight.* The second being that maybe it was our souls that had known each other before and just couldn't wrap our brains around meeting again. I'm revealing a bit of the cynical side when I say that I don't believe in either of those things. So, I still have no answer. I learned later that my sister and he had a sexual relationship, and it broke my heart.

Not long after that meeting, my sister got sent to a girl's camp for troubled teens. She was out of control. She'd started some of the bad habits that are still not-so-desirable influences on her life today. Drinking, drugs, promiscuity, you get the point.

My brother moved out of the house to my grandparents initially, and then to his own apartment. He was married soon after and started a family. After Kelle's release from Salesmanship youth camp, she got married also. I was the only child left at home, essentially from the time I was fourteen.

Other than seeing him at my grandparents' house from time to time, it would be many years before I saw their friend Jack again, but I never stopped thinking about him or wondering what he was up to or how he was. I don't think anyone ever forgets their first crush.

One day I came home from school to learn that we were moving *again*. My parents had purchased some property in East Texas and wanted to sell everything and move out there. I was not about to agree to that. I called my absent biological father and moved in with him, his wife and their youngest daughter.

I was miserable. Mainly because my father was never home. Which proved to me, without a doubt, that man did not like me. While I was there, I attended high school, and it happened to be the same school that my cousin Misty attended. I had my best friend again. I tried out for drill team, made the team and got quite popular with my certain little group. I was still uncomfortable with crowds but made the best of it because I loved performing.

Living with my father didn't last long. I was lonely for my mother.

She rented a cheap apartment across from the school so I could finish the year. I was a sophomore when I moved back in with my mom and Wess.

The apartment was small, with only one bedroom. I slept on the couch. She was never home, and so he picked up where he'd left off. When he got up for work and my momma wasn't there, he woke me up from the couch to move to the bedroom to sleep. Then, after his shower, he would always come touch me. Stroking my thighs or shoulders. He kissed my back, face, or neck. He was getting bolder in his attempts. I always tried to pull away and act as if I were asleep. I just didn't know what to do or how to respond. It was awful. It kept me upset, and I didn't want to go home anymore. I stayed with Misty as much as I could, but still had to go home regularly, and it was pretty traumatic.

I am not saying that is all that happened. I am going to say that he never had sex with me. I was still a virgin and was pretty terrified of anyone trying to take that from me. I hadn't even dated yet. It doesn't help anyone for me to go into those details.

I don't feel that Wess was a pervert or even an awful person. I've come to realize after all these years that he was very mentally immature and probably didn't completely have a handle on his feelings for me. I grew up in front of his eyes, but we weren't blood related. I feel like he loved me very much and just didn't grasp the concept of deep love not ending in sex. I'm not making excuses for him in any way; I'm just taking the position of the devil's advocate here.

I've always excelled at seeing both sides of any situation. For me, he had the mentality of a sixteen-year-old boy and just didn't know how to show love any other way. He was the only father figure

I'd ever really known. I know he loved me, and he never completely raped me. But those years were a living hell, wondering and worrying about the possibility that he might. It made home an unsafe place for me, and I'd always preferred to be at home.

In the middle of tenth grade, they decided that the three of us were moving to the land they'd purchased, to live in tents while they built a house. Again, I didn't want to leave. So, my grandfather agreed to let me stay with them until the end of the school year. He would drive me to practice and school every day.

Living with my grandparents was the most wonderful time for me. I'd taken Vance's old room; they loved me and doted on me. My grandfather was a brilliant man, and he used to help me with my schoolwork. He loved to teach me algebra. There was always someone home to talk to, and he was available to take me anywhere I wanted to go. For the first time in my life, I actually had a social life; my grandfather made sure of it.

I really was happy there. I loved going out to eat with them every Friday night to the local cafeteria. He enjoyed telling the staff and servers there that I was his granddaughter.

He was proud of me, and I felt it. Looking back, that was the best part of my teenage years.

Before long, the school year ended, and my momma came and got me to live in the woods, in a tent with no electricity, while they built a house. I was alone and completely miserable. I hated every single second of it and just wanted to return to high school with my friends.

I have always hated change. I find comfort in consistency and knowing what comes next. With my parents, that was never an option.

Another starting over period that I had no decision in, and I fell into horrible depression. I felt like I hated them both. Looking back, I realize that my depression and unhappiness, combined with my age and naivety, made a perfect conduit for anything that seemed better to my inexperienced mind and soul to effortlessly make its way in and thrive.

What, or rather, *who* I allowed in to initially console me, ended up changing everything about me and my future.

CHAPTER 6

It is never easy to describe one's own looks or beauty. This is true, especially for me, but I will try.

At fifteen, I stood 5'2, 115 lbs., with a small waist, round hips, and a somewhat muscular build I had developed from the high school drill team. Hazel eyes, full lips, and dimples. I had a flawless olive complexion. Auburn hair that I usually wore in a shoulder-length bob. My grandfather said that I was a classic beauty, but I never really believed it. Looking at pictures from that time, I can say now that I was a very pretty girl. I really had no idea how lovely I was. I dare to say that I was beautiful. However, I didn't see myself as anything but common in appearance. Although I acted with confidence, I was *anything* but.

The summer I turned sixteen was the year that would change the direction of my life. Every single thing in the years to follow was altered because of the long-term decisions I made in those few months, with no care, concern, or thought for my future. I was a child making grown-up choices with no one that had my best interest at heart to guide me.

It started when I moved with my momma and Wess on the acreage they'd purchased in east Texas. It was a beautiful plot of heavily wooded land, and they had chosen to build a small house to live in while they built their dream home. I was just along for the ride.

I read and helped when I was made to, but honestly, I just pouted and complained more than anything. All I wanted to do was go back to my grandparent's house and continue going to the school that I had grown to love. I was drained from having to start over. Like any teen-age girl in my position, I was angry and unhappy concerning my current circumstances.

There was another family living on land right next to ours. They were living in a camper while having their home built. Mom and Wess became friends with them. We went over to their place for dinner from time to time, especially on weekends.

They had a son, and during one of our visits, I was introduced to him. He was six years my senior, and to this day, I can say with complete truth, that he is one of the most handsome men I have ever met. His name was Conor.

Conor stood about 6'2" with broad shoulders, brown eyes, a heart-shaped face, and dark brown wavy hair. When he smiled, he revealed a set of dimples. He had a piercing gaze that could look right through a person. He commanded respect when he spoke, and he was serious about most everything. His appearance was a cross between Elvis and Ray Liotta. He was breathtakingly gorgeous.

We started talking one evening, and he just had a lot to say. Even though he was much older than I, he still enjoyed some of the same music and activities. He was like no one I'd ever met, with his knowledge of everything and willingness to share it with me. He loved books too, and we spent much of our time talking about classic literature. I will never change my mind or opinion that Conor was and is one of the smartest men I've ever met.

My grandfather once warned me that the closer a person is to genius, the closer they are to being crazy. Like every other person advising me at that time, I chose to ignore him.

Whenever I went next door, Conor and I took off on long walks. We walked for miles and stayed gone for hours at a time. No one raised an eyebrow or shut it down. Even when summer was coming to a close, all of my extra time was spent in the company of the neighbors. I preferred being over there around his family, instead of at my house with my own.

When I considered what I would write about him, I had to really think long and hard about it. Mainly because I'm still in touch with him—and have ties to—his family, and I didn't want to dig up old wounds or hurt anyone over this. After careful consideration, I concluded that this is my history; it's my story, from my point of view. It is mine to tell any way I see fit, and although I've come to care for his family throughout the years, there are many things that could have been much easier on every person involved had they just acknowledged what was going on at the time, instead of living in denial. So, while I will only relay part of our lives together, I will relay it. With as much delicacy and accuracy as I can.

Conor and I were always together. Although he had a girlfriend that he and his family called an ex, she had recently given birth to their son. They also had a daughter. They'd known each other since high school.

I was young, naive, and thought I was in love. My mom figured out pretty quick what was going on between us and forbade me to see him. Being her strong-willed daughter, I left her a pretty heartbreaking letter and ran away from home. At sixteen, I knew everything.

I went to Nina's house. She lived in an apartment next to the high school I was desperately trying to get back to. I got a job at a local K-Mart and decided I was going to continue going to school.

I'm not sure what I was planning to do. My little part-time job wasn't going to support me, and Conor didn't have a job. I was blindly optimistic that everything would work out. I wasn't ready to give up on my education. I was determined to graduate. I entertained ideas of being a doctor or archaeologist. I was not convinced exactly what I was going to choose as a career; I only knew that without graduating high school, I would never accomplish anything.

School started, I enrolled and went. Conor started showing up every day in the hallways. I saw him before school, during school, and after school. He was always popping up. I never went anywhere that he didn't either show up or go with me. If it was school or work, he was always there, waiting afterward. I realized pretty quick that this was not out of love or affection, but more to keep tabs on me. He was insanely jealous. Extremely untrusting and paranoid about who I associated with.

Had I been older, I would have seen the abundance of obvious red flags. Like I said, no one could tell me anything. I thought I knew it all.

When we were together, he was very sweet, charming, and attentive. That seemed to change when other men were in the room. If I looked at or spoke to another male, he got angry and accused me of having sex with them. At that point, I hadn't even had sex with him! We'd gotten close a few times, always making out in his car at the lake or park, but we had never gone all the way. For me, I was still in the mindset that I wasn't having sex until I got married.

Conor was Catholic. He was very religious and fanatical as a matter of fact. All of his time not spent in school or following me around was spent studying the Bible, praying, or going to church, from what I could see. On days that we spent together, it became all he ever wanted to talk about.

He could talk for hours. All night, all day, and then some if I let him. He obsessed over scripture. He felt the need to repeat it and preach to me constantly. As a young girl, I thought that meant he was a good person. I hadn't grown up going to church and at first found it interesting and exciting. I came to believe that God had somehow had a hand in meeting this man to save my soul. Which strengthened my belief that I was in love with him. I was as loyal to him as a dog.

I was so inexperienced and innocent at that point in my life. I'd really never been around boys or men and wasn't old enough for my mother to let me date. I didn't go to school parties like all of my friends and had absolutely no knowledge of anything sexual except what had been forced on me at a very young age. It was all new, and the more I had it explained to me, the more I learned, and the more scared I became of it.

I'd only started my cycle at around fifteen, so I was as green as anyone could be. Not just in the physical sense, but emotionally. I was completely blind to the game's men play. I was dumb to anything concerning relationships; I'd never even had a boyfriend. At best, there were only two boys, aside from Jack, that I'd had an interest in the whole time I was in high school. I was never allowed to be alone with them or see them outside of school or a school dance. All of the grown-up things that were being presented to me just made me more confused.

I was extremely simple in my thoughts and my actions. Anything outside of my self-contained bubble, I had no interest in understanding. Until it directly affected me, I had no knowledge of it.

As the months went by, I realized that going to school was not something I was going to be able to continue. I had to quit to support myself. My pride and feelings for Conor were enough to keep me from going back home.

I gathered up as much money as I could and rented an apartment in the same apartments that I'd lived in with my family at thirteen. I had to lie to the leasing agent about my age to get the place. Conor and I moved in together. We had sex for the first time on that apartment floor. It was the lowest point for me. I hated it. Everything about it. It was awful. I was nervous, and I felt pushed.

He was older, and I thought it was something I needed to do to keep him. The truth being that the actual act of sex with him felt like an assault on my immature, unadulterated, romantic mind. It was never enjoyed, always tolerated. On my part, it was the emotional closeness I was trying to achieve but never could. In my mind, I felt that meant that there had to be something wrong with me. From everything I'd heard, shouldn't it be amazing and magnificent to be joined that way in pleasure with another person? Especially someone I loved? I only felt guilt and disdain.

I had to act as if I wanted it or else suffer the outrage it invoked in him. After each time I had to listen to him tell me all of the things I should do or didn't do correctly. If I acted like I knew what I was doing, he insisted I was no virgin and had acquired the knowledge from someone else. There was no winning.

Two weeks after moving into that apartment, my mom, terrified that I would end up pregnant, signed a consent for us to get married; I was seventeen. We both took a day off of work, went down to the justice of the peace, and got married. It was about as eventful as going to get a library card.

That evening, on our wedding day, he beat me for the first time.

We got home, had some food, and consummated our marriage. I went to take a bath. While I was laying in the bathtub, my new husband came in, and to my shock and horror, he hit me so hard upside my head that I hit the wall. He was ranting and raving and screaming about how I had not been a virgin. He just kept telling me to tell him the truth. Had I fucked my brother? Had I fucked my father? He accused me of having sex with my sister's husband and every other man I knew.

That attack seemed to go on forever. When I thought it was over because he left the room, I stood up to get out of the cold bath. He ran in and shoved me back down.

There was a hairdryer plugged in beside the bathroom sink. He took it into his hands, sat himself down on the toilet, and held the dryer over the bath water. He started preaching. Reciting scripture from memory, in between the scripture he told me to pay attention and acted as if he would drop the hairdryer into the water. He called me a whore, and other vulgar names.

His face looked evil, contorted, and spit flew from his mouth as he screamed. A vein protruded from his forehead. He looked like a different person entirely. I did not know the man in front of me.

My ears were ringing from the blows to the head, and my lip was swollen and bloody. My shoulder hurt from being grabbed so many times, and my bathwater was freezing cold.

I sat there, naked, wet, shivering and crying. I stayed in that position and did not make a sound for hours while he preached; Humiliated and weeping. I sat there with him until I honestly stopped caring if he dropped the hairdryer into the water. I was numb and terrified and couldn't process what he'd done, what he was doing, and who I'd just married. I was so confused as to what was going on. My new husband was acting like a monster.

Hours into his tirade, something changed. As quickly as he'd gotten enraged, he returned to normal. His face softened, his voice became calm, and he stopped—he simply stopped it all.

He placed the hairdryer back on the counter and left the room. I *did not move* from that tub. A few minutes later, he came back to me with a clean towel, and he was smiling. Actually *Smiling*.

He pulled the stopper out of the bath to let the water out and told me to stand up. I did, but I was shaking violently from fear and anxiety and still cowered in the corner.

He tenderly wrapped me in the towel, helped me out of the bath, and when I stepped out, he lovingly, gently picked me up and carried me to the bedroom—to have sex again.

Afterward, I was exhausted, but it was the next morning before I finally slept. Bruised, sore, swollen, and confused. When I woke, he was gone. I didn't see him again for three days. I was afraid to leave the apartment, equally afraid to stay. I didn't know what to do, so I just stayed and waited.

I didn't call my mom; I knew she would see the bruises. The side of my face was purple; on the other side of my head, my ear and neck were black. There was a huge lump on my temple. My shoulder was bruised with his fingerprints, and there were scratches along my chest and throat. I didn't want anyone to see me. I didn't want anyone to see what he had done. I wanted to hide my mistake. I didn't go to work or *anywhere* until the marks faded.

By the end of that week, I'd lost my job. I had never gotten my drivers permit and had no vehicle. I was completely dependent on a man I was afraid of. I had nowhere to go and no one to turn to. All I could do was sleep for the next few weeks. I discovered pretty quickly that sleep was a mode of escape. In my vain attempt to forget everything, I slept as often as I could.

In between sleeping, he woke me up periodically to summon me to the dining room to sit and learn scripture. To listen to him preach hour after hour. To slap me or threaten me if I'm not paying enough attention.

I get good at it. I get really good at knowing what to say and when to say it. When to act the most interested and when to add my knowledge to the conversation. Whatever it takes to keep him out of a rage—I do. Most of the time, it's still not enough. Half of the time ending in another altercation I can't prevent.

It was almost a form of brainwashing. Constantly making me recite right from wrong according to God. The promises of marriage and vowels and the consequences of divorce. It kept me loyal to him for fear of going to hell. I really absorbed and believed every word that man said. I took it all in as truth, even when it was distorted, or explained the way he interpreted it. I was a sponge. I wore those words in my soul the way I wore my skin. No matter what he did, I didn't see any of it as a good enough reason to leave. I felt that God would see my reasons as an excuse and I would be punished.

I just wanted the fairy tale ending he had made me believe was possible in the beginning. I thought I would never be forgiven if I left him and gave my body to another man. I was convinced that if I did that, it would always be considered adultery.

Through his teaching, I came to believe that no matter what a piece of paper said, God had joined us and we couldn't be separated.

What I've learned since is that Conor was obsessed with religion as a way to keep his guilt under control, but it did the opposite. He would teach and preach all of his knowledge, but it was only temporary relief, as it went against everything he was doing in his own life. Then he would get angry with himself for all of his shortcomings and lash out at whoever was around him. That was either me or Marsha, his ex. The mother of his children.

His manic episodes lasted for days, or sometimes, weeks. All she and I could do was ride it out, and try to keep him from getting angry. We split his abuse between the two of us. We were both equally scared of him. When Marsha saw me after days of periodic absence, she would always say, "I am glad it is you and not me."

Out of everyone that knew us, she understood what I was going through better than anyone.

One day, Marsha dropped their son off for Conor to watch so that she could work. It was early; I was still in bed. When I heard the door, I got up and went out to see who was there. The last thing I remember was he and the toddler sitting on the floor in the living room. With things under control, I went back to bed.

When I woke a few hours later, I went back to the living room, only to see Conor sitting by himself in front of our two open front windows. His Bible was open in his lap. I didn't see the baby. When I asked him where the child was, he looked at me as if I'd startled him out of some kind of trance. He immediately flew out of the chair and started searching the apartment for the boy. He was not there.

I threw on a robe and shoes, and we spent the next hour scouring the complex, searching everywhere, yelling his name, and asking anyone outside if they'd seen him. I had genuine concern that he'd been taken or drowned in our apartment swimming pool.

Eventually, a middle-aged guy came walking up with the toddler in his arms. He handed him to Conor; we were both relieved and shaken. We walked back to our home; happy things had turned out the way they had.

As I entered the apartment and the door close behind me, I heard Conor shut the two front windows. I assumed to prevent another escape. What it actually was, was an attempt to hide what he was about to do to me from the outside world.

Before I knew what was happening, I felt a sharp pain in the back of my head. The blow is so tremendous it knocks me to the ground. My ears are ringing. He grabs my hair and pulls me to my feet with it. The next few hours were the worst nightmare I could have ever imagine. Hours of getting hit, slapped, spit on, kicked. He took his time to completely torture me that day. I was actually looking at my hair in great gobs, lying all over the apartment floor. My mouth was bleeding, and the baby was crying.

He leaves to take his son and lay him down for a nap. I believe it is so he can continue without interruption. As he picks him up, he turns to me, grabbing my chin with his free hand. He looks directly into my eyes, and through gritted teeth, in a deep growl, he says,

"Maybe in the future, *fear will make you watch my son.*"

When he leaves the room, and without thinking, I run to the front door, and unlock the chain and bolt in record time. I take off running. Running like there is no tomorrow. I run until my lungs are burning, searching for anyone who can help me. I knock on doors that no one answers. Trying to get as far away from Conor as possible, as quickly as possible.

I run through parking lots looking for anyone who might be coming or going. I was looking everywhere for another human. All the while assuming that Conor was right behind me.

I finally run right into a man who is walking towards the apartment building. It turns out he was going back to grab something he'd forgotten. I almost knock the poor man over. He knows immediately something is desperately wrong. His car is still running, right behind him, door ajar.

He spins around quickly on his heels, no questions asked, and directs me to his waiting automobile. The urgency to get me out of that complex is something I didn't have to verbalize; he knew by looking at my bruised face, split lips, and disheveled hair.

Through my tears and terror, I just tell him to drive—to please get me out of there! And he does. Within moments, we were merging into traffic on the main road. I have an immediate meltdown. Crying hysterically and trying to catch my breath. He doesn't expect an explanation. He just drives without question until we are far enough away that I can calm down and tell him where to take me. I direct him to my brother's house on the other side of town.

He only stops long enough to go into a store, get me a few cubes of ice wrapped in a paper towel, and a soda, then he delivers me to Ricky's house. I will never forget the kindness of a complete stranger and his willingness to get involved. I was saved.

Thank God for that man.

CHAPTER 7
From Hell to Holy Land

In an attempt to escape the monotony of being stuck in the city while the virus has changed all of the rules of everyday living, I choose to go to the little seaside town of Dahab for a rest.

I have spent weeks recovering, and I've gotten some of my strength back.

It is quite tricky to set up transportation for this, as every tour bus and normal means of transportation have been halted for now. I finally manage to secure a seat on a minibus with other people trying to do the same thing. All of us wearing masks and trying to be as socially responsible as possible.

It all goes well until we get there and are denied entry past the city gates.

Where there is a will, there is a way.

We separate into a few groups and have private taxis come outside of the entrance to pick us up and take us in that way. We succeed.

I rented a small bungalow about a mile from the sea. The first few weeks, I just enjoy the sea and the fact there are hardly any people there. Not a ghost town by any means, but sparsely populated when compared to Giza or Cairo.

It is so enjoyable spending my days with my toes in the sand on the virtually empty beach. Reading, eating, relaxing.

I feel my health improving, and I'm gaining some of the weight back that I lost during my illness.

The local police allow people on the beach for a few hours a day as long as we observe social distancing protocol, and it is renewing to my spirit to be so close and have access to the water.

Dahab sits deep in a valley, surrounded by mountains.

Imagine in your mind a short drive to the beautiful mountains, a few miles along the Red Sea shoreline. Not just any mountains, Egyptian mountains, made of sand and sparkling granite. Different hues of pink, brown, green, and black.

You arrive at a canyon, there is a warm breeze, and you hike up and through for a couple of hours. The whole time knowing that Moses as well as Jesus traveled this same area. Your actually in what is considered *holy land.* The view is completely breathtaking. It's one of the few times I have ever been speechless.

You come down, crack open a bottle of red wine, and start a fire.

As the sun goes down behind the mountains, it makes the skyline glow its usual orange and fuchsia, as well as the mountains themselves. It's a quarter moon, and the clear sky is filled with unbelievably bright stars. (They really do, absolutely twinkle here.)

A local man is playing a guitar next to you and the sweet sound echoes through the canyon. It's the most amazing music because it is as if each string is being plucked individually, and it sounds different than anything you have ever heard. As you look up into the night, you see an intriguing lighted object fly straight across the sky, and then another one. It isn't a plane; it's too bright, too high, and way too fast.

Everyone here discusses the fact that whatever they are is not of this world, and it just adds to the already indescribable magic and mystery of this place.

You drink the wine, you drink in the people, and you absorb the vibe so that you can try and hold it in your memory forever. You savor the calm and spiritual nature of it all because you know that, without a doubt, this is a once in a lifetime experience, and you are not likely to ever have another evening like this.

That was how I spent my day. It was amazing and beautiful. This country touches my soul and has claimed my heart.

Sometimes it shocks me—where I came from and what hell I've been through. To end up on such precious soil is a gift—a gift that I truly cherish.

CHAPTER 8

Back in the little house with my mother, and after a few hundred "I told you-so's," it took her only a few days to know what I did not. I was pregnant.

My due date was February 1987. Which means I had conceived the week we got married. I was devastated and scared to death. I'd never considered having a child. It hadn't one time entered my mind at seventeen. My life was officially running me.

We lived in the house in east Texas that was meant to be a temporary home while they built the new one. It was one room, with a sleeping loft and a small kitchen; more like a cottage.

Conor left the apartment we'd shared and went back to live with his parents next door. It didn't take long for me to forgive and forget what had happened.

He seemed genuinely sorry. I was naive and simple and just wanted a happy ending. I had a baby to consider and didn't want to raise our child on my own. I reconciled with him.

I moved into his parent's home next door. I felt like somehow that would keep me safe. I assumed he wouldn't do anything that would alert his family and mine of his real nature. I have never been so wrong.

He continued right where he left off, but this time with much more anger and viciousness. He felt that I'd betrayed him. This was the reason behind every single beating I received. He didn't care who heard us; he felt comfortable doing whatever he wanted behind a locked bedroom door. He tried to keep bruises and marks only from my neck down, so that they could be covered with clothing. Hardly a day went by that he didn't lash out and hurt me.

At times, the abuse lasted for days. Preaching, hitting, name-calling, and vulgar insinuations that his paranoia sparked. I couldn't protect or defend myself against any of it. The occasions were getting more frequent and worse in intensity.

One time he forgot himself and gave me two black eyes. He moved me into his parent's camper beside their house until I could cover the bruises effectively with make-up.

His family was around for the start of some of those occasions. At first, I would scream for help, hoping they would intervene. To no avail. It just made him much angrier. After a while, I gave up and stopped making a sound. Whatever I needed to do to get through it with as little damage as possible.

I realized that when the abuse started, they would usually leave the house. They just got into their car and left. I remember the sinking feeling I used to have when I heard them leave. As terrifying as he could be, it was magnified when I knew we were completely alone.

In their opinion, I was a grown woman and whatever was happening was none of their business. We, as Catholics, should settle our disagreements and do whatever it takes to make it work.

When my belly started growing, my mother wanted me to come over so that she could measure me for maternity clothes, and when I did, she saw a bruise. She lifted my shirt to see them all. She was horrified. I immediately confessed everything.

I was sobbing from relief, but also in fear of the punishment I would receive if he found out I'd told anyone.

She rushed me to my grandparent's house. I left with only the clothes on my back. I was safe, if only temporarily.

When I left, Conor joined the United States Coast Guard. He was gone for basic training, and when he came back, I agreed to see him. He took me out to dinner and back to his hotel room. Where we had sex, and at barely seven months pregnant, I went into labor. A labor that the doctors, no matter how hard they tried, couldn't stop.

With no symptoms of pregnancy until over three months along and going into labor so early, it seemed such a short time. I never even had the chance to get used to the idea of having a baby. They were concerned I was having a miscarriage, so when the little guy made his appearance on Christmas Eve, 1986, and he was alive and healthy, it seemed like a miracle.

I named him Jet. He was perfect, but very tiny, at just under five pounds. He had to spend six weeks in the hospital, while I got sent home in four days.

Conor returned to the coast guard; I had no car or way to go to the hospital to feed my newborn, or spend any time with him. I spent those weeks just trying to recover and getting things ready for him to come home. I rented a small apartment and collected diapers and things I would need. I was really on my own.

When he was finally released from the hospital and came home to me, it was the most difficult thing I'd ever undertaken. I had a little person dependent on me that I hadn't bonded with, and didn't have the first clue how to take care of. I had no experience with babies.

There were no personal feelings, or that expected automatic motherly love and instinct everyone spoke about. He was a cranky baby who fussed all of the time, and I would usually sit exhausted and cry with him. I was a child with a child, and I was failing miserably. I felt overwhelmingly guilty for my lack of what I considered *normal* motherly devotion.

When Jet was almost two months old, Conor came back to visit and detailed what our future would hold. Two weeks later, I would pack up what few things I had and join him at his new station on the Texas southern coast of Sabine Pass.

If I thought having a baby and a new location would change things, I was wrong again. The abuse continued. The amount and consistency were becoming so bad that I flinched or cringed if he moved too quickly around me; much like a cowed dog.

He began taking out his frustrations on Jet as well. He didn't physically abuse our son, but he was less tolerant of normal baby behavior and started placing him in closets or laundry hampers when he'd had enough of him.

I didn't have the normal motherly affection for my son, but I did have the feeling of being responsible for his well-being.

There was a sick kind of jealousy Conor had for Jet. He hated for me be too attentive to him or act as if I loved him more. He said that in God's eyes it was wrong to love a child more than your husband. Which just made me draw closer to my baby, and I got to where I didn't want to put him down. I always had him in my arms. That became another reason for us to fight. Trust me, we didn't need another reason.

I couldn't continue denying what I had suspected all along: Conor was mentally ill.

He would go through phases where he acted a bit normal, and then out of the blue, he would lapse into manic episodes that made him see and hear things that weren't there. Severe paranoia, usually followed by rage. I was frightened all of the time. I felt helpless and hopeless.

At one point, he burned every bit of clothing I owned. He considered them immodest. He was so obsessed with control and thought that other men were looking at me and having sexual thoughts. It occupied his mind more than anything else. Especially since I had, in his mind, been disloyal when I left him.

I did, however, discover exactly how much I loved Jet. While I was holding him one day, I ran my hand across the crown of his little head and found a huge lump. I immediately suspected Conor of doing something to cause it and rushed him to the doctor. It turned out that Jet's premature skull had shifted a bit during his rapid growth.

I'll never forget how worried and upset I was. The thought of anyone hurting him overwhelmed me and caused me to feel physically sick to my stomach. I sat in that waiting room, holding him in my arms and crying. I realized then that I would rather die than have anything happen to my little boy. From that day forward, I felt different. I felt like a mother. Finally.

It was a turning point for me, not just as a mother but as a human. I realized that I loved someone else far more than I loved myself, and he was mine. To hold and love and take care of. I began to relish every single second of having and caring for him. He became my comfort and my purpose. With that realization, nothing else really mattered.

The abuse continued; I just began to accept it. I knew that I'd made the choices that brought me to that point.

Conor rented a house away from the military post instead of staying in military housing. I know that it was to keep our private lives a secret. I was more alone and scared than I'd ever been before. With no job, no support system, and no way of escape. I kept my mouth shut, never accepted invitations to go anywhere, and I'd become a recluse.

All I knew was that I had to provide for and protect my son. To add to my concerns, I found out I was expecting another child. I'd gotten pregnant on Conor's visit when Jet was not yet two months old. At that point, I gave up any hope of a normal life. It was a situation I had absolutely no way out of.

Marsha came to visit us. She realized things had gotten worse; I didn't have to tell her. I was gaunt, thin, and again bruised. At the end of the week, she privately confided in me that she too was pregnant. I shared the news of my own, and we quickly devised a plan to get us out of there.

One morning after he left for work, we loaded up her car, and she drove Jet and me home. That time, I didn't look back. I never again returned to him. It was finally over.

Her plan was to return home, pick up their son, Michael, and go to Arkansas to a place for unwed mothers called the ABBA House. It was a place run by Catholic nuns that condoned adoption instead of abortion and it was safe. Away from Conor or anyone that would know until she had time to think and plan her future. Not really having a plan of my own, or a better option, I decided to go with her.

We arrived back in Dallas, loaded up her car again, and with her son and mine, we took off.

ABBA HOUSE was an old Victorian-style, three-story house in Little Rock, Arkansas. It was home to many women and young girls with different stories and backgrounds. We settled in pretty quickly to our routine.

Daily chores, dish duties, masses, spiritual growth, and weekly group sessions that focused on our emotions.

Neither of us had drug or alcohol addictions so it made us different than most of the other girls. She and I spent much of our time in prayer or Bible study. The day-to-day life of taking care of our children kept us busy.

I still had my heart set on getting my high school diploma, so I enrolled in courses to catch up so that I could take a series of three-day tests to receive it. I was hoping that one day I could use it to attend college. So, four days a week, Marsha watched Jet while I went to class.

It was the best part of living there for me; I still loved to study. It made me feel as if I was preparing for a future and that there was a possibility that one day, everything would somehow get back on track in my life.

In August, when I was six months pregnant, just after my nineteenth birthday, I was ready to take the three-day exam.

I am going to take a minute to speak to you directly as the reader.

I have spent many years with countless therapists, doctors, prescriptions, religious endeavors, and anything else you could imagine to try and forget this part of my story.

All I ever wanted was to put it behind me and erase it from my memory. To this day, it is the subject of my nightmares and the reason for my phobias. Recounting it has proved to be an act of betrayal against myself and all of the efforts I've made to keep certain details a secret.

I had to walk away from my writing for a few weeks just to think about it and convince myself it would all be over with, and I would get better just by letting it out of me.

Telling someone, putting it into actual words, might bring the relief I have prayed so hard for. Thanks to the type of memory I possess, I will be able to recount this with stunning and vivid accuracy, because it has never been far from my mind and thoughts since the day it happened.

I choose to tell this in all of its disgusting detail so that I may release it. So that I can finally tell it all and perhaps rid myself of some of this shame or blame that I still carry with me. My growth as a human being, as a survivor, depends on it.

It has taken many years for me to understand and fully accept what it has done to me, what it continues to do, and what this event *took* from me.

So, I offer this next part of my life, not as a story for you to carry in your heart or even for you to understand or sympathize with, but more to help make sense of some of my later decisions.

It is more of a cautionary tale, where I get to tell the truth for the first time, and you get to realize at the end of the day, I cannot be held accountable for all of my failings. I never learned the tools to address or deal with trauma. Especially this one.

I find that I am shaking, and bile is rising up in my throat just to be this close to putting it down for anyone to read. With that said, I will continue; I have delayed long enough.

It was a Thursday morning and the nuns dropped me off at the school for my last day of testing. I only remember what day of the week it was because after my tests, we would have a long weekend. It was a day that regular high school students had already been dismissed at noon. My testing was completed around 2:30 pm. I felt hungry and drained when I left the building to wait for the sisters to come and pick me up.

I rushed out of the building with such a feeling of relief; I was pleased with the way the test had gone. I was confident that my grades would be high.

I walked around to the back of the building, where I usually waited. I'd finished earlier than anticipated, so I sat down on the steps.

It was a hot day but there was a breeze, so I didn't mind waiting. I could sit and feel satisfied that I'd achieved a goal that I had always had for myself. I would receive a high school diploma. I remember feeling almost giddy with pride. I was in a great mood.

The school was an older one, with large grand concrete steps and pillars on either side of them at the top, right outside of the back entrance. The side where I was waiting was locked up already. It had a wall that ran from where I was sitting, the length of the building. On the other side of that wall was a steep stairwell that led down to the art department.

As I waited, a man approached me. Another man followed. They both walked up the steps and seated themselves behind me, much higher up. One of them had a large radio. In those days, we called them *jam boxes.*

After a few minutes, one of them climbed back down the steps to meet another man that was walking towards us. I didn't think anything of it.

The man sitting closest to me started asking questions. Simple questions pertaining to the school. Was the school open? Was anyone inside? Was the door locked? Questions that should have been red flags to me, but I was so inexperienced with social interaction and did not have a suspicious bone in my body. I assumed he was waiting for someone still inside testing, and so I answered him.

I answered his questions and basically gave him all of the information that he needed to feel safe enough to do what he did next.

From behind, I felt an arm go across my neck, and in a split second, I was in a chokehold. There was something sharp against my neck, poking me.

I try to scream, but my air is cut off; I can't suck air into my lungs. His hand moves over my mouth. I am struggling. Using every ounce of my strength to push him off of me, but it's no use. There is another man at my feet, and I am half dragged and half carried to the basement steps—where we become invisible, we are hidden from view—the wall is covering us.

I break free, but as I do, I receive a blow to my face. And then again.

We are on the staircase but somehow, we've made it to the bottom of the steps. I am trying to scream, but there is no sound coming out of my mouth. I have lost the ability to scream. My brain is confused; I don't know what is happening. All I could do is cover my stomach and drop into a fetal position while they continue assaulting me.

The hits are hard; they can't be using fists. What were they hitting me with?

In a moment of clarity, I consider the fact that maybe they're going to rob me. I am wearing gold rings. I sat up and started trying to remove my jewelry, but I am trembling and can't get them off—but I still try. Thinking that if I give it to them, they will leave me and it will be over.

That's when the real terror sets in, because they laugh. They didn't want my jewelry. Oh, God. My mind just won't consider what else they may be after.

I sit there on my knees, weeping. Out of control weeping.

They try to get the art department door open. I think they will kill me. I see a chance while they were trying to open that door. For a minute, their attention isn't on me. I jump up and try to run. My voice has come back, and I am screaming as loud as my lungs will allow.

As fast as I can, with every ounce of strength I possess, I start climbing the stairs. My eyes are starting to swell, and it is difficult to see through the swelling and the tears. I keep missing the steps; I keep stumbling, falling, and getting back up.

I manage to make it half-way when another man appears in front of me. Where did he come from? Then I remember him from the parking lot.

He drags me back down. There are three of them, and the one who has me wrapped in a bear hug from behind is the largest of them. I am kicking and yelling until he clasps his hand over my mouth and my nose. I can't breathe. I bite his hand and taste blood in my mouth. As he removes his hand from my face, I feel excruciating pain to the back of my head. I hit the ground face down. My head is throbbing, and I finally accept that I am trapped. There is no way out; I'm at their mercy.

My gaze is on the ground in front of me, and my eyes are focused on a large pair of steel scissors. Oh God, please. I repeat over and over.

Was I saying that out loud or in my head?

As one of them grabs me by the hair and uses it to lift me up, I hear myself. In a voice that doesn't even sound like my own, I say,

"Please don't hurt me; I am pregnant."

He responds, "Are you sure?"

I think at that point I've lost my mind; all I could do is stare at him through the swollen slits that are my eyes, and I chuckle. I actually giggle. It was obvious to me that I was; couldn't he see?

More than my odd reaction to laugh in that situation, I remember the look on his face. He looks as if he wants to apologize. A fleeting look of sorrow, regret, and guilt. It only lasted a few seconds, but I am sure I saw it.

With no success getting the art room door open, they do what they came to do right there at the bottom of the staircase.

The first man grabs my face with his hands, pulls me close, and tells me that I will do whatever they tell me to, or I will not walk away from there. He also informs me that there is no use trying to escape, as there is another *friend* just out of sight.

Then, it becomes a flurry of activity between the three of them. There is only a concrete wall between us and the rest of the world. A cruel fact for me at the time. A few inches of concrete give them enough privacy and confidence to damage me for life, as the rest of the population, unaware, goes about their daily lives.

They took turns raping me. Through my half-removed pants were patches of blood that were seeping through from my knees. While one was behind me, the other was in my mouth. The smell of their bodies and breath is ingrained into my brain, sweat and alcohol and filth. I can't stand it. It was enough to make me vomit on one of them. I will never be free of that smell.

At one point, while lying on my back, I could see the blue sky. Just a little, but I could see it through my swollen eyes, and I wondered why no one was coming to save me. I silently lay there and cried. I stopped fighting back.

Then, the most surprising thing happened. If I ever doubted that there was a God, those doubts were put to rest that day. I have never doubted it since. Because, all of a sudden, I was not in my body. I was not in pain from the injuries. I stopped being afraid; the shaking ceased. I simply was not present any longer. I somehow left myself. As it was happening, I was not there. My mind left me. I was on the outside looking in. I could see them. I could hear them. But not from my eyes, from somewhere else, somewhere safe, hovering above us. I became calm as I complied.

The calmness washed over me, replacing the terror. I felt an odd kind of hope, and it felt warm. As if someone poured a warm bucket of water over my head, only it wasn't water. It was love and hope.

I stopped crying. I was lifted up and away and didn't have to endure it any longer. Had it happened any other way, I think I would have lost my mind that day. I do not think my soul could have survived it. It was as if something just plucked me out of my body and took me away.

When they were finished, they instructed me not to move. I was hit again, and lost consciousness. I was so exhausted; I just went to sleep. It stopped hurting. I gave into the darkness, and I didn't feel the abuse to my body anymore. I was completely numb. until I woke up; I felt no pain.

I don't know how long I laid there. I woke up because my baby was kicking me in the bladder, and even that part of me was sore. The sun was low in the sky when I came to. I couldn't open my eyes to see it, but I felt the difference in the air around me; it felt like late afternoon or evening. I had to dress myself and feel along the wall to walk back up the stairs. All of the while praying that if they were still close, they wouldn't see me alive. I was sure they had not intended to leave me that way.

It seemed to take forever to feel my way around the school wall to find the front of the building. Feeling along the outside brick and trying every available entrance on the way. When I finally found an open door, I walked in.

I used tiny little half steps and waved my hands against the air in front of me because I couldn't see. I heard a female. She let out a yell. A short, high-pitched yelp. I'm assuming I looked pretty rough.

I only remember collapsing. I honestly do not remember anything else until I got to the hospital. Someone gave me a cup of water; someone else wrapped a blanket around my shoulders.

Their talking around me was a low roar in my ears. I knew they were speaking, but I couldn't make out the words. It was a hum, a foreign language, and I'm not sure why. As if we were all under water.

I have never felt so alone. Complete disassociation from everyone and everything around me.

Hours later at the hospital, the police asked me questions. I felt too ashamed to tell them everything. I simplified it to a version that made me less damaged. I still feel that they knew what I wasn't saying.

In this frame of time in American history, when this type of assault took place, there was always an underlying feeling or unspoken blame from the police and outsiders. The sentence never said but always inferred was *what did the victim do to deserve it*. I felt it; silent or not, it was shown in their demeanor.

The doctors gave me shots to prevent sexually transmitted diseases and cleaned me out. Which for me, was a whole different kind of hell because of my modesty. I do not know if they took DNA swabs; I don't know if that was the procedure at the time. I was there physically, but in no other way was I present that day.

The nuns came and took me home. They'd shown up at the school and couldn't find me.

Had they walked a few feet from where they surely drove the van, they would have heard me. But, instead, they'd given up when I wasn't waiting at the prearranged spot. Until they got the call from the police.

The following few weeks are a blur. I didn't want to eat, I couldn't sleep without nightmares, and I didn't want to talk. Or pray. Or live. I couldn't even take care of my son.

When I was awake, I could only cry. I felt like a different person. I felt dirty and ashamed. Like somehow my virtue was taken. I was not a virgin, but the only man I'd ever known was my husband. I felt like a piece of trash. I couldn't escape the feeling that it was somehow my fault. My innocence was gone.

I was so violated, and it wasn't just physical. It was mental and emotional. Every time I looked in the mirror or walked across the room, I was reminded of what had happened when I saw my reflection or felt the pain. I still have a scar beside my eye where the bone was chipped; so, I am still reminded.

They had taken something that I considered a holy act and made it dirty, cheap, and disgusting. Those weeks following the incident are gone to me. I have absolutely no recollection of anything that happened. Marsha pretty much led me by the hand to accomplish anything I needed to do to get through those days and live.

I was alive; my unborn baby was alive, but I felt dead. Everything I was before was gone. I was just scared and sad, nothing else. I walked around in a daze.

Somehow, I'd been mentally removed at the time it occurred, which helped me live through it. The problem was that I had not returned to my body since. I didn't know how—I wasn't sure if I wanted to.

I walked around a shell of the person I used to be. I was damaged goods. The night before the assault was the last time I slept without interruption.

I realized then that life was not to be lived and enjoyed but instead *endured*. At nineteen years old, I didn't want to find out what else life had in store for me. I was afraid. I was afraid of everything.

CHAPTER 9
Right On Time

Arabic is a difficult language for most; I believe it has been more so for myself because many of the words are quite literally the same words of some of the other languages I've most recently learned, with entirely different translations. So, I am always getting my languages crossed. It is tricky!

Today, I left my home to go to one of the many falafel restaurants in my neighborhood. While waiting, an older Egyptian woman and her adult daughter started talking to me in Arabic. This happens a lot. I just tell them in my broken Arabic to speak slowly that I have limited understanding, which they do.

They ask me where I am originally from. I tell them America. The mother speaks to me, making small talk. She comments about the high quality of the food in the shop and something about the weather. Then, she comes closer to me, wraps her arms around me, kisses me on the cheek, and tells me I am "gamila." Which means beautiful.

A bead on her hijab caught in my hair as she pulled away from what I can honestly say was one of the most heartfelt, warm, and greatly needed hugs I have ever received. An amazing, loving, motherly gesture that was right on time.

She smiled wide as we struggled to find out exactly where my hair was caught.

Both of us giggling and the world around us dissolving, we stood there with her hand on my cheek. Her daughter gives me a side hug and runs her fingers through my ponytail. By now, tears were about to spill down my very flushed face. (I really needed that hug!)

She again tells me how lovely I am and says she felt goodness in my eyes. (Although I knew she was saying something about my eyes, I had to come home and look that part up in my translator. But I still felt the weight of it in the moment.)

By then, the shop was getting a bit busy. So, misty-eyed, I step up to order my food.

Imagine ordering at a busy Subway sandwich shop and needing to know every single word for every preference you have, from bread to about ten other items. Quickly, and in a completely foreign language.

I had two different orders.

I have lived on this street a while, but today I managed to place my order perfectly, with no pointing, and I understood the man as he spoke to me while serving me. In addition, I understood the amount of money he needed.

That man's pride in me showed in his grin that kept getting bigger with each correct Arabic word I spoke.

As he handed me my change, the people around me, including my Egyptian sisters from earlier, clapped and patted me on the back. They were all thrilled and cheerful to see this small accomplishment with my new language skills! Lots of congratulations to me and smiles so big I felt like a winning game show contestant!

And that, folks, is why I love this place and these people so much.

I've been having a pretty rough time emotionally, and today was a particularly hard day. These beautiful humans have a sixth sense I cannot completely understand. It touches my heart and soul in ways I can't explain. I went to grab dinner and came back with my spirit renewed. The timing couldn't have been more perfect.

My God, how lucky I feel.

CHAPTER 10

Following the rape, I do not remember how I got home to Dallas. Whether it was a plane, train, or bus. I have a faint memory of holding Jet in my lap on some type of mass transit; I just don't know which. I found out months later that I'd passed my tests with honors. That diploma cost me more than I could have imagined, but I finally had it.

My momma and sister were there to pick me up. I remember that when I saw my mom, she had a sad, worried look on her face. It was very difficult to be strong when I saw her eyes well up with tears. She looked heartbroken, which cemented the fact in my mind that I'd been irrevocably damaged. I despised being pitied!

But my clearest recollection of that day is of my sister Kelle.

My face, even after weeks, was still bruised quite badly. The black, purple, and yellow marks were impossible to conceal. When she saw me, her eyes became wide and she exclaimed,

"Jamie, what on earth happened to your face?"

At that moment, my soul, or whatever life force it was that had abandoned me the day it happened, rushed back into my shell of a body, and I started to laugh. Not just a giggle, but a full outburst of laughter. It felt like waking up.

They probably thought I'd lost my mind. But I hadn't. It just hit me as so hilarious that she couldn't remember what happened. Something so life-changing had been utterly forgotten by someone who loves me—and in such a small span of time.

It put it into perspective.

I realized in that one comment from her that life had gone on. I mean, no matter how evil and awful it was, no matter how life-altering it had been for me, I was the only one carrying around the pain and memory of it. Everyone else in the world were basically living their normal lives. They were unaffected. That was a huge eye-opener.

Life was being lived, with or without me. People were moving forward, and I was expected to also.

So, I just stood there laughing. Until tears rolled from my eyes, I laughed.

Kelle remembered right after she made the comment and was apologizing profusely. I had to collect myself long enough so that I could think, for the first time in weeks. All I could do was stand there, looking daft, and laugh until I cried.

After coming home, I still had nightmares and fear, but I was able to learn how to live and act normal. I never talked about it. No one ever asked me about it. Let's face it, not one person desires to hear about things like that. Nobody wants affirmation that there is that kind of evil lurking around us. No one wants to feel bad. No loved one wants to recount something that hurt someone they love when they can't do anything to fix it. It was in the past. I just moved on and pretended like it had never happened.

***

I quickly adapted to the many side effects that were a direct result of what happened to me.

I stopped going out after dark. I would not be left alone with any man in any room, office, or corridor. Even in public, I became ultra-sensitive and aware of my surroundings. I found that when I did go out to eat or into a store or business, I immediately scanned the room for a possible escape route—I still do this. I trusted no one in a public setting and went so far as to only be seated with my back against a wall. If I had to get onto an elevator and there were only men on that elevator, I skipped it and waited for the next. I was hyper-vigilant about locking doors to my home and car. My tolerance for being touched or even having someone too close behind me became nil. I was afraid of the dark and slept with a light on. I tried not to go anywhere I didn't have to go, and never alone.

I was suffering, but I'd become an expert at hiding it and acting normal. After a while, it just became who I was. I felt like I was somehow building strength by being unaffected. Each day behind me was a win as far as I was concerned. No matter how I'd won it.

On November 3rd, 1987, seven weeks before Jet's first birthday, my second precious son Beau was born. Against all odds, he was healthy and full-term. Whereas Jet had an olive complexion, brown eyes, and dark curly hair, Beau was fair-skinned, blue-eyed, and blond-headed. They were opposite from their looks to their personalities and temperaments. I was in love with them both.

Jet with his thick, long eyelashes and sweet, serious nature, and my Beau, who seemed to laugh and push himself forcefully through the world. His full lips were always ready to smile. He was not born with a shy bone in his body and rarely cried or got upset about anything. He was fearless.

They are the same age for seven weeks out of each year. They were very close to one another then, and still are. They made my life worth living.

In those days, Marsha and I lived together most of the time. Not only to help each other, but also so that we could raise our children together. We had both been through a lot, and it created a strong bond between us.

She'd suffered a miscarriage while at Abba House and needed to heal as well. I'm not sure I would have survived if we weren't such good friends. We all became family. Our children were siblings, and she became like a sister to me. It was tough raising the boys alone, but she took up some slack.

We spent a lot of time laughing and she is Jet and Beau's godmother. Every Sunday we went to her parent's house for her dad's famous spaghetti, and they treated me like an extra daughter. Everyone around us found our relationship odd, but to us, it felt perfectly natural.

We weren't completely rid of Conor. We knew we never would be; he was still the father of our children. Their daughter and my Jet looked too much like him to ever forget it. Not that we wanted to; we both just wanted a smooth transition into our future. Whatever that meant.

Conor's illness started to reveal itself in new and odd ways. He'd begun to hang out behind our house, in a field, just beyond our chain link fence, for hours at a time; sometimes all night. With his Bible in his hand, he would stand and watch our house and our activity. The neighbors noticed first and called the police.

When the officers approached him and asked him why he was there, he simply said he was praying for his family. Since he wasn't bothersome or threatening in any way, there was nothing they could do.

Eventually just being there was not enough for him, and he became brave enough to knock on our door. We ignored him. He attempted off and on for weeks to get us to answer, until one night he'd had enough of being ignored and lost patience. He physically punched his fist through our solid oak door, reached in, unlocked it, and let himself in.

Dealing with him those years, Marsha and I had already devised a plan for such an incident. I climbed out of our bedroom window and called the police at the neighbor's house. He left before they got there, and we didn't see him for a while after that. But the fear and constant concern about him reappearing never left either of us.

Eventually I landed a job at a bank working the night shift, and she stayed home with the kids. Which allowed me, for the first time, to support my own family.

It was the perfect job for me. I could no longer sleep well at night anyway, and in my down time I could read as much as I liked. I worked in data processing, which included tape drives, microfiche, and other business done at night, to process the daytime banking activity.

I enjoyed it tremendously. I was basically on my feet running all night long, operating various machines, and I made good money doing it. I started to gain some self-esteem, and it felt great to learn again.

After a year, I managed to save enough money to get into my first apartment as a parent. I rented an apartment for my little family, and it was rewarding after all I'd been through.

That was the winter I lost my grandfather. The only man I had in my life that I could depend on. He'd been in the hospital and I'd gone to see him one day on my way to work. By the time I reached my area and began my shift, my supervisor informed me of his passing. I was the last one to see him alive, and it was a huge loss.

He was really the only man who acted like a normal father figure throughout my life. He meant the world to me, and I miss him still. Losing someone I love never got easier, and in fact, it just got more difficult.

It was also the year I met a man that would again alter my life. But this time, it wasn't all bad.

His name was Sam. He was eight years my senior and had worked at the bank for years before I was hired.

He was not a large man, at 5'9, but to me, he was attractive in his own way. He had a kind and beautiful disposition. Extremely smart and quiet. He was a writer and he was in the Navy reserves.

We shared a love of books and poetry. He was still taking college courses while working at the bank, and he trained me in our area to do my particular job. We became fast friends.

The love we began to share was the product of the mutual respect we had for one another. Our friendship was a slow, deliberate collaboration that we put an equal amount of effort into. He was the only man I've ever known who truly made me love myself. He believed in me, and made sure that I knew what I was capable of.

We went to lunch together often and really enjoyed each other's company.

I am smiling thinking about him right now. While I will try to give a better description, it feels as though no matter what I say about him, I won't do him justice.

Sam was a gymnast in college, so his build was muscular and defined. He loved tennis and math. He played on a tennis league in his spare time, and I loved to go and watch him compete in tournaments. Very soft spoken; his voice was smooth and calm. Silky, if that makes sense.

Although mostly serious, he had a great quirky sense of humor and loved to laugh. When he laughed, he held nothing back. He was the kind of man that I would describe as the all-American boy. The guy next door. The type that had respect for people around him and had to work hard for anything that he wanted. He had no problem working for material things.

He went after everything in life the same way. Meticulously and passionately. He had character, integrity, and no shortage of self-esteem. A lover of music, he often went to concerts, and when at work, he listened to his favorites through his headphones.

He loved his parents and was very close to his four brothers. He was in constant pursuit of knowledge and usually stayed enrolled at the local community college. He was predictable and steady. But mostly, he was a good father who loved his son.

He had a young son when we met. He shared with me details of his failing marriage and told me all about his little boy over our lunch one day. Sam was an amateur photographer, and his child was the most frequent subject of his photos. I came to care for him very much, as he did for me.

Things progressed the way things do, and eventually we took it too far. What I mean is that, as friends we were amazing, and it should have stayed that way. We were both lonely, and too many drinks one night turned into a relationship neither of us was prepared for. The spur of the moment decisions made over the course of a few weeks had long-term consequences.

Less than two years after having Beau, I was pregnant again.

That time, it would not be an easy pregnancy, and I spent most of it in the hospital. I kept going into premature labor. When I was not in the hospital, I was on bed rest or had to wear a monitor strapped to my stomach to record contractions. Work had to cease for me. It made it challenging to take care of the two little boys I had at home.

Sam and I got an apartment together, but everything was moving too fast for both of us. I loved him, more than I can relay in words, but it was not the right kind of love. It was a respect and friendship love that obviously came with sexual attraction, but nothing more. He was still in love with his ex-wife.

So, we coexisted. Which made us feel trapped and lonely for what we did not have between us. I would have given anything for him to have loved me as much as I loved him, but he didn't.

I'd never experienced being *in love*. To me, what we had was enough to build a future together. Sam knew the difference. Looking back, he was correct. He tried to be good to the boys and me, but his heart was never all of the way in it.

He was an expert at compartmentalizing his feelings, and he could put them aside and be very distant and absent emotionally. Those days he was cold most of the time, and I didn't know how to draw him out when he closed himself off. I am a reactor, so my only recourse was to act the same. I mirrored whatever he did. It became toxic for both of us.

Thinking about this, I realize that not one time, the whole time we were together, did we ever have an actual fight or disagreement. If we discussed something and had a difference of opinion, there was no vulgar name-calling or disrespect from either of us. No matter how mad we may have gotten, we always spoke to one another with care, or we didn't speak at all.

I gave birth to my third son, Fin, on December 15th, 1989. A beautiful, quiet baby who melted my heart then and he still does.

After a few months, I was allowed to return to work. We hired someone to stay at our home at night with the boys while we both worked and took alternating shifts during the day to sleep.

One afternoon, Sam woke me up to tell me that Jet had injured his leg and he was worried. When I saw my four-year-old baby with his thigh as large as an adult man, I knew immediately something was very wrong. When I questioned him a second time about what had happened, he told me he had spanked Jet for wetting his pants, and he hadn't been able to walk since. I called 911.

Later at the hospital, we discovered that his leg was fractured. His femur bone was damaged so badly it was completely separated. I've never been as surprised and hurt as I was to hear that news. I cried for days. The emotional turmoil inside of me was crippling. I cried while they put my sweet boy in traction, and when he cried, I sobbed even harder.

I never left his side. I refused to leave. I didn't even go home for a shower or clothes. I lived at the hospital. I felt so much pain in my heart.

To believe that someone I loved and trusted had hurt my firstborn was something I couldn't come to terms with; I felt responsible. He was my son; my reason for living. I just could not wrap my head around the fact that that sweet and gentle man could hurt anyone, especially a child I knew he had grown to love.

All I could do was weep and hold Jet's hand while he lay there in a hospital crib in constant pain. It was more pain than I thought I could ever bear. I still feel sick and full of despair as I write about it now.

Child protective services got involved, as they should have. I had to repeat the story a dozen times in those few weeks. Each time was like reopening a wound.

They interviewed Sam and called in specialists. It was worse than any nightmare. My little boy was sent home in a full body cast, from under his little arms to his toes. With only an open place around his genital area.

The surgeon who was treating him finally released his findings that Jet's leg was not broken by a blow to the leg, but instead, he felt it had gotten twisted in a hole while the boys were playing.

I believe it was a combination of both. When I looked over the facts, I came to the conclusion that the spanking Sam delivered to Jet probably wasn't a severe one. It was probably the position of Jet's leg when he was spanked.

Either way, child protective services dropped the case. But the pain and doubt I had for Sam after that was overwhelming. Our relationship never really recovered.

I felt I'd failed at protecting my baby, and that in itself was too painful for me. I never once doubted that Sam was innocent of the intent. He never got mad or lost his temper and was gentle and loving with the boys. He really did love them. I could never shake the feeling that he didn't care enough to inform me the minute it happened, and it made it appear that he was hiding something.

Although I went back to our shared apartment while my son recovered, it was never the same. I was hurt for my little boy, a hurt that still feels awful now, and I blamed Sam.

I put a huge wall up, and although I still loved him very much, I unintentionally chose sides. Between my son and a man, I was going to side with my child every time. Whether he did it or not, Jet was in his care that day. I blamed him.

I moved from our place into my own shortly after. Not having a sitter at night, I quit my job at the bank. After that, I went months that I didn't hear from Sam at all.

I didn't understand it. I thought he loved me, and I knew he loved Fin, and yet he acted like we didn't exist. So quickly and easily he turned his back on us.

At first, I thought it was his guilt, and that was hard for me. It felt like a silent admission. I clung to Fin like he was baby Jesus. He always slept with me; I never left him with a babysitter or let him out of my sight. He was mine, and he had so many qualities that his father had, I just couldn't get enough of him. He was a product of what we'd shared. He was my little Sam. He loved me as much as I loved him, and it fed my lonely soul.

I had three little boys in four years that needed love and basic life necessities, and I was their sole provider. People say that their children are their world; there is no truer statement for me. They were my everything. For over a year, I grieved the loss of Sam as my friend. I grieved for the loss of him as the father of my son. Once again, I was abandoned by someone I thought would be in my life forever. I was discarded. *We* were discarded.

My kids became a source of strength for me; I had nothing else. I needed nothing else. They were my most difficult endeavor and my most rewarding blessing.

The love I felt for those little boys is what kept me putting one foot in front of the other. Starting over had become second nature by then. As long as I had them, I would start my life again and again a hundred times if needed. Each time getting stronger and better at it. Always hoping that happiness was just around the corner. But that time, it actually was.

CHAPTER 11

Sleepless In Giza

I wake up sometimes and forget where I am. like now. Sleep is a skill I still have not mastered. I find myself pacing the floor all night if I don't write.

I can't even delve into a good book anymore. Something I've always enjoyed; I can't seem to do. My own past seems more pressing and is always on my mind these days. The only real relief seems to come from my never-ending need to meditate. I feel as if I am going to meditate myself into another dimension.

And this, my friends, is the part of being off of all drugs and pharmaceutical medications that emotionally struggling people do not discuss.

The fact I am doing everything in my power to create good endorphins to counteract all of the side effects of a negative history I find myself reliving every day doesn't matter. I battle against it now because I tried to take shortcuts then.

You can swallow a pill, snort a line, or pop a top. The outcome will remain the same. Eventually you are going to have to feel whatever you're dedicated to *not feeling*. One way or another, you will have to process it. Better sooner than later. It is obvious which one I chose. The one that has me writing about Egypt to keep from thinking of less attractive subjects at 3 am.

I hear the car horns and Egyptian music coming from the outside world. I lay in my bed always half-awake. The only time I manage to nap or achieve any type of rest or sleep is during the day. I've had dark curtains made especially for this reason. It's still never a deep sleep.

Giza is my home now. Until the pandemic is under control, this is home to me.

However, I could probably live here another twenty years and not ever completely feel like it is. I'm reminded every single day in every way that I am a foreigner here and it's not my country. Even going to get food and supplies is, at times, an unwanted adventure.

In America, if you need household supplies or food, you simply go to one of the many grocery stores. Oh, the lazy part of me misses the convenience of that!

Here, I live in the middle of a huge dirt cross. A large intersection overshadowed by six- to ten-story apartment buildings. Dozens of them, side-by-side for blocks. Three of the closest corners have traditional restaurants on them; a small cigarette and soda pop type of 'convenience store' occupies the fourth. It is actually more similar to an old-fashioned newspaper stand. You can't go into it, but instead, climb a few steps and tell the shopkeeper what you need, and he retrieves it for you.

Shopping on a larger scale is a bit of an experience. Especially if you're not accustomed to it.

If I need milk, I must go to the small grocer that has fresh milk. They ladle it out of a large steel vat, and I must bring it home and boil it before consumption. I had no idea until now that milk could be so sweet, creamy, and delicious.

If I need bread, I go to one of the bread makers who have small shops set up along my street. Household goods, like cleaner or toilet paper, require a different store that only sells those particular types of items. What about shampoo, soap, or even toothpaste? That involves a trip to the pharmacy. Spices, coffee, or tea? Yup, you guessed it; I must go to the spice shop. Which, by the way, is my favorite place to go. I feel as if I'm stepping back in time when I go there.

The walls are lined with cubbies that are filled with spices, and they measure them out with large copper scoops and sell them by weight. The floors have large burlap sacks filled with rice, beans, and corn. Just like an old-fashioned turn-of-the-century mercantile. I am not sure why these appeal to me so much, but they do.

All of the shops are side-by-side and face the street, like a big outside mall. Apartment homes above them. Some with traditional doors and some equipped with roll-down steel enclosures. Similar to garage doors.

Heaven help me if I need shoes or clothing. That's a different part of the city entirely. Do you have a clear picture yet?

The motto in this country should be, "If it isn't broken, don't fix it!". They have seriously resisted change.

I can set out to grab a few things and easily spend two hours and go into five or more shops. Add the language barrier to that fact, and some days I just don't have it in me. I come home feeling exhausted after a prolonged game of charades.

My Arabic, though much improved, is still awful. I use hand gestures like a full-blown street pantomime most of the time to get my point across. Thank God for these beautiful Egyptian's patience. I suppose that's part of this country's charm. I think my opinion on this depends of what kind of mood I'm in.

The way the city is set up makes sense. Giza, just like Cairo and every other town here, has smaller roads that cross over the larger highways. Like a train track or waffle. The smaller roadways are still dirt and sand. When I was living near the pyramids, it felt like a habit trail. You know, the things hamsters live in? There are a million different alleyways and paths snaking their way around and through different colored concrete buildings. It's a maze. For me, it remains one of the most exciting and childlike experiences to find my way around, through those little-known secretive pathways that only the locals use. I know I have used the movie *ALADDIN* as a reference before, but there is truly no better description.

The older generation here is in a class all by themselves. Although the men do spend much of their off time in coffee/shisha shops, when they come home in the evening, you can find them on the *stoop* in front of their apartment buildings. Sometimes sitting in a plastic chair, surrounded by other men from the neighborhood. With their wives, watching their children or grandchildren play.

They sit there all evening and occasionally you'll see them with a fold-up table playing backgammon or dominoes. They don't get loud and excited the way Americans do when they play. It's somehow a letdown when I pass them and they do *not* slam down the domino and holler, like any domino player anywhere else in the world would do.

I live on a louder, dustier, busier *Sesame Street*. Where the letter of the day is always the one I cannot pronounce.

The children of Egypt are kept busy. They are very much a part of their parent's everyday life and career. It always surprises me when I go into a food establishment or other type of store and get waited on by a child as young as five or six years old. They are put to work and seem eager and happy to help.

When men in this country greet each other, they are related to, or longtime friends with, they embrace and kiss one another on both cheeks. From twenty years old to eighty, it seems second nature to them. It's not uncommon for men and young boys to walk down the street arm-in-arm. Women and girls of all ages hold hands or loop their arms together. Affection is common here but expressed so differently than in any other country I have been.

To witness it makes me feel more alone. Human touch is essential to one's mental and emotional health. Just by walking down my street on a quick errand and observing the locals, I'm reminded that there is a huge deficit of this particular human necessity in my life. The love, respect, and connection these people feel for each other is palpable. Especially with their elders.

My new neighbors know me now and I get an excited feeling in my belly when I walk down the street and they wave and yell out to me from their shop doors, "Hello!"

I have a few who laugh with me over my Arabic. It is safe to say that they have accepted me. They look after me, and some even refer to me as the Texas Egyptian. I have more than accepted them.

It's the little things that make me smile. Like when shop merchants don't have change, they give out gum, chocolate, or hard candy to complete the sale. Because of this, I have a never-ending bowl of candy on my coffee table.

Or like yesterday, when I saw a street kid walk up to the vegetable stand and pick up a tomato. He waited to catch the shopkeeper's eye, and when the man nodded his okay, the boy wiped the tomato on his shirt and took a bite as he continued his walk down the street. After taking a few steps away from us, he stopped and turned back around. With tomato dribbling down his chin, he yelled out, "Shukran!" (thank you in Arabic). The shopkeeper smiled and waved. It was a sweet exchange I was delighted to witness.

Earlier, I went to my favorite corner eatery and ordered a pizza. While I sat outside and waited for it, I watched the ducks and rabbits directly across the street from me. Not in cages, but up on a platform. Unaware of their fate, they don't try to escape. That particular restaurant, like so many others, allows the customer to choose their live dinner (i.e., duck, rabbit, chicken, etc.), then they dispatch it, cook it the way it's ordered and serve it up or wrap it up to go.

I sat there with the overwhelming urge to just go buy them all, so I would know they were safe. Then I visualized me with ten spotted bunnies and ducks in my apartment and laughed out loud at myself. I would have to go down each block and buy thousands to make a difference. Where in the hell would I even put them? So, I will continue to endure that sight and suppress that urge as long as I'm here. It seems to get more difficult daily.

The thing inside of me that got hard and uncaring in America towards how we got our meat has somehow changed.

I never thought twice about grabbing a package of chicken or steak at the grocery store then. It seems my empathy is not just for other humans anymore. It feels weird being one of those vegetarians I used to make fun of. Now I feel guilty for trying to make them feel stupid about it or even arguing the point. They, it seems, were further in their walk than I was at the time. They had a greater knowledge and understanding of our connection to each living being sharing this planet than I did. Had I shut my mouth and listened to them for even just a minute, I'm quite sure they would have shared valuable knowledge with me. I was too busy defending Texas barbecue.

My new home and surroundings are always teaching me something. I'm not as eager to learn as I was when I first got here, but, in my day-to-day life, somehow, I still absorb the knowledge anyway.

Maybe, just maybe, this is what it's supposed to be about. Is it possible that the lesson I'm supposed to get from all of this is that in between the big adventures and traveling, I am to find my inner peace and strength that will see me through? Is it the lonely, sleepless downtime that's my true teacher?

Times like these, when there's no flight to catch and nothing fantastic in front of me to occupy my thoughts.

Is it the slow rehashing that is teaching me to give up trying to make sense of it, and accept the fact that those things are unchangeable? If so, will I magically wake up one day and be able to process all of this and lay it to rest? At the end of the day, will there be less guilt and remorse?

I have to keep reminding myself to just try and live in the present. The past and future are only in my head.

Today I'm tired, impatient and inquisitive. But oh, so sure I'm on the right path. I wish the path included more sleep.

CHAPTER 12

The years 1990-1991 were a challenge. I was a busy and broke mother of three young sons. With minimal work experience and just a high school diploma, employers were not exactly beating down my door to offer me a job.

Finding work that I could earn enough to pay the bills and pay a daycare was next to impossible. I struggled in every way a human can struggle. I was emotionally pretty torn up over Sam. I'd lost my best friend and I missed him terribly. Made worse every time I saw my little boy display one of his father's expressions or do something that growing babies do for the first time. I wanted to share those milestones with someone. It was a lonely feeling.

I was still just a kid learning the ropes of what it took to be an adult. On top of the fact I was walking around with unresolved trauma that caused me to feel unsure of everything.

No matter. I was in a little bit of a fantasy land. My world was crumbling around me, and I remember not really having the common sense to worry about it. My days were so full.

I spent all day, every day, with my babies. There was so much happiness and comfort in the tasks I completed to care for them. I remember at the end of an exhausting day, with my boys fresh from the bathtub, with their hair still wet, snuggling on the couch with them while we watched television or had a snack.

I don't remember ever being frustrated or eager for them to be put to bed. I was content with them in my lap, letting me rub their back. I still mourn the loss of those days. I used to let them stay up later than they should, because once they were asleep, I was alone.

Many times, I let them fall asleep and carried them to my bed to sleep with me. I still had a terrible fear of being alone in the dark.

Those were the days without cellphones or computers in every home. We had each other, and maybe fifteen television channels, a video cassette player, and a stack of movies. I was lucky and actually had a landline home phone, but back then, we didn't dream of hanging out on the phone. I was never into clubbing or drinking, but occasionally I went out with Marsha and Kelle. I always preferred to be at home with my kids.

To make ends meet, I watched other people's children in my home during the day while they worked. When I think back to that time in my life, my biggest regret is that I didn't appreciate it more.

That was dear time with my sons, and although I really did enjoy it, I didn't think about it or assign it weight. In other words, I felt like a failure for having so many children so young and not completing my education, so I didn't value myself and what I was doing with my life. Even though I experienced immense joy being their mom.

Being a stay-at-home mother didn't keep the lights on or the rent paid. I had to do something.

During that time, and after over twenty years of marriage, my mother and Wess separated. He'd fallen for another woman and had an affair. My momma filed for divorce, locked up the little house, and left to attend truck driving school in another city. I had nowhere to go. No home to go back to. It was sink or swim.

Nina knew that I was struggling to find a job that would pay enough to hire a sitter and came to stay with me. She stayed with the boys while I looked for work. She had recently become a mother herself and brought her beautiful six-month-old daughter Toni with her. I loved having a little girl in the house. Having my Nina with me always made me feel safe, and there wasn't a soul on Earth I trusted more to watch the boys.

Marsha's father gave me a job as his office secretary. I hated it, and I sucked at it. No other way to say it. I was young and inexperienced and he was impatient and set in his ways. I loved that man when we went to their house on Sundays for spaghetti, but as a boss, whew! He was tough.

One day at the office, I developed a horrible toothache. Seeing my jaw swollen and painful was too much for my kindhearted boss, and he sent me to his dentist.

Later, at the dental office, high on nitrous oxide, I opened my eyes to see whose hands were in my mouth. I looked up to a set of baby blue eyes, sandy blond hair, and a smile that anyone would appreciate.

After giving me a few numbing injections, the nitrous oxide (in my voice) asked him if he was married. He laughed and told me no, he was not. My reply? I asked him if he wanted to be!

He said his name was Dr. Chase Logan, and that he felt he should introduce himself if we were to be married. And, just like that, the next chapter of my life began.

Later, we both agreed that if there was such thing as love at first sight, that was it.

When I left that office, I was on cloud nine. I actually told my mother that day that I was going to marry my dentist. The root canal he'd started would need several more visits to finish. I would have to return the following week. I could think of nothing else the days leading up to the next appointment. If I sucked at my job before, it paled in comparison to the dreamy-eyed, absent-minded employee I was by the end of the week.

Generally speaking, I'm terrified of having injections in my mouth, but not that time. I was more than willing to plop down into that dental chair and get twenty shots if it meant I was going to see him again. A three-visit root canal turned into six visits, and before my permanent crown had even been placed in my mouth, we were dating.

It happened on the third visit. I had a late afternoon appointment, and was his last patient of the day. I had plans to go out with Marsha and Kelle that evening, so I was dressed to do so. Apparently, it was obvious to him I was going out because he asked me if I had plans for the evening. I told him I did. He gave me the usual injections and finished my treatment in about an hour.

Afterward, as I headed to my car, he came out from the back door of the office, and we reached my vehicle at the same time.

With not an ounce of obvious hesitation in that man's body, he asked me to come have a drink with him.

I repeated what I'd told him earlier about already having plans. He then smiled in a way that I can only describe as the Cheshire cat, and explained to me that he'd injected me with the long-term numbing medicine. I would need to call my "date" and cancel because I would be numb for at least eight hours!

There I was, standing with keys in hand, staring up at this man who stood about 6'1. My only concern being the possibility that I might have drool running out of the corner of my completely numb mouth. I nodded yes to his invitation while my insides did cartwheels.

That evening was one of the most wonderful and nerve-wracking of my entire life. He was so handsome. Smart, funny, and such a gentleman. He had a way of making me feel cherished and considered in every single thing he did. He was older by seven years, but he acted like a man from a bygone era. Opening doors, pulling out my chair, and asking me if I was comfortable. Impeccable manners. He spoke softly, with a deep, even tone. Like a purr. Everything he did put me at ease. He was so confident and assured. It was obvious to me that he'd been one of the popular kids in school.

His attention never wavered; it was focused solely on me. At one point, he even reached up with a napkin to wipe something from the still quite unfeeling side of my mouth. It was a simple gesture really, but he did it with care and an odd familiarity. Like a parent to a child. I spent many hours that night with my cheeks burning and flushed.

To us, we were the only two people in that restaurant, and he hung on to my every word. He asked me questions and waited, with eye contact and patience, for each answer. As if he had all the time in the world.

We sat in that establishment talking until they closed. It was close to midnight. My mouth was still numb, but starting that annoying tingling it does as the medicine starts to wear off.

Leaving in his car, I'd never felt as relaxed as I was with him. He drove me back to the dental office, where my car was parked, and he came around to open the passenger door.

As I put my feet onto the asphalt, he had his right hand extended to help me out. I put my hand in his for the first time, and it felt right. It just felt like my hand had always been missing his.

We stood there in the dimly lit parking lot staring at each other. I started to tell him thank you, but before I could utter a word, he reached up and placed his hands on either side of my face. I remember they felt very warm—too warm. They were hot, or was that the blood rushing to my cheeks?

Right there behind the dental office where we'd met a few weeks earlier, Chase gently pulled my lips to his and kissed me with the passion I'd waited for my whole adult life. I was weak with pleasure and happiness. My head was spinning. It felt like my first kiss.

With that kiss, he owned my soul.

Later that night, as I lay in my own bed thinking about all that had happened that day, it never occurred to me that that feeling could ever be anything but right and good. I was romantic and immature. I lay there blissfully unaware of the dangers that come with allowing myself to trust anyone that quickly.

***

The next morning, I awoke to someone persistently knocking on my door. Groggy and in a daze, I answered it and couldn't believe my eyes. The person standing in my doorway was none other than—Sam.

I must have looked crazy, because I just stood there, rubbing my eyes for what seemed like a really long time. I'm sure I wasn't concealing my shock. I've never been great at hiding facial expression. I know that my mouth must have been literally hanging open.

I hadn't seen him in at least eight months. I guess I didn't know what to do and he didn't either, because we awkwardly stood there looking at each other.

He finally broke the silence and asked if he could come in. Before I knew it, we were seated in my living room. He skipped the small talk and got right to the point of his visit.

He said that he'd stayed away to give himself time to think, and the longer he stayed away, the more difficult it became to come back. Knowing that was a lousy excuse, he looked ashamed while he explained himself. I sat calmly and allowed him to speak.

To summarize, he'd missed me, decided he couldn't live without me, and felt guilt for leaving me alone all of that time to handle raising our son. Then, all of a sudden, while I'm sitting in my robe still trying to wake up and comprehend the fact he was even there, he does something I will never understand. Sam pulls a diamond ring out of his pocket and asks me to marry him.

After abandoning me for all of those months, he came to my house out of the clear blue to profess his love and propose.

I'd been hurt and grief-stricken in one way or another for a few years over him. I had experienced so much pain and rejection for so long, and I'd cried until there were no more tears for me to shed.

I had done it all alone. He had left me *alone*.

I realized that minute I was long past needing him. He couldn't hurt me any more than he already had.

After explaining to him that I'd met someone else and I couldn't consider his offer, he reluctantly went to the door to leave. I followed him out. Just before he left, he asked me when it had happened. When did I get over him? How long ago had I stopped loving him? When did I meet this other man?

"Yesterday," I answered.

I will never forget the look on his face or what he said next. With a half-hearted smile and tears in his eyes, he replied,

"I am always a day late and a dollar short."

And then he left.

I sat down and put my head in my hands and cried. Not because I still loved him, but because I didn't. At least; not the same way. The weight of the pain I'd carried around for so long, my unreciprocated love was so very heavy. It was as if I was waiting for him, and closed myself off to anyone else for those years.

It was very lonely, loving Sam.

When he left that day, it felt like a stone had been taken from around my neck. It still hurt me to hurt him, but nothing compared to the pain of waiting to feel worthy of someone's time and attention.

The saddest days are the ones where the promise of love ends. No matter who's fault it is.

CHAPTER 13

My life became a fairy tale. For the next few months, I was living a dream, and Dr. Chase Logan was the dream weaver.

It was candlelit dinners in quaint little out-of-the-way bistros, and brunch in downtown sidewalk cafes. One evening we would dine at a five-star restaurant in the city and have cocktails at some swanky piano bar, while the next we might pick up Chinese takeout and eat it from the carton at the lake with a bottle of wine. It's because of him that I have an appreciation for wine.

If he invited me somewhere ritzy and I didn't have a dress that was appropriate, he took me to some in-vogue clothing shop to buy one.

My first taste of prime rib and Yorkshire pudding was memorable. To say the least.

These were the type of establishments that only employed the best chefs and, in some cases, had lengthy waiting lists. The kind with Maître Ds and servers wearing expensive suits with a crisp white towel laid over their arm. I found it odd the first time one of them placed a cloth napkin across my lap and, once seated, helped me adjust my chair closer to the table. I still don't know how he managed to get us into such places.

We went to the theater to see live productions, and to the stadium, where he had season tickets, to watch the Cowboys play. He took me to my first ballet. He bought me my first martini. Outdoor concerts on a blanket under the stars and late-night conversations laughing until we cried. He even took me out of state to Louisiana to the horse races, where we won a ton of money on a horse I chose, and gambled at a beautiful resort casino until the sun came up. Both being firsts for me.

There were countless firsts. To be courted by that man was no joke. He spared no expense and enjoyed showing me how the "other half lived." I felt like Julia Roberts in Pretty Woman, and I have often wondered if he wasn't, in many ways, mimicking that movie. He didn't seem pretentious but more entitled and accustomed to that lifestyle. Although it was a bit overwhelming at times, I enjoyed every single second of it. He treated me like a princess. I couldn't get enough of him.

Is *suave* even a word used to describe men anymore? If so, that is him, by definition. I felt valued and beloved, and with him, I felt like a lady.

In the midst of my fairy tale, and two weeks before Christmas of that year, I lost my job. Actually, Marsha's father fired me, and I did not blame the man one bit.

I hated my job, and it really pained me every second I was there. I was never good at sitting behind a desk and answering phones. Bookkeeping was never a strong point either. I honestly deserved to be let go long before I was.

My mother and her new boyfriend, Kurt, had moved back into my mom's house in the woods in east Texas. They agreed to take the boys while I stayed in the city to hunt for a job. Ricky was separated from his wife and offered me his spare room. Nina stayed in my apartment with little Toni, and I just went back and forth between the three places.

I took the first job I could find as a waitress at Chili's Bar and Grill. I needed money, I was good with people, and anything was better than sitting behind a desk all day. I had cash in hand at the end of each shift, and although it was not enough to pay the bills, it kept gas in my car while I continued to look for a better opportunity. Waitressing was a trade I would turn to off-and-on for the rest of my life. It was always a great way to make quick cash. Surprisingly, it came naturally to me, and I was good at it.

Chase and I continued to see each other. And even though I was constantly driving back and forth between my mom's to be with the boys and the city to work, rarely a day went by that we didn't find time to be together. If I was working a double shift, he would stop in to my workplace for lunch or dinner, just to see me.

He consistently sent flowers. I felt embarrassed to see the florist pull up in front of the restaurant so often. I was the envy of all the women at work. I could not have been more infatuated with him, and vice versa. Which is precisely why it was so God-damn surprising to find out after all of those glorious adventures and an exuberant amount of time spent in each other's company that Chase had a fiancé— a fiancé that *lived* with him.

Ricky was the first one to notice that I'd never been invited to the good doctor's home. I didn't even know *where* he lived.

Ricky wasn't as naive as I was, so it was obvious to him. We always went out or to my house, and I was not suspicious by character, so I really hadn't given it much thought. I waited until our next date and just flat-out asked him if he was in a relationship with anyone else. He didn't lie to me, and I was crushed when he admitted to it, but I didn't hesitate. I very calmly asked him to take me home.

When we arrived at my brother's house, I told him I had no interest in ever seeing him again. I walked into the house, closed the door, went to my room, and cried myself to sleep.

But I was okay. Even the next morning, I realized that I was fine. I just carried on like I'd never met him. I still don't know how I did that. How I was able to shut down that emotion goes against everything I am. But somehow, I did it.

The next three weeks were excruciating. He called constantly. I told my brother to tell him I was not home. Every single time he rang or came by. I made a point not to answer the phone and I stayed busy.

He sent flowers to my home and job numerous times. Cards, letters, and gifts were on my doorstep or at the reception desk at work. He'd even left money in an envelope in my mailbox, marked *RENT*.

As flattering as all of that was, I felt so disrespected that it didn't matter. After almost a month, he appeared to have given up. I figured it was fun while it lasted and that was that. Painfully confusing. The only way to describe those days.

A man plagued by obsession wasn't going to be denied for long. He was a man who was used to getting what he wanted.

After five weeks of no contact and my complete avoidance, he'd had enough, and showed up at Ricky's house at 3 am. My sleepy and annoyed brother let him in and pointed him in the direction of my room on his way back to bed.

When Chase woke me, I knew immediately he was drunk. He looked exhausted, disheveled, and miserable. He'd come to tell me that she had moved out. He was no longer engaged. He was asking for my forgiveness for lying to me. Actually, he was begging.

Look, this was a rich, good-looking guy who treated me like a queen; he without sin, feel free to cast the first stone. Of course I forgave him. I was offended and hurt, but in my mind, the good far outweighed the bad.

There couldn't have possibly been more red flags, but I ignored them. I'm good at that. It's another one of my special gifts.

I still feel as if some of my negative fortune is a bit of karma over that girl he cast aside for me, and it still feels awful. Even though I told him I wouldn't be the cause of someone else's pain, I was—and I knew it. I never asked him for details; I didn't want to feel more guilt than I already felt.

That night at my brother's house, in my little sparsely furnished room, lying there in the dark with him, I knew that I loved him.

For the first time, I became fearful. Loving another like that takes away your control. It makes you feel powerless over the direction of your own life in too many ways. Common sense is replaced with the need to overlook things to keep feeding the sensation that your heart gets accustomed to. It's like a drug addiction. But I couldn't imagine not having him in my life. I needed to love him. But mostly, I craved the validation of him loving me. I can admit that now.

I had persevered by not ever completely giving in to love. By claiming him and the life he promised, I was going against the way of life that had kept me intact and sure of my own personal survival. That night I realized my heart had already made the choice for me, and I was incapable of backing out. I justified myself and my weakness with the belief that he was some type of reward. Like, God took pity on me for all I'd been through and was handing me happiness on a silver platter. You know, like,

"I know you have been through hell and years of misery; here's your consolation prize." — I'm actually laughing out loud at my younger self right now.

I really, truly believed that he was my God-sent knight in shining armor. And that night, I finally, completely gave into him.

Making love with him was just, *wow*. I understood why the poets constantly write about it and why it's the subject of so many songs. I'm not exaggerating when I say it took me to a different place. Not just physically, but also mentally and emotionally.

In the months that followed, he took his time introducing me to things I had never experienced, and he did everything with perfect timing, patience, and gentleness.

We spent countless hours soaking in bubble baths and talking. Even though some touches are not meant to be sexual, every touch from him was. A current of electricity ran through both of us just to hold hands. It was a constant needing and longing to touch and be touched. Nagging and almost painful want for his hands to be on my body and for mine to be on his. Just to lay with my head on his chest, with my hands lingering on his bare skin, was ecstasy. Calming and exciting, reassuring and empowering.

With us, we took great pains to make our nights longer than our days. We never got bored of one another. We survived on very little sleep, waking multiple times a night to enjoy one another. Even now, I think of those days as some of the most beautiful of my life. The connection we had was undeniable. The passion between us was mind-blowing. The more we had of each other, the more we wanted, and it was truly the first time I had experienced sexual pleasure. I was like a kid with a new toy.

Nothing was taboo, and it was all sacred and honest. It was a high. We gave each other a thrill that felt like we were intoxicated all of the time. I'm sure part of the euphoria was all of the oxytocin surging through my body, but whatever it was, it was glorious.

For the first time in my life, I didn't feel alone. I felt feminine, sexy, and confident. I felt proud. In every way, a person can feel pride.

I felt safe.

Now, my mother used to tell Kelle and me that it was just as easy to fall in love with a rich man as it is with a poor one. I have come to the conclusion that it's actually much easier. Rich men have got a leg up on the poor ones, for sure. Hear me out.

In my opinion, it's much easier to give your heart away to someone when you are not in distress about the things you need in life that only money can obtain. When there is no need to be concerned with how you're going to eat or pay rent, your mind is freer to choose. You observe and appreciate all of the little things in a potential partner that you would have probably missed had your mind been focused on expenses and termination notices. You have more time to devote to developing a relationship and getting to know a love interest if you're not working long hours to make ends meet. You're simply fresher, and it allows for you to be more attentive with your brain less cluttered.

Take the worry and stress out of everyday life challenges that *lack* of money brings to the table, and it's a whole different ball game of sorts.

What that translated to for me was that I got to quit my job and make plans to finally attend college. Within a few months he had purchased a home in an affluent upper middle-class neighborhood, and our time was spent at his place. He set up a room for my boys, and they were with us most of the time as well.

The house was an older one, the 1950's art deco style. The whole neighborhood was filled with these wonderful little homes with character. Not like cookie-cutter houses, but more mid-century modern. Lawns were all well-manicured, with large, magnificent trees.

A few senior couples still lived on the street, but recently it had become an area very desirable to the yuppie type, and so we fit right in. It seemed like it was a safe area and a good neighborhood to raise a family.

And, I'm quite sure the next revelation won't come as any great shock to you, as the reader. Within a couple of months of getting back together, I was expecting our child.

Now, at this point you're probably wondering if I just didn't use birth control, or maybe I'd held on to my Catholic teaching about it. Or possibly I was just unbelievably irresponsible. You would be wrong on all accounts. I was on the pill, and the contraceptive sponge served as a backup for my third son, as well as this time. None of them worked, obviously. With this one, I was on the strongest pill available.

I am going to insert a fun fact here that most people are probably unaware of. If you are on the birth control pill and you take certain medications, such as the antibiotic I was on for a kidney infection at the time, it lowers the effectiveness of the pill by half. And, of course, we reaped the rewards of this little unknown gem of information.

The boys and I were spending the weekend at my mother's house, and her hawk-eye when it came to me was at an all-time high. She mentioned that I looked puffy. Whatever that means. In the past, she'd always been correct, and I was gripped with panic.

After a quick trip to the pharmacy and a home pregnancy test, her intuition was confirmed. I was mortified. I was scared to tell Chase, and he happened to be on his way to get me. Anxiety had me in tears when he showed up. I told him in the car.

His reaction was one I was not ready for. He looked like a deer caught in headlights. After pulling up to a stop sign, he just sat there. Not speaking. Then he said he felt like he already knew.

As we drove to the city in silence, I cried.

***

Could I not ever do anything in order? My fairytale was out of sequence, and after his reaction, I was in fear of losing it all together.

Again, as much as I loved him, things were happening too fast.

That night, during the long, quiet drive to his house, we didn't hold hands or utter a word. I felt that reaction and behavior told me everything I needed to know.

Chapter 14

The Logans were the reason for his reaction. His concern and respect for his parents.

They were traditional, upper-class people who went to church every Sunday and had never had or considered such *accidents*. They, by all appearances, were mistake-free.

They hadn't come from wealth, but had worked very hard their whole marriage to achieve the level of comfortably rich they'd become. They and their family before them had put their money into farmland in and around the Dallas area and had sold it off bit-by-bit to developers and then invested the money. All while still working regular nine-to-five jobs until retirement.

I'd only met them once. A few months earlier, while I was sick. They'd put me in their spare room to take care of while Chase was at a dental convention. I had a pretty severe kidney and bladder infection and was bedridden for ten days.

They were nice people and were very accommodating and friendly towards me.

But all of that changed.

While having lunch at their house, we told them the big news. His mom wept, and his father just sat there staring at Chase. I wanted to run from the room. As lunch was cleared from the table, I was asked a litany of questions.

Who were my parents? What did they do for a living? Did I have a career? Did I have medical insurance? Did I have an education? Did I believe in abortion? Adoption?

I was humiliated and insulted. But I was strong. I simply answered their questions, as nicely as I could, and told them they didn't need to worry. I wasn't asking for anything. I would have the child, and I could take care of us both. I didn't need their money or their sympathy.

Then, with as much dignity as I could muster, I stood up to leave. I'd had enough insults to last the rest of my life. There was a churning deep in the pit of my stomach that threatened to throw lunch back out the same avenue it had gone in.

I'm not sure if it was my nerves or the beginning of the hatred I developed for them.

I headed toward the door, wondering if Chase would follow. Surprised the hell out of me that he indeed, did follow.

After helping me with my jacket, he hugged his mother, shook his father's hand, and told them in a very firm voice and soft manner that he loved me and wanted to marry me. They'd better get used to the idea. He also told them that he had accepted my three other boys as his own, and when they were ready, he would introduce them.

By the time we were in the car, driving down the road, I was shaking.

These people made their opinion of me very clear. I was not good enough for their son. They were condescending and rude, and it broke my heart and pissed me off. Tears were already streaming down my face. I started to say something about the *nerve* of *them*, when Chase grabbed my hand, stopped the car, and apologized. He apologized for them and said they were just shocked. They would get over it. They would grow to love me and the boys the same way he did. I just needed to give them time.

It soothed me for the moment, but I never forgot it. It hurt. I'd never seen myself as anything other than simply a good person with good intentions, and they'd made me feel like trash. Like I was after his money. Like I'd gotten pregnant intentionally to trap him. What they failed to realize is that he prescribed that medication and knew what the side effects were with birth control pills—I didn't.

Either way, I was going to have baby number four. As the truth settled in, I became excited. I was hopeful it would be a girl, but it didn't matter. I was expecting a little Chase and Jamie, and I was ecstatic.

Shortly after that lunch fiasco, the boys and I permanently moved into the house. It was what he called a starter home. It was a small three-bedroom, one bath. It had original hardwood floors that I loved, and to me, it was perfect.

We spent our time decorating the boy's room, the baby's room, and updating the rest of the house. My sons finally had a stable home, a backyard, and lots of neighborhood children to play with.

Chase's parents became good grandparents to them. Especially Fin. His father loved Fin, and Fin loved him. That was his Pepaw; she was their Memaw. We began living a life none of us had planned, and it just came naturally. We worked together to get things ready for the new baby. My excitement was infectious.

Everyone in his family looked forward to our child being born. Although Chase had a sister, he was the favorite in that family, and it showed. I was quickly extended invitations to lunch meetings with aunts, uncles, cousins, nieces, nephews, and his grandmother. It seemed as though he had a million relatives, and I was meeting them all. It was a good life for us. The boys thrived, and I got extra family. The kind of family that couldn't seem to do enough for us. A family that loved and doted on my children.

In that new life, I was able to enjoy things I'd never experienced before. Happiness and serenity. It seemed my world had evolved into a pleasant succession of holidays and time spent with his very involved kin. Jet, Beau, Fin, and I were accepted as one of them and taken in with their whole hearts.

I could enjoy all of this without the care or concern about running out of food or paying bills. Thoughts that had plagued my mind for years became a worry of the past. I experienced the one-of-a-kind feeling of belonging and being completely loved and valued. I had no time for the lurking melancholic thoughts.

At some point, I ceased living in survival mode. It was absolutely wonderful. I could consider letting go of my past, and simply focus on our future.

Wess became a frequent dinner guest at our home on Sundays to watch the races or ball game with Chase. Ricky came to visit often, and Kelle did as well.

Wess suffered a heart attack that year and had to have open heart surgery. He came out of the hospital a different man. He honestly acted so much older and normal for his age. He was quiet, caring, and mature. He and Chase got along well, and it made me happy.

I loved Wess. He was the only man that was similar to a father I'd ever had, with the exception of my grandfather. So, I buried the past transgression and accepted the new man he had become through his illness, and it was nice.

When I was around five months pregnant, Kelle came over after a fight with her husband. She wanted me to go out with her to a club. A large country and western dance hall. She didn't want to go alone. Chase was waiting for his friend to come over to watch a game, and they would possibly meet us there later. And so, I agreed. I couldn't drink, so what could possibly go wrong?

We'd been there about two hours when Chase and his buddy showed up. Kelle and Chase were both already quite drunk. I danced a little with his friend rather than just sit. I didn't look pregnant, and in fact, I was still wearing my normal jeans.

After we came off of the dance floor, we were both seated at our table. Kelle and Chase were nowhere to be found. He told me he was going to the men's room earlier and never came back. It was 2:00 am, and the club was about to close. Lights went on, and Chase's friend and I searched all over that club and couldn't find either of them.

Kelle had her car keys, but her car was still in the parking lot. We were there until after 3 am. Searching and Waiting. My stomach was in my throat. I had no way home; Chase had our car keys. My mind absolutely wouldn't accept what had to have happened. I felt so sick. I didn't shed a tear and just kept hoping for a difference explanation than the obvious. One that did not include my fiancée and my sister together somewhere.

His friend took me back to his house, where his wife was waiting up for us. She put me in their guest room for the night. I cried myself to sleep; I was exhausted.

The next morning at 11:00 am., I called the club. I told them that my husband and I had been there the night before with a couple of friends and that we couldn't find them. The man didn't hesitate to answer. He said,

"Ma'am, we found your husband and your friend on a pool table having sex at 4:00 am. This morning. I had to stop them and escort them out. They walked in the direction of the hotel across the street. Sorry lady."

I couldn't even tell the man goodbye. I felt as though I had been punched in the stomach. It sounded like an ocean in my ears, and I physically became ill. I had to vomit. I couldn't catch my breath. I was so shocked and hurt, nothing I can write now will ever relay to someone who has not experienced it, exactly how excruciatingly painful that was. A physical pain in my chest; my heart actually wounded.

This would not be the last time he would inflict that kind of hurt on me. It seemed like once it started coming, it didn't stop.

I took a cab to Nina. She was still living in my old apartment, and I laid my head in her lap, curled up, and bawled like a baby. She rubbed my back and let me sob. I cried for so long and so hard I lost my voice. That was the pain I'd always been afraid of; I'd always protected myself from it, to no avail. When I felt it, it was so much worse than I had anticipated.

The anguish matched the love. As much as you allow yourself to love someone is the depth of the pain you'll feel when hurt by them. I wanted to die.

I was betrayed by both the father of my unborn child and my sister. They did it together. Neither of them cared enough to stop it. They left me, five months pregnant, in a nightclub to go have sex and didn't even care enough to hide it from me. No discretion or compassion from either of them.

It shattered every idea I had in my head of what I thought Chase was. The sister I thought loved me and would rather die than hurt me had just ripped my heart from my chest. All of my faith was in those two people. The two persons I trusted most in the world. The only two people I was close to had *chosen* to betray me for the physical act of sex, and it almost killed me.

It changed every single perception I had about life, and somehow the world looked ugly after that. At first, I struggled to believe it even though I knew it had happened.

Neither of them bothered to contact me that day.

I—at the very least—expected enough empathy from them that they would try to explain. A lie seemed better than silence. But, nope.

It wasn't until the next afternoon that damage control began.

I wasn't ready to hear them. I went to Ricky's house to spend time with him. Although he was sympathetic, nothing Kelle ever did surprised him.

He told me I had to make a choice. He said if I loved Chase and my children were already involved, I needed to go back. I needed to try and put it behind me and take care of myself and the child I was carrying. He pointed out that I didn't really have another option.

He said that people make mistakes and that he'd once done something similar and regretted it. I should go back and give him a second chance. I had more to consider than myself.

I was going to have to go back and forgive someone who never apologized or even admitted what they'd done. That took strength I didn't know I had—until I did it.

I think my saving grace was that I didn't ask for the story. I didn't want to know. I knew I had to go back, and had I known the details, I wouldn't have been able to.

A few years later, while Kelle was drunk, she did in fact fill me in on all of the details, and I still struggle with the things she told me. She has always needed to clear her conscience, even if it made others feel horrible. It made her feel better by her accountability, and that was all that mattered to her.

At the time, I made the right choice by refusing to listen to them and in returning home.

I didn't just return to him, but I never mentioned it to him again. I didn't even think of it *at all* after a few weeks. My brain just couldn't process that trauma, and so I pretended it didn't happen. My defense mechanism, I suppose.

I needed my family to be intact. So, I blocked it from my mind. What else could I have done?

I found out shortly after that incident that I was going to have another son.

***

The next three months were filled with maternity check-ups that Chase never missed. Baby showers, painting the nursery, and buying whatever our little guy needed—and loads of Chase going the extra mile to somehow try and make up for what he'd done.

If I even hinted that I wanted something, he bought it. If I gazed too long into a store window at something, he went back and purchased it for me, had it wrapped, and surprised me with it later.

He treated me as if I were ill or fragile. He did laundry, cooked supper, and did yard work. He was the picture-perfect partner.

There were late-night trips to the store for blueberry cheesecake ice cream, because that is what I craved, and when my belly got too big for me to be able to shave my own legs, he did it for me. Not to mention the steady stream of flowers that seemed to be delivered to our door. Guilt is a powerful emotion.

It made forgiveness easy, and I was eager to forgive. I would have given anything to go back to the way it was before.

At eight months pregnant, I was standing in the kitchen ironing a set of curtains I'd made for the boy's room. I borrowed my sister's sewing machine, and I was pretty proud of my handy work. It was late when the phone rang. I answered expecting it to be Chase; it wasn't.

It was a woman on the line. She had a three-way conversation going, similar to a party call we used to use back in the days of landlines. I was pretty quickly informed that she and the other women on the line were all women Chase had been sleeping with. The woman said that he was also having a sexual relationship with his dental assistant. I was told that he was not playing poker that night but was with his assistant. She sounded upset as she gave me details about certain weekends that she had been with him, while I had been under the impression that he was bird hunting with his buddies.

Chase was always off to some kind of hunting trip, boy's poker night, or weekend dental convention—so I *thought*.

My first reaction was to deny what she was saying, but she knew way too many details of my life, and even repeated conversations between him and me. She was able to do that because she'd been sitting right beside him when he had called and lied to me.

Although I acted calm, I was shaking on the inside. I just listened to all she had to say. I thanked her for calling—as if she had been some kind of cold-call salesman or someone telling me some mundane detail about an appointment reschedule, or like my serviced car was ready to be picked up. It was odd, but fight or flight mode for me had become the norm.

Fleeing was always my choice; I've always despised fighting. Three weeks before my due date, I hung up the phone, got my three small children out of bed, called a taxi, packed a suitcase, and went to Kelle's house.

Hurt again, and with every intention to make that the last time I was made a fool of, I wasn't going back. Not that time.

Chase came home to an empty house, and after a few days of refusing to speak to him, his mother called.

When I spoke with her, she said that no matter what had happened, he loved me and the boys. She said they all loved us. Whatever he'd done, he was too ashamed to tell her, and he was so sorry. He was miserable and couldn't live without us. She asked me to please come back.

When I spoke to him, he explained that what that woman told me needed to be exposed and that he was glad that it was out in the open. His guilt was out of control, trying to prevent hurting me and making the ones around him happy enough not to tell. He felt that since there were no more secrets, he could do better; he could be better. We could start over with a clean slate. There was nothing else to hide. The boys and I were all he wanted.

I didn't have the luxury of time to decide or make a well-thought-out decision. The next day, I went into labor. The boys and I returned home. They were early contractions brought on by emotional upset, I am sure. But for the next two weeks, off and on, I had them.

On May 12th, 1992, on Mother's Day, I gave birth to my beautiful fourth son. We named him Dean. Olive skin, green eyes, and brown hair. He was a cross in looks between the two of us. He was perfect.

I adored him from the second he was born. But honestly, I couldn't help feeling like I'd just been an incubator for the Logan's.

I lay in the hospital so proud of my newborn and in fear of what would change for myself and Jet, Beau, and Fin now that Dean was not safely inside of me anymore. I was still trying to process the information I'd just received a few weeks earlier concerning Chase's indiscretions.

Although his parents seemed genuinely sympathetic about what Chase had done, once I came back, they were unconcerned. They acted as if it never happened. I couldn't escape the feeling that my services for them were complete, and I was afraid of the amount of control they had over all of us.

His birthday was a *happy* day; experience taught me that those are always followed with some type of tragedy or something bad that I would need to prepare myself for. So, I was on high alert and truly exhausted. In a blissful, full of narcotics way.

I felt an immediate need to protect him, to hold onto him. When I considered leaving Chase, I experienced pure anxiety of having Dean taken away from me. I knew if anyone could, it would be my soon-to-be in-laws. I felt it in my soul.

I decided to make the best of the situation and again, forgave and forgot. At some point, I guess I slipped slowly back into survival mode. It was not just that; I truly loved Chase. I was not going to give up on him that easily.

On June 6th, 1992, before Dean was one month old, the only father I'd ever known, Wess, had a heart attack at home and passed away.

He died alone, and it was two days later, when he didn't show up for work, that his body was found.

That was especially hard for me because he was supposed to be at our house for dinner the evening he died and never showed up. I wanted to check on him, but Chase and I were arguing, and he didn't want me to leave.

I stayed to keep the peace, but felt uneasy about it until I got the call two days later. Wess never passed up pot roast, and I knew he would have called if something came up. There was anger in my heart toward Chase for not caring enough to be concerned. It was honestly more than my overemotional postpartum self could handle, and it sent me into deep depression and despair. It just added to an already full plate, as people say.

My sister and I had to go clean out his apartment, and I will never forget the odor. If you've never smelled death, there is simply no way to describe it. It isn't an odor like a dead animal on the side of the road as you would imagine. It's a different smell entirely. Like chemicals mixed with fresh blood or sulfur.

Nina had to go remove the couch that he'd died on from the apartment, so Kelle and I could stomach the job ahead of us. We cried nonstop.

One of the more disturbing days of my life. I experienced unbelievable grief and indescribable inner turmoil.

I never had the chance to tell him I forgave him, and I'd never even hugged him as an adult. I never told him I loved him. It was—and still is—confusing for me.

I know I should have hated him or held him accountable for the damage he'd bestowed on my young mind. The sadness over losing him is still very real and fresh.

I didn't take advantage of the person he had become after his heart surgery. It was a small window in between the immature, sick Wess and the emotionally more stable father figure type of man he'd become. I let it slip by. And so, it still felt unfinished. I guess it always will.

I struggle more than most with death, and it added to the already chaotic home environment I was living in. No matter what had happened, he was still one of the few people who'd been around as long as I could remember. My entire life included Wess. I was running out of people like that in my life, and it was frightening to me.

Even now, when I think back to the birth of Dean, I think of Wess's death.

***

Now, I need to clarify a few things in the lives of Chase and Jamie.

First of all, we were in *no way* rich. Chase had only been out of dental school practicing a few short years before we met. The money he made, while decent, was not nearly enough to cover his tastes for the finer things.

He could spend money like no one I'd ever seen.

He owned every credit card you can imagine. From gas cards, Visa, American Express, and department stores. You name it, he had it. They were all maxed.

All of the beautiful places he took me in the beginning were all funded by plastic. The credit card bills that had to be paid at the end of every month were astronomical. We were living way beyond our means.

My beloved also had a huge gambling problem. Football, baseball, basketball, fights, and anything else that could be bet on, he did. Not just small amounts of cash either; we're talking hundreds of dollars on one game.

He sat and watched sports with friends, and while they enjoyed the game, he would observe with a certain tenseness and concern that he just couldn't hide. So, he drank. He drank a lot. He also enjoyed his fair share of narcotics.

Pharmaceutical representatives made weekly visits to his office and left him with a rather large supply to dispense to patients. Chase brought them home instead, and we had cases of them stacked in our closets. There were always packets of pain pills in our desk drawers. He took them every single day. To be fair, most dentists and doctors at that time did the same. It was considered one of the perks of the profession.

He also smoked marijuana daily. These were all the little things I was finding out along the way. I was always learning something else new and distasteful about my love. I was the queen of denial and made every excuse in the world when it came to him.

At my six-week post-baby checkup, I had birth control implants put into my arm. It consisted of six tiny tubes that were placed under my skin that released a low-dose hormone. It was meant to keep me baby-free for six years. One less worry, right?

Although Chase's parents seemed to be good people who treated me and all of their grandkids well, I never could completely trust them. They were constantly doing things to keep my security just on the edge.

For example, one day they had to meet with Chase's ex-fiancée to give her something that had been left in their care when she and he were a couple. I remember they had Dean with them that day.

Later, when they came to bring him home, Chase's mother told me the day's events with an odd and a bit of cruel satisfaction. She told me that she'd intentionally taken Dean with them and that the girl looked surprised to see Chase's son. It had hurt her, and his mom smiled, telling me about it.

That always bothered me.

So quickly they had discarded a woman who was almost their daughter-in-law. A woman they supposedly loved and who had been around for many years.

The cruelty of that day didn't escape my attention. I felt real empathy for her, and I saw that I could just as easily be discarded. It was not me that they loved; it was the grandchild I had born for them that made me a temporary favorite. Nothing more.

A grandchild that they initially did not even want. I had to stand my ground and fight to bring my son into the world. They simply had no choice; I was going to have him with or without their approval. So, they had chosen to embrace him, and I was just extra.

Through all of those little secrets and financial woes, I still felt a certain satisfaction in it. Having a home, the man I loved, and my boys. His parents were pushing us to marry soon, for social respectability, I'm quite sure, and so we started making wedding plans. It all seemed perfect to anyone on the outside. Hell—it was more perfect than I'd ever had, and I was on the inside.

It's good for all of us to remember that a whole different life is just one decision away. One choice made in an instant can turn a fairytale into a nightmare.

Please allow me to remind you that, as I told you earlier, my track record with decision-making is sketchy.

CHAPTER 15

There will be a point in your life when you will make a decision, and that decision will become something that you'll look back on the rest of your life as a turning point. The decision of all decisions. The choice that will come to define you. The one fork in the road where you choose the wrong road and you feel regret and pain for it the rest of your life. The one decision that you make, and you know, without a doubt, that had you not made that particular call, your life would be completely different from what it is now.

Sometimes we only see one road; we don't see another one. Whereas other times we do, and we simply choose the wrong road intentionally. We've all done it.

It reminds me of Marsha and me when we were young and broke.

We would buy what we called *disposable cars*. They would cost a few hundred dollars and would have some major defect, like no lights, so we couldn't drive them after dark. Maybe it required a quart of oil a day, or the windows were plex-glass. No heat meant we bundled ourselves and our children up in the winter to go anywhere. Marsha actually had a light switch her father had installed on the dashboard in one of those cars that she had to flip to the *ON* position to get it to start. You get the point.

Anyway, with a disposable vehicle, it could last a month, or, if we were lucky, a year. We were on God's good graces just to make it from point A to point B. And, when they finally died at an intersection, in traffic, or on the side of the highway, we just shrugged our shoulders and said our goodbyes. Then we'd empty out all of our personal possessions and leave them wherever they had decided to give their last little surge and permanently croak. More times than not, in a blue cloud of smoke, when there was somewhere we had to be and it was freezing or raining outside, and usually with a car full of kids.

It's what we signed up for by not spending the extra money and effort to get a reliable car.

Because they were cheap and we considered them disposable, we didn't take care of them either. No oil changes or new tires. We did the bare minimum. Just enough to get an inspection sticker slapped on the windshield.

The choice was clear when the car of the month left us stranded. It was cheaper to leave them where they died and move on. No tow trucks or repair shops. We just had to be glad for what we had while we had it, and then we'd start making plans to find another one. When what we should have done was save a little more money and bought a better car to begin with.

Hindsight is indeed 20/20.

Two roads, and we chose the cheaper, easier route. We chose it by buying the crappy car to begin with, and we chose the easier path by walking away from them afterwards.

And there you have it. Spur-of-the-moment careless decisions with no thought to long-term repercussions.

Temporary band-aids. Young minds make poor choices.

We kept choosing the same path over and over again. Hence the term *"disposable cars"*.

We did it so often, we even assigned it a category.

I explained all of that so that I could tell you all of this:

My fiancée, the father of my son and love of my life, had a drug and alcohol problem.

All through my pregnancy, his friends would come to the house for dinner or to watch a football game or whatever sport was in season. But they didn't just come over for a few hours, and none of them ever really ate. Long after I retired to the bedroom exhausted, they would stay—all night. They stayed in the living room playing dice or cards until the sun came up.

I mean, these were respectable people with careers and good jobs. Yet they stayed up all night long drinking. I knew that most of them enjoyed their marijuana; Chase smoked every day. That was the only drug I had any experience with. So, I couldn't understand how or why they were doing it.

I mentioned to Chase that I didn't sleep well with a house full of people, and I didn't want the boys to think that was normal—or something to that effect.

All that did was ensure that he would be gone a few nights a week at someone else's house instead. Then I didn't sleep any because I worried about where he was and when he was coming home. Too frequently, he didn't come home at all. This pattern continued after Dean was born, and I was baffled.

I'd started taking courses at the local community college soon after having the baby. My cousin Misty and her husband lived in an apartment on the way to my school. On occasion, I dropped in to visit.

One evening I was explaining to her what was going on at my place. I wanted her input and opinion. She was much more street smart than I was. She knew immediately.

When she mentioned that it had to be drugs, I became very indignant. I couldn't fathom these businessmen and "pillars of the community" doing anything illegal.

Especially hard drugs. I left her apartment, but what she said stayed with me for days. It gnawed at me, not letting my mind accept any other explanation.

I invited her over while Chase was at work, and together, she and I searched my home. I wasn't even sure what we were looking for, but she was.

It took her a whopping thirty minutes to find drugs in my house.

Up in our closet, tucked inside the brim of a baseball cap, was a little bag with white powder in it.

She dipped her pinkie into the bag, touched it to her tongue, and then, in a rather matter-of-fact way, she announced that it was cocaine.

It sparked a rage in me. I was furious. There were drugs in my home with my children. I started going through all of the drawers, and we pried open the locked top drawer of Chase' file cabinet. Where we found drug scales and other paraphernalia.

That was it. I was livid. Once again, I packed our bags and left the house.

Only that time, I was mad in a whole different way. I was not just angry that he was doing drugs; I was hurt that he was hiding it from me. Another lie. I was always being lied to.

Even though I was very much against illegal drug use, I was pissed off that he was treating me like a naive child. I didn't understand why he would want to enjoy something that I imagined was so enjoyable without me. Also, deep down, I felt that he couldn't possibly be content with our life together if he felt the need to do drugs at all. The fact he was doing them and keeping it from me meant he didn't trust me. I started to second-guess everything.

And then, everything from the past year or so started to make so much sense. I had a scape goat.

I blamed the drugs for all of his bad behavior and shortcomings. It had to be why we were struggling financially. Wasn't a drug habit expensive? It was the drugs' fault, not his.

He wasn't out all night with other women; in my mind, he stayed out all night to do drugs so that I wouldn't find out. Or, it was because he loved us so much and wanted to keep us safe. Blah,

blah, blah. Insert every excuse under the sun for every unacceptable thing he did to me right here. I was a gullible idiot and needed to blame something or someone for everything gone awry in my world.

The amusing thing, is that this time, it really *was* the truth. The drugs were his other love, and alcohol was definitely his "wingman". And not just the cheap stuff; he preferred the $100 bottles of aged scotch. Nothing but the best.

If there is one sure thing I've learned, it is that a person can either love the drugs and alcohol, or love their family. But they cannot do both at the same time. I didn't know that then. That's something I would have to learn later, through experience.

I only stayed gone for the weekend. The boys missed the man who'd become their father, and I missed him as well. I came home and allowed him to explain.

He made it seem so trivial. So inconsequential. It—the cocaine—was just something he did to relax sometimes. It was just for fun. He wasn't addicted. He didn't need it. Hell, he rarely even did it! I was not to worry; if I wanted him to

221

stop, he would. He would never bring it into the house again.

Okay, let's stop right here.

Had I had any street smarts or knowledge of the drug world at all, I would have recognized the fact that that man was a poster child for addiction. From the alcohol to the gambling, spending money we didn't have, and even his choice in career. He did not ever half-ass do anything. He was gluttonous when it came to the tangible pleasures in life. They were all of his little *"rewards."*

Whether that was a $100 plate of food at the best dining establishment in the city or a bottle of scotch, he didn't have a simple or cheap bone in his body. He loved all things that money could buy.

Although initially I was taken aback by the knowledge he did drugs, I never found it surprising at all that he chose what was known as "the rich man's drug" over all other drug choices to use. He even had to have some level of class in his addiction.

With that said, a few weeks later at one of our gatherings in our house, with all of our best friends seated in the living room watching a football game, I found myself seated backwards on our toilet, with a line of cocaine in front of me and a rolled-up dollar bill in my hand. The instructions I'd been given echoing in my head as I snorted my first line. My first illicit drug.

And this, my friends, is the life-altering bad choice I was talking about.

I didn't want to be on the outside of the circle anymore. I didn't want him to hide things from me or feel the need to go away sometimes to do it. I wanted to experience everything that he did. Together, with him.

Up to that point, I was an outsider in my own home. They were all part of some secret club. Going in and out of my bathroom, experiencing a feeling I'd never felt. I wanted to understand, but I also did not want to feel like a child in the midst of a bunch of adults anymore. I'd never been good at interacting in social situations, and I just wanted to feel normal. Like one of them.

I didn't want to be the naive partner of his that everyone had to whisper around and protect. *Everyone* was doing it, so how bad could it be?

These were smart people with their lives together; surely if it was as harmful as I'd heard, I would have seen some sign of its destruction in our social circle.

They always treated me like the Sunday school teacher of the group. My sister still referred to me as *"goody-two shoes."* Our friends approached me with kid gloves and watched their language around me.

I know it was out of respect, but to me it perpetuated my feelings of alienation.

For once, I needed to feel like I belonged. Even if belonging made me feel bad inside—and it did.

I felt it in the pit of my stomach. I was immediately changed after that night. Not because of the cocaine, but because I had lost my integrity. My core standards were blurred. I lost class in my own eyes. It affected my self-esteem and opened the door for anything to be acceptable.

All from a few lines? You bet!

I started tolerating and accepting bad behavior months earlier. With each new behavior I allowed, I was teaching him what he could get away with. From sexual indiscretions to drugs. By staying, I was saying it was okay, and then I willingly became a participant. It was easier to join in than stand my ground and expect change.

Maybe in the back of my mind I knew it was a losing battle. Acceptance was just the logical, easy choice.

I lost myself. All for the sake of trying to obtain my fairy tale ending. I lost my self-respect that night, and later it became evident that he had too.

I made a choice. A conscious choice to do what I knew was wrong, to temporarily fix a problem. You can't build a house on a shaky foundation any more than you can build a marriage on one. Same goes for putting your trust in an unreliable car to get you to your chosen destination.

Our relationship was fragile enough, and I kept giving into things that had never before been acceptable to me. I put my trust in a man who was making all of the worst decisions and expected to end up at the destination of my imagination— our happy ending.

Similar to driving a disposable car on a cross-country vacation. Yeah, *exactly* like that.

Don't misunderstand me; that night was a good one. It was oddly satisfying.

For the first time, I didn't feel awkward in a group of people. They were all high as well, so they weren't paying attention to me. Instead of sitting next to Chase and listening to their jokes and conversation, I found my voice and joined in. It was such a weird experience. The taste in the back of my throat, my numb lips and nose, and the way my hair tickled. Yes, I meant to write that.

Time went by so quickly, and everything felt new. My senses were all being tantalized simultaneously. Sounds were louder and crisper; to be touched sparked every nerve in my body. There were no thoughts or concerns in my head except what was going on right in front of me.

Chase's parents had the boys, so I didn't have to be concerned with anything else. My cheeks physically hurt from smiling all night, and everything was funny. Life became so much more interesting. Until the sun came up and the cocaine ran out.

That part was *AWFUL*. Coming down from that particular drug is what makes people turn to crime, including armed robbery and, in the worst-case scenario, murder. I don't feel I need to give it a better description. That sums it up perfectly.

It took all week to feel myself again. Lots of sleep and huge amounts of water. By the time I felt better, it was the weekend again, and it started all over.

Every. Single. Week.

It became what we both looked forward to and lived for. That quick. It's what any extra money we had was spent on, and there was many a kid's soccer game we attended higher than the Empire State Building.

Family functions were the worst, and his family was always having some kind of get-together that we were expected to attend. It got to where we didn't want to leave the house for any reason.

A few months into that addiction, we changed our drug of choice to methamphetamine. It just made more sense. It was cheaper, the high lasted much longer, and we didn't have to constantly find a place to do a line. In our drug-induced stupor, we thought it was a more functional drug.

The whole time we were throwing ourselves into the path that would eventually tear everything apart, and at that time, we were planning our own wedding.

Days. We went three or four days with no sleep. No food. Just alcohol and meth. We didn't drink alcohol to get drunk, but it was used more to keep us on an even keel. I'd always been pretty obsessive-compulsive when it came to a clean house or the kids clothing and things like that, but with nothing but sleepless time on my hands, it went into overdrive. I was actually of the opinion that I was a better mother on that shit.

We didn't do anything different; we just got to where we never left our house for anything. With the exception of Chase going to work, taking the kids to school, or simple errands, we stayed home.

We both lost an unbelievable amount of weight. We were pale, and I had a new affliction that started sometime in the middle of our full-blown addiction. I had hives.

Not the simple whelps that Benadryl or a steroid would take care of, but more like watery-filled blisters all over me. If I felt anxiety or got upset, I broke out in them. Once started, I couldn't stop it. It left sores and scars. I went to the doctor and dermatologist many times and couldn't get an answer. I wasn't sure if it was the drugs, hormonal, or a side effect of the severe nervous energy surrounding me with my life being out of control and our wedding rapidly approaching.

Whatever it was, I wasn't going to leave my house for people to see me looking like that.

I looked sick. I felt sick. I acted sick.

Then came the fighting. We started to fight a different way. It wasn't just arguing anymore; it was physical altercations with horrible disrespect from both of us. It's as if nothing was off-limits. The words that came out of his mouth didn't even sound like him.

He went straight for the jugular every time. It was like a competition to see who could hurt the other one the most. I am no judge, but I'm going to say he won. That man was quick-witted and had the sharpest of tongues, and he knew where all my touchy spots were.

We hated each other, and we adored each other. We were obsessed, and it didn't bring the good out in us like it did before. As horrible as our fights would get, the make-up sex later was always much better. The worse the fight, the better the sexual satisfaction. That in itself became an addiction.

Then, on March 25th, 1993, we stopped doing meth long enough to attend our own wedding. A wedding that I hardly had a thing to do with planning. Except for the chapel choice and the flowers, which I insisted on, Mrs. Logan did all of the planning, the execution, as well as the funding of our wedding.

It was a small service in a quaint little church, but the reception was anything but. It felt like the whole city was invited.

Our buffet dinner included prime rib and all the trimmings. The only thing she didn't approve was an open bar—the smartest decision of them all.

I was thin; I was in the middle of a full-blown drug addiction, and even though I was finally getting to marry the man of my dreams, I didn't enjoy one second of it.

There are few things I remember about that day, but one thing I do remember clearly is that my groom was high. We had sworn to each other we would abstain from use that day, but he was clearly as high as a kite. I knew then that one day I would think back to our wedding day, and that's what I would recall. Here I am, after all of these years, doing exactly that. It's still hurtful.

After a few hours of our reception, toasts had been made and dinner eaten, cake had been cut, and pictures taken, I ran up to our room to change.

When I walked into our suite, it was full of people. There had to have been twenty or more of our friends crammed into our room, and they were getting high. There was a party in my room, bigger than the one downstairs.

When his parents got on the elevator to come say their goodbyes, one of Chase's buddies took the stairs and managed to get to us just in time for a warning.

We literally shoved everyone in the bathroom! I am laughing now. That was actually funny. Twenty people in formal dresses and suits practically on top of each other to hide from his parents is still a funny picture in my mind, even though it shouldn't be.

I'm not sure I realized how sad and abnormal that really was until right this second.

The next morning, we got on a plane for a short honeymoon in San Diego, California. We were coming off of drugs and spent the first two days asleep in our room.

Seriously, could that be more depressing?

We did manage to go to Disney Land and spend a few days enjoying the city before the trip ended, but thinking back, it was the worst honeymoon ever. I still have photos from that trip, and we looked really bad. We looked sad, unhealthy, and miserable.

As we flew back home to Dallas to start our married life, I knew that things had to change.

I promised myself on that plane that I would do whatever it took to get us back to the way we were. We loved each other too much to continue sabotaging our future. I still believed we both had it in us to have our fairytale ending. I was thinking with a sober and clear head for the first time in months. Being sober gave me the impression of hope. It allowed me to slip back on my rose-colored glasses.

Our only issue was drug addiction, and we would just simply stop using.

CHAPTER 16
Eid Al-Adha
Egypt During the Holiday

Eid Al-Adha, also known as the festival of sacrifice, this year is celebrated from July 30th until August 3rd, 2020. This is a Muslim holiday and honors the willingness of Ibrahim to sacrifice his own son Ismael as an act of obedience to God's command. But, before Ibrahim could sacrifice his son, God provided a lamb to sacrifice instead.

For the last few weeks, there was a makeshift animal pen right outside of my apartment building. I live at a four-way intersection of sorts, so it allowed for a very large area to contain them.

I walked past it every day. It held fifty or more goats, lambs, and sheep.

I enjoyed seeing them being tended to by a few older gentlemen and what I assumed to be their young sons, dressed in their traditional Egyptian attire.

They set up chairs at one end of the enclosure and played music, and I watched them hand-feed the animals. Little children gathered around the wooden fence panels and petted them or fed them herbs or grass.

It was so adorable to watch the children interact with them and giggle with excitement when they were permitted to take care of them or touch them.

However, I was unaware exactly *why* they were there.

Apparently, they were sacrificial meat for the religious feast that is taking place over the next few days.

This morning, I left my flat for my usual walk to get supplies. The smell of blood was so thick in the air I fought back the urge to gag. As I walked down the road to the market, there were pools of blood everywhere. The whole street was completely covered in thick, dark red blood.

I was wearing open-toed sandals. They were emptying buckets of water onto the street to wash the blood away, reduce the inevitable collection of flies, and keep the smell to a minimum. The mixture seeped up and saturated my feet and got in between my toes.

I looked to the pen. Where there had previously been so many animals—it only contained a few. All huddled in a corner, and I could see in their eyes that they knew what was coming and were scared. Fear is recognizable in any species.

If you've never experienced this, I highly recommend that you skip it. It's awful.

The mood was festive. Locals were lined up at many stalls placed down my street waiting for their share of meat, while butchers work endlessly to dispatch each one, expertly cut them up, and pack them.

It doesn't matter to me that they were treated well and killed the Halal way; it's still heartbreaking.

After a short walk, I couldn't avert my eyes any longer. I had to look up to see where I was going to avoid getting hit by a car. I wish I hadn't even ventured outside today.

I think back to who I was a few short years ago. I was born and raised in Texas, and we love our barbeque. I've always been a part of a family that loved to hunt wild boar and deer. I myself have field-dressed animals numerous times without hesitation or concern. I wonder when I changed?

The thought now of killing or consuming meat upsets me. It goes against every empathetic fiber of my being. I didn't set out on this journey to change the part of me that enjoys a good steak, and it's baffling. The unintentional change of my spirit and consciousness is a mystery.

I've pondered on this for a bit and still have no answer.

I have an idea, however, that the closer I get to my fellow man and every living thing around me, the more I value them. With value of another being's life, the more empathy is created in my heart, and the next logical step is to stop enjoying anything that creates pain or death. No matter how much I miss having a cheeseburger, I just cannot justify it.

Today, I turn fifty-two years old. In two years, every aspect of my values and beliefs has changed. I go through life now and consider every single detail. From the way I treat people to my diet.

I no longer hold onto religious dogma or the rules I was always taught as a child or as a young adult involved in the church.

It feels as if I have truly started over. I am a blank slate, and my new understanding of the world around me is my moral compass. All of the things I used to be opinionated about no longer matter. I'm open to learning and receiving a new perception of everything. One that makes more sense to my soul. It just feels right.

Letting go of who I've always been has been challenging. But, as I sit here in my flat, writing this, I'm calm, and my mind is free of turmoil. Even if I am alone on my birthday, I don't wish to find company or try and be free of my loneliness. Instead, I embrace it as part of this process.

I am building a new kind of strength. One that doesn't require others approval or company. Instead of being in survival mode, like I have been for so many years, I'm just living in the moment. Whatever that moment has to offer, I receive it and value it for what it is.

I'm immensely grateful for the ability to go through this when so many are denied the chance. I look forward to whatever the next year holds.

But today, in Egypt, it proved to be a bit much for my newly developed sensitive understanding of what eating meat really means.

I mourn for those animals I saw every day and the hope they received each time they were fed.

I truly hope I find peace in this. I am working on it.

CHAPTER 17

King Henry the 8th and Anne Boleyn's relationship, from beginning to end, lasted approximately one thousand days. The courting, the birth of Elizabeth, the changing of the Church and divorce law, their marriage, as well as her beheading and all of the personal and political history in between, was crammed into three years—roughly 23,000 hours.

That, it seems, was plenty of time for their love and obsession for one another to run its course. Apparently, it's enough time for anyone. A whole lifetime filled with joy and sadness, as well as regret and tragedy, can be lived in that very short period of time.

Two weeks before our first anniversary, a month before our son's second birthday, I filed for divorce.

The drug use didn't stop. It had only gotten worse. The fighting was out of control, and I'd ended up with a few rather serious injuries from some of them. I had a fractured tailbone and black eyes, among other things. I weighed 94 pounds. I cried all of the time, and my emotions were what fueled every single thing I said or did.

Anger is what fueled him. I felt lost and just didn't know how to keep our lives from spiraling out of control. The only time we actually got along anymore was when we were high.

Being high for me was the only time in as long as I could remember that I was not scared. I did not relive my past trauma while I was using and never thought about things I didn't want to. It was different for me. I even began to refer to it as my *medicine*.

Mental illness was not acceptable to Chase or his family, and giving them another reason to feel I was defective was not something I was going to do.

I needed to see a psychiatrist; I needed help. I'd still never told a soul most of what had happened to me. I craved compassion and understanding. Talking about it would have been a great idea. The problem was that I still felt so ashamed and guilty. In my mind, it would somehow tarnish my *girl next door* appearance.

Also, I didn't want them to feel sorry for me. All I could do is self-medicate.

By putting down the drug, I would need to heal or suppress my emotional turmoil and anxiety in another way. I simply did not know how.

In his family, appearance was everything. If he or I admitted we had a problem and sought help, that was a social stigma. He was not about to let his parents know about his flaws or mine. So, it just continued.

By outward appearances, we were the perfect all-American upper-middle class family. There was no evidence of drug use except for the fact we had both lost a tremendous amount of weight.

The house was spotless, he continued to work, our kids were involved in sports and activities, and I was a member of the PTA. I cooked supper every evening, and we sat down with the boys for them to eat. We attended family barbeques and anything else that was required of us. Unless you were one of the few people in our inner social circle, you wouldn't have had a clue as to what was going on behind closed doors. The money he made was enough to keep up the addiction and facade. And so, it kept on, until the day that I truly couldn't take it one more minute.

What I need you as the reader to understand the most right now is that although I did in fact eventually file for divorce, I did not do it to end our marriage. I didn't want a divorce. What I wanted was a reaction. What I needed was for the love of my life to understand that he had to make a choice. The drugs and alcohol, or me and the kids. I never intended for it to actually happen. I never in a million years would have imagined that by filing for a divorce, I would actually end up with one. I just didn't see any other way to get his attention.

I hired a lawyer and filed secretly. It just so happened that while I was receiving one hundred long stemmed red roses for our one-year wedding anniversary, he was being served with divorce papers. I never intended for it to play out that way.

I was still madly in love with him, and he was with me. It was madly toxic.

I was trying to salvage us. But I went about it the wrong way, and to say it backfired is the understatement of all understatements.

Out of fear of what I would bring up in court, he immediately went to his parents and told them I was a drug addict. He gave them a story he could live with, not owning his share of personal responsibility or even the fact that he too was an addict.

My so-called soulmate threw me under the bus.

It had never once entered my mind to tell my attorney about anything other than the infidelity and the fact we weren't getting along. Even in the drastic action I was taking, I was still protecting him.

Like I said, I didn't want or anticipate a divorce. I just wanted him to stop and do what he needed to do to heal our family and stay together.

In true Chase fashion, he was putting himself in the position to win—at all costs.

I was shocked when my lawyer told me that my husband had accused me of doing drugs. I never would have told anyone.

The battle began. I knew then that I had made a terrible decision that was not going to get the outcome I longed for.

Imagine the worst divorce movie you have ever seen. *War of the Roses* comes to mind, or even *Kramer vs. Kramer*. All of them. Consider all of them. Not one of them comes close to how bad our divorce was.

It turned into an actual trial, filled with pride and hate and lies and angry betrayal. Instead of getting the man I loved back to me and clean, he turned his back on me and told the court anything he could to win. He paid people off to lie, or whatever he had to do to convince his parents, who were sitting in that courtroom every day, that he was blame-free. I'd injured his pride, and he lashed out.

Once he'd made me out to be a monster, he couldn't go back. It was our final undoing. Even though I was the one who'd filed, I wasn't prepared for the outcome.

The day I decided to file for divorce, I quit doing drugs and cleaned my house of anything drug-related. I'd lost everything I loved over that crap, and I hated it.

Within a few months I moved into an apartment with the boys, and we shared temporary custody of Dean. Chase had purchased the house before we were married, and I didn't want anything that belonged to him. Especially anything that reminded me of him. It was too difficult. I never wanted anything from him except love and loyalty. All of the material possessions were just for show, and I never required any of them.

It turned into month after month of court dates and painful testimony, and a staggering amount of money. Our friends were subpoenaed to court; clear sides were chosen. His parents hired a private investigator to follow me around. Twenty-four hours a day, seven days a week.

The Logan's' completely turned their backs on Jet, Beau, and Fin. Chase did as well, and my boys didn't understand why the man they called Daddy was not coming around anymore. That was the most heartbreaking thing of it all. They couldn't wrap their little minds around the fact that Chase or his parents came to get Dean and left them behind. It wasn't just my heart that was broken; it was my sweet little boys that were being punished.

It was torture. Slow, intentional torture. They used my children to manipulate the outcome. They would have their way at any cost.

I recalled the time they'd met with Chase's ex-fiancée, and even though I always knew our ending would probably be the same way, when it finally happened, there was no way to prepare for the actual pain of it. For that, I consider all of them cold-hearted monsters. My opinion will never waiver on this subject. For me as an adult, I could handle it. My children were treated worse than discarded puppies, and it was not gradual; it was overnight.

We spent a lot of time with Ricky as that part of my life unfolded. I needed his level head and counsel more than ever. He agreed with *why* I'd done it, but he did not agree with *how*.

One night, while he and I shared a beer, I confessed what I was considering.

I'd done so much growing up as of late and looked at the state of my own family.

A family that consisted of my mother and her boyfriend, who was only two years older than myself. They were long-haul truck drivers and were always traveling cross-country. They were both doing meth to stay awake for those long trips. While they were in between those hauls, they stayed with us. We partied together, sometimes for weeks at a time. Staying up all night, playing board games or cards and doing drugs.

While I was growing up, her job or endeavors made her an absent parent more times than not, and whilst I did not hold that against her, I included those details in my decision-making.

My own father had nothing to do with me, and in fact, the only time I'd seen him in many years was at our wedding. The only thing I'd ever done for him to be proud of enough to warrant his attendance or have pride in me.

I had an alcoholic sister with a failing marriage that I couldn't trust and a brother who had a full plate with his own family and concerns.

There was no one else.

Marsha was married and had her own babies and marriage to contend with, and if I'm telling the truth, once I married Chase, I'd completely abandoned any friendships or family ties, and claimed his instead.

I considered what my husband's family was and what they had to offer my son.

They were a respected family, with money and stability, and there were so many of them. literally dozens of family members that would drop everything in an instant to help one another. The choice just seemed clear.

As painful as the decision was, I had to do what was best for Dean.

I also knew for a fact that had I kept him, they would one day find a way to take him. It was only a matter of time. I would always be under their scrutiny, just like I had been for the last few years. They had the desire, the money, and the means to get their way.

People around me at the time tried to counsel me against it, including the judge presiding over our divorce and custody case. I had to search my soul and really put my pride and selfishness aside to come to such a devastating conclusion.

(according to the judge), with the amount of child support I would have been awarded from Chase, it would have made my life, as well as my children's lives so much easier, but that wasn't fair to Dean.

I knew that even with the money, I would always be splitting my time and attention between three other children, a job, and school. I didn't have the kind of support system from extended family and friends that Chase had. I knew what I needed to do.

My brother cried with me when I told him. He told me he loved me and hugged me. Then, before he left my house, he turned to me and said that even though it was the right decision for Dean, I would someday regret it. He said that eventually it would tear me apart. My brother was always right. He was always right in matters of the heart.

I agreed to give Chase custody, and in return I had their solemn promise that they would never intentionally keep him or take him from me. I needed the court and attorney costs to end, and I couldn't stomach seeing the pain in my children's eyes any longer. I had to return my boys to some type of normal life—a new one that, again, would not include a father and traditional grandparents.

Dean would live with Chase, and I would get him on weekends and holidays. It wasn't a win-or-lose situation to me. My only care or concern was what was best for my son. I will stand behind that choice, as painful as it was, to this day. I did the right thing, and it almost killed me. I think that in my mind, I always felt it was going to be temporary. I still clung to the belief we would be together in the end.

***

After documents were signed, lawyers paid, and winners were crowned, Chase and I started seeing each other again. Almost every night. We missed each other.

It was so messed up. The power we still had over one another and the need to be together never went away. We snuck around and hid our continued relationship. He was always showing up at my apartment in the middle of the night, or I went to the house and parked my car down the street in case his parents drove by. It was exciting. But it was stupid because it kept feeding my hope for reconciliation.

He was an excellent manipulator and always led me to believe one day we would get back together. I was still in love enough to believe it. I was breaking my own heart.

I saw signs around the house when I was over that he was seeing other women. I ignored them to feel better about us. He was my worst addiction.

I had a friend; her name was Lacy. She was beautiful, smart, and funny. I had met her only a few months before filing for divorce. At the time we met, drug addiction was our common bond. Together, we were a mess.

After the divorce, we attended concerts together and anything else she could talk me into doing to get me out and about. She was my savior at the time, honestly. Through thick and thin, she was always there. She hated Chase, even though it was a friend of his that had introduced us. She saw what he really was and what he was doing.

She had invited me to a concert one night. It was *The Eagles*, "Hell Freezes Over" concert. I had to cancel plans with Chase to go with her.

We went and had a good time; I even bought him a t-shirt.

Afterwards, I decided to drop by his house, which was not out of the ordinary at that time. I wanted to see him and give him his shirt. I had been drinking a little. It seemed like a good idea.

I drove over around 2 am. I knocked but did not get an answer. Cell phones had just come out; I had one and gave him a quick call; no answer. I figured he was just asleep. I knew he always kept the bathroom window open for when he smoked a joint after work, so I checked. Sure enough, it was open. I pushed a bucket up to the window and let myself in. I was wanting to surprise him.

As I entered the house, I heard the bedroom door lock.

Oh man, that's when it hit me. There was someone else in the room with him. I knocked on the bedroom door. He didn't answer.

I started to shake uncontrollably. I'm not sure what possessed me that night, but whatever it was, it has me filled with anxiety even now, after all these years. I had just left him, and we had just made love earlier that day.

Long story short, he eventually came out of the bedroom, and it was closed and locked behind him. I went absolutely, temporarily *insane*. The quiet, reserved woman I'd always been turned into a raving maniac. We had a physical altercation in the living room, and when I left, the shirt he'd been wearing lay on the ground in shreds, and he had a bloody scratch down the side of his face. A scratch that was so deep it would leave a scar.

I don't remember getting into my car. I don't remember driving away. I actually do not remember anything besides the searing and unbelievable pain in my chest. The most physically painful pain I have ever encountered.

I was so upset; I had to pull my car over and vomit. Somehow, I managed to arrive at Lacy's; I must have driven on autopilot. She answered her door, and only because she told me later do I know that I said,

"It hurts so bad."

And in her words, I fell into her arms, sobbing and repeating myself. My legs were shaking so violently they wouldn't support me any longer, and I laid down, right inside of her door, and experienced a total, 100% complete meltdown. I couldn't even tell her what had happened. I was crying too hard. The betrayal was catastrophic. I laid on her bed, and bawled for hours.

And, just like that, I was a full-blown drug addict again.

I gave no shit to what kind of drug either. If it made the pain subside, I was willing to do it. I didn't want to sleep. I knew that when I did, I would be faced with the nightmares involving my past, and I would have to wake up and feel that sick, awful fucking pain over my current situation. Every single time I woke up. I had to realize it again and go through a new sensation of being stabbed in my heart. Reliving it over and over.

Heartbreak is a real thing, people, and it is soul crushingly painful. It made my addiction so much worse. My only goal in life at that time was to numb all feelings.

The oddest thing about that is the fact I'd never thought about he and Kelle or even the other affairs. Not once since they'd happened.

What made this one different was that I had actually caught him; I could no longer deny the facts. I believe I was feeling the pain from all of the past acts of his indiscretion, all at once. They all became real. All of them became real for the first time that day. Which means I also lost the time I felt was beautiful and solid in between this time and the first. In other words, our whole relationship had been a lie, and we had no future.

The joke was on me. The worst part was that everyone else knew *except* me. I had been played and I was the last to know.

It was not about losing a man. It was about rearranging my mind and imagining a future I had never considered. It never dawned on me that my life would not include him, all of my sons, and our plans that we had made together. Plans that we still continued to discuss, even after the divorce was final.

I just couldn't accept it, no matter how hard I tried. He was supposed to be my reward for all of the horrible years I had suffered; remember? For me, it felt like he was my husband. God had joined us, and with my religious understanding, there was no way we could be separated. We had been married by a minister in a church. I simply wasn't equipped to comprehend anything else.

My poor friend. I ended up putting all of my personal possessions into a storage unit and moved in with her. When I did manage to sleep, Lacy made sure she was awake first.

It was a ritual of sorts. I would wake, and within a few minutes of my eyes opening, I would be overwrought with anguish and sobbing like a two-year-old. She never left my side those months. People can judge all they want, but she was only doing what she needed to do so that I would gain the ability to function.

She was keeping me alive the only way she knew how. If that meant spoon-feeding me Captain Crunch cereal like she would a toddler or making sure I had drugs for the day, she was helping me live because I'd given up. All of the years I had been strong, through so much for so long. I couldn't call on my inner strength anymore. I hadn't any left. It was gone.

When I woke, she had whatever I needed in front of me. There were times she would wake me up gently with a crackpipe already up to my lips and would quietly tell me to suck. Other times it could be a line of coke or meth. Sometimes, on the rare occasion we were out of the illegal stuff, she would hand me a glass of straight bourbon or vodka, and I would down the whole glass.

Had she not done this, I would not be alive to write what I am writing right now. That grief was too much for me to bear. To lose my whole future, my son, the man I loved, and to realize that the past was all a lie as well. The last betrayal had been the proverbial '*straw.*'

I was not just destroyed; I was so hurt and broken I couldn't function or get through a day without having a meltdown. I absolutely did not want to live. No matter what happened between Chase and me, my trust and faith in him to do the right thing never wavered. I genuinely believed him when he said he was still in love with me. I never doubted that we would be back together. Not one second did I think our divorce was final. Not one time did I ever allow myself to believe that he was a liar or that he was anything but genuine in his actions and words. It was a feeling of getting the wind knocked out of me every time I thought about the night I caught him.

No matter how good of a writer I am or will ever be, the dictionary doesn't even include words to describe how awful that hurt.

I am being under dramatic when I say that my mind, heart, and soul were shattered.

Simply put, he didn't want me, the boys, or our life together. Period.

He was the one who had started all of the things that led to our undoing, yet I was the one who'd lost it all and was suffering, whilst he came out smelling like a rose. He just moved on.

Why? Why did he keep up the facade? Was it just to continue having sex with me when he was clearly getting it elsewhere? He was a good-looking dentist; it just didn't make sense; it still doesn't.

Anyway, I took my boys to my mother's house and spent all of my time trying to make enough money to either send to her for the kids or to support my drug habit—*all of them, I was doing them all*. I didn't care if I lived or died.

I was walking around an empty shell of the person I had been before. I had no purpose and no future, just anguish and pain. I was physically ill. All my energy went to keeping myself numb, and it still wasn't enough.

Each day away from my children, I felt more shame. I blamed God and felt that I was being punished again. With no clear reason what I was being punished for. I didn't know what I'd done to disserve any of it. What had I done to make God turn his back on me so many times?

That went on for months. I learned at that time that people are opportunistic by nature.

Men that had been friends of mine and Chase's when we were a couple called up out of the clear blue sky to meet me for a drink, you know, just to "check on me." Those meetings would always end the same way: with a cheap, insulting proposition, and my feelings hurt. Disgusting.

No matter how many or what kind of drugs I did, my heart, as broken as it was, still belonged to Chase. I couldn't even consider giving myself sexually or any other way to another man. I was never someone who lost my moral compass. I'm sure there were a few things I might have done that were questionable, but I still remained a good person.

As absurd as it sounds, I was an honest drug addict and tried to inflict damage only on myself. I wasn't street smart enough to be any other way.

I was too hurt to have the ability to hurt someone else, if that makes sense. I never lost my empathy for others, and in fact, I believe my empathy became stronger because I understood.

Originally, when I started using, being high made me more social. I was able to talk and not feel awkward. At some point it flipped and had the opposite effect. I wanted to stay high, stay quiet, and avoid people.

Lacy was extremely social, so I was just along for the ride. She kept us busy. She had a day job, and I wallpapered homes or apartments when I needed cash. I actually ended up with a full-blown wall paper business that did very well and kept me busy most days and nights.

It was a job that allowed me to show up high; no one to answer to. It was rare that we ever ran out of substances to abuse. Two very damaged souls, clinging to whatever we could to keep us moving forward.

There came a day when I was so exhausted because of my chosen lifestyle and self-abuse that I drove myself to my cousin Misty's house and asked her to take me to the hospital.

The drugs weren't working to numb the pain any longer. I had reached a point that I feared for my own safety; I was afraid of what I would do to myself. I had lost all hope.

With tears in her eyes, she did exactly that.

I was hospitalized for a month and was clean for a short time after, but it didn't last.

Since I'd discovered Chase that evening, he had no reason to hide it. So, he didn't. His dental assistant and her daughter became an almost permanent fixture at his house. I had to face them every single time I picked up my son. A re-wounding of sorts. Every Wednesday and every other weekend. It was not conducive to my sobriety. Especially when he himself answered the door high.

When one drug stopped working for me, I tried another. I just kept finding stronger drugs or different ways to use them.

And then, finally, in the midst of all of the pain and chaos that was my life, one night I found myself sitting in a dirty apartment with no furniture or electricity. An extension cord running through a window to a lamp on the floor.

I missed my children, and I felt completely alienated from every other living creature on the planet.

Lacy was in one of her countless stints in a rehab facility. I had exactly zero self-worth at the time.

I have no clue who that house belonged to. I must have been pretty messed up, because I don't remember anyone else being with me, but it was not my house.

Maybe it was in a moment of desperation, but I much prefer to call it a moment of clarity. I picked up my cell phone, and I called the only person I could think to call.

The only person in the world that I was sure loved me.

I called Sam.

CHAPTER 18

He picked me up within thirty minutes of my call. From the side of the road in a rough area, littered with drug peddlers, crackheads, and prostitutes doing their leisurely nightly stroll. Somewhere near downtown Dallas, Texas, in the rain, I got into his truck.

It was the first time I'd seen him since the day he left my apartment years earlier. Immediately, I felt love around me again. He had Fin with him. He'd gone to get him from my mom's a couple of months before, and he had become my son's father, sole provider, and caregiver. I got to hug them both.

Sam held me while I cried for a very, very long time. It was complete relief; I felt safe.

When we arrived at his apartment and after a hot bath, I laid down with Fin in his bed. It had only been a few months. Normally I saw them at my mom's house on the weekends and holidays. More recently, I had started skipping them. I didn't want them to see me that way. It seemed like it had been a lifetime. I snuggled up to his little body with my nose against his hair and fell into an exhausted, peaceful sleep.

Just like Jenny Gump, I slept for days. I was emotionally, mentally, and physically drained in a way I'd never been. For weeks, all I could do was wake up and eat, shower, and sleep more. My body needed to heal. My mind had to recuperate. It was not going to allow anything else.

The beautiful thing about Sam was that he didn't ask questions. He was not looking for answers, and he didn't expect me to function. He was a silent, endearing pillar of strength that just *was*. He invited me to heal. His unassuming, lovely nature didn't just allow me into his heart and space again; the truth was that he would not have accepted anything else.

It was as if he was making up for what he'd done the only way he knew how. Not from guilt; it was from complete compassion, understanding, and love. The only time I have ever felt that from anyone.

Because of him, I am alive, and I will always love him.

If you ever read this, Sam, I love you with every piece of my now capable heart.

I felt safe and warm for the first time in a long time, and I thank God for Sam. He showed true unselfishness and friendship, as if we had never parted ways, and it was good.

He made sure I ate when I needed to, and we had no problem quickly returning to the best friends we had been before. Even though I was still faced with unspeakable horror in my dreams, he was always there to soothe me and help me feel safe enough to fall back to sleep.

We liked being at home, ordering takeout, and just being in the same space with one another. Just the three of us.

I was getting more strength and weight back daily, and with Fin, my soul was being fed. I was cautiously optimistic.

Jet and Beau were with us every weekend as well, but they were still enrolled in school near my mom's house, so until I got better, it was a good situation.

They loved Sam very much, and they were older, so they developed a real kinship with him. They brought their homework when they came over, and Sam enjoyed teaching them math, history, or algebra.

He took me to the doctor to see if I could find out why I was getting hives. Something my husband had never thought or cared to do. They never went away and plagued me at the most inopportune times.

Within minutes of being examined, the doctor knew what the cause was. I was allergic to the hormone that was continuously surging through my bloodstream given off by the birth control implants that were still in my arm. He set me up for immediate surgery and removed them at no cost.

Apparently, this was a common side effect of that particular birth control, and he gave me a handful of pamphlets and phone numbers before I left. There was a class-action lawsuit against the pharmaceutical company, and he encouraged me to file. He said whatever happened, after that day, I would get much better.

After the removal of those implants, the anxiety, emotional distress, and hives subsided. Almost immediately. The fog seemed to clear a little for me. I stopped crying at the drop of a hat. That was a solid win in my book. I'm not saying I didn't have major mental and emotional challenges ahead of me, but there was a glimmer of hope.

***

There was a problem every week and every other weekend that still remained: picking up Dean.

It was torture. If I was late to get him, Chase left the house, so I didn't get my visit at all. If I was late bringing him home, he bitched me out and threatened me about losing my future visits. Holidays that were mine, I never got him. They used excuses that I didn't live in a normal, safe environment, yet we lived in a very nice area, and Sam was more respectable than Chase had ever been.

Sam and I were both nervous wrecks every time we had a visit. When we did manage to get him, we made sure he was brought back clean and without a scratch. I was extremely careful and nervous when I had my own son.

Chase decided that Dean was not allowed to spend the night or weekends at my house either. He knew I didn't have the money to fight it. There was always the threat of not getting to see him at all. I cried every time I dropped him off. I missed him so much.

Little by little, I was losing my child.

A few months after moving in with Sam, I made a decision. With his unwavering confidence in me, as well as his help getting a loan, I enrolled as a student at the American Airlines Academy.

It was a course to guarantee a good career and good benefits in the travel industry. My hope was to one day become a flight attendant that stayed local, so I could stay close to the kids.

Sam helped me study, and I got accepted. I had to live in the dorms on site, but it was something I was willing to do to develop some type of worthwhile career at my age. I'd always planned on finishing school, and my classes had gone very well with high grades from the community college. I felt it was a good stepping stone.

I moved into the dorms and got to work. Classes were difficult, but I managed. What started to occur after I was actually in school and doing well is beyond belief.

Chase began coming up to the airline center to see me, and sometimes he brought Dean.

He came and took me to dinner or lunch and sent me flowers a few times. There were even occasions that he came to pick me up and drove me back to the house in Dallas to spend the night. I was stumped. Though, not so confused, I didn't allow it.

Every time I started to get better, got a stable life-plan going, or got used to the fact we would never be together, he would appear.

There he'd be to give me new hope.

The truth is that he didn't want me, but he couldn't stand the thought of anyone else having me either.

Sam caught wind of this fact and stopped coming around. He was hurt, and I understood it. But my true love had always been for my children and Chase, and I was too stupid to stop it. I would forever be the girl that kept putting my hand back into the flame to make sure it still burned.

The fact is that the heart wants what the heart wants. You have no control over who you fall in love with. It is like a sickness, and once felt, it closes your heart off to the possibility of any other.

If you try and get temporary relief from a different human than the one who owns your heart, you injure them. When all they are trying to do is look for the same thing that you have already found.

Millions of jaded people walking around the planet have been someone's stepping stone to get over a heartbreak.

Once you've felt that kind of love, you never know if you'll experience it again. I believe that is why we—who have experienced it—hold onto it with every ounce of strength and determination that we have. We believe it may be the last time we'll ever feel connected to another soul. That's a pretty devastating thought, so you just don't want to give it up. It becomes who you are. It became who I was.

I often think about what would have happened all those years ago had Sam just shown up at the door of my apartment two days earlier. I loved him enough then that we would have had a happy life together. At that point, I'd never experienced being *in love.*

Both of us would have skipped so many tragic parts of what is now our collective history. The sad product of an ill-timed visit. He was *just* a day late. *One Goddamned day.* Or was Chase a day early?

When I left the apartment that Sam and I shared, Lacy and he became friends. And that was okay. I loved them both. I was even a bit hopeful for a love connection between the two of them.

She was a beautiful bombshell with a stellar personality, a wonderful steady job with an advertising company that she'd been with for years, and a lovely house in a very desirable part of the city. He was a solid, good man who had everything going for him.

He was honestly the most wholesome man I'd ever known. The connection they formed was not the love connection I had imagined, but instead somehow became a starting point for Sam's drug use.

Lacy and I had been closer than any two females on the planet. No matter what we did, in between her many stints in rehab and my constant life changes, we always ended up back together. We used to say,

"I'll catch you on the other side." When we would part for any amount of time.

We always knew we were toxic for one another, but we had been through so much together. We knew the only way either of us were going to stay clean and get our lives straight was to stay apart. We just never could.

Too much shared pain and too many common secrets between us. We knew each other better than anyone else. She was the *ying* to my *yang*.

She was outgoing, fun-loving, and full of self-esteem. She had not one ounce of fear in her gorgeous body. We were exact opposites. When it came right down to it, I was *our* conscience. I kept her more level-headed; she got me to be more adventurous. She had street smarts, where I had absolutely none. She was always very protective of me. We loved one another knowing all there was to know, without judgment.

I knew when I'd invited her over to Sam's to see me what would come next if the visits continued. I would throw sobriety and everything else I had worked for out the window. We made a pact the day I left for school to never look for each other. It's something we always did, but it would only last a few weeks or months. We always found our way back together. That time, we both meant it; we had to.

Our last evening in each other's company, we sat cross-legged on Sam's floor, and we were both honest as we expressed our feelings. We were listening to the Pearl Jam song, Black.

She sat opposite me and sang every word in her husky, sweet voice. Then, we told each other in actual words what we meant to each other. Once again, we were parting ways. Our foreheads pressed against each another's; tears streaming down both of our cheeks. Somehow, we both knew we probably wouldn't see each other again. That time was different.

We repeated the words that became our final promise, to never look for each other.

I am crying now. Not just over the loss, but also over the unbelievable love and care we had to have felt between us to even make such a promise.

I left for school the next day, and she continued to go see Sam. Needy and hurting souls, leaning on other needy and hurting souls. Even now, I take responsibility for that.

The guilt over it is felt deeply. I was hurting him the same way Chase was hurting me. He turned to drugs for the same reason I had, and it remains one of my deepest regrets.

***

School went by quickly. I still let drugs slip in periodically. I could count on Chase to have them every time I saw him.

I would love to say I prevailed and received my certificate, but with drugs so readily available again, even if only on the weekends, I failed one of my classes and was faced with having to repeat it. I could not afford to do that.

With my new failure added to my resume of screw-ups, I left the academy and went back to my mom's house. It seemed that Sam was now wrapped up in a drug addiction of his own, and it wasn't long before Fin was back with me.

My parents, (by then, they were married) had a wrought iron fence company. It was doing very well. They needed help with it, and I had my health back. I was sober and needed the work, so I dove right in. My stepfather spent hours teaching me how to weld. I learned first with a MIG and later with an ARC welder. I became excellent at it, and soon I had my own crew, and we were building and installing fences, gates, and railings all over the Dallas-Fort Worth area.

It was difficult work for a small woman, but it kept me physically as well as mentally busy, so I didn't mind. From 5 am until late in the evenings, I worked. In the summer, I worked so much that I was able to buy a truck, and I was proud.

On the weekends, I shined boots at the local honky-tonk for extra cash. I worked hard, kept my mind busy, and relished every second that I wasn't working and got to be home with the boys.

I rented a house next door to my sister's home, out in the country, and we spent a lot of time together. Our homes were just around the corner from my mother's place. Kelle had four boys by that time, so our children played together, and somehow, we just made it work. During off-season for the fence company, I went back to data processing. She and I got similar jobs in the city and drove in together each morning.

I will never forget that time in my life or those long drives to work with her. We laughed so hard sometimes; I had to pull the car over until we got ourselves together. She and I, 5 am, caught in Dallas traffic, on the side of the road hysterical and weeping from laughter. Not drug or alcohol-induced; just real, genuine laughter with my sister.

Between the fence company, the bar, and the side jobs, I worked all of the time. If I was installing a fence in the Dallas area, Chase periodically popped in. He appeared with birthday presents on my birthday or brought Dean to see me. It was so damn confusing. It kept me from ever moving forward or getting involved with anyone else. Looking back, I'm sure that was the intent.

In the middle of 1997, I was healthy, relatively happy, and completely drug-free. I had my sobriety for a few years at that point, and rarely considered even having a drink. I just didn't think about it anymore.

After seeing Chase one afternoon, he somewhat casually informed me that he was getting married.

He announced it with less care than someone would if telling me the mailman was running late.

Although it was a crushing blow, initially, I didn't react. What I eventually did was far worse than what an immediate dramatic reaction would have been.

It went something like this:

There was a man on my fence crew; his name was Seth. I loved him as you would a friend or a coworker. Seth had a crush on me. He was married. Before I knew what was happening, he'd left his wife and five children.

I honestly believed that particular choice was not because of me. I thought they just didn't get along. I do not feel it necessary to go into that time in my life in too much detail, but I am opting instead to give a short synopsis explaining just what you would need to know to understand. Mostly because I have nothing bad to say about Seth. Other than the fact he gave me one of my most valued treasures, we really don't share enough history to discuss.

Not that it was uneventful, but it would be rehashing so much of what you've already heard. He too had his demons and drug issues. But somehow, in the beginning, he appealed to the soft and needy side of me. The side of me that wanted to be worshiped and taken care of a bit. He showed me attention at a time in my life that I really desired it.

I took advantage of him that way. I allowed certain actions and displays of affection that in any other time in my life I wouldn't have. I was trying to deal with the new blow I'd been dealt concerning Chase.

I was wrong.

That being said, now I somehow feel that it's unfair not to give Seth more weight in my story, so I will paint you a clearer picture of who he is as a person.

He is Mexican American. (I would call him Hispanic, but he used to say he was not from *Hispania*, and he didn't even know where that was.)

He was very handsome. Seth stood about 5'8 with a muscular build acquired from years of doing manual labor. Dark smooth skin, large brown eyes, and a beautiful smile. He was clean-shaven, which softened his otherwise rugged good looks. Charming personality and proud. Very respectful of others, always addressing people as "sir" or "ma'am.".

He was the kind of man that would stop and help a stranger change a tire on the side of the road, even if it was cold and rainy outside and he was exhausted. One of the hardest workers I've ever met. Shy and quiet most of the time, he embarrassed easily. We all made the extra effort to make him blush. It was quite adorable to witness his cheeks turn crimson while he looked down at his feet.

Serious isn't a strong enough word to use concerning his demeanor. He was the epitome of a strong, sensitive male. He had a passion for classic cars and trucks. He wasn't book smart and had not finished high school, but he made up for it with common sense.

Seth was a simple man of few words. He liked Mexican music, Mexican beer, and Mexican food. Pressed blue jeans, cowboy boots, and button downs. With a clear understanding of English and Spanish, most of the time he spoke Spanish. When he spoke English, he did it with not even a hint of an accent. One of the many reasons he was an asset to have on my crew. Most of the employees were Mexican.

I'm sure by now you've figured out that I absolutely do not have a type. With men who warrant my attention, it's never been about looks, careers, money, or the lack thereof, but always about the attraction or vibe. I either find them attractive or I don't. In most cases, I do not.

There has to be something special in a man that captures my attention and keeps it for any length of time. I'm not entirely sure that I shouldn't replace the word "special" with "aloof" or emotionally unavailable.

In December of 1998, I gave birth to my fifth son, Tris. The light of my life, the apple of my eye. The one I am the closest to, even now. As a proud mother of five sons, I would be remiss if I didn't clarify that I love all of my children, equally, of course. I'm just closer to the youngest, and we have a better understanding of one another. He is the most gentle and nonjudgmental soul I have ever encountered.

The only way I can make sense of—or explain to you as the reader—how I managed to get pregnant again is to tell you that it wasn't about passion.

It was more that sex had become a way to give back to a sweet friend—a friend that had been good to me. As if I felt he "earned" it. After the birth control implants were taken out, I started taking the pill, but I wasn't sleeping around, and wasn't good at consistency. And there you have it.

I am not sure why, as humans, more often than not, we seem to mistake friendship for love. Or is that just me? It didn't help that I had been lonely for a very, very long time.

***

Tris. He was the most beautiful little boy I'd ever seen. He looked like a little native Indian papoose. Chubby, olive-skinned, and laughing all of the time. He had a thick head of dark curls that I never wanted to cut, so he had long ringlets down his back. Jet, Beau, Fin, and even Dean loved him to pieces. All of Seth's other children did as well. That child was passed around and unbelievably spoiled. We all kind of worshiped the little guy.

He was always happy and brought joy into all of our lives. Sweet, quiet, funny, and kind. He had extra personality and wore his feelings on his sleeve. All traits that he kept. I was genuinely in love with that little boy. I still am.

Eventually my parents decided to sell the property in east Texas and moved down south. They moved to Lampasas, Texas. Where my stepfather's family lived.

Seth and I tried to make a go of it for a short time after Tris was born, but that time I had the strength and will to walk away from what I knew wasn't healthy. I didn't want anything to do with anyone who used drugs or alcohol. I just wanted more for myself.

It also made the drug too easily accessible to me, and again, I was not beyond doing it on occasion. I was all too familiar with how quickly it could become a way of life. I was done with loss attributed to any substance. I was not in love with Seth any more than I had been with Sam, and he and I both knew it.

Karma with a side of Karma, anyone?

By 1999, I was 31 years old. I had five sons. The eldest, Jet, was only thirteen. I was a waitress at a steak restaurant, I'd been divorced twice and hadn't completed college. I'd beat an almost two-year drug addiction but I'd spent the last eight years of my life trying to get over the most recent ex-husband.

I gave him everything, so materialistically, I owned nothing of value. I was single again and still had massive amounts of unresolved trauma. All of the idiosyncrasies I'd gained from my past were still very much a daily battle for me. Without anything to take the edge off or any way to deal with them, I wore them like I wore my skin.

Sleep still eluded me no matter what I did. I had a crappy disposable truck and worked so much I didn't get to spend time with my children like I wanted or needed to.

I was again, in constant survival mode. Unable to settle into a routine of day-to-day life.

Although I could get into relationships and bare sons that any Chinaman or King of England would have been proud of, the rest of what was considered "adulting" was evidently just not my cup of tea.

And then, for the first time in my life, something unforeseen and pretty great happened. Something, not someone, that came along at such a perfect time that it can only be considered good luck.

As unlucky as I have always been, you, as the reader, should have been nervous as hell to even read that last statement.

CHAPTER 19
Tethered

Periodically, I go to the pyramids. There is a hostel there that has a perfect view of them. I go to the rooftop and meditate, enjoy the scenery, or just absorb the vibe.

"Vibe" is not a word I would have used two years ago, but I find in Egypt, I use it a lot. The energy here is indescribable. Even for someone who didn't used to believe in the everyday ebb and flow of it, it's impossible to ignore.

There's something about this place and those pyramids that will set a person's mind at ease while simultaneously questioning all. I believe it would make anyone give serious thought to the *why* in every single thing. From birth to purpose and everything in between.

So many of my years have been spent in the work, eat, and entertainment mentality of living here on Earth. I never really felt the need to consider anything else. Maybe because I could never slow down enough to catch my breath or ever had a chance to give into second guessing.

I look back and feel now that although I made all of the life-directing decisions concerning myself, each one was made as a result of another. I just adapted along the way, even at times when I shouldn't have.

In retrospect, I have been as a leaf in a river. Just floating down stream and having no real control or anything to hold onto. I might have gotten hung up on a rock or limb along the way, giving me a view of the stream and which direction would have been the most beneficial, but was never in that position long enough to see a clear picture or form a plan. The next current or wind would pick me up and carry me forward too soon, and I would just adapt and go with the flow. It was like,

"Oh, this is what we are doing now? Okay."

Then I would set about making the best of it.

However obvious it is to me now that I should have taken control to shift my mind and produce a more favorable outcome, I didn't have that knowledge then. I am pretty certain that even if I had, I would have lacked the courage.

When I came to Egypt, I was so wrapped up in seeing all of the tourist attractions. Taking pictures, and as most travelers do, running from one amazing historical site to another. All so that I could say, show, and commit to memory that I had been there. Which is comical to me now—the thought that I would ever forget *any* of this. I am not sure when it started to change, but it certainly did.

While I do still consider what I would like to see next, it's more about the experience of feeling and enjoying the rich and solid vibe. The vibration of this country is real. It is real, and at times difficult to comprehend.

If you choose to make this country a must-see for yourself, you need to realize a few things first.

One of the most important things on that list is that if you come here with any silver dental work in your mouth, expect it to hurt. It will. As a matter of fact, I have had every single filling in my mouth either fall out or cause so much discomfort that I have had to have them all replaced.

Since my own experience, I've heard countless stories from other travelers along the same lines. There is no explanation, except that the vibration of this place is on a whole different level. Your body will actually start to reject anything that is unnatural or harmful.

Maybe I sound a bit crazy, and a few months ago, I would have felt anyone telling me this was a bit "touched." But it is a very real phenomenon.

I even saw a dentist before I came here and had a routine check-up and maintenance done to make sure I wouldn't have any issues. Still, not enough preparation and foresight.

When I walk through Giza or get close to the pyramids, there is an overwhelming power in the air. The hair on my arms and head stands up. As if it were statically charged. That isn't where it stops. The energy seems to rise up from my core, much like an excitement or adrenalin rush. It cannot be subdued. At first, I wasn't sure what was going on. It felt as if I was being overstimulated. I perceived it as nerves.

Lucid dreams of all aspects of my life were every-night occurrences, not just the one awful incident. I am not sure if anyone has ever written about this being part of the Egyptian experience, but I feel it is very important to relay.

I had to relocate and give myself more distance from that area until I could learn to grip that energy in a more effective and less mind-scrambling way.

The ground here is a Tesla ball, and all of us are walking on it, absorbing its life. When a person is new to it and not aware, it will feel disconcerting and nauseating.

Even if you do not consider yourself religious, Egypt is a spiritual place.

Again, I am not sure when it happened that I changed. At some point, instead of feeling like an individual or lone soul walking these deserts and streets, I started to feel connected. A connection to everyone and everything. Although I've never been here before, it all feels familiar. I do not feel alone, but instead feel that wherever I go and whatever I do,

I do it with a crowd. Hypothetically, of course.

For the first time in my life, I don't feel disconnected or singular. It is as if everyone here has a cord connected to one another.

A better analogy would be a lightning bolt. A surge of electricity with all of its little tentacles of power, but instead of power connecting that energy, here—it's people.

It goes much deeper than that.

Not only are we all part of the same bolt, but somehow, we are all part of the source of the outburst of power. The part we cannot see—way up in the universe. I am tethered to something unseen; only felt. Even though I can walk away from a group and find myself alone, I never really am. I don't feel as if I am on a short leash, but one made with infinite expansion material. I can go as far as I want. It is my soul, heart, or energy that will always find its way back to others and the main source.

This feeling has a glorious side effect: safety. I feel safe.

These people have something inside of them different than any other humans I've lived around. They have a want and need to be a part of everyone and everything around them. With sincere effort on their part to connect as much as possible. They have grace and gratitude.

When I'd only been here a few months, my dentist asked me where I lived. I told him I lived in Indonesia. His reply surprised me.

He said that he had been there once and that he was not fond of it because the people were cold. He said he felt no real human connection. I didn't understand him having that opinion. I thought about that for days.

Mainly because I love that country, and compared to Americans, there is no lack of feeling their love. Now I realize that he was comparing it to here. If that is the case, I'm not so sure that every country wouldn't be a bit unfeeling and cold when put next to Egypt—perspective.

Even though most people here do not speak English, choosing instead to be fluent in French or even Russian, they *try* to communicate. They *want* to talk to me.

These people *need* to feel human connection.

In the beginning, I didn't understand. I almost felt aggravated or put out when I realized Arabic is mostly all they speak. In my mind, this is a very touristy country. I didn't see selfishness in my expectation that they should all know English as a second language.

What I have come to realize is that the little bit of Arabic that I have learned to speak has built a bridge between me and them. A smile and a few words and we interact perfectly. Understanding each other goes beyond a fluent language. They focus on our commonality.

I feel it when they touch my arm as they slow down their speech trying to teach me. While I teach them the English version. They yank the smiles, love, and laughter straight out of my soul. It doesn't matter how busy they are; there is never an occasion that they do not make time for a smile, a wave, or a moment of showing their pleasure in my presence. It touches a place in my heart that I cannot completely understand myself.

It's an everyday, open exchange of our inner power and source. A dance of sorts between each and every living being in this country. I didn't have to decide to participate; the universe decided for me. It is truly the most eye-opening and marvelous thing I have ever experienced.

I had forgotten how to cry until I came here. Which I thought was strength, but I'd also forgotten how to feel true joy for life. The two go hand-in-hand. Pain and joy. You cannot truly experience one without the other. You learn depth of feeling when you learn to give into both. You must give each its turn, or you will never experience life the way it's intended.

I believe as humans we do ourselves such a huge injustice considering the way we view happiness. I myself have my own view, as I am sure everyone does.

When my son Fin was in high school and about to graduate, the senior class was interviewed and asked individual questions.

The question presented to him was something to the effect of who his hero was. Who motivated him the most? His answer was published in the newspaper the next day. I was unaware of its existence until a friend called me and told me to go grab a local paper.

So, I did.

I sat in my car scanning the pages for a clue as to why she would tell me to go out and buy one, and then I saw it.

In the middle section were pictures of some of the graduating students. When I spotted my son, under his picture, I read.

His answer to who his hero was? His mom. It was me.

He went on to say that I was strong and determined, and for that he looked up to me. This was—and remains to be—my definition of happiness. It is all the validation I should ever want or need. Through all that was going on in my life, no matter my struggles or failures, one of the main purposes in my life that kept me marching forward was watching. He saw me.

Not only did he see me, he appreciated and valued me to such an amazing extent that he didn't care how lame it might have appeared to other young adults his age by making it known. Simply put, he loved me back.

I was touched so, that I sat in my car and cried.

As wonderful as that feeling was and is, I will compare every other feeling of happiness I ever have to the minute I read that newspaper. I will, without intention, overlook happiness that doesn't measure up to that moment in time. The feeling of being loved by one that I love is what life is about. It doesn't mean I shouldn't truly appreciate all other forms of joy.

We must stop assigning different degrees to happiness. Any happiness is to be cherished and appreciated. There truly is always going to be another great heartfelt pleasure in our lives. None greater than the next unless we deem it so in our own minds.

We limit ourselves. The love that brings joy and vice versa should be limitless. Each and every single second is a gift. Emotions those moments bring are to be included; not rated.

I walk around in the midst of these people as if I am wearing a space suit that is equipped with happiness, gratitude, and love pouring in and around me through a lifesaving tube. I simply cannot feel any other way.

I feel my soul in Egypt. I have found myself here.

PART 2

CHAPTER 20

I am running through a maze of white brick buildings; all of them have huge round pillars in front, holding up the eves. It's dark and dim, but the sun is clearly in the sky, as if in the midst of a solar eclipse. I am trying to scream; I think I am, but no sound is coming out. Silent calls for help that take every ounce of my energy and produce nothing to aid me. It doesn't matter how fast I believe I am running; they are always at my heels.

It's consistently the same nightmare. Over and over again, for the last thirty-four years. It replays almost nightly, just to make sure I haven't forgotten.

The dreams are much worse than the actual occurrence. Mainly because while I am reliving it, I already know what is about to happen. My subconscious knows the outcome; I will not be able to stop it. And so, it goes...

When my boys were small, I would go into their room every night and check on them. Cover untucked arms or legs and touch their soft, dimpled hands and cheeks. Kiss their little foreheads. Not just for the pleasure of kissing them, but also for their smell. Innocence has the most calming aroma in the whole world. Hands down, my favorite smell.

So many nights I either crawled into their beds with them or brought them into mine. Sometimes sleeping with my hand on one of their chests, feeling it go up and down. Listening to their little, light snoring brought me comfort. Even as they got older and into their teen years, I would awaken after one of my dreams, or I would just poke my head in their door on my way to the bathroom.

Countless times I stood by their beds, with only the light from the hallway illuminating their faces, just staring at them. It has taken me a long time to realize that now, when I wake up, there is no one else here to check on.

It is not until just this minute that I realize how much responsibility I pushed onto my children. I made them carry the weight that came from giving me some kind of peace and purpose. It became more so as they grew. They were always my comfort, much more than I was theirs. When I was sad or crying and had one of my babies crawl up into my lap or wipe my tears away, that was a whole different level of relief.

As they grew, so did their empathy. Beau, Fin, or Tris could never stand to see me cry. Jet hated it also, but he was always the strong voice of reason, standing at a distance with his own eyes watering and giving me words of encouragement.

The phase of my life I was about to enter is just as liable for who I am today as the rest, but it is different in my mind because it involved my growing boys. I feel responsible for the decisions I made that didn't just affect me. As older children, they should have had a say in some of it; I should have considered how they felt. But that first life-changing decision seemed more like a lucky break, and in the beginning, it was great.

***

Laurie was a coworker at the steakhouse where I worked. If my memory serves me correctly, she had been there for almost ten years. One day she came in and quit. Before my shift ended, she took me aside and told me she had a new job at a sports bar and said she was making an incredible amount of money. She gave me the name of the place and told me to come check it out.

One week later, I too was putting in my notice at the steakhouse. I had lucked out, and one of the waitresses at the sports bar was not working out; I was hired.

The place was called SCOOTERS, and it was in my hometown of Garland. It was a smaller "cheers" type of place in a shopping strip at an intersection that proved to be a great location. Pool tables, food, drinks. Everything you would expect from a bar. The difference being that when the clock struck 10 pm, the lights went down, the music went up, and it turned into a full-blown nightclub. It was a karaoke bar, and it was a favorite of people from all around the Dallas/Ft. Worth area.

Every night karaoke and DJ, pool and dart tournaments, as well as poker. It was packed with people seven nights a week. I used to wonder if those people had jobs, because many of them came in at happy hour and didn't leave until closing at 2 am—every day.

The owner's name was Scott, and my first impression of him was not at all what he turned out to be. I thought he was a jerk. He was a man who had been in the business long enough to know exactly what he wanted for his club and what he didn't, and he wouldn't accept anything else. It was his way or the highway. He was tough.

He had this phenomenal ability to call people stupid without ever using the actual *word*. He was the type of guy that could have you bawling your eyes out one minute and, in the next, hand you two thousand bucks for your car repairs or rent. One of the sweetest assholes you would ever meet.

Genuine. No matter what mood he was in or what side of him you saw, it was guaranteed to be real. The man did not have a fake bone in his body and had no interest in people-pleasing or pretending. If your feelings happened to be on your sleeve that day, and you expected differently from him, well—that was on you.

I had to have pretty thick skin around him, but that was okay. I had plenty of time to grow it, and he would make sure that I did. I tried to embrace the painful growth.

I have since realized that being blunt seems to be a side effect of integrity. I appreciated and valued him, even if I didn't completely understand his methods. I had always been a "frustrated crier." I spent more time than I would like to admit trying to escape from his view before he could see tears welling up in my eyes. I would have rather died than have him see that weakness in me.

The few times I didn't get away quick enough to hide it, he would have to walk away. He would always come to me later, after he had calmed down, and either explain himself or apologize in his way. A conversation that usually started with why *I* was wrong but was said in a gentler manner.

I hate to admit it, but he was right more times than not. He was rough in attitude but kindhearted in nature. I was never sure if I wanted to hug him or throw a bottle at him. Most of the time I wanted to do *both*. Once I conceded to shut up and listen, he was always teaching me something. I was so hard-headed and full of pride; I was a difficult student.

What comes to mind when I think of him is the phrase "if you're going to be dumb, you're going to have to be tough." A point he made, one way or another, daily. If he cared for someone, he cared. If he didn't, he just didn't. He acted accordingly. No one had ever had my back like him, and no one has since.

What also comes to mind is the fact he reminded me so much of my brother Ricky—in appearance and attitude.

Scott had a great, infectious laugh. He didn't laugh often, so when he did, it made everyone within earshot relax a bit and giggle too. Which was not so great when I was mad.

He had this habit of cracking up when I was furious! The angrier I acted, the more he found it funny. So many times, I stomped away, fists clenched, fighting back tears, and biting my tongue. Serving drinks to patrons seated around the bar, laced with my tears.

There were a few times he would leave the club out the back door, and as soon as I heard his car leave, I would throw something at that door. He was so frustrating! I am grinning right now, ear-to-ear. Why in the hell is this such a fond memory for me?

I started as a waitress, and at first, I doubted I'd made a good choice in quitting the steakhouse. It was the most different work environment I had ever experienced. For a few weeks, I only made half of what I was used to.

I had to put up with the smoke and the intoxicated patrons, and I had to work twice as hard. Not to mention the foul language. I had never heard the word *fuck* used to that extent. It slid out of everyone's mouth as easily as saying hello. I myself didn't use it at the time, and it offended the crap out of me.

Then, I'm not entirely sure what happened. Maybe the regulars got used to me or I got better at my job. I made over two hundred dollars in one night, and it wasn't a fluke. It began to happen every night. The harder I worked, the more money I made.

We didn't have assigned sections; each waitress just had to run for their own money. It was a system that worked for everyone involved. The customer received great service, and we all made good money.

One evening, one of our bartenders didn't show up for her shift. Without a replacement, I ended up behind the bar making drinks. I had no idea what I was doing. I didn't drink, and the only thing I knew for sure was which beer was which.

It was Labor Day. Our bar was always a favorite for people at the end of a holiday. By 11 pm, I was three to four people deep all of the way around the bar. The dance floor was packed, with pool tables all occupied and no empty dining tables. We did not have bar-backs—ever. If we needed ice, beer, or alcohol, we had to leave the bar and get it ourselves. I had one waitress on the floor that night, and I was getting her drink orders too. There was a small card catalog beside the well with drink recipes in it. I didn't have the time for that, so I just started asking them what color the drink was they wanted and made it up as I went along.

Somewhere in between learning how to change a keg, serving colorful mystery drinks, popping tops, restocking beer and ice, and doing dishes, I eased into a groove of some kind and lost the anxiety over it. Once I settled in, it became easier, and I managed.

By "managed," I mean it felt like I had been doing it my whole life.

Later, after everyone was out of the bar and clean-up was completed, I counted tips and couldn't believe my eyes. I had made over four hundred dollars. In one night. Without taking my clothes off.

After that night, I received real training behind the bar. I worked as much as I could and never turned down the offer to take someone's shift. Money was an excellent motivator. I was making it hand over fist, with no time to spend it.

The boys had spent the summer with Kelle, and because my job required me to be there at 1:30 pm, and often times I didn't get home until after 4:00 am, she enrolled them in school with her boys. I took that time and worked. I worked every single day if I could. For the money as well as the fact that at the end of the day, I was so exhausted I could fall asleep. For the first time in years, I was sleeping.

After each shift, I counted my money, took out just enough to pay for gas or whatever I needed, and I put the rest into a bank bag and hid it at the bar. I did that for months.

By the time I had a day off and decided to count the money, I had close to $10,000. Within a week I had rented a new apartment by the lake and filled it with all new furnishings. I picked up the boys from Kelle and brought them home.

I have to say that the way I spent money at the time is comparable to handing a fifteen-year-old a stack of cash and instructing them to "spend it wisely.".

A great example of this would be as follows:

We had a hailstorm one night in our town. The next day, on the way to work, I passed a Ford dealership. There were lots of shiny new, hail-damaged Mustang sports cars on the lot. I had always wanted a Mustang. The next day, before work, I went and bought one.

I bought a brand new, black, standard shift, fully loaded Mustang. The girl with five children *purchased a 2-door sports car.*

Although I loved that car, and I got a great deal because of the two hail dings, I still do not know what I was thinking. I guess what I am trying to say is that I could have benefited from some kind of advice on making major financial decisions. I learned that just because I could didn't mean I should.

Scott, with his hilarious gift with words, called it my "family mobile." That time I would have understood, had he just called me stupid.

I worked *a lot*. When I was off work, the boys and I had a blast. We shopped, went to the movies, and ordered Chinese takeout or pizza. Whatever they wanted. For the first time in my adult single life, money and paying bills were not a concern. All of us were happy.

I felt extremely tired most of the time, but much less preoccupied. I did not like it that they were alone most of the night, but I trusted them. They were always good and responsible.

I gained self-esteem. Working in that place was the most physically and mentally demanding job I have ever had, but the money reflected exactly what I put into it. Which fueled me to work harder. I have jokingly said that working for Scott made me a badass. Jokes aside, much of my strength and attitude that I still possess, came from that job and him.

Some people are good musicians; some are great dancers or swimmers. Those people that excel particularly well at those professions will tell you it just came natural to them. Oh, how I wish I could say that I was born with one of those more reputable talents. It just so happens that my gift is bar tending.

Although I have never been really great at dealing with people, that job taught me how. I was socially awkward, obsessive, hyper, and eager to do my best to support my family without help. That job was not just a solution; it was God-send! I had much to prove—to myself more than anyone.

It consisted of constantly thinking about the next chore while handling the last customer, and the countless other responsibilities it takes to run a bar, while a million other things are going on in the background, in the loudest and sometimes most obnoxious environment you can dream of.

Remembering ten drink orders, making them, delivering them, collecting the money, making change, and somewhere in the middle, re-stocking, doing dishes, and handling the waitress' as well as delivering food orders. On repeat for hours. No time to think, sit, or even run to the bathroom. It was enough to make anyone feel like a badass.

Autopilot for long hours, so I had to know what I was doing. Being aware of everything going on around me and behind me came naturally since the *incident*. My kids always said I had eyes in the back of my head, at Scooters, I used them. I could feel a fight coming long before the actual brawl.

I used to have customers that came in that didn't even drink alcohol. They ordered soda and told me they came to watch the "show." They just enjoyed watching me work; I was fascinating to them.

Working behind that bar made me fit. I would have to go retrieve ice for the well and our huge beer bins at the beginning of the shift and periodically all night. I carried four full ten-gallon buckets of ice at a time, twenty times a night. We had a dolly cart, but I never used it. I could stack four or five cases of beer in my arms and carry them out to restock. I was strong and lean.

The best feeling came at the end of the night when I emptied the tip jars and counted money. It was immediate gratification, every day. It was as if the money I was making gave me value. If that is the case, I was worth around fifteen hundred a week in the winter months, much more during the holidays, less in the summer. I guess you could say I felt pretty validated.

I think what made me fall in love with that life is the fact that when I was working, I thought of nothing else. It was time off from anything and everything that brought me pain or anxiety. There was no time or space for melancholy. It gave me an emotional and mental break.

When my shift was over and I was back at home, I was too exhausted to feel anything. I just tried to be with the boys and enjoy them. More times than not, I would fall asleep on the couch on my days off, but it was comforting to have my kids around me making noise and messes.

I was working and supporting my family by myself. We were in need of nothing. Whatever it took to make them healthy and happy, I was providing. There was never a greater feeling.

I finally settled into a consistent and predictable lifestyle—just me and my boys. It would prove to be one of the only periods of time I can claim that, and it went by entirely too fast.

CHAPTER 21

I would like to use loneliness as an excuse, but I wasn't. I wish I could blame my choice on needing financial help or wanting to have some type of normal family dynamic, but I cannot. I have no answer to why I made my next life choice, except I guess it was just time.

I had been unattached for a few years, but I was actually without a real romantic love since the final ending with Chase. Even with Seth, I kept my heart to myself. A kind of sick loyalty I had concerning my most recent ex-husband.

I still compared everyone I considered, or who considered me, to him. No one stood a chance with me. Because to me, not one person measured up.

I was never the type of woman who had one-night stands. Random sexual trysts were not a part of who I was and never interested me. I wasn't having lots of sex in my younger days; it just so happened that each time I did get involved with someone, the relationship seemed to produce a child.

For me, I had to slowly develop a friendship with someone to even be attracted enough to want to be intimate.

The few times I've tried to subdue my loneliness by inviting someone into my bed prematurely, it just made me feel bad. It also had the side effect of my need to immediately sever the relationship all together. I basically never wanted to see them again. I sincerely have never been able to achieve sexual gratification unless I do, in fact, care deeply for the person I am with. It's a waste of time and energy.

I am the epitome of a serial monogamist. Choosing to remain celibate in between my horrible choices in partners.

Honestly, I really never had many men interested enough to ask me out on a date. Not just then, but most of my adult life. I was used to being alone; I was not going to settle for anything less than what I thought I deserved. Even if the idea of what I did deserve was foggy and unclear at that point.

Not long after I started bar tending, Chase, Dean, and his new wife, as well as his parents, moved to Longview, Texas. Although every step I made was partly to prove how much I didn't need Chase and how well I could do on my own, they were not around to see it. I still considered them and what they would think in almost every decision I made. So, other men were off the table.

The Logan's didn't consider me at all. I didn't even have a phone number or a way to reach them.

The last time I saw Dean, he was eight years old. I picked him up and took him to a local park. I'd bought him a toy bug collection set that included a net, magnifying glass, tweezers, etc., and a belt to carry them in.

It was a Wednesday, and I remember sitting at a Picnic table, watching him. He was on his knees, with a magnifying glass against his eye, excitedly observing a critter of some kind in the grass. I enjoyed his enthusiasm and listening to him chatter like a magpie. He had the cutest little lisp when he spoke.

He crawled up into my lap and told me that even though he had a new mother, I would always be his mommy. I held him and cried. I somehow knew I wouldn't see him again. I was intentionally late taking him home that day.

Had I known for certain that would be our last hug, kiss, and "I love you," I would have held him in my arms much longer. I should have held onto him long enough to memorize his smell. I can still recall how his little sweaty neck felt against my cheek. Longview might as well have been Alaska; I had no way to go and see him with the job I had and funds available to me. I had to stay focused on his brothers.

They'd always witnessed my distress when it came to Dean and his father. Yet, I still tried to make the best choices just in case. I was always trying to prove my worth to those people.

Anyway, I had no time to actually feel the tremendous pain. I put it into my box of unresolved issues and placed it somewhere out of reach in order to function. I had a club to run, and my boys at home were my main reason to work hard and provide. Always telling myself that someday I would be able to do something to correct what had happened with Dean.

**

At the bar, the new never wore off. I still had Scott, always pleased with my work and expecting more from me. He wanted me to become financially independent, and I believe he saw something in me that I didn't. He had developed more faith in me than I had in myself. Which used to be part of his frustration.

It was not a normal Karaoke style bar. Scooters attracted some amazing talent. With a few of them going on to become famous. Definitely not run-of-the-mill singers.

There was a man that used to come in five or six nights a week; sometimes he sang. He chose songs from Led Zeppelin, or AC/DC. He had the voice for it, and usually his performance got everyone up on their feet and riled up. For sure, someone everyone knew.

He occasionally did some electrical work for Scott when he was in a pinch. I never really paid attention to him. He was a very large, overbearing biker-looking guy. Leather coats, tattoos, Bourbon, loud and boisterous. Many times, causing fights or disruptions on purpose because of his choice in women. It was a neighborhood soap opera of sorts. He was not my type, even if I'd had one.

His name was Derek, and after developing a crush on me, he became persistent. After months of asking me out and my refusing to go against my strict rule to never date customers, I thought I had ended his interest—not a chance. He just kept pulling out all of the stops. It was getting quite difficult to turn him down.

He stood about 6'2 with almost black naturally curly hair that he wore in long ringlets down his back. It was longer than mine. Fair skin and neon blue eyes. Broad shoulders, barrel chest, and a meticulously groomed goatee. He had a rather large skull tattoo across his upper arm. Not exactly what normally interests me.

I think what made me finally agree to see him was his personality. He was funny. Usually corny, dad type of jokes, but he always looked happy. Except when he got so drunk he left his card at the bar and had to come get it the next day. Then he was serious, well-mannered, articulate, and dressed nice. Ruggedly charming. He was very persistent, and after months of asking, I finally agreed to meet with him for drinks.

Thinking back, I really should have considered, or at least questioned, the validity of a man who spent so much of his time in a bar.

We met up at another popular club on the other side of town. What started out as some happy-hour cocktails ended up being a twelve-hour date and my first tattoo. My attraction to him was not immediate, but instead took many hours of his charm and conversation to create an interest.

He had a magnetic personality. A cross between a gentleman and a tough guy who knew all the right things to say and do to make a girl feel good. He was rough around the edges for sure, but not tacky.

I knew even then that those moves had taken years of practice to get to the level of confidence he possessed. He only used the ones that worked and was very smooth about it. The more he revealed his personality, the more handsome he became. Sex appeal he had in spades.

He had a strong, powerful, and positive persona. He radiated self-esteem. He wasn't uneducated but was not a college graduate. He had chosen a field that was lucrative and allowed him to continue his nightly shenanigans. He was a commercial electrician and made quite decent money. He didn't seem needy or desperate like most men I'd been around, but rather secure and happy with himself. Annoyingly cocky and proud.

When Scott heard that I was seeing him, he was genuinely concerned. He had known Derek long enough to develop a not-so-favorable opinion of him. He warned me, but I was a know-it-all and wouldn't listen to anyone. I liked the attention of this strange, loud, sexy guy. The most different of any man I had ever spent time with. It was odd how he made me feel lucky to be in his company.

I am at a complete loss to explain *why* I would feel that way. Especially since I later found out that he had spent many of his younger years in prison. That would normally have been a deal-breaker for me. He didn't act low-class; it seemed that he had been raised right. He is really hard for me to put into words.

We were opposite in every single detail. I was small, framed at 5'2; he was huge compared to me. He was outgoing and loved loud social situations; I hated them and became quiet and nervous. His manners left something to be desired, and he had absolutely no couth. He loved heavy rock and alcohol; I enjoyed country music and being sober. Opposites in every way; they do, in fact, attract.

He was fun, and when I was with him, I became less serious and couldn't help but loosen up and follow his lead.

I guess what it came down to is that I actually *felt* something with him. Which, for me, was not a common occurrence. I felt attracted to him and enjoyed his company. I had not felt that in many years. I never wanted anyone to touch me since Chase, until Derek. Human touch is a deeply seeded need in all of us, I think, and I'd been deprived for so long. He came along at the right moment in time.

As with every single relationship I have ever had, ours went way too fast. He came to my apartment one weekend to meet my boys, and they absolutely hated him. He was pushy, sarcastic, and had a foul mouth. They immediately saw what he was and didn't like any of it. From his personality to his manners, they disliked it all.

He came in trying to run something, even making the mistakes of reprimanding Beau over the way he spoke to me. That was not an enjoyable day.

After ten months of dating, I was running into issues with my schedule at the bar without someone to watch Tris at night. The boys were exhausted and going to school on no sleep, not to mention not having parental guidance at night. They were alone all of the time. I felt guilt even then, but in order to raise them and provide everything that goes along with it, I had to work almost every day.

Derek owned a home in the nearby town of Mesquite and asked me/us to move in with him. He said he loved me, and I felt something like love or infatuation; I'm not entirely sure what I felt. Even though we had only been dating a short time, I'd known him for almost two years and felt he was a fairly sincere guy. I had a problem, and he presented a solution. So, we moved into his little three-bedroom home and settled in.

For me, it was a relief that the boys had someone around when I was working. They wouldn't be left to their own devices all of the time.

Things were good in the beginning. I bought a family dog—a Sheltie we named Shelby. The sweetest little addition. The boys loved him, but that was Tris's best buddy.

One night I came home from work early. Derek had been at the bar drinking that night, and something in the way he was acting was unsettling to me.

It's strange that when I stopped doing drugs years before, I simply erased all knowledge and didn't think about any aspect of it anymore.

I had been made aware of the fact it was going on around me one night, when one of our door men threw a pack of matches to someone across the club, and I intercepted it. When I opened it, there was a little bag of cocaine inside. I started to take notice after that.

The signs were all around me. It seemed that everyone was doing it. Including people I worked with. I ignored it. That was a road I had already been down and didn't care to revisit.

It was always an insult to me when someone would ask me jokingly what I was on. It really made me angry that people assumed I had to be on something because I was a hard worker. Like I would need an illegal substance just to do my job.

Anyway, something in the way Derek left the bar so quickly that particular night, along with an odd look he had in his eyes, was bothersome. So, I saw that the bar was taken care of and just went home.

When I got there, I went in and asked where Derek was. The kids said that he had been in the bedroom for hours; they thought he was asleep. When I went to the bedroom, I was locked out. I basically had to break into my own bedroom. Once inside, I saw that he was in the bathroom. I knocked and knocked and became concerned. When he finally did open that door, what I saw took a while to register.

In all of the time I had done drugs, there were only a hand full of times I had done them any other way other than smoke or snort them, and a nurse friend of mine had done it for me. I had not considered ever being so addicted to a high that I would administer it intravenously to myself.

A spoon, a lighter, a syringe, and a bag of what looked like cocaine lay out on the bathroom vanity. His arm was still tied off.

I had to sit down on the bed. I was so surprised. I really had no clue before that minute he did drugs. It was more than doing drugs. When I saw that setup, I immediately labeled him. I was devastated. I had brought my children to live with a junkie. Even in the drug world, the people that choose that method of using are judged. He was in the same house with my teenagers and my toddler shooting up. Wow. What had I done? How stupid could I be?

My reaction was swift and precise. I quit my job, packed up my children, and left for my mother's house within a week.

At first, he was not invited. But then he made a plea to come that I couldn't refuse. He said he had battled drug addiction for years and felt confident that if he could change his surroundings and get away from the people that did it, he could stay clean.

What I should have thought about first was why, in hell, I kept ending up with broken men. What was it about me that attracted that type of toxic masculinity? Men that appeared to have their lives together and have motivation and self-esteem always ended up being the exact opposite.

I seemed to be a magnet for such people in general. I never stopped and evaluated myself or even saw a pattern. The types of men I chose all being so different from each other, with only the drug use in common. Signs that were painfully obvious escaped me.

It was easy to feel empathetic towards him. He was an only child who did not have a close connection with his family.

His father had passed away a few years before, and he didn't seem to have a relationship with his mother. He was alone, and that tugged at my heart a bit. We were all he had. It made it harder for me to walk away, and so we all moved down south for a fresh start.

We decided to help with my parent's fence company until we found jobs, and that is exactly what we did.

Although it worked for a while, he and I didn't get along. I worked for the fence company as well as a few neighborhood bars; he always found a way to drink. He was an alcoholic.

When he drank, he was loud, obnoxious, and verbally abusive. If you think my boys disliked him before then, it was nothing compared to how bad they hated him after we moved. Although he managed to remain drug free, he did not give up the booze. My stepfather as well as my sister were always drinking, so he had drinking buddies.

After living with my mom for a few months, I realized the move had not been such a good idea. I was going back to

Dallas. I needed regular work. Neither of us could find stable employment.

I remember that day as if it were yesterday. The day I made the decision to retreat back to my hometown.

My folks lived on a twelve-acre track, most of it wooded. My stepfather was using binoculars at the window in the dining room when he observed a deer that seemed to be stuck in a barbed wire fence that ran down the side of the property. He grabbed his gun and wire cutters and headed down to try and release the animal. I went with him.

When we reached the doe, she'd been stuck for too long. She was barely clinging to life. He had no other choice; I turned my head while he put her out of her misery.

Like we had done countless times before, he began to field dress the deer. As I stood there talking to him and watching, lending a hand when he needed me to, her blood started to run and seep into the dirt. Thick, red, and starting to coagulate. A strong irony smell permeated the air.

I looked down to see Kristy, the family dog, lapping up the warm blood. The air was crisp and a bit cool, so there was a slight steam rising from the puddle. I couldn't control myself and didn't get two steps away before I started vomiting.

An event that I had been a part of countless times in the past with no side effects made me immediately and violently ill. I apologized and excused myself. I was confused. Before I reached the top of the hill headed to the house, it registered with me, and I knew. I was pregnant.

I was going to have a sixth child. From past experience, a baby was not going to make our relationship better. My life was running me again.

CHAPTER 22
Sharks Bay Umbi
Sharm El Sheikh

As I and dozens of other passengers bumped along the dusty highway, I tried to sleep. I chose to take the night bus so that I could rest along the way. Miles and miles of desert and mountains seemed like a good opportunity to nap. Not a chance.

I'd selected a small diving village in Sharm El Sheikh for a short getaway in hopes that a change of scenery would help me catch up on sleep and possibly some writing. With only my backpack and laptop in tow, I boarded the bus at 11:30 pm in Cairo.

Because of my travel history, I have become accustomed to being around people who don't speak English; I've learned to stay to myself and not expect verbal exchanges for prolonged periods of time. Which is why this particular part of my journey has made it into my story.

There was a man seated next to me on the bus. Half-way through the long ride, I realized that he spoke English. Foregoing the normally awkward beginning phase of any relationship, we rapidly fell into easy conversation.

After initial introductions, I found myself looking into a set of beautiful, intelligent Egyptian eyes, amber in color with thick black lashes. So thick, in fact, they had the appearance of being lined with charcoal eyeliner. He possessed a soothing voice; it didn't take long for me to feel right at home. As though I had known him always.

Classic good looks, articulate, quick-witted, and charming. He was the epitome of the old phrase "tall, dark, and handsome." Any anxiety I had seemed to melt away, and I found myself secretly wishing our arrival would be delayed. I felt safer and more relaxed with him occupying the seat beside mine, and I do not understand why. I'm still confused as to whether I should attribute our meeting to a brilliant stroke of happenstance or if I should accept it as fate. I believe if there is such a thing as kismet, our meeting the way we did would be the best example of its existence to date.

He departed the bus four hours before my final destination but not before exchanging contact information. I will revisit this person and our relationship later in my story, but not before making clear that no matter how I view the circumstances of our meeting, I did gain a friend that day. The story he and I share did not end at the conclusion of that trip. I will eventually elaborate, but all in due time.

Traveling to certain destinations in Egypt is an exercise in patience, to say the least. Because it borders the Gaza Strip, there are security checkpoints all along the highway leading into the Sinai Peninsula. Each one equipped with military and police. Their presence is strong everywhere here. In Cairo because of the recent revolution. In the Sinai because it has been the center of a long-running insurgency and was attacked in 2019 with a high death toll for Egyptian soldiers.

Each time I felt sleep overtaking me, we would reach one of those checkpoints.

Every stop involved all of us getting off of the bus and going around to the luggage compartment to claim our bags. We would then open them and stand in a long line as they were searched. When they finished, we'd place our luggage back into the luggage compartment and reload back onto the bus. The driver would stop again after leaving the search area, at the entrance to the highway, and allow a military official to board the bus and check all passenger's identification. Each time retaining up to five of them to take and check validity as well as backgrounds.

Although I appreciate the security measures and understand that it is for our own safety, I arrived after almost eleven hours, exhausted.

I sat on the beach the first night having a coffee. Lulled by the waves of the Red Sea and listening to the sweet soulful sound of Egyptian music. I couldn't help but already feel that it was one of the most worthwhile trips and best decisions I have ever made.

As amazing and beautiful as I already found this country, none of my experiences to date hold a candle to this place. I just keep falling more in love with it here. The locals say I am a born native. I am starting to agree with them.

The sea slips into the bay. The water seems to ease in slowly, lazily. Not dramatically like the waves of the ocean. It is a consistent and hypnotic flow. It's so still in the evening; it is like glass. Mirroring the lights from the buildings on shore.

There are white, adobe-type structures and homes built in tiers, seemingly chiseled into the side of the cliff sides and sandy hills. Palm trees dot the spaces in between. Large clay pots are lit up with red lighting and strategically placed all across and down one side, facing the cove. The effect of those lights bouncing off of the water is unreal. Except for the clay pots, all of the lights here are the same shade of white with a slight orange tint, which is a feat in itself because there are thousands. There is so much loveliness in the consistency and amount of those lights. It is intentional and it is mesmerizing.

The owners of the little village-type hotel where I am staying are Bedouin people, and they are constantly here to handle all details concerning every aspect of this little community. We all feel like family.

The short explanation of Bedouin being *Arabic-speaking people of the Middle East and followers of Islam. Usually occupying middle eastern deserts, especially North Africa, the Arabian Peninsula, Egypt, Israel, Iraq, Syria, and Jordan. Traditionally, they are nomadic, desert dwelling, living in tents and moving their herds across vast areas of land in search of grazing areas. Things have changed for them drastically the last few decades due to tourism.

My experience with these people has always been a pleasure. They are kind, quiet, serious, and give thought to all they say and do. I like them very much. They are genuine and hospitable. Normally dressed the same as their fellow Egyptians in a long white or beige gallabiyah, distinguishable in appearance only by their headdress and their very thick, unique accent. I have gotten pretty good at understanding enough Arabic to usually get the gist, but I can't understand a word when spoken by a Bedouin. I was told by an Egyptian friend not to worry, that he too had trouble with their particular dialect as well.

The attention to detail has created an exotic and calming atmosphere. Low to the ground, sofas line the inside perimeter of the large concrete and wooden tent type of structure. It resembles one huge conversation pit, with short wooden tables placed in front of each section on two different levels. With only one wall against the back, it's a semi-circle, and the view of the water is perfect no matter where a person chooses to sit. Heavy, dark, rich material covers everything from ceiling to couch cushions to floor. The wooden slats of the ceiling are adorned with rough woven textured fabric in shades of gold, orange, brown, burgundy, and cream. Macramé fringe hangs about two feet down all around the outer edges of the structure, and it sways with the breeze.

The oversized ceiling fans, with their enormous blades, seem to spin to the tempo of the music, stirring the air just enough to keep it fresh and cool. Ornate copper lanterns strategically hung inside as well as out. The lighting is not bright and intrusive, but dim and gives a warm glow to everyone and everything under the canopy. It feels comfortable and unforced; intimate and romantic.

Once the sun goes down, other than the reflection from the lights ashore, there are no lights from anything else on the water. No fishing vessels or boats, just complete darkness. It's as if we are far away from the rest of the world. A self-contained and hidden paradise. There is no noise from traffic or hustle and bustle from the world outside. Just the sound of the sea, the Arabic melody from the small random speakers placed about, and the low hum of conversation from people seen and unseen.

It has been difficult to write about this particular place. Not because of a lack of subject matter, but more because I feel a strong responsibility to relay it as descriptively and accurately as possible to give it the justice it deserves.

When I first arrived, I had my doubts. I mean, I was dropped off at a large empty bus station, basically in the middle of nowhere. Surrounded by white sand and nothing more. A short cab ride, and this place appeared out of nowhere—like a mirage. In the blink of an eye, the vacant hills turned into a green oasis, complete with deep blue sea and palm trees.

I spend my days laying in the sun reading and watching. Drinking in all of the exquisiteness of my new surroundings and trying to commit it to memory. The sheer beauty of this cove is overwhelming.

Little dark-skinned, topless children run down the beach, darting in and out of the water. Screaming their delight at the multicolored fish visible through the crystal-clear water. I fill many of my hours snorkeling. It is my new favorite past-time. The underwater reefs here are breathtaking.

It is home to every type of sea creature you can possibly imagine and a countless array of bright and cheerful-looking fish. Spotted or striped, they look as if they have been dyed or painted. Coral in hues of purple, pink, yellow, blue, and white, as well as enormous clams, are sprinkled across the bottom of the sea with crimson or violet trim. They look fake. Tim Burton couldn't have filmed this to be more of a feast for the eyes than it is.

Although this place has all of the earmarks of a tourist destination and I truly expected to see the California surfer-type of people pop up, they have not. It feels as if I have found a secret haven.

Egyptians have quickly made the top of my list of favorite humans. They come equipped with an undeniable sixth sense. Knowing by looking at others if they require alone time and peace or need conversation, and they respond accordingly. I have not one time been approached by anyone or had conversation or interaction forced on me. It is as if they *feel* me.

I previously wrote about the exchange of energy. It is even more so here. If I do not have positive and contented emotions or energy, they seem to loan me theirs. It is an obvious yet silent exchange; them replacing my not-so-favorable feelings with life-giving, happy ones. Being this willing to give into smiling as much as I do is still such a new and amazing experience for me. One of the most treasured gifts I have received is the ability to genuinely smile.

When I spend time with people here, it's always beautiful. For the first time in my adult life, I can be one hundred percent myself. I do not need to tone down my enthusiasm or alter my sometimes-loud personality. They care for me just as I am. If I am feeling especially quiet or melancholy, one of them silently nods in my direction or smiles at me, just to let me know I am not alone; then they leave me in peace. Unspoken kinship and regard. I really, truly do not ever have to voice how I feel; these intuitive people just know. I have never felt so transparent. Egyptian people see *me*—they see each other.

Time is taken to observe whoever shares space with them, and they acknowledge and wholeheartedly rise up and meet the vibe. If I am excited, they are excited. If I am inquisitive, they patiently and joyfully answer my questions.

Each day I feel myself becoming more of the person I have tried to hide and tuck away for so long. I have not discovered one jaded person here. They offer love and friendship like children on a playground. I can't say enough that I've never felt so valued as part of the human race.

I am reminded constantly by my surroundings that this is an Islamic nation. It can't be ignored or forgotten.

Even when swimming or frolicking in the sun, these women wear modest clothing. Consisting of special swimwear that covers the neck, wrists, and ankles. Most have special hijabs made for water to keep their heads covered. We are obviously so different, but so much the same. These are my true soul sisters. I enjoy their company immensely. Undoubtedly the sweetest, most wholesome and feminine ladies I have ever had the pleasure of meeting. Just having them around me somehow makes me behave and feel like a better person.

They do not speak ill of each other; there is no gossip or cliques. Just understanding and tolerance. Compassion and love for their fellow man.

Although they have cell phones here, everyone is not always paying attention to them. Even though sometimes I get asked to pose for a picture with complete strangers here (especially by teenagers), selfies are not their constant habit. They are living in their moment rather than trying to memorialize them for later. I find so much happiness in watching them; observing them live as if social media is the last thing on their minds.

Italians are the second group of common nationality here. They come here to spend the winter. They too are truly a wonder to me. So full of life and humor. Automatic friends from the minute we meet. We are all just enjoying this experience together.

I spend so much time laughing at them. They have now become my family, in every way. When they talk about *anything,* it is said with their mouths and explained with their hands. Using phrases like "mama mia!" (how ever you said that in your head is exactly how they say it.) I am not kidding. With a serious and undeniable Italian draw at the end of each word. They are a dramatic and radiant type of people; animated.

They are experts at socializing and love to laugh. These people have mastered the art of living and enjoying every second of it. My affection for them was immediate, and I have made plans to spend some time in Italy very soon.

After ten glorious days at Sharks Bay, I must return to Giza, if only temporarily.

You see, I have decided to pack up my apartment and move to Sharm El Sheikh for the winter. Another step toward the goal of decluttering my heart and mind. With mild temperatures year-round, the sea, and these lovely new friends, I simply feel I cannot do otherwise.

CHAPTER 23

Back in Dallas, I sat down with Scott. I was afraid to tell him I was pregnant. Of all the people in the world, his respect meant the most to me. I didn't want to disappoint him, but I knew I could only hide it for so long, and I needed to work again. More than that, I needed to feel the security of having him in my corner. I was terrified.

I could tell he was, in fact, disappointed in me, but he hired me back on the spot. He paid for my first doctor visit, and when the pregnancy was confirmed, he assured me that my job was secure and that he would be there to help any way he could. Words that calmed me and gave me the strength I needed to proceed with my life.

Through thick and thin, that man never withdrew his support and friendship. Sometimes it came with a lecture, but I could always depend on him.

We moved back into the little house in Mesquite, and that is when we met Gage.

Gage was a neighbor boy who was constantly at our house. He went to school with Jet and Beau, and his mom had her own drug issues. He became a constant visitor and eventually a full-blown member of our family. One year older than Jet, he just fit in. He is what I consider my adopted son.

From that time until now, he has remained my extra child. He even looks like me with his green eyes and olive skin.

Even though at first, I was cautious, because he seemed like a wild child. I learned that he was and still is a beautiful person with a heart of gold. I have watched him grow into a wonderful young man, and I feel lucky to have him in our lives. He is my "hippy" child.

My whole pregnancy consisted of working all of the time and trying to keep Derek out of the bar. He was still drinking, and most nights that I was gone, he was off somewhere and not at home with the kids. He had just stopped bringing the drugs to the house; he hadn't stopped doing them.

I remember going out with him one night when I was seven months along. We went to meet some of his friends at a local bar. The night ended with me being left there. When the bar closed, I had to have them call me a taxi. Derek had gone somewhere earlier and never returned. He had all of the money on him, so I couldn't even pay the taxi driver.

When I got to the house, I had to crawl in a window and break into my bedroom again. Same situation as before. Cocaine is a conscience killer. The user loses all ability to be rational or have concern for anything or anyone around them.

I obviously had no self-esteem. In hindsight, I was pathetic. I just kept digging myself a deeper hole, clinging to my mistakes.

I had to hide the cash for bills, or he found it and spent it on partying. Eventually he lost his job over it, and it left me as the sole provider. I was exhausted. He managed to secure another job a few weeks before I gave birth, only to lose that one as well. A consistent theme for anyone addicted to drugs and alcohol.

I developed gestational diabetes and had to go to the doctor five times a week to have my blood sugar tested, and I felt awful and sick most of the time.

One night, while closing the club, I had long since quit smoking cigarettes, but someone had left an open box of cigars at the bar. While I counted money and did paperwork that night, I was alone except for one waitress. I took one of the cigars, thinking it would ease some of my stress. I lit it and took a few puffs. It had an odd effect on me. My head spun, and I had to throw up in the trashcan next to the bar. It took me a while to feel normal; my knees were shaking. I let it pass and attributed it to the fact I hadn't smoked in so long.

The next night, while at work behind the bar, I went into labor. I couldn't find Derek. I lay in the hospital all night, but the contractions never became consistent. He finally showed up drunk and high in the morning. I sent him home. I was embarrassed. I went home a few hours later to wait for labor to progress.

The following night, my water broke, and I started bleeding profusely. Something I'd never encountered with the other children. Derek was home and drove me to the hospital, where sixteen of the most difficult hours of labor played out. On September 5th, 2001, I gave birth to my sixth and last child, my baby girl, my only daughter, Ellinore.

She was chubby, dark-haired, and blue-eyed. The most beautiful little girl I had ever seen. I finally had my daughter. Even after they handed her to me, I just couldn't believe I finally had a daughter. I kept unwrapping her and checking her girl parts. I was in awe.

When they brought her to me to feed, is when I realized something was wrong. They wouldn't allow me to breastfeed her. I breastfed all of my children, and I didn't understand—until the nurse informed me that I had tested positive for cocaine. I was shocked.

My mouth went dry, my eyes filled with tears, and I felt rage. I was being accused of doing drugs while I was pregnant when I wouldn't even consider taking Tylenol! I had even quit smoking cigarettes. And then it hit me.

While I sat there in tears, angrily proclaiming my innocence, I remembered the cigar a few days earlier at the bar. It was what we call an "outlaw" cigar. The difference between those and regular cigars is that they are rough cut and wrapped. It would have been very easy for it to have been laced and rolled back up and not look any different. It was a common thing for addicts locally, and I became scared at the thought.

The absolute worst part of having a past drug addiction is the fact that it doesn't matter how long you're clean; everyone around you that knows will always assume you're doing them.

After I walked away from that lifestyle, it was not a struggle for me. In fact, at some point I would have forgotten about that part of my history completely if there were not so many people in my life to remind me. Periodically, I still had people actually ask me if I could acquire this or that certain narcotic. It was so insulting.

Why must every joyful day be tainted with some hidden cause for fear and sorrow? How come the days that should be the most memorable because of their beauty or an amazing event are instead overshadowed and shrouded in darkness?

It seems that there were always some unforeseen and devastating circumstances surrounding my most precious days. Particulars that even now, I still recall alongside the long-awaited birth of my only daughter. Unnecessary clutter on an otherwise perfect occasion. Fifteen years and five sons later, I had my baby girl, and I was in very real danger of losing her.

Social workers came to talk to me, and the only reason I could fathom for a positive drug screen was that cigar three days before. I had not one other explanation. I assure you; I had not done drugs in years.

They were going to do a final test on Ellinore's meconium to ensure that was the case. I was humiliated. Of course, the test came back negative, and I was vindicated.

Even though I knew I would never consider doing cocaine whether I was pregnant or not, convincing them was a whole different story. Even after it was scientifically proven I was telling the truth; I was treated with disdain and contempt. It was horrible.

I sat in the hospital for four extra days to wait for an available operating room so that I could have my tubes tied, and then we were sent home.

Two days later, while I sat at home breastfeeding Ellinore, I watched the television in horror as the World Trade Center was attacked. It was one of the most memorable and horrific days in America's history, and I will never forget it. The next day, child protective services showed up at my door.

I allowed them into my home and tried to be as compliant as I could be. I didn't understand why they were there. They had opened up an investigation because of the false positive drug test in the hospital. Which is exactly what it was. I had assumed there was something in the cigar I smoked, but two urine samples, one positive, one negative. Ellinore's meconium tested negative. They had also tested my blood; negative.

I was treated awfully in that first interview. I allowed them to search my home, check my cupboards, and take pictures. Whatever they needed to do. I had nothing to hide. They had intended to do a six-month investigation with pop-in visits and interviews with my children, among other things. I didn't see that I had a choice. They popped in when they felt like it, walked through my home, drug tested me, and did everything else you would imagine they would do. I allowed it.

I would also like to add that once they were seemingly convinced of my innocence in the matter, in time, they became helpful. One occasion they paid a past-due water bill and brought the kids coats. They became a necessary evil.

I just wanted it behind me. The good thing about that time was that it kept Derek on the straight and narrow. He was terrified of losing Ellinore, so he stopped drinking and became committed to trying to be a good father. During the investigation at least. When it was completed, he went right back to the old Derek.

So many nights Ellinore sat in the office with Scott. While I worked, he took care of her. I was able to take breaks and go back and feed her. The boys were older and could take care of themselves, as well as tend to Tris. But she was a fussy baby who didn't like bottles and needed my attention.

More than a few times Derek brought her up to my work, mid-shift, and I had to take her back to the office to feed her and quiet her. Many times, he showed up at the bar to party and left her at home with the boys. It infuriated me.

Then again, he lost his job. He could not maintain the work and lifestyle he enjoyed.

When she was almost a year old, I had had enough. I packed up all we owned, Jet, Beau, Fin, Tris, Gage, Ellinore, and Shelby, and we headed back down south to my mother's—again.

I wasn't sure what to do anymore, and I needed my mother's help and advice. Dallas was always an easy place to obtain drugs if someone was looking. I longed for the safety and security of my mom, but I also needed the money from work at the bar; I couldn't have both at the same time. I was like a yoyo, always going back and forth.

What I didn't realize then is that no matter where a person runs, if they want drugs, they will find them.

The move seemed to work at first. I immediately got hired as a bartender in a neighboring town; he secured an electrical job, and the drugs and alcohol came to an abrupt stop. I was encouraged. So, when he wanted to go out one night together and have dinner and cocktails, I was not against the idea at all. He hadn't had a drink in months.

The evening started out at a local restaurant, and afterwards we went to a sports bar to play pool or darts. It was fun until Derek became drunk. He drank way too fast at the bar. He was so drunk he almost had a fist fight with someone, so I got him out of there.

On the drive home, his whole disposition changed. He went from happy, loud, and silly to irate and outraged. I too had been drinking, and it adds to why I still can't piece together everything that happened.

From what I remember, we were driving down the highway, arguing over something. He hit me while he was still driving. He hit me hard enough for my nose to sling blood across the windshield of my mom's truck. I must have said or done something pretty infuriating, because honestly, he pulled the truck over to the side of the road and beat me so badly that all I can recall from that point on was arriving home. Running into my mother's room so that she could see my face. What he had done to me.

I remember entering her room, flipping the light on, and her shrill scream. I remember her horror. She looked so scared that she scared *me*. I woke up later in the hospital with a fractured jaw, two black eyes, and a face that was unrecognizable. My sister came to visit me, and she and her boyfriend thought they had the wrong room. I had a morphine button I could push for pain relief, and it still was not enough. I was destroyed psychologically and emotionally. My physical injuries were bad, but nothing compared to my beaten mental state.

I refused to press charges. Mainly because I took my own amount of personal responsibility for what happened. I too was drinking, and I know that I can have a disrespectful mouth. Seriously, under the right circumstances, I have the ability to piss off the pope. I assumed I'd surely done something to enrage him.

Later, my mom told me that the police came and Derek ran. He'd managed to escape justice for that beating. The truck, she said, was absolutely covered in blood. The policeman said it looked as if someone had been murdered in the cab of that vehicle. He said that it was difficult to believe that much blood could come from someone who was still alive.

Two weeks later, I came home to mom's house, and Derek.

My boys never really got over that. They tolerated him at best, but they couldn't stand him. I stayed because I had always run, and I didn't have any answers. I was exhausted from running. I didn't want to fight, but I lacked the courage and energy to run anymore.

I was the opposite of co-dependent. I was constantly leaving situations and relationships that were distasteful instead of addressing the issues and working through them to build a future. It was easier to leave than work on fixing anything. So, it became a habit for me. At the time, I had a daughter to consider—a daughter that needed her father.

I also believe I stayed through that time because, no matter how awful it got, I knew he was loyal. For me, because of my past relationships, I put so much weight on whether a man cheated or not, and I knew he was trustworthy in that department.

I might have to get him through a substance abuse problem, but in my mind, at least I didn't have to question his integrity when it came to other women. Isn't that what successful married couples do for one another?

I knew he loved me, and I had come to love him, and he reminded me often that we were all he had.

Anyway, the difference in him after that incident was immediate and drastic.

He stopped drinking, stopped doing drugs, and started insisting all of us go to church. He secured a great job and went to work every day. He was supporting his family.

He became loving towards the kids and everyone. He started attending a men's group at church. He literally became a different person overnight.

I think that is when I truly started to trust him and could rely on him. He became responsible and respectful. Within a year, he had reinvented himself. He was kinder and gentler, and he became a wonderful father.

We moved out of my mother's house and into our own home.

That was a good time in our lives. Simple living and dependable circumstances. Being at home with the children and getting to be a mother to Ellinore the way I had not been able to with the boys was incredible. We were all in love with her. Derek worshiped her. She was smart, and he had the brightest blue eyes.

No one wanted to see her cry, so we all spoiled her. She and Tris and Shelby were always together. We all loved to hear her talk. She had the most adorable voice and giggle. She was my little doll that I loved to dress up in pink. Braiding her hair and painting her little finger nails. That little girl brought her sweet attitude and smile with her wherever she went, and still does.

The boys passed her around. Played with her and helped take care of her. Jet taught her numbers and colors; he always had her in his arms. He'd been the same way with Tris, but with her, she brought out his soft side. She was crazy about her brothers, as they were about her.

I remember that time so vividly. Family dinners together. Gage teaching Shelby to roll over and speak. Shelby looked like Lassie, so he taught him to speak if we said, "Is Timmy stuck in the well?"

That year Derek worked overtime and side jobs so that we could buy Beau a set of drums and the other boy's guitars for Christmas. It really was a good year. Our house was always filled with noise. We surely had the loudest house on the block with six kids, two adults, and a dog always barking. Add drums and guitars, loud music and video games, fighting teenagers, and it was, at times, out of control! It was beautiful.

When Ellinore was almost three years old, I went back to work. We wanted to buy a house, and honestly, we needed the income.

I applied to work at the Texas Department of Criminal Justice. My mother worked as an officer and had great pay and benefits, so I thought I would give it a try. I got accepted into the training academy and became a prison guard. In 2004, Derek and I made it official and got married. Everything seemed to be good and normal. All of us were healthy and content.

We took a few short family vacations to Sea World, San Antonio, and everything was comfortable and predictable. I cannot accurately describe how much I truly miss those days. My heart aches to turn back time to when we were all together under the same roof. There was so much laughter—so much to be grateful for.

As is common in my life, all good things must come to an end. I will always look back at that time as the quiet before the storm. I had no idea that I was headed down the real path of destruction. Even had I known, I am not sure I could have stopped it.

CHAPTER 24

Is anxiety a real thing if a person doesn't give it space? I mean, if you don't label it, is it to be considered? I was not raised in a generation that used the words "anxiety" or "toxic" when referring to mental illness or distasteful side effects of a person's ability or inability to handle stressful scenarios in life. So, have I always had anxiety, or did it become prominent after I understood what the word meant?

I always assumed it was, by definition, an attack where you can't breathe and cannot cope with what is going on at the time. To include sweating, shaking, and out of control nervousness. If that is the case, I can say that I didn't have outward signs of anxiety until I was around seventeen.

My understanding never exceeded that explanation until I got a complete picture of the real realm of possibilities concerning this particular affliction. I always assumed it was a larger expression of panic. This isn't the case at all.

Anxiety is walking around with your jaw clenched so tight and for so long that it gives you an actual headache—when you don't even realize that you're doing it. It is being wound up inside so tightly that your shoulders physically pull forward, affecting your posture and giving the appearance of being slumped over.

It's the dread of having to speak on the phone when you're uncomfortable with it, or the hours you lay awake the night before an appointment or event because you know you are going to have to interact and participate the next day. It's replaying a million different scenarios over and over in your head about something that hasn't happened yet, and in some cases, won't happen at all. It is an obsession with detail so you can judge from every possible angle and prepare for each one.

It's walking around on high alert and on edge because you aren't sure the urge you have to run away or lose your shit in certain situations is not going to have its way. Such a deep-seeded urge that you spend most of the time trying to control every little facet around you so it won't be triggered.

It is, in fact, the loss of all the control you have over your emotional and mental state at any given moment and the fear that is your constant companion because you know it is just a matter of time before it does. The person experiencing this is a slave to it. Knowing that it's always just under the surface but never being able to guess when it will hit.

Certain movies, sounds, smells, and situations are no longer tolerable. It is wanting to scream or cry and not knowing exactly why. Energy inside of your soul begging to be heard and the belief that the sickness in the pit of your stomach is a warning somehow installed to protect you.

It honestly feels like a bomb inside of your chest; that is always just one random uncomfortable situation away from exploding. Causing you to miss out on so many great opportunities and beautiful days in life trying to avoid the one in a million chance of a bad one.

It is exhausting, confusing, and frustrating. So much of your energy is spent hiding it. As it progresses, you find yourself adapting in some pretty unhealthy and questionable ways.

I recently realized that at some point I ceased to enjoy watching new movies, but I choose instead to re-watch those I've seen many times before so that I know the content and outcome. It's as much of a part of me as breathing, eating, or sleeping. Stronger than the best or the worst emotion because it slowly starts to rule them all.

For me, my brow stayed furrowed for so many years that it became natural. The muscles in my face never relaxed, and the tenseness radiated through my neck, back, and skull.

The side effects of anxiety are numerous and manifest differently for each individual. All equally awful. I never realized I was experiencing anxiety at all. Had I known all of this back then, I would have given much more consideration to my decisions concerning my work environment.

Believe me when I say, being a correctional officer should have *never* been on my list of career choices. It was a gradual murdering of what was left of my sanity. My healthy coping mechanisms were long gone, and I piled more things to have to deal with onto an already very full plate.

I could write a complete book on the subject of the Texas prison system. Working there changed me in more ways than I can count—none of them good.

I worked at a maximum-security women's unit; twelve-hour shifts, four days on, four days off. If you consider the hour drive to get there and the almost hour-long shift change, it amounted to around fifteen hours. Endless days of cell searches, strip searches and pat searches. Constant and repetitive paperwork, counting humans, and chow hall. Most days I felt like a referee in a boxing ring.

The first day I was off each week, I was rendered useless from exhaustion. Two days were spent catching up on chores and things that weren't done while I was working. The final day, when I started to feel a bit normal again, I spent getting ready to go back to work.

The boys were teenagers and involved in school activities, like soccer and tennis, football, and such. I was missing out on the things I was working so diligently to provide.

Inmates are a whole different group of women. They have twenty-four hours a day, seven days a week, to scheme and manipulate situations. They are housed, fed, and given basic necessities, but lack what we need as humans to thrive.

Many of the women on my unit were there for life or had long sentences. These were not hot check writers but more violent crime, narcotics, and gang bangers, among other things. They were felons.

For a while I transferred them from our unit to others in Texas, so I had access to their files. Some of them did things that still haunt me.

The feeling on that unit was hopeless and sad. Violence was a daily occurrence. It didn't matter how happy you were when you went to work; once you entered those gates, if you possessed any empathy at all, it was going to affect you.

How apropos that our uniforms were gray, like the dark cloud and mood that hung over that place. To make matters worse; many of the officers were callous and unfeeling, angry and mean. They seemed to take pleasure in adding to the inmate's already shitty life. I will always believe that the reason for that stems from the fact they had no power in their own personal lives, so they chose to work as a guard to feel better about themselves. To have control in one area was better than having none.

I tried, but I absolutely could never leave my job at the gate when I left. It stayed on my mind whether I was there or not.

Not to say that I was not good at it; I was. I have always been one to work hard and become good at anything I do, but there was absolutely no gratification in it. It takes a special kind of human to have that career and not be impacted negatively. I was not one of those.

I find it almost amusing that it was called Texas Department of Corrections when the system was not correcting a thing, and in fact, serving a sentence there did the opposite. These *offenders* came out of the system worse than they went in. It was like a crash course in crime for them, and they got out with better criminal knowledge and skill than they went in with. Add that to the fact that once they served their time and were released, they hadn't a chance in Hell when they put their incarceration on a job or apartment application. Most employers do criminal background checks. It was a set-up for failure.

I could go on and on about this subject, but instead I will approach this part of my story in a simpler and more methodical way.

There are six major things that come to mind while working those years at the prison. I will simply focus on those.

Number one:

I was in my third year of employment there when one day I was called to the front gate, where I was served by a constable with papers. Not having a clue as to why I would be served, I took them back onto the unit.

Sitting in the sergeant's office, with inmates just outside the door, I opened them. They were papers formally requesting the absolution of my parental right to Dean. Attached was a handwritten letter from my then thirteen-year-old son asking me to please sign the papers so that his new mother could adopt him. It was written in pencil and looked to be written by a child, but they were obviously not the words of a child. Regardless, I got the point.

I sat there and read that letter several times before its weight actually hit me. When it did, I started to shake, and I handed those very personal papers to my sergeant without thinking. He sent me home.

I had to sit in the office a long time to gain enough composure to leave and walk down the main road to the front gate. The cell-block building that I was working in that day sat at the farthest point from the front gate. It took every ounce of strength that I had to hold back tears so that the inmates I passed on the way out didn't see me cry.

That's the thing with them. As an officer, you can never be weak in their presence; they will use it against you later. An officer has to be strong, and then it is always possible to loosen up later if the occasion calls for it, but it is never in anyone's best interest to let them see emotional distress. I recall that walk feeling like the longest walk of my life.

I left the unit. I cried all of the way home and took a few days off to consult an attorney. There was no way I could afford to fight it. We'd just bought a new house, and it took both of us working to pay the bills. I absolutely agonized over it. I am agonizing now as I write about it.

In the end, I signed the papers. The loss of my son was complete. He honestly wanted nothing to do with me then, and still doesn't to this day. This has never gotten easier. In all of my detailed writing, these were the most difficult paragraphs to write so far. I'm struggling to continue through my tears. I miss him every single day. Suddenly I understand why Forest Gump kept saying, "And that's all I have to say about that." Because it is. For me, if I am to continue, it has to be. I am breaking my own heart. Time does not heal all wounds.

Number two:

My physical health went to shit. There really is no other way to put that.

It started with a slip down a few steps one night while working in segregation. An inmate got feisty, and I fell and landed on my tailbone. The next day I woke up and couldn't walk, and later I couldn't move my head. It was the beginning of years of treatment, including nerve injections in my lower back and physical therapy.

Long-term side effects were sciatica, headaches, and excessive periods of time spent in bed unable to use my arms— excruciating pain. Something that still plagues me today.

It was also the beginning of my prescription narcotics use. Vicodin, muscle relaxers, Gabapentin, and Xanex were a daily regiment for me, among others.

After a routine gynecologic check-up revealed cancerous cells, that year I would also have a partial hysterectomy. Cervical cancer was a real possibility and concern, so I was immediately sent in for surgery. A few months later, after a mammogram, a lump was discovered in my left breast. It was removed, but they were unclear as to what kind of mass it was. Cancer runs in my family, and although it was found not to be, I was a mess.

Number three:

Derek started drinking again. I was working nights. That left him with a lot of alone time on his hands. He got into a habit of drinking with my sister. A few times in those years, Kelle and her boys stayed with us. She was having issues with her husband at the time, and we all tried to help each other. Many nights I called home during my break at work, and he and Kelle were at a club or just drinking at the house. On my four days off, I often joined them.

Working for the prison gave me a lot of things I wanted to forget, and it was never-ending. Memories I struggle with even now that I wish I could erase.

There was always another horrible incident to try and make sense of, or try to put out of my head. Alcohol was a way to do it. Occurrences that go on daily in those facilities are indescribable and pretty sickening. Relief was necessary in one way or another. With my past, I didn't cope well with violence and overwhelming sorrow to that degree.

Number four: this one is tough.

Segregation is a building where the prison houses the worst offenders. They spend twenty-three hours a-day in a small closet-sized cell, with one hour of recreation.

One night, like many other times before, I was assigned to work that building. It was count time. I finished counting the bottom row and was headed to the picket to turn it in. An inmate called me over to her door; she didn't sound in distress, so I felt no hurry. I told her I would be right back. I turned in the count to the control room and made my way back to her cell.

She was young, attractive, and usually fairly happy—as happy as one can be in that situation. She was actually someone I kind of liked because she'd always been very predictable. I went to her and asked what she needed.

She was standing at her cell door, silently crying. Tears streamed down her cheeks. I will never, ever forget her words or the look on her face while she said them.

"Mrs. C, I'm sorry."

And then, before I realized what was happening, she calmly stepped back, took a razor blade and stuck it just under her left ear, and sliced her own neck from one side to the other—without flinching. I stood there in shock, not completely understanding what had just taken place, until the top of her white prison uniform gradually started to saturate with her own blood. As I called and waited for help, I watched that young girl's bleached white shirt turn crimson.

She had no intention of surviving. That cut was not a shallow, apprehensive cry for help. It was one that she intended to end her life with. I cannot describe the feeling that washes over you when you witness that type of hopelessness. It is, without a doubt, one of the worst feelings I have ever experienced.

It felt like watching a puppy get hit by a car, unable to get to it, stop it, or render aid because of traffic.

I stood there and watched someone who felt so hopeless, unloved, and inconsequential that they were willing to put an end to their own life. I watched her suffer through the window of a steel door. The most tragic thing I have ever witnessed. If you do not think that I go over that in my mind often and beat myself up for not being able to prevent it, you are wrong. I am still quite heartbroken over that particular failure.

Number five:

A woman arrived on our unit one day, and like so many others, she was crying. It always takes the new arrivals a while to accept their situation and adjust. The first few weeks are the toughest for them.

She was in her late thirties or early forties, slender, attractive, and scared. I had spoken with her a few times the week she came to us and observed her struggle to settle in. Sometimes they just need to talk to feel better. I was always of the opinion that my job was not to judge. I just tried to be firm, fair, and humane.

Human connection is important when you're treated like a second-class citizen for months leading up to the actual day you land in a cell.

She was well spoken and soft in her nature and demeanor. All of her time she spent reading her Bible or writing to her mother or children. Over the course of that week, I learned she had many small children at home. I honestly cannot remember what she was in for; it has somehow lost importance to me. I know that it wasn't murder or child abuse; those are the two crimes I would never forget. I also recall that she was only going to serve a fairly short amount of time compared to the usual lengthy sentences of most criminals that came to us on that unit.

I came on shift, and during my first count, I realized pretty quickly that she was not okay.

She wasn't responding to general conversation and laid on her bunk with a blank, hollow expression. I could tell that she hadn't showered for a while, and she didn't want food when chow was served. It was not habit for me to concern myself with things like that, but something about her made me take notice. I am not sure exactly what it was.

I discussed it with the officer that I was working with and went out for my second break of the night. I was only gone for thirty minutes. When I returned, the first thing I did was head up the stairs to her cell to check on her.

She was the first cell on the second floor, which was generally where I started my required thirty-minute well checks anyway. When I got to her door, I was horrified to discover her hanging by a sheet from the light fixture. The sheet was twisted and wrapped tightly around her throat. Her face was gray; foam was around her mouth.

By the time another officer joined me and we rolled the door, it was too late. We got her down and called medical, but she lay on that concrete floor unresponsive. She was taken to the hospital but never regained consciousness.

She was a mother to children that she missed and was grieving over. She was someone's daughter. She was a wife and granddaughter. More than that, she was a human being. A human being that had lost all hope and felt completely alone. In less than two months, I had witnessed two suicides and countless other atrocities.

Humans are cruel and, when caged, are capable of behaving more like animals. Which brings me to the final memory from working in the prison system that I will share.

Number six:

I FINALLY AND COMPLETELY LOST MY FUCKING MIND. Not slightly or gradually, but fully and all at once.

I came home one day in a daze, and then, out of the clear blue, I started to cry. I started to cry and could not stop. Not a silent weeping, but a full-on snot-slinging bawl like a toddler does after falling and scraping their knee. I seriously couldn't catch my breath.

I guess you could say there were some symptoms I was headed that direction. I'd started to get paranoid. I couldn't stop thinking about all of my life events, my failures and secrets. I couldn't sleep at all, for days at a time. The more I didn't sleep, the more I couldn't sleep, which added to my irrationality. I couldn't think straight. Such despair and fear; it was crippling.

I was absolutely convinced that Derek was sleeping with Kelle, even though they hadn't gotten along for some time and seemed to dislike each other tremendously. When I accused him, he looked hurt and questioned my sanity. In my mind, I knew it was because of what had happened with Chase, but I couldn't stop being suspicious.

I analyzed and second-guessed everything either of them told me. I found myself watching them when they were in the same room together. For the first time, I started to doubt his loyalty when he had given me not one reason to. I actually felt a bit crazy. I didn't believe my thoughts; I knew it was irrational, but it didn't prevent me from thinking them. I couldn't figure out why I was fixated on that of all things.

I started to become overly concerned about my children and obsessed over the thought of something happening to them. I was in physical pain all of the time. I had no appetite, and I'm not at all sure what the final straw was.

I only know that for two days; I couldn't do anything but cry.

At that point, suicide was becoming a reasonable option. Prevalent in my mind because of the recent events at work. I almost envied the two for their courage. It was as if all of the years I held it in and filed things away so that I could function finally resurfaced. I'd heard of people having "nervous breakdowns" but never understood what that actually entailed—until that day.

Just because I was operating at full capacity with my physical endeavors at work and my hectic home life, it did not mean I was functioning. On the contrary, being obsessively busy is a trauma response. Made worse by the fact I never felt like I was measuring up.

I'd spent years running from my past and trying to obtain the level of respect and financial stability that I enjoyed with Chase, which was impossible. I'd set an impossible standard for myself. Anything less; I viewed it as failure.

Every job I chose was one that required a title, a show, or the production of something to be praised by other people. I needed validity in that way, and let's face it, that is simply not conducive to a healthy self-esteem or life. Putting happiness in other people's hands, so to speak. I had done it for so long. I simply didn't know any other way.

Although I was impressive to my bosses at the prison, I was failing the people incarcerated that I had a responsibility to. By allowing myself to view them as humans, I took my work home with me. In doing that, my children never got all of me. I was failing them also. Even though, by all outward appearances, I had my life together and was doing well, I was in fact—unraveling.

I got into my car and drove to my mom's. I was shaking so violently that I had trouble keeping my hands on the steering wheel. My teeth were chattering, and my thoughts were skipping around. Jumping from one subject to the next, past, present, and future. It was as if a film projector was playing highlights of all the horror I'd experienced in my life—on repeat. It became unclear what was real and what was not.

When I got to her house, through uncontrollable sobbing, I tried to explain to her how I felt and my crazy, all-consuming thoughts about Derek and my unnatural fear concerning my children.

I begged her to take me to the hospital. I was ready to admit that I needed help. I didn't have a choice.

I remember that drive. My stepfather drove while my mom let me lay in her lap and sob. I was rambling. I couldn't shut up, and she was crying with me as she rubbed my back.

Thinking about this now, I realize that she must have been frightened. I was not making any sense.

She just kept telling me that she loved me and that everything would be okay.

"My Jamie," my momma kept repeating. Over and over again.

I consider that another turning point in my life. As much as I needed to believe it would be a good one, it was anything but.

CHAPTER 25

I spent seven weeks in a mental health facility in Temple, Texas. It took the staff two days to finally figure out what to give me so that I could sleep. Even with heavy sedation, I only slept for four hours at a time.

Once I sat down with the psychiatrist and finally started sharing and revealing my past, the pharmaceuticals started. Once they started, I might as well have had a conveyor belt going to my mouth.

There were so many medications. Pills for sleep, anxiety, pain, depression, and then more pills just to counteract the side effects of those pills. I felt like a zombie for weeks while they experimented with different drugs.

I'd disclosed some of my past, but not all of it. I still carefully guarded awful secrets.

Doctors are not magicians. They can only diagnose from what they are told. A patient tells them their symptoms; they make an educated guess and proceed from there. As much as I wanted and needed help, I still clung to a feeling of blame when it came to so much of my trauma. Things that, in my mind, made me a bad person.

Personal responsibility has always been ingrained in my head; figuring out what to take responsibility for and what I should not was beyond my abilities at the time. I felt then much like I still feel now.

Many of the things that happened to me were direct products of my negligent decisions. Consequences that, in some cases, I felt I deserved; some, I did not. It was difficult to distinguish which was which. So, I suffered guilt for all.

Mentally ill. A label I'd spent most of my life trying to avoid, and oh boy, did I get labeled.

I was diagnosed as bipolar on the depressive end of the scale, with obsessive-compulsive tendencies. I was also diagnosed with an anxiety disorder. I spent weeks on suicide watch. I had so many drugs in my system, I'm surprised I wasn't drooling. One of the things I've always battled is the fact that medication has never worked for me as it is intended. It usually has the opposite effect.

If they prescribed something to relax me, it gave me insomnia. Things meant to make me focus and induce serotonin put me to sleep. All of the pharmaceuticals they were giving me were working against each other. I felt worse than when I went in.

When I'd done illegal narcotics, it was the same. Methamphetamine made me quiet and subdued, as did cocaine, whereas marijuana, pain pills, or Xanax hyped me up. Alcohol made me bounce off of the walls as well.

Being bipolar meant that I would go on sprees of feeling full of energy and hope, only to come down at some point and feel exhausted and full of loathing, depression, and despair. With OCD and anxiety, it was a touch of hell. Keeping everything around me under control and perfect was my primary concern. It was an impossible task, and so depression would set in. After a while the anxiety would rear its ugly head and force me to obsess over past or upcoming failures, and then to combat that, my mind switched into my manic state of handling everything and making it all perfect again. It was a vicious cycle.

After my psychological disorders were diagnosed and explained to me, it made sense. It didn't give me relief, but at least I saw what I was up against. I come by my crazy honestly.

I come from a long line of mental illness and unhappiness. My mother was miserable while I was growing up. She was very codependent. Her mother was miserable, and my grandmother before that, from the stories I have heard. My sister isn't the happiest girl I have known, and many of the women in my family struggle with some form of depression or OCD. I am not sure if it is chemical, hormonal, or learned.

The whole nature-nurture thing is a mystery to me. All that I know for sure is that I was just carrying on what had been going on for generations.

Although I do feel strongly that mine certainly had something to do with my inability to make decent life choices. My boys seem to be better at it, thank God. My daughter has also always seemed to make the right decisions. Maybe the generational curse has been broken. I can only hope so.

My children saw what I lived through and decided early on what *not* to do. They saw the worst of the worst and decided to run in the opposite direction of anything resembling my life. I guess all of that drama that I heaped on myself became teachable moments. Without even realizing it.

They wanted a different outcome, so they chose different paths. I am extremely grateful for that rather huge blessing.

When I was released from the hospital, I was sent home on a regiment of medications that had to be taken punctually, several times a day. I had to return weekly to see the psychiatrist. I was in a fog most of the time. Jet called the medications my "personality killers."

They really were. I only knew that if I continued to take them, I was promised more normal and livable mental and emotional health. I held onto that hopeful outcome and did what I was told to do by the professionals.

Most of my marriage to Derek was riddled with disagreements, complications, and countless separations.

I blamed myself for much of that and felt that I was a difficult person who was challenging to live with. Whatever the reasons, it didn't get better after I settled into a routine of medications and a constant dark outlook.

I lived life sedated and detached. My saving graces were my relationships with my children and Ricky. At that point, my boys were growing up and leaving the nest. Something I hated more than anything else; I struggled with it.

My brother had always been such a touchstone for me. My main support system and strong voice of reason. Calm, reassuring, steady, and loving. I leaned on him during every single trying time in my life. One of the only men I had ever had to look up to and trust. I could always count on his no-nonsense approach to life. He was forever my counselor and stuck by me through my countless mistakes. He had the biggest heart of anyone I'd ever met, and he had a soft spot for his little sister.

Ricky didn't have it easy growing up in any way. Looking back, his life was so often about survival. I mean that in the literal sense. Including the never-ending injuries caused by he and Vance's shenanigans. So many of my memories of him involve hospitals.

When he was eight years old, he and some friends were crossing a busy street when he got hit by a car. He spent months in the hospital and suffered through countless reconstructive surgeries to repair the damage done to his face and teeth. I was too young to remember, but from what I understand, he spent a short time in a coma and was not expected to survive, but he did.

Later, at the age of fifteen, he was diagnosed with scoliosis. He had a pretty severe spinal curve, which required surgery to insert a steel rod along his spine to prevent it from causing damage to his organs.

The operation was not an immediate success, and a few weeks after having it, he started to bleed internally and he had to go back and have it repeated. He was in the hospital most of his sixteenth year and wore a body cast that went from under his arms down to his hips for another eight months.

As a teenager who had always been more comfortable blending into the woodwork, it was very distressing for him. When he did go back to school, his classmates were not nice. His soft heart was bruised, and so he just stopped attending school. It was hurtful to his sweet nature as well as his self-esteem. He became sullen and eventually turned to drugs and alcohol. Mostly marijuana.

Although it was not a habit he continued as an adult, those years changed him. Coming out on the other side of that very traumatic event as a more guarded, sad, and withdrawn young man. I recall it taking him a while to regain his confidence and become comfortable in his own skin again. But when he did, he became something of a comedian. He made his way through life with a cocky attitude, goofy dad jokes, and hilarious sarcasm; he kept us laughing.

As an adult, he was the kind of brother that had his own life but never once forgot a birthday or holiday when it came to calling me. All through my life, I could always count on hearing from my brother at least a few times a month. He adored my kids and took a special interest in them when he had free time. He bought Tris his first bow and arrow and spent days teaching him how to use it. He was the most precious uncle and brother I could have ever hoped for.

He was funny, affectionate, and calm. Serious with a quirky sense of humor. He sincerely appreciated everyone and everything around him. One of the most sensitive men I have ever encountered. He took great pleasure in deer hunting, grilling outdoors, and spending time with his children. He adored being a father.

Vacations were spent deep-sea diving, and he was a frequent traveler to Mexico to do so. An animal lover, especially dogs; he was attentive, tender, tolerant, and understanding. He was a proud man, but there was no fragility to his masculinity.

He never lived like he had to prove anything to anyone. He loved his country, family, friends, parents, and grandparents, and he had no issues with letting anyone he cared about know it.

So, when he called me one day out of the blue and asked me to come visit for the weekend, I didn't hesitate to pack a few things and immediately go. His voice on the phone was different than I'd ever heard it, and I wasn't sure why. It was unsettling. So, Ellinore, Tris, and I went.

When we arrived, as soon as we dropped our bags, his arms were around me. He buried his head in my hair and sobbed. The most heartbreaking, guttural cry I have ever heard.

His wife had taken their two youngest children and left him, and he was shattered.

For him, it was a cruel pain that he had difficulty coping with. We stayed for a couple of days, and from that day on, every weekend I went to be with my brother.

For months, all of my thoughts and free time were spent with him. Sometimes with my children, most of the time without. Mainly because I didn't want them to see him that way.

All he could do to stifle the pain was drink. He drank from the minute he woke up until he finally gave into exhaustion.

All of the minutes in between were filled with anxiety, loss, and pain.

By far, the most helpless I have ever felt.

I knew and understood that particular pain better than anyone, and there was absolutely nothing I could do except be there and hold him while he wept. I listened and supported him the only way I knew how. That kind of pain just has to be felt, and it was horrible to watch him suffer.

In December 2007, I was still spending every minute I could at his place. Weekends I escaped to his house, and he and I spent from Friday afternoon until Sunday night together. Talking, cooking, drinking, or just occupying the same space.

In this new sibling relationship, he was the one asking the hard questions, inviting my advice at every turn. It was a role unfamiliar to me, but I did my best. All I had was my own past experience with heartbreak to refer to, which hadn't turned out well.

He had good days and bad days. Although he had always been a tough person, most of his days at that time were emotional chaos.

As I was cutting his hair one weekend, I noticed a small sore on his neck that had been there since the last time I'd trimmed it. The mark didn't look like it was healing, and in fact, his neck, hairline, and down his shoulder appeared to be red and inflamed. I brought it to his attention. He knew it was uncomfortable but wasn't concerned—I was.

I told him that the next weekend when I was expected back, if it didn't look any better, I wanted him to go to the doctor and have it checked out. I even remarked that if it was worse, I would take him to the hospital. He shrugged it off and made a wisecrack about how it would take a lot more than that to make him go to see a doctor! He showed me a cut he had on his hand. It was a small cut he had gotten at work; it also looked questionable.

He worked as a manager in the parts department of the same auto dealership since his early twenties, and car parts came in from all over the world. It briefly crossed my mind that bacteria from a foreign country could be a culprit, but I quickly dismissed the thought, attributing it to my ever-growing paranoia when it came to the people I loved.

However, I was concerned at the possibility that because he was not eating or sleeping regularly or taking care of himself, his body was just too run down to heal any type of wound. No matter how much I cooked when we were together, his emotional state rendered him unable to eat.

As I headed out the door at the end of the weekend, I honestly did not want to go. I'd stayed an extra day, and it was Monday night. Something made me uncomfortable about leaving that time, and I lingered on the front porch saying my good-byes. I just didn't want to leave him. Much more than usual.

When I finally made my move to go, he did something I'll never forget. He grabbed me in a tight embrace—a longer and stronger hug than normal. When he pulled away, he looked me square in the eyes; his hands were placed on my shoulders, and he said,

"Thank you. Thank you for being here for me. You are the best; I'm proud you're my sister; I love you so much."

Overcome with emotion, and at a loss for words, I basically repeated his words back to him. We stood there in the doorway, in the cold, shivering with tears in our eyes. I finally let go of his hand and told him we were being ridiculous because I would be back in four days.

I took solace in the fact I knew his two adult children, a son and a daughter, would be there to check on him during the week when I was not. They were as concerned as I was and were consistent in their visits.

So, with plans to return that following weekend, I got into my car and drove the four hours back home. His words echoed in my head the whole time.

Later, at my house, I was exhausted but couldn't sleep. I laid in bed thinking of my only brother and what he was going through. He had always been a pillar of strength, but this devastation had essentially reduced him to an unsure, hurt, and psychologically damaged little boy. I finally drifted off after the sun came up. Only to dream about him.

I woke up and went down my hallway to my living room, where he was sitting in my favorite overstuffed chair in front of my bay window. A smile on his face, his arms outstretched to me. The sun coming in the window was brilliant, and I could barely see his face. He was bathed in the light, and colors bounced off of him like a prism. I went and sat down at his feet and rested my cheek on his knees. His hand felt warm on the crown of my head. He was calm, and unlike recent days past, he wasn't upset. He kept repeating the same thing over and over.

"I am going to be alright; it's going to be okay; I promise. Please don't be sad; I love you."

I was startled awake by my sister and mother in my bedroom. They were both frantic. My sister had a firm grip on my upper arm. My momma was crying. Kelle told me to get up; something was wrong with Ricky. We had to rush to Garland to the hospital immediately.

Once I realized that this time, I was awake and shook the cobwebs from my brain enough to think, I admit my first thought went to his possible suicide. Thankfully that was not the case; they told me what little they knew in the car on the way.

That was the longest drive I have ever experienced. Suicide or not, I knew in my gut that a few hours earlier, on the porch of his home, would be the last time I would see my brother alive.

Arriving at the hospital, we were all informed of what had happened. He had woken up sometime in the night with a swollen arm and neck. It was painful enough to warrant taking himself to the hospital. The emergency room physicians realized rather quickly that he had an infection in the soft tissue of his arm that required immediate surgery. To remove what was already damaged, clean the area, and contain it. The plan was direct and would be the only chance to save his life if followed up with antibiotics.

Due to the fact that time was of the essence and it was an emergency, he didn't call any of us to come. He went into the operating room alone, with no family in the waiting room. No final goodbyes or thoughts to share. From what I understand, his last words to the surgeon were,

"Do what you need to do."

In hearing that detail, my heart broke even more. In true Ricky fashion, he didn't want to worry us. I am sure he figured he would just talk to us afterwards.

Things didn't go as planned. He had contracted necrotizing fasciitis—a flesh-eating bacterium. When the infected area was opened up, the virus moved into his bloodstream and very quickly ravaged his worn-out body, shutting down all of his internal organs. He never woke up after surgery.

He lay in the hospital for days on life support, and on December 15th, at forty-three years old, my beloved brother left this world. After all of the other life-threatening battles he'd won, this was truly shocking.

I remember every single moment of those days in limbo. I have never prayed as much as I did then.

Illness and death have an odd way of bringing people together. Nina was there, and I saw my father for the first time (and the last time) for many years. Aunts, uncles, cousins, and family friends.

What I recall most is the minute we were told he was not going to make it. The moment the consent was given to unplug the machines. The excruciating pain as I grabbed my son Fin and finally let go of my emotions and allowed the anguish to take hold. My baby boy had to hold me up; my legs just weren't up to the task. I lost my brother on Fin's birthday.

***

As with any unforeseen and tragic death, members of the family needed something or someone to blame. Some way to make sense of it so that the fact he was gone so quickly could be digested. I became the receiver and target of the wild and outrageous theories. In hindsight, that is probably due to the fact I was the last one to see him alive, as well as the one spending so much time with him during those weeks leading up to his demise. It still didn't make the accusations hurt any less.

Allegations aimed toward me included the fact that even though I had been free of an illegal drug habit since 1994, I had given him something that killed him, essentially making me his murderer.

Then, after finding pictures we had taken one weekend at his house of the two of us having a normal affectionate embrace and kiss, we were accused of having an incestuous relationship. It was not just hurtful; it was disgusting and preposterous. Especially during a time that all I needed to do was grieve.

I was so upset I couldn't defend myself. I did not even try. Even at the funeral, their suspicions were felt. They didn't bother to hide their disdain and resentment.

It was hell. I was excluded from the family pictures that were displayed at the funeral home for the service, and to this day, I have no clear reason why. I am not sure what horrible thing they decided I'd done, but whatever it was, it wasn't true, and I suffered the extra cruelty in silence. Alone. On top of losing him.

As much as I wanted to be there for my mother, something in my soul and mind split the day he died. Catastrophic pain. It was the greatest loss I have suffered to date. I still cannot fathom how my mother lived through it. I still struggle daily. Mothers should never outlive their babies.

Since that day, I have felt like a trapeze artist without a safety net. The world lost its luster somehow. He was my friend, my confidant, my sibling, my adviser, my shoulder to cry on, my greatest fan, and my scolding fill-in father when needed. He was everything to me. He was good.

I have to live with the fact I was the last one to see him and I didn't recognize how ill he already was. Or at the very least, urge him to go to the doctor sooner. Something that I will regret the rest of my life.

I guess what defines a life is how a person is viewed by others once they are gone. By the affect they had on our lives.

At some point, he became my hero.

Although he didn't feel it, he was extraordinary. Ricky was often down on himself in his last days, habitually pointing out what he considered his shortcomings. But he had mastered the thing in which all humans should strive to achieve: the ability to unconditionally love. He didn't just love; he had the ability to make a person *feel* completely loved. Which is rare indeed.

That love came at the ultimate price, for I will always feel that he died from a broken heart. With the constant pain he was enduring, he simply gave up. He didn't want to live in a world without her beside him. A fact he had stated to me many times in the weeks leading up to his death.

In writing this part of my story, I have realized three things.

The first being that my beautiful brother was simply "on loan" to us. We were never entitled to keep him. The world is just too callous and cruel for some, and they can never completely adapt.

Those types of people live a life of struggle and emotional unrest. As if they are simply born into the wrong era, family, or planet.

Though they work tirelessly and consistently to understand and give back to the world around them while they are here, these types of people never seem to be a real *part* of it. Never quite mastering the art of blending in. Their souls are crushed at some point, and their bodies seem to follow.

My second realization is what an incredible gift I received by spending so much time with him those months before he passed.

I got to know him, and he revealed parts of himself to me that I'd never seen or appreciated before. When he left, he did so after bequeathing to me the overwhelming and indisputable knowledge of how much he loved me. For that, I shall be eternally grateful.

The last painful realization being that these tears that I shed for him will never, ever dry up.

I know now beyond question that I will always mourn him and feel his absence. Missing him has become a way of life, even though living without him hasn't.

He was, and still is, my favorite human that I have ever had the pleasure of knowing.

Having Ricky as a brother, growing up with him, loving him, and being loved by him made me a better person. In his gentle way, he always expected more from me. Pushing me to become the best version of myself. But, no matter how much I failed, he never judged or lectured. He just seemed to show me even more support on my worst days.

Other than my children, I know that I will never enjoy that strong of a bond with anyone else for the rest of my life.

The most challenging thing we face in life is learning an effective way of letting go.

CHAPTER 26

The next year of my life was spent much like those weeks in the hospital for my brother, hovering somewhere in between life and death. I hadn't completely ducked out, but I wasn't living either.

I have few people left in my life who I have known since birth. My mother, my sister, two aunts on my mother's side, my biological father, and his brother; my favorite uncle. I have cousins that I saw on holidays as a child and a handful that I speak to on social media. For all intents and purposes, I am left with my mother and sister.

My sister.

Now would be a good time to describe in detail the very complex and somewhat irrational relation that is my sister.

Kelle, short for Kellene. The middle child. Two years older than myself, two years younger than Ricky. Because of the smaller age gap, they shared a much closer relationship while we were young.

She and I are as opposite as night and day. No two people could be as different as she and I are, to include our looks.

She is blonde, fair-skinned, and blue-eyed. I am dark-headed with olive skin and hazel eyes. Dissimilarities in our appearance are just the tip of the iceberg.

My first memory of growing up with her kind of sets the tone for all of the years that have followed.

When we were about four and six years old, my mother took us to the store with her and told us that if we were good, we could pick out a toy afterwards. We were, and she did. For Kelle's selection, I truly can't recall what she chose. I only know that within a brief time, whatever it was became either broken or uninteresting.

I chose a brand-new box of crayons and a color book.

I was lying alone on my stomach on the floor in our bedroom, with my color book open; coloring a picture. Removing each crayon one at a time, replacing them as I was finished with it back into the box. To me, crayons were my new treasure. I loved to color.

She came into the room obviously upset about something; maybe my peace? She grabbed the box of crayons, dumped them onto the carpet, and stomped on them. When they didn't all crush under the weight of her feet, she bent down and grabbed one and snapped it into two pieces. As I started to let out my cry to alert my mother, she took from my hands the picture I had been coloring, ripped it from the book, then tore it in half. This has been the mood of our relationship our whole lives.

Though it is important to note that if someone else had done that to me, she would have knocked them out! It was only okay for *her* to torture me; no one else!

She was genuinely protective of me in any other situation. Which has always been extra confusing. More so as an adult than as a child.

I grew up in her shadow. She was a beauty.

Physically, she was and still is every single thing that is appealing to the opposite sex. She literally oozes sex appeal. From her small, petite frame to her shoulder-length blond hair, that she learned at an early age to flip just the right way. She walks, speaks, and radiates self-esteem and confidence. Something from the inside that just screams, "Follow me to fun."

Unlike myself, she has not one socially awkward bone in her body. She liked attention, demanded it, and thrived on it.

Whereas I was always more comfortable being on the outside looking in, within a few minutes of being in a crowded room or bar, she easily and intentionally became the main focus. Effortlessly commanding adoration. Men were like moths to a flame.

We used to participate in talent shows at school when we were little. I always played the boy of our singing duo, even though she was the tomboy.

It was never uncommon for her to have multiple male admirers, and she was always surrounded by friends.

Kelle was the life of the party, even if there was no party. Any situation was an opportunity for her to shine. The downside was that whatever she felt or did, she did to the extreme.

If she was laughing, she demanded that the world laugh with her. If she was mad, everyone had better get the hell out of her way.

To this day, when she gets angry, she becomes possessed with a superhuman strength. I have personally witnessed her toss a man twice her height and three times her weight as if he were nothing more than a load of laundry or an empty suitcase. She is a little bulldozer—a force of nature. Loud and pushy is just her style. In all honesty, she is a bully.

With that said, it's important to relay also that most times when she loses her temper, it is eventually followed by guilt and a need for her to make things right again.

My modesty was often the subject of her teasing. She has never had issues showing skin and prefers her jeans and shirts very tight in fit. I was softer spoken; she was loud.

Her make-up skills have been honed since she was thirteen, and she has become somewhat of an expert at accentuating what God gave her in every flattering way possible, from clothing to hair and everything in between. She has never been overly ladylike, but more rough and edgy.

Mom calls her a bull in a China closet.

A damsel in distress she certainly is *not*, and yet, every man within earshot seems to be racing to save her. Even her walk and mannerisms are somehow seductive.

As a child, she cried more than most. Like me, tears were usually a product of frustration or anger. The difference being the intensity and frequency of hers.

Kelle can be hateful, heartless, and cruel. I have been on the receiving end of that side of her many times in my life. But she can be equally sweet, loving, and sympathetic.

Someone who loves her is in a constant state of confusion as to what they have done to turn her from one of her personalities to the other.

There is an anxiety and fear that comes with being close to her, because one never knows when she will get mad or what she will do when she does. A ticking time bomb—and it is always just a matter of time.

It is not an exaggeration to say we walked on eggshells around her. We still do.

There is simply no telling what is going to set her off. She does things without thought of long-term consequences. Usually, the actions in any given situation are fueled by anger or her wanting or needing immediate gratification. She is a slave to her emotions, which are fleeting.

I always admired my sister. She was everything I wasn't. Facing life head-on and with strength I can only try and mimic.

Recall in your mind the way the sky looks right before a big storm. That period of time when it's dark and gray and the clouds are somehow more beautiful as they haphazardly swirl around in a rush. Even though we know the chaos they are about to bring with their downpour, there is just something in the electricity they are surrounded by that we, as humans, cannot help but love. It is exciting and intriguing due to the fact that it isn't clear if nature is going to give us a light shower that will pass soon or a torrential downpour. Either way, most of us usually stare at the sky in awe. We just can't help ourselves.

That is the best description I can give of my sister.

Love her, appreciate her, and always be prepared for the worst the storm could bring. I wish it was as simple as always having an umbrella.

When she was a teen, she was a bit wild. Sneaking out of the bedroom window often to attend parties and concerts. Sometimes my mother would realize she and Ricky were gone and lock the bedroom window and front door. I would sneak in and unlock them, or simply let them come in through mine. I hated to see them get into trouble. I always hoped that one day they would invite me to go with them.

That day finally came when I was fifteen and living with my grandparents.

Kelle decided we were going to go to a male strip club to see a guy she was dating who worked there. She was dropped off earlier in the evening. I dressed to look as mature as possible, and we secretly met a taxicab a block away to get there. I didn't drink or smoke, but that night I did both. I was so dreadfully uncomfortable about everything involved in that situation.

As we crept back in as quiet as possible that night, we realized pretty quickly that my grandparents, as well as my mother, knew that we were gone and were waiting up for us.

Although she'd coached me repeatedly on what to say if that should happen, I broke immediately under the questioning by my mother and confessed everything. I just couldn't lie.

That was the end of my being invited to go with her! I tried sneaking out on my own once and went to a concert. I got dumped at the after-party because I wouldn't have sex with my much older crush, and Kelle had to come rescue me. Our mother was never the wiser. I guess I just wasn't cut out to do that kind of stuff. I was never any good at it.

She too has always been afflicted with the inability to make good life choices. Out of the three of us siblings, Ricky seemed to be the only one blessed with the sense God gave a goat when it came to making decent long-term decisions.

So, as a result of that fact, between both of our failed relationships and life hardships, she stayed with me. Off and on for most of our adult lives, with the exception of a period of time after Ricky died. I didn't see her much that year for whatever reason.

I don't know whether I would consider us close by other people's standards. It has always been a love/hate relationship.

We got along, as long as it wasn't for an extended period of time. I love her and miss her, but after a day or so of being with her, I am usually exhausted.

When she isn't having a good day, she can seemingly suck the air out of a room within minutes. I am an empath, and her energy or mood always has adverse effects on mine. To put it bluntly, she makes me feel bad.

Happiness or calmness has never been a long-term state for Kelle. I end up feeling on edge the entirety of our time together, never knowing when something is going to enrage her. I don't ever want to be in the path of her hurricane once it begins.

She learned to drink alcohol and smoke at a young age; both habits she still retains to this day. You will rarely see her without a beer or mixed drink in her hand. The later in the day it is, the more disagreeable she will be. She is a semi-functioning alcoholic.

She is talented artistically, and she can be very generous. Under the right circumstances, I have also witnessed her as fiercely loyal and protective. This side is seen mostly when it comes to her children.

She has five boys. Much of our childbearing years, we seemed to be pregnant at the same time. The result of that is that all of our children are extremely close. They share more of a brotherhood than cousins.

At times in our lives, I have felt like I know her better than anyone else in the world. While other times it is quite clear that I do not know her at all.

No matter what she has ever done to me, I seem to have the inability to hate or dislike her. She is my sister, and although

I know now that I can never really trust her, I love her. Because of that, I seem to have an unlimited amount of forgiveness when it comes to her.

I assumed that writing about my deceased sibling would be much more difficult than writing about the living one; I was wrong. Both come with very valid, if not very different, pain.

After a year of grieving the loss of Ricky, I needed a distraction. Although I never ceased trying to be a good mother to Ellinore and Tris, staying busy with their school activities, soccer practices and games, and every other detail of being a stay-at-home wife and mom, I just needed more.

Any free time on my hands was undesirable time. My mind needed to be occupied during the day while they were at school as well as in the evening when they were asleep—or all night when I couldn't.

I came up with a solution.

I enrolled in classes at the local community college. The first semester had gone well, and I was nearing the end of my second.

I was studying for final exams in our local laundry mat while waiting on my clothes to dry. When a young man came in that I'd known years before. He he'd been our neighbor for some time while he was in his teens, and we fell into conversation.

After a while, he asked me how Derek was. I jokingly commented that I didn't know (Simply because he worked all of the time, but I didn't make that clear.) and he got the impression that he and I were no longer together.

By complete mistake, I opened a door that changed my life in a matter of minutes.

He said he knew it would just be a matter of time before I found out what was going on between Derek and Kelle.

What?

He said it so casually, it took me a minute to understand what he was insinuating. I closed my textbook and started to remove and fold my laundry. My insides were boiling, but I wanted to continue learning what he supposedly knew, so I played along. I acted as if it was old news.

While I stood there trying not to show my complete shock and surprise, he kept talking.

He had walked in on them a few times while I was working nights at the prison. By 'walked in on them', he meant he actually caught them in the act. As he continued with the details, I started to get a roar in my ears, like an ocean. I was shaking so badly I could hardly get my clothes loaded into a basket and into my car. This was not happening.

I said my goodbyes and got out of there as quickly and calmly as possible. I went straight to my mother to tell her what I had just learned.

To say I was upset or hurt is the greatest understatement of all understatements. It was like being kicked in the stomach; I was struggling to breathe.

By the time I arrived at mom's house, I was fairly calm. Through tears, I proceeded to tell her and my stepfather the story.

Initially, they both sat there without speaking. Acting *really odd*. Looking down, not making eye contact, not asking questions, but not in shock either. I sat there at their dining room table, upset, mad and in disbelief for a couple of hours before my stepfather finally looked to my mother and said,

"Go ahead and tell her Charlotte."

Tell me *what* exactly?

My parents knew. They admitted that they knew because years before they'd also caught Derek and Kelle at their house in the same compromising position. More than once.

They had kept it from me all of that time, and they were perfectly honest in telling me they weren't sure if it was still going on.

My mother, stepfather, neighbors, and only Lord knows who else knew that they were having an affair and kept it a secret.

Dear God—*What in the actual fuck?*

CHAPTER 27
London

Cold, gray, and drizzly. These are the most common words used to describe England. In all of my years of reading classic novels and watching cinematic depictions, this was my complete understanding and overall picture in my mind of this country. It is inexplicably the truth.

The sky weeps incessantly. It seems to teeter on the edge of a torrential downpour that never fulfills its promise. If allowed, it adds to the feeling of what could be described as impending doom.

However, I choose to see it differently.

Imagine every Jane Austin novel turned movie: Mr. Darcy or some other love-enthralled main male character sitting at a secretary in front of a large window, quill pen in hand, writing a letter on a piece of parchment paper. The glass and window seal perfectly framing a picturesque view of the grounds of some grand London estate. The sky beyond the antique glass possessing proverbial and continual misty eyes, releasing just enough moisture to send trickles of tear-like steams down each pain that lends to the dark and dismal feeling of the collective scene. It is a very real likeness of this place.

It is in the cold or dreary that we appreciate and long for warmth. This mood sits differently. It adds to the mystery and curiosity of what will come after such a forced and prolonged attitude. Comparable to a bear's rest or hibernation. A restorative reprieve from the habitual over-interaction we must endure as adult humans. Somehow the damp drizzle lends to the feeling that it is acceptable to stay in our homes, read our books, drink our tea, or whatever simplicity it is that brings us soothing comfort. It somehow gently pushes us to reflection and self-awareness—of simply being.

Collecting thoughts and making effort to entertain our minds or emotions instead of practicing our abilities in action-based exchanges that we have become much more comfortable and adept to. I see this as an extraordinary gift that is just a part of the London charm. No wonder so many literary masterpieces were written in this country. It certainly expects to be written about or photographed. It demands it.

Emotions that a person would otherwise have control over are quickly taken over by romantic and cliché inclinations. It is unexplainable.

I have a friend here in London who extended an invitation to come visit. Although I adore Egypt, my mind needed new material. Not for writing, but for just the opposite. A long overdue rest of sorts.

I feel at home in Sharm El Sheikh. It is, in fact, my home. The thought of actively conversing with another English speaker and enjoying a hug, or the smallest hope of experiencing the long-lost feeling of family, was something I desperately needed. A different human connection; a more familiar one. I packed my backpack and landed in Heathrow-London on February 5th, 2021. The country went into its second full lockdown the following day. I immediately entered into self-isolation.

From what I understand, it rarely snows in London. It has been snowing here the last two days. It is a welcome sight, and I am grateful. It even seems to snow differently here; or maybe I'm just inclined to perceive it that way.

The ever-large flakes do not just fall from the sky or trail down in any kind of order; they are both graceful and haphazard. They float down, aimless and lackadaisical. Dancing in swirls on the light winter breeze, entangling together before they land on the barren tree limbs or wet ground below. Giving the appearance of being inside of a snow globe. The weather here begs for a couple to walk hand-in-hand along the riverways, parks, or on one of the many beautiful bridges. The English landscape craves to be appreciated in pairs rather than singularly. This atmosphere beckons its subjects to take the ones they love in their arms and kiss them on the forehead or lips. A scene that is often played out in front of my eyes, not just in my head.

While walking around alone, there is an overwhelming loneliness and complete awareness of the need to embrace and feel another soul just as enamored with the scenery. London in the winter is a wonderland to be appreciated. It would be criminal to take it for granted.

It sparks so much passion and romance that it is almost painful not to be able to comply. A warm hand in mine, a shared cup of coffee, or to stand under an awning waiting for a bus would never be simple and mundane. The atmosphere just wouldn't allow it.

There is an unspoken formal class attitude here like no other place I've been. The inherited or learned decorum is palatable. From the way these people speak to the way they eat with two pieces of cutlery. There is always a hint of formality in any of their activities or actions. What is to be expected from an educated country still having a reigning queen, I suppose. They have manners and self-control. There is an odd comfort in that for me. I cannot explain it or elaborate; it just is.

After my two-week quarantine, I took some time to explore London a bit and take in some sights that I have dreamed of seeing since I was a small girl.

Buckingham Palace, London Tower, and Westminster Abbey. I was not disappointed; they are all magnificent. I enjoyed every single second of my explorations. With one major catch.

I have spent years of my life scared. It wasn't until my departure from the United States that some of that anxiety started to fall away. The last year being Collectively, the months that have gotten rid of it almost entirely. Only to resurface the minute I landed in Europe.

It has come to my attention that the relaxed and carefree feelings for my personal safety were not here to stay. I have returned to the girl who always seems to be looking over my shoulder, and I have again become hyper-vigilant, aware, and untrusting of the people around me. This has me stumped. Maybe it's the fact I am again smack-dab in the middle of a culture where crime is as prevalent as it is in America? I am alerted to this fact with every police or ambulance siren I hear from my temporary room in this otherwise cozy London flat.

With that being said, I feel the need to try and relay a bit of the London vibe the only way I know how. Using a familiar constant as a comparison: the ever-present sentiment of love.

In any and every country, human beings have their own way of doing things. From transportation, worship, relationships, raising children, their manners, to what they eat. I find that the greatest difference can be seen and felt in each place with the way they display love or affection. The way they express themselves in this area seems to set the tone for that country's vibe. It is an undeniable fact. One that I will expand on. I am taking this opportunity to delve into the emotion of love itself and verbalize a little bit of what I have learned on the subject.

The need for love is primal. It is just that—a need. An instinct that each of us is born with. This statement is not up for debate. It is the truth.

However, to what degree we need or want it or even ways of acceptable expression is indeed debatable. There also seems to be a never-settled argument as to where the emotion derives. Is it hardwired into our brain? Is it our chemical or biological makeup? Many believe it comes from our unseen, and so far, unproven, soul. We have to this day no factual data supporting any of these explanations. They are all still, and will probably remain, theories.

We are taught from the time we are born how to love, how to express it, and apply it to our day-to-day lives. Whether there is a correct way to do all of this is a topic that is not scientific in nature but instead more of a personal preference laced with social acceptability. A learned personal preference that eventually becomes our own.

Nothing, and I do mean *nothing*, adds to the evolution pertaining to the way we individually love as much as trial and error. Humans have always learned best through grief and pain, as I suspect we always will.

Watching our parents or grandparents love one another, religious upbringing and teachings, social standards and rules, and the relationship we have with our pets, friends, and siblings are all things that mold the way we perceive and practice our personal habits concerning loving and being loved.

Wrong or right, we are all little human sponges when it comes to learning anything as children, and so we learn. Even though the people raising and teaching us this important skill are still learning themselves. We absorb and mimic the dysfunctional as well as the functional. The sad part being that we, in turn, pass all of our knowledge in this area to our children, who will then teach the next generation. We lead by example. Which usually gives our children a snowball's chance in hell to get it right.

Generally, by the time we get better at it, we are trying to teach our children how to love their children the 'better' way that we have picked up from experience, which goes over much like a lead balloon would. Simply because the years we spent showing them the wrong way are by then ingrained into their minds. On repeat, generation after generation. This is the ugly truth.

Not one of us has this figured out; it is like the blind leading the blind. The consequences of this are pretty pathetic. As unintentional as it may be, humans seem to be getting worse rather than better at it. Maybe because sex has replaced so much of what should be non-sexual contact? We have filled in what we are lacking with physical touch. Always looking for a connection but never really finding it. Trying to get our emotional needs met the only way we know how when we were never really equipped with the skills to do so to begin with. At least, not properly.

So much of the way we express our feelings is inhibited by past trauma, betrayal, and social acceptability. It has become carefully orchestrated and overanalyzed before we even say the first "I love you" or decide to give into the first kiss. We consider what others will think or how it will affect our lives or make us look. In this day and age, we perceive this needed and unavoidable state of the heart as a weakness.

Love takes practice with someone who is willing to match our effort and learn along with us. No one seems to devote the amount of time and attention it would take to learn healthy habits in this area.

Yet we will go to great lengths to learn a musical instrument, cook, or even something as trivial as learning to swim. I do know that when someone wants something bad enough, they will dig deep and somehow find in themselves the energy, as well as the time to do it. The problem being that something has to be pretty incredible to catch our attention enough for us to decide to give up our coveted time to the cause.

We as a race, are overstimulated. We expect more but are willing to give less. We are a culture that never seems to be satisfied, and we are unwilling to dedicate our precious moments to anything that isn't sure, thrilling, or mysterious. It seems that we only deem things important if there is a financial or social gain, even when considering love.

I said all of that so I could say this.

In Egypt, there is a beautiful human connection that, above all else, can be felt. I have discovered that this is not the case in most countries.

Although, once outside of the United States, all countries I have traveled have their own unique feeling of love and appreciation for their fellow humans. Southeast Asia is especially warm and inviting to all walks of life.

As an American, I've become accustomed to constantly question intent. Nothing feels real or genuine. It seems that people were always saying and doing everything that would give the appearance of loving one another, but not following through. There is anger in their feelings. As if to make up for their inability to completely love or trust. It is shared instead by displaced or overstated passion. More times than not, it is temporary. As a nation, we are fickle, and it is the accepted norm.

Then there is the United Kingdom. Different from the countries previously mentioned. Feelings are kept close to the breast. Decorum and social standards are felt. Which gives it a very cold and untouchable vibe. Every single questionable method to relay wanted or even unwanted feelings that I just explained to you can literally and figuratively be felt here. Surrounded by people who you can touch with your hand but never with your soul. The rat race seems to have consumed them all, and emotions have been put in a jar on a shelf somewhere just out of reach. The detachment is felt. Completely and utterly. It feels like people are just going through the motions. Never allowing the true drama of life to permeate them.

I feel unfair in my analogy. So, I will try and soften the blow a bit.

There is a definite reason that I have chosen to write all about my thoughts on the subject of love from this country. It does, in fact, inspire it.

This is without a doubt the most romantic place I've ever been.

The architecture, the history, and the weather all lend to the feeling that we want and need to explore and be involved on a deeper level with someone. Being surrounded by beauty of this magnitude is so damn stimulating. Mentally, emotionally, and physically—I want to bathe in it.

Although it appears cold and uncaring, you can actually tell there is so much more just under the surface. As if the boiling point has been reached underneath a pot lid on the stove. There is no doubt that it is there; the question is how to tap into it. It becomes a subconscious need to find the source and prove that it is in fact real. All of the senses are piqued, and so it makes a person act more rigid to have some kind of control. Although it is all very prim and proper and orderly, if one pays attention, it also relays a dreamy storybook type of vibe that I cannot seem to get enough of. A person knows, without a doubt, if they want a happy ending, they can surely find it here.

There are two types of people on the planet. Ones that love without perimeters, and the ones that have them. The persons without perimeters love naturally, freely, and sometimes illogically, from the time they are old enough to do so.

Even through the sometimes-horrible side effects of being that way, they will never give up on finding someone on this planet that will reciprocate the way their souls crave—the way they know is possible. They need it, like they need air in their lungs. Those people give their whole heart, time after time. Even when the outcome is clear, it is always worth being consumed by something so beautiful.

They hope for a favorable result, but each occasion they do so becomes less about the ending and more about the growth and experience. Realizing that the sheer joy of love given or shared is worth more than the outcome. Always searching, but oh so very happy to the core when they have a shot at it and when they have it. No matter how fleeting.

The ones with perimeters do not suffer as much. They analyze, make rational decisions concerning their partners, choosing consistency and the known over the dramatic, and that is okay.

I do not believe one is better than the other. It is up to the individual. Although they are not as quick to invest, it does not make their feelings of esteem or love less valuable. On many levels, it says the opposite. The overthinkers of the world can be trusted with their affection because they have spent so long trying to talk themselves out of it. It just comes with copious amounts of caution. They have surely analyzed and weighed out every single angle and option.

I have always been without boundaries when it comes to giving love. I like the return. A few months of that electric feeling being reciprocated is enough to run on for a very, very long time. I always say that I am not a slave to my emotions, but I think in some ways I always will be.

I have stopped looking for the happy ending—at least the ending that I used to dream of. Now I am fueled by the actual act of loving itself. It feeds my soul. As I have grown older, I have also become an overthinker. Even though I have acquired very solid personal perimeters as of late, my heart still wins most of the time. Not because I do not know any better; it is a choice.

At the point in a relationship when I have already figured out the outcome and know beyond a doubt it isn't going to work in my favor, I still choose to invest. Love is worth that to me. I realize it will end with me in tears at some point, and yet it is so rare in this day and age to feel anything for another person that I am prone to choose the inevitable pain.

In England, they have very clear and rather obvious boundaries.

My English friend witnessed me kiss a male friend on the lips as we parted ways one evening. He told me later that it was awkward and weird to him, whereas for me, it felt normal and natural. When I explained to him that my grown children still kiss me on the lips and that my siblings did also, he couldn't wrap his head around it. The difference in the way we were raised to express care is the culprit.

It takes some navigation. I have no doubt that once anyone is submerged in the culture and figures out the route, it's worth it. No matter what idea someone has in their mind of what that might entail, they just have to work a little harder and dig a little deeper. Until then, the surreal surroundings here are just a catapult.

I personally cannot fathom a better example of *extra*.

CHAPTER 28

I am a lover of words. I am a romantic fool for them. I kind of have to be; I'm a writer. But I love and value them in the true sense. I get excited about reading and learning new ones—their meanings and multiple uses. I adore how I can absorb them from a story, and the creator of the literature has them arranged in a particular order to set the mood or make the most impact.

I learned at an early age that I could be transported by them. To other places. New places I'd never been that fed my dreams. Words and imagination enabled me to visit the happier lives of the mostly made-up characters.

I relish the gorgeous artistic flow of the syllables themselves that add depth of understanding and feeling from the writer's perspective. Intentionally drawing me in. If written well and with passion, I can almost smell the damp room, coffee brewing, or whatever it is being described. Getting lost in the pages is one of my true joys in life.

I love writing them for the same reason. The English language is a beautiful and intricate tool to use at our disposal. In most classic literary works, they are used with such skill they have created magic. To be able to master words in such a way they can take the reader on an adventure. A previously unknown place to explore. Being able to induce feelings of fear, joy, love, empathy, Sadness, or pain, has to be the most amazing of gifts. Voltaire said that writing is, in fact, painting with words. I even love that analogy.

I spend so much of my adult life expanding my vocabulary and trying to become better at articulating perfectly from my mind to paper. As I've grown in these endeavors, I have also acquired the desire to learn languages other than English. I really do delight in this way of expression. Acquiring the ability to use them to your advantage is really the key to communicating with other humans. If everyone knew what vocabulary to use and adjusted their tone while doing so, I believe we would have a much narrower gap between us. We would understand one another better and would react more appropriately. One step closer to world peace. I wholeheartedly believe this.

So, when I say that when I found out about Kelle and Derek, I was hurt in such a way that I can't explain in words how bad it felt; you know what I mean.

I just don't have anything but common or general descriptive words to use. Such as betrayal, anger, heartbreak, and sadness. This description will just never do. But it has to. I could try and use a hundred words, or just one; either way, it won't begin to relay how awful it really was.

If I had to choose one word though, it would be lonesome. From the minute I heard, I was completely and utterly alone. Everyone who knew my husband and my sister knew. I was the last to find out. I have never felt so lonely.

It was something I wished I didn't know. I wanted the cat back in the bag. At least before that day, I knew I had a husband and a sister who loved me. The adult people I was closest to in the world betrayed me *AGAIN*.

I didn't just lose them; I lost my whole family. My trust in everyone was destroyed. Who I was and what I believed in was absolutely shaken.

That time was so different. I reacted with anger like I'd never experienced or displayed. When pushed that far, I found my strength.

No pill was going to help me forget the fact that they all allowed me to think myself crazy, and as a matter of fact, I became filled with animosity every time I took my medication. They had, without interference, watched me commit myself to a mental facility.

All of them watched me suffer and patted me on the back and encouraged me to seek help over something *they knew to be true*. Being found out was more important to them than me. The lie was worth covering up at all costs. That was the hardest part of all of it. No one cared about me as a daughter, friend, wife, or sister enough to tell me. Even when I convinced myself that I was crazy and started taking loads of medication to combat my paranoia and calm my inner voice, they simply let me. Oh! That hurt! It made the pills actually that much harder to swallow—literally.

The impact that had on me was what I will refer to as the beginning of my final descent to self-destruction. It was unequivocally the catalyst of all of my decisions that led me to where I am now.

As much as I appreciate where I am on my journey, as well as where I am in the world, I wish I could have skipped the seven years leading up to it.

What does a person do in that situation? I'm not sure what anyone else would do, but the only answer for me was to leave. Leave Derek, leave my family, and leave my town. I had to distance myself from anything that made me feel like a fool or anyone I felt had betrayed me. Which was pretty much everyone I knew except for my children.

I hadn't seen Scott in years, but I picked up the phone and called him. I didn't tell him what was going on, but I know he knew. He immediately offered me a job and a room to stay in until I could get my own place. Through thick and thin, that man was always there.

I packed a suitcase, and with Ellinore and Tris and Shelby in tow, I left for Dallas.

Time had changed both of us. I was on a litany of medications, and when I came back, he and I both started drinking too much. We were on shaky ground even as friends; as a boss and employee, it was explosive. We were bad for each other in every damn way possible.

The bar was not doing as well as it had years before. It was in one of its stagnate phases. It still paid the bills, but without the same joy and assuredness I had enjoyed years prior. It was hard to keep my head in the game.

I realize now, in retrospect, that it probably had less to do with where either of us were in our lives and more to do with the fact I heaped a whole lot of expectation onto the situation and him. He'd always been a fixer of my problems. For years when anything went wrong, he and his business became a beacon for a new beginning. Anything less was going to be a letdown, no matter what it was in actuality. I kept returning each time to relive a time in my youth that induced feelings of self-worth and independence. It wasn't fair to him, and it was a set-up for failure for me.

That particular time, it didn't work out like all of the times before, and after a few short months, we went our separate ways.

I chose to remain in Dallas, and when things became too difficult to handle financially, I eventually allowed Derek to come back. Amid promises of fidelity and sobriety. Two things I knew in my soul he would never be able to live up to.

His sincerity was never the question; it was his inability to follow through. As painful as it always was, I don't blame him for that particular fault. I had my own issues to be held accountable for.

Prescription medication was a way of life for me then. The way I saw it, if it came out of a bottle and had been prescribed by a doctor, I was doing nothing wrong. Even when I took way too many or went through them twice as fast as I should have. I had an excuse for everything. I was the queen of self-medication and denial.

It was only a matter of time before the thought of introducing illegal narcotics back into my life was not such a bad idea. The prescribed ones were not working. I longed for relief; I was desperate for it.

There were a few weekends where that was the case. Those weekends rapidly escalated into occasions I spent the rest of the week looking forward to, and before I knew it, I was in over my head.

We were living in a lovely three-bedroom home in the suburbs. It was beautiful in its simplicity. A nice, established neighborhood with large pecan trees lining the streets. Tris's middle school was just across the road from us, and Ellinore's primary school was a short walk. Per usual, Tris was involved in baseball and football and quickly became quite the popular young man. Our house was always full of his friends. Beau was staying with us at the time as well as my nephew Van, and if there was ever a time to be at peace, that should have been it—not a chance.

I was living with a man I no longer trusted. A man who refused to completely admit or even discuss what he'd done to cause the new pain I was trying to escape. Upon his return, I was expected to let it go. Pretend it never happened. No apologies or personal responsibility. Forgiving someone who was only sorry for getting caught was an impossible task for me.

Essentially, I was strung out on prescription narcotics. The weekend warrior mentality that included street drugs added fuel to the flame. I was not sleeping and lived to get through each day so that I could take a handful of pills and not feel anything for a few hours. The nightmares were increasing in detail and frequency. I grieved the loss of my brother; I missed my sister and family, and all I could think about was ending it. I was completely alone. In a busy home, store, or social event, I was still painfully aware of my singularity. That kind of loneliness is indescribable. For the woman who was everyone's rock; I had not one person I could turn to and trust.

It became too much. There was no escape that I could think of except one, and it consumed my thoughts every minute of every day. It became the one and only road I saw out.

One evening after four days of sleep deprivation, I scribbled a quick note and tucked it into a journal I'd been keeping. It was a simple good-bye letter. With a heavy heart and non-stop tears, I took a bottle of tranquilizers and some soma. The thought of living one more second with that emptiness and pain was not realistic. I was done.

I woke up in a mental health ward of a state hospital. Whatever happened between taking that handful of pharmaceutical medications and ending up there, thankfully, I don't remember.

Beau sensed something in my demeanor that evening and alerted Derek. I left by ambulance. He caught me in time; I was still alive. When I woke up and realized that fact, I was mad and a little more than distraught. I couldn't even kill myself properly. Another failure.

I was transferred to a private hospital where, for the first time in my adult life,

I decided to actively participate in my own recovery and mental health.

After forty-three years of keeping secrets, I finally told the doctor everything. After finishing my story, my assigned hospital psychiatrist actually wiped tears from his own eyes and hugged me. That doctor spent at least two hours a day with me, every day, the entire time I was in the hospital. He'd even put off his own vacation to do so. It was then that I realized the magnitude of all of the collective trauma I'd been running from.

On top of the original diagnosis, he added post-traumatic stress disorder to the list. This was the one diagnosis that would make sense of all the others.

The doctors finally had the whole picture. I received intense therapy and all new medications. For three weeks, the focus was mostly about getting me to sleep longer than two hours at a time. I walked those hospital floors more times than not, but eventually they found a cocktail that worked. I was sleeping again, and my body was just as exhausted as my mind. After two months, I was released back into the toxic home life I had opted to check out of, with foreseeable consequences. But I had nowhere else to go.

A few months after coming home, I suppose Derek's temporary good behavior became tiresome for him, because he went right back to the habits and self-destructive behavior he'd always relied on.

We went to visit a friend one evening, and he had way too much to drink. He wouldn't allow me to drive home. On the way, he told me we were going by the dealer's house to pick up some cocaine. I wasn't having it. That time I was putting my foot down. An argument ensued. The next thing I knew, I was covered in blood. He had punched me out of anger.

A car driving beside us witnessed it and called the police. We were pulled over. I left by ambulance to a hospital; he left in a patrol car to jail.

I had a gash from my nose to my lip that took several stitches to close. I will never forget lying on the hospital bed, the surgeon stitching up my face as she cooed words of solace to me with the policeman just inside the door.

They were patiently waiting to question me, whispering to each other about what they were witnessing and the paperwork on the assault. My shirt was then saturated in my own blood, mascara ran down my face, while a never-ending supply of fresh tears mutely slid from my eyes and soaked my pillow. My throat was so constricted I couldn't seem to do something that should have been second nature to me: inhale oxygen.

I didn't experience the physical pain but was overwhelmed with emotion instead. I felt hopeless, stupid, scared, and confused. But mostly I felt helplessly trapped.

No matter what I'd done to get mentally healthy and happy, I kept repeating the same behavior that landed me right back to square one. Ten steps forward, fifteen back. Being miserable was a way of life that I evidently felt some source of comfort in. There was comfort in the familiarity. A sick kind of dependence on the routine and the known chaos and pain.

Addiction to sadness, I suppose. It was the one emotion I had plenty of experience with. I've never been a fan of the unknown, and so I chose the consistency of the horribly redundant instead. Breaking the cycle was something I just did not know how to do, so it continued.

There were always periods of time that Derek was a good husband and father. There was never any doubt that he loved the kids and wanted to do what was right. He had his own unresolved trauma and ways of self-medicating. I was never strong enough for the both of us. When he fell, he generally took both of us with him, and vice versa. My loyalty and compassion for my husband always kept the door open for his return.

***

There seemed to be a lengthy reprieve in 2014 for both of us.

He got a good job in Dallas, and after working quite hard and diligently, he'd moved his way up the ladder and became a foreman. The money involved in that was more than he had ever made, and for the first real time in our marriage, finances were not a concern.

For a while it was like living a materialistic dream, which made the rest a bit more bearable. We rented a huge home in Richardson, Texas. It was by far the nicest home either of us had ever lived in.

Upper-middle-class neighborhood filled with professionals; doctors, lawyers, and such. Our home included four rather large bedrooms, a formal dining room, a spacious kitchen, and three bathrooms. We enjoyed a 22,000-gallon built-in saltwater pool and jacuzzi in our backyard. Beau came to stay with us, and everything seemed to be going better than it ever had.

As history had proven time and time again, it was not something I should have gotten used to or comfortable with. It was only the calm before the final storm that would end life as I knew it, in every single possible way.

That particular time, the results of the events would prove to be unmendable. I would become a felon within the year.

CHAPTER 29

There seems to be a point in everyone's life that things get stale or stagnant. For most, it is temporary. For me, the predictable life was something I should have welcomed and relished after years of struggle and failure. All attempts to get to a point of being able to enjoy instead of just survive seemed to be fruitless.

I'm not sure exactly when it happened. One day it just did. Food lost its taste; excitement about anything was just dead. I ate, but only to sustain my life. I knew I needed to eat, and so I did. Nothing tasted sweet, no pleasure or joy in it. Not just food but every single thing.

Life; I had no hunger for it. I was buried in a never-ending routine of doing what was necessary to get from one day to the next.

We were living well and had gotten another family member. A Pitbull terrier we called Odin. All the affection I had inside of me to give, I heaped onto the children and the family pets. No matter what I showed to the outside world and family, I was still very sick.

I was a shell of the person I had been. So forlorn and lonely. My game face had been perfected.

I spoke a lot with Nina at that time. She was my long-distance Savior. Often lending advice and love. She knew; she always knew. She was the last person left in the trust department. Those daily talks kept my heart afloat. She was always a second mother.

In October of 2014, she lost her battle with a long-term heart condition and died. I was devastated. It nearly killed me. I knew even then that she was the last person actively in my life who hadn't betrayed me. The absolute last person I could trust was gone; permanently.

Quivering chin up, I still forged forward. Hectic mom schedule kept me on autopilot. I couldn't show a chink in my armor. There were too many people looking to me. I buried the pain and kept moving ahead, never properly grieving or acknowledging the loss. No one would ever know how damaged and hurt I was.

Perfect conditions for an emotional meltdown had I allowed it. Which I refused.

Christmas that year came and went without extended family visits. Otherwise, all seemed to be as it should be.

Until I received a cut-off notice on the door one day for our electricity. I was baffled. We were not in any way short on cash to pay our bills. When I asked Derek about it, he simply said he'd forgotten to pay it. I accepted his explanation and didn't give it one more thought.

However, it wasn't long before an eviction notice showed up as well. We were apparently many months behind on rent. Thousands of dollars. I just didn't understand.

When I did get to the bottom of it, I was flabbergasted. All of the overtime, weekends, and nights I thought he was at work, he wasn't. He'd developed a drug issue again. That time it had been going on long enough to put us in such financial turmoil; I was not prepared.

Almost overnight we were financially destitute. Although he still had his job, we had no savings, no money, and nothing to fall back on. It was all gone. Reality was that I had put my complete trust in him again and hadn't given it a second thought in months. I had to act fast.

I want to take a minute to speak directly if I may. It's about to get a whole lot worse before it gets better. But trust me when I say—it does get better. My story is about to take a seriously dark turn, and as much as I would love to blame anyone else in the world for the events I am about to describe, I can't blame anyone else but myself. Just know that although you are about to go on a little bit of an uncomfortable voyage as you read this, my story does, in fact, end up to be a victorious tale. So, keep that in mind.

I feel it is important that, as you read this, you know I am not proud of my behavior and am not trying to make excuses for any of this. Although not my finest hour, I claim it. I wouldn't be where I am now without the disastrous past, and I wouldn't trade where I am now for anything in the world. I find comfort and complete gratitude now in relaying it, knowing the outcome. So, bear with me a little bit while I tell this to the best of my ability.

Back to the story.

We were in the midst of financial disaster; our marriage had long since been over in every way possible, and neither of us would let go, and although off-and-on we were on the wagon, truth be told, it would be more accurate to say we were always just running beside it.

I went to my mom's one weekend to visit and realized pretty quickly that everyone in that household and in that little town was strung out on methamphetamines. That is where the idea first entered my mind.

My stepfather told me that everyone was struggling to feed their addiction at the time; all of the dealers they knew had been caught and locked up. He asked me if I knew where to get it. I hadn't touched that particular drug in almost twenty years, but I did know where to get it. I lived in Dallas. In a city that big, it was everywhere. The next day I drove back, pondering that fact.

Faced with eviction and not knowing where we would go if it actually came to pass, I contacted a longtime acquaintance, who I knew for certain could give me details on obtaining some and what the cost would be. I considered the risk, but I was desperately trying to keep from uprooting my kids again. It was a serious thought that if I didn't figure something out, we would end up in a shelter. That fact, more than any other, fueled my actions.

I made up my mind. I would pick up a few ounces at a very low cost and deliver for a huge profit. If my calculations were correct, I would have us out of the red and back on our feet with a few trips down south.

As far as financial gain, the plan worked out beautifully. Within a few months, our bills were paid. But the results came with devastating side effects.

My schedule was packed with constant trips to drop off and pick up product and money. I couldn't keep up. I started taking the drug to get me through the trips. What started out as something to keep me from falling asleep on the road turned into a habit pretty damn quick. Not just for me, but for Derek as well. His drug of choice switched from cocaine to meth. Mainly because it was so readily available, which was my doing.

During that time, another thing changed that I have to confess. Mostly to lend some understanding of where my head could have been and how I ever allowed things to get so bad.

The first time I ever took meth, the alternative way, was while I was making those ten- to twelve-hour round-trips. I allowed my husband to inject me the first time. Not to get a better high or push the envelope, but more out of my growing paranoia of getting caught. I was too scared to travel with anything I couldn't hide up my skirt, if you know what I mean. Pipes were not easily hidden, and snorting a line didn't have the same effect.

I could do one shot and get through the long trip with ease. The steady stream of poison in my bloodstream seemed to last longer and stay at an even level.

Listen, even people in full-blown addiction judge each other by the way other addicts partake of their drug of choice. People who resort to the injection method are labeled junkies. No ifs ands or buts. I even saw myself as trash. So, I kept it a secret.

I didn't trust Derek at the time with anything. As much as I hate needles and am still scared of them to this day, I learned to do it myself. I didn't want to put my health in his hands. I was in fear of being overdosed by accident. I also wanted to be confident beyond anything else that I was using a clean, new syringe each time. That was the only way to ensure both. I simply watched a video on the Internet one day on how it was done, mustered up the courage, and did it.

I used my ankle so that there would be no marks or track lines. My arms have always been such a difficult place for even the most skilled nurses to hit a vein and draw blood; it just made more sense.

It also cut back on the amount of drug I was consuming. I hated the act of having to inject so badly, and the effects lasted so much longer. I would only have to use it once every few days. Two or three times a week, in very small doses.

I still have difficulty thinking about who the hell I could have been to be able to do that to myself. I generally love writing. My writing this is accompanied by so much contentment and animosity for myself that I seriously loathe each word.

Did I not learn anything from the 90's? Apparently not. Addiction creeps up on a person so quickly that by the time it is realized, it's too late.

Derek lost his job over a random drug test. My short-term plan ended up being something I couldn't quit. I was the only one making money. Eventually we got evicted anyway. From the frying pan and into the fire.

We found another house not too far away so that the kids could stay in the same schools. The catch was that it was being remodeled and would not be available for a few weeks.

Instead of staying in a hotel, we moved all of our household goods into a storage unit and headed down south to my mom's house. It was only going to be about a month. I had notified Ellinore's school of the plan to return and asked them if I should check her out of school for that period of time. After some consideration about our situation, the answer was no. They agreed to hold her place and not count her absent as long as she returned within the frame of time discussed.

We took only what we needed. With a loaded-down SUV, Derek, Ellinore, Odin, Shelby, and myself went on a temporary, if not forced, short holiday. Tris remained behind with a distant relative who lived walking distance from his high school. He couldn't afford to get behind in his studies.

When I think back to that decision and why it was made, I feel so overcome with guilt, shame, and disgust. It's making me sick to my stomach. Telling this part of my life is by far the most difficult and painful thing I have done to date. Probably due to the fact that that was the last time that I had all of the things I hold most precious still in my life. All at the same time. I and I alone threw it away with both hands. What kind of person does such a thing?

I can't summarize what happened next. I wish so much that I could, just to get it out of me and be done with it. As much as I want to, I have to relay each painful detail to take the blame and somehow digest it in a way I can live with myself. Even though my actions will never make enough sense to me to be able to live guiltless. I know that now.

Staying with my mom was short-lived. Odin was huge and didn't get along well with my family, honestly. Although I had control of him, I couldn't always be around. Kelle was staying at the house also, and with her and Derek's past, it was uncomfortable, to say the least.

We moved to a hotel in town. Once we left my mother's house, I stopped selling the drug. I refused. I was done, and I just wanted to help Derek get clean also. He resisted with anger and every bit of drug addict reasoning you can imagine.

Four days before we were to leave and head back to Dallas, he got pulled over on the way to my mother's house. He had an outstanding warrant for past traffic tickets and was taken to jail. The policeman was nice enough to allow him to give me a call, and I went to retrieve the truck so it wouldn't be towed. Odin was with him that particular day, and I have often wondered if it was the officers fear of having to deal with our huge and anxious Pitbull or his compassion that made that possible. Either way, the truck was past due on registration, and I was scared to drive it back to the hotel. I called my stepfather, who came and picked up the truck, helped me empty all the contents into our hotel room, and then drove it back to their house.

While he was in jail, my mother came and stayed with me at the hotel. She and I searched that room, through Derek's luggage, and in every single nook and cranny for drugs or paraphernalia. We trashed everything. Made sure it was spotless of anything for him to come back to when he got out.

I spent almost every dime I had bonding him out of jail. It put us back at square one. We were broke again. So broke, in fact, that we didn't even have the money to head back to Dallas, and certainly no money for the first month's rent and bills on the new place.

My stepfather had a solution. Although I hadn't made any trips to pick up product recently, he suggested that I do it one more time. Just to replace the money I had to spend getting Derek out of jail so that we could get back home to Dallas.

It didn't take much to convince me. He made it easy and even set up a ride with what was a complete stranger. I still marvel at the fact I took that ride, but I did. I'm sure there was another way out. I just didn't see it.

In all of my trips back and forth during the most active times of my short-lived drug selling days, I had only dealt with one person. A girl my stepdad introduced me to. A girl I'd come to trust. I always put the drugs in her hands. She always paid promptly.

What I didn't know at the time is that she'd been arrested and got out of jail with the promise to help the police capture the person bringing in the meth. Yup, that person was me.

When I returned that particular time, from what I considered my very last time, I put the drugs into her hands once again. All accept a small amount that was promised to my stepdad. Within a few days, I got my regular early retirement check, plus the money she owed me. I was back on track and ready to leave. Derek was not.

I couldn't get him to stop doing drugs long enough to get us out of there. I made up my mind that the next day I was taking my daughter and leaving on a train—without him.

I'm not sure why I didn't find it curious that even though I'd just given a substantial amount of drugs to the girl a few days before and she needed more so quickly. I am not sure why I didn't second guess the fact that she'd picked up my daughter from my mom's house and brought her to the hotel room. I don't know. I don't know anything about where my head was. Months of toxic levels of poison will do that to a person, I guess.

I do know that when she showed up, Odin, who generally loved her, acted out of control. Strange. His behavior was one I had never seen before; she was acting equally strange. So much so that I told her to leave.

A girl that I'd always liked and trusted. A girl who I had grown to truly care for. On a recent occasion, I'd driven five hours with backup to escort her abusive boyfriend off of her property. There were times in the last few months that I'd paid her electric bill, loaned her money, and even trusted her around my children. As with anyone I considered a friend, I had her back, and I assumed she had mine.

That particular night, something in her mannerism was off. I felt so uncomfortable that I *told her to leave my room*. All of the red flags were there; I just didn't take note of them. My grandfather used to say,

"There's no honor among thieves."

Nothing could be truer.

CHAPTER 30

"GET THE DOG!" Someone was yelling loudly.

Odin was barking like crazy. He wouldn't let up, and that is what jolted me awake.

I'd slept with headphones on for as long as I could remember. I would go to sleep with intense rock music. It seemed to be the only way I could make my thoughts dissipate long enough to fall asleep. It kept the nightmares at bay.

I woke up to my new nightmare.

I opened my eyes to see so many blue uniforms in our hotel room. Police officers, standing in the SWAT position you see in movies, all at the foot of our bed with guns drawn.

Ellinore and I had gone to sleep in the bed, while Derek stayed up on the computer. I had intended to leave that morning and never look back. To that town, the drugs, or that chapter of my life. I'd waited too late. One day earlier, and my whole life would have been so different. Hindsight does me no good now.

They were screaming to us to put our hands up and to GET THE DOG!

It's odd to me the things that we as humans recollect when thinking back to a traumatic event. (Even if the situation is one we created ourselves, it is trauma nonetheless.)

My half-awake daughter made the comment to the officer that she could either get her hands up or get the dog, but she couldn't do both. He needed to make up his mind. I'm sure she didn't intend for it to come out as smart-ass as it had, but she was thirteen, and everything at that age that came out of her mouth sounded sarcastic and disrespectful.

I could go into great detail about every single thing that happened that morning; I remember every second of it. Every single second. But I won't. Because all that really matters is that I was wrong; they were right. I was the criminal; they were doing their jobs.

The most important thing to say is that that day probably saved my life, no matter how awful it came about. I couldn't have continued on that path and, looking back, I am not certain I would have ever escaped the addiction and dysfunction without some type of intervention. I would have preferred it to have played out another way, but that isn't the way it happened. I have to live with that.

I will say that I generally change names in my story, but there is one person I will not do that to. He deserves better; he will get a mention from me. A police officer named Fidel.

He showed compassion when it came to my daughter, my dog, and myself that day. He acted as a good human being while simultaneously doing his job. I will forever be grateful to him for making a horrible situation a little easier to look back on.

That said, Derek and I went to jail. Odin went to a local animal shelter, and Ellinore went into the temporary custody of Marsha's daughter. Child protective services were now in her life to stay until she came of age. It was June, three months shy of her fourteenth birthday. The magnitude of that as well as the extent of exactly how much trouble I was in had not hit me yet. But it would.

After forty-eight hours in lock-up, we were released with a bondsman and an eventual court date. We had nowhere to go. A friend of mine had an old house twelve miles outside of town she offered to us. That is where we went.

In less than a year, we'd gone from living in a huge home, having plenty of money, and frequent pool parties for our daughter and son. Two vehicles and no real concerns, to living in a run-down shack basically in the middle of nowhere. No jobs, no money, no children. We weren't even allowed out of the county. Forced to stay around people who were in the exact situation that we were supposed to recover from.

It was a set-up for failure, but I tried to make the best of it. I wanted to get my daughter back, and the only way to do that was to do what I was told to the best of my ability.

Of course, within a few weeks, drugs were made available, and no matter what I did, I couldn't get them away from me or out of my life. At that point, I wanted to hide more than I ever had. I didn't have my children. The fact I was childless for the first time since the age of seventeen was the hardest thing I'd ever faced. I missed them so bad all I could do was lay in bed and cry. I was completely dysfunctional. For months.

I took the drugs to stop thinking or feeling so I could face the day and do what I needed to do. It was a horrible cycle. I had no family to turn to that was not addicted to either drugs or alcohol, and I had absolutely no idea how to turn things around.

I settled into a life of just trying to focus on getting through each day the only way I knew how. Derek and I lived under the same roof, but we fought constantly. When he was using, I was scared to death of him. I was a coward.

The only things that kept me sane at that time were Odin and Shelby. Yes, they are dogs, but they were all I had to take care of and love. They loved me back and gave me a reason to function. I needed a reason—any reason. They were it. I was okay as long as I had them to look after.

The unconditional love they offered kept my heart alive, I suppose.

The day that Odin got off of his lead in our front yard is a day I will never be able to erase from my memory. I still consider it to be one of the most painful days of my life.

He somehow removed his harness and got out of our yard as we stood there arguing. We were always arguing. Honestly, we fought from sun-up to sun-down. Everyday. Odin didn't like it when there was any fussing or disagreement around him. It made him fidget and get uncomfortable. Much like it would a child. He was so much like a child.

Before he could get out of sight, I told Derek that he needed to go after him. He did. Odin had made it to the neighbor's yard and was cutting across the far corner of the acreage. Just running through it. I saw the man go into his house and come out to his porch with a gun. I ran to the fence line and started screaming to the man. All I could yell was "NO!, NO!. Derek had almost reached Odin at that point.

Three loud shots rang out. I saw my baby drop. I dropped. I saw Derek drop to Odin's side.

Odin was huge. Derek picked him up like a baby and was half running, half stumbling, with tears streaming down his cheeks; he carried Odin to me. By the time he reached me, he could barely speak. He laid his half-alive body down on the hood of our truck and begged me to save him. I knew I couldn't. He had been shot in the lungs. To watch him lay there and gasp for breath was one of the worst things I have ever had to witness.

He was my constant companion for months. He walked with me, watched me while I planted and took care of my vegetable garden. He dug holes ahead of me when I planted flowers in my flower bed. When I cried, he sat patiently with his head or paw in my lap. Eager to learn anything I taught him, and he was always my protector. He and Shelby were everything to me. They had become more than pets; they were family. They were my children. They were truly all I had at the time. They kept me from being alone.

He was so smart. In the weeks previous, I had taught him to say, "I love you." He always sounded like Scooby Doo when he said it. That moment wasn't any different. His last act before he succumbed to the gunshot wound was to say those words. His last act of love. Man, that hurt.

Something in me snapped that day. Another disconnect of some kind. The pain was too great. One of my main reasons for existing was murdered in front of my eyes, and I couldn't think properly. All of these things just kept chipping away at my softness, producing a more hard, cold, and unfeeling me.

Two days later, we packed the truck with a few things and, going against the court order to stay in the county, we headed to Dallas to get our things out of storage. The plan was to sell it and come back and pay attorneys. Better ones than what the court was providing.

While we were back in our hometown, the truck broke down, and we missed our court date. Somehow, law enforcement knew exactly where we were and picked us up the same afternoon as the missed court appearance. We went back to jail and were held a few weeks there before being transferred to the charging county, where another two months went by in lock-up.

I am not trying to minimize my failure by not going into greater detail of these months. I am faced now with the truth of the fact that there is just too much to tell. Too much to relay and stories from that time that are not fair or that I just can't digest enough to even elaborate on. It is still so fresh. Even writing what I am is making me angry and sad. I don't do well with things that are not fair or don't make sense.

It seems that when a person admits they are at fault in this world and assumes responsibility, they are not considered really sorry unless they admit and accept all of the things they are accused of. That just isn't something I can do. There was so much injustice in this part of my life. Even though I made the mistakes that put me in those positions, I will not and cannot accept the sheer magnitude of the injustice. I will forever be of the opinion that a person is only allowed the justice they can afford. It is a sad reality, and it was so difficult to learn it the way I did.

Eventually, I got myself out of jail. With the money I saved by sitting in jail, I hired a new attorney. Then I got Derek out of jail. But even after months of being clean due to his incarceration, he got out and went straight back to doing drugs. I shouldn't have gotten him out. I know that now.

When Ellinore was taken into child protective custody, Tris was afraid of being put into the system, and at almost seventeen, he ran. He avoided what he considered his own injustice.

He did come back after a few months and met with the caseworkers and allowed them to do their investigation. The investigator on his case reported back to the court that he was one of the most well-adjusted and smart young men he had ever come into contact with. He further stated that Tris had not suffered any abuse or neglect and, in fact, felt that it was just the opposite, stating that he was well-rounded and emotionally stable, if not even a bit spoiled. Case closed.

He was not placed in foster care, so he was allowed to live on his own. Unequipped and with no real way to support himself.

Even though Ellinore was raised across the hall from her brother and in the same house, they reported the exact opposite for her. The fight to get her was not ever going to be easy. No matter what I did, I failed.

Although all court-mandated drug tests were clean, getting to the office to get them when required became almost impossible. I lived too far outside of town, and our truck was still broken down and left behind in our home town.

I moved to a house inside the city limits, walking distance from the office where the urine samples were collected for my drug test, but they changed the office later to seven miles outside of town, and I just couldn't get to them. Every time I didn't make these same-day appointments, they were considered a fail. The same as if they had detected drugs in them.

We went to court and received our sentence. Both of us took plea deals.

Felony 2 convictions. Five years' probation with court costs, probation fees and for me it was worse. I was ordered to get back onto all of the psychiatric medications—medications that attributed to my downfall to begin with. I was monitored to ensure I was taking them.

The side effects of all of those prescriptions, along with some new ones that were added to my daily regiment, made me crazy. I became a complete agoraphobic. I refused to leave my house, and when I did, I spent the whole time I was gone filled with so much anxiety. I physically shook until I could get back home. Simple trips to the grocery store or doctor took every ounce of my strength.

Another thing I was dealing with was the realization of what came along with being convicted of a felony. Many of the jobs and skills I had counted on for an income before, I couldn't any longer. Such as working as a correctional officer or special needs teacher in any public school. They did background checks.

As part of my plea deal, I was not allowed to work anywhere that alcohol was served. I couldn't go back to bartending or waitressing to pay my bills or court fines. I was basically stuck in a bad situation that kept getting worse with every month I couldn't pay them.

I do not know how people get out of such situations. Even now, I have to think that if a person doesn't have family to support them or to live with, there can't be a way out of it. I strongly believe that is why the recidivism rate is so high in the United States for felons. If a person can't work to get themselves out of a situation or they don't have a car or roof over their heads, they go back to what they know for survival; crime. I am not saying they are right or wrong; only that now, I can understand them.

Anyway, in the midst of my self-created midlife crisis, I went to a court date for Ellinore one day. I was under the impression that it was just another court date. To see our progress, drug test us, and make the plan for the following month.

That particular morning, Derek refused to go. He said he was sick. But he was acting so strange. I didn't understand why anyone would miss a court date when it involved their daughter. I walked the ten blocks to court alone. I was side-swiped.

The day was not like previous court appearances. I had no idea what I was walking into. I suspect now that he knew exactly what was about to happen. It is why he didn't go. Maybe the attorney assigned to our case emailed or called him; I guess I'll never know. I only know that I was unaware.

The worst day of my life was that day. After a few hours of testimony about the drug case, the sexual aids found in a bag under the bathroom cabinet, and the fact there was only one bed in our hotel, it was obvious to me what was happening. This was a hearing to take my daughter permanently. I was caught off guard.

This could be the part where I insert all kinds of excuses to make myself feel better or to get sympathy. But I won't. It is all my fault. I did this; no one else.

I will add for clarification that the only reason there was a duffel bag of sex toys under our bathroom vanity was the simple fact we had to empty the truck out the day Derek was taken to jail, and that bag had been brought up with the rest of them.

There was in fact only one bed in our hotel room. I tried to switch rooms many times once he got out of jail, but they never seemed to have one available. Either way, we all did not sleep in one bed, and even if we had, I could not and will never be able to wrap my head around what I was being accused of. Sexual abuse? Some warped idea of me and my little girl? Offended doesn't cover how sick inside I felt over that accusation.

I had to leave the courtroom, run to the ladies' room, and throw up. I couldn't stop vomiting. After a morning of testimony and getting grilled on the witness stand, it was over. They took me across the street to get a urine sample, which was clean, and when court convened, I was stripped of my parental rights and obligations to my one and only little girl. I had lost her.

I lost my reason for breathing, existing, and trying. The only piece of hope I had clung to in the world was taken from me. That was it. I walked home in a daze. Physically shaking and sobbing. I freaking wanted to die. The pain was excruciating. The end of all I was. The rest of who I was ended that day. I knew I would never be the same. I am not the same. My heart was completely broken. I was completely broken.

I came into my house, went to bed, and cried. For days, I just cried. I couldn't eat. I just slept and wept.

Within a few weeks, Derek would return to jail. His drug addiction was out of control, and he was paranoid and abusive. At times he was so paranoid he wedged pieces of wood under the door knobs or walked around with a baseball bat. He kept hearing voices and thought I had put cameras all around the house.

His form of abuse was so degrading. He spit on me, pulled knives, and threatened me, and sometimes he walked around breaking everything he could touch in the house. I was scared all of the time.

Until one day, he and Kelle had words in my front yard, and he lost his temper and pushed her. I called the police. They finally took him to jail. Where he would spend the next three years. The district attorney in Dallas had never dropped the case for the assault that had resulted in my stitches after he punched me in the face in 2012. So, he was convicted on that old charge.

A short time after Derek was incarcerated, and at almost twenty years old, Shelby passed. He deteriorated quickly over the course of that year, and my poor sweet boy could no longer walk or go outside to do what he needed to. It seemed selfish and cruel to prolong his life any longer. It was a difficult decision, but it was the right one.

Every single thing attached to my old life was gone. Everything I loved was gone. I'd lost it all. I had to start all over. Emotionally, mentally, financially, and physically. Completely.

***

When Derek went, things started to get a bit better for me. I started a business refinishing furniture. I was able to pay court fines just enough to keep them appeased, and I paid my bills. I bought a truck and could finally see the light at the end of the tunnel. I worked hard to try and put myself into a better position. I was timidly starting to feel a little proud of myself again. I was climbing out of the hole. It took every bit of my strength, but I was doing it.

Although the agoraphobia was still crippling, I managed by running my business out of my house. But honestly, all of the antidepressants in the world weren't going to help my brain. I was moving forward in the same old survival mindset. Void of emotion or any form of happiness in my actions.

Every single day I managed during that time I considered a win. I hired people to work for me that could leave my house and run my errands so I didn't have to, which perpetuated my phobia of leaving the house.

Somewhere in that time I gained the respect of some of the community, and my business became quite popular in our small town. I was on the right road. I was putting all of my energy into trying to get some kind of life back. Hopefully a life I could be proud of. That's it, nothing more. It was my last shot as far as I was concerned. One day at a time was my motto.

I didn't realize how right I was to keep my dreams so small.

CHAPTER 31

The Man on The Bus

I fell in love once. At twenty-one, I was blissfully, completely, naively, 100% in love. There was no apprehension or second guessing. I gave into my emotions and the sheer delight of it. Loving another person that way was beautiful when you took away the fear that would generally accompany that particular state. Pure, honest, and reckless.

The love I experienced was what I now consider a once in a lifetime one. Not to say that someone gets one opportunity to get it right and that's it, but if it comes around again, we just cannot experience it the same way.

As much as a person loves equals the amount and depth of pain when it ends, and so it just won't ever be felt as deeply or as innocently. To love with an untainted heart is a whole different kind of loving. Even though I know now it was dysfunctional, it doesn't make what I felt less real or important.

We were both consumed by it. We needed each other to feel alive. To be separated for any amount of time left us empty and longing. We were addicted to the feeling we could only get from each other. It was amazing and also heartbreaking. It left me with the reality that to accept anything else would be settling. I have settled for too many other things in my life; I refuse to settle for some half-hearted attempt at love. So, I avoid it. Not intentionally, of course, but I can admit to myself now that it is always in the back of my mind. The back of my mind is a faraway place when it comes to hopes and dreams of any kind of real connection with men, or anyone, to be honest.

In October, I took a bus to Sharm El Sheikh. On that bus, seated beside me was an Egyptian man I have mentioned already. Now I will elaborate. I will call him Adham.

That day was just like any other, marked only by the meeting of another human on his own journey. Two people who happen to be sharing side-by-side seats for an extended period of time. The two of us obviously had more to share than the same row of seats and conversation we had on that trip. Sometimes more time is needed, I suppose. For us, this holds true.

We exchanged information then and started messaging back and forth. At first it was simple content about the weather or timid questioning aimed at getting to know each other better. As with all things, at some point it started to evolve. Not into a romance, but a friendship. Based on complete honesty.

I really viewed him as a man I would probably never see again, and so all answers and expressions were uncluttered with the usual flirtatious embellishment. We just simply became phone "pen pals.". It was nice at the end of the day to periodically get a message asking me how I was doing or what I did that day. It was even nicer to have someone I could ask the same questions. So, it went.

Our first meeting after that bus ride was on the rooftop of my hostel. As we sat chatting with a few other people that evening, against the backdrop of the

Great Pyramids of Giza, I watched him. There was something so calm and sure in his manner. Deliberate, inquisitive, focused, and kind. Yes, he is attractive and devilishly charming in action and appearance, but I didn't see that then.

When he spoke, I heard his words, but it was all in the way he said them. His voice was strong and velvety; it's melodious. Hearing the meaning behind what he was trying to relay became an act of serious intent on my part. Even after that first evening together, I didn't view him as a romantic interest. A lovely person, yes, but not anything else.

As I do with all important characters in my life, I will try and give an accurate description of him.

Tall, he stands about 5'11. Broad shoulders, masculine but average build. His legs are lean. The kind of muscle tone one gets from playing sports. If I had to guess, I would surmise at some point in his youth he had played soccer. His complexion is soft, smooth, and even toned. A few shades lighter than you would imagine a Middle Eastern man's skin. I am assuming, from the more recent years being spent indoors in a classroom, not as much exposure to the relentless Egyptian sun. His thick head of hair is black and curly and is kept short and neat, which suits him and showcases his classic widow's peak. I have seen pictures of him with a short beard, but the whole time I have known him, he has kept it neatly edged and trimmed. Which always looks to be a meticulously kept five o'clock shadow. Flawlessly proportioned, from his body to the shape of his face, including his facial features. He has a strong nose, which adds a unique edge to his overall appearance. He has the most incredible mouth. His lips look as if they have been copied from a Michelangelo painting; full and perfectly sculpted.

If eyes are the windows to the soul, then his soul is magnificent. His are anything but common. They are an unusually rich hue of brown, resembling that of dark cedar, and accentuated with thick, long lashes. When he smiles, not only does he show a beautiful even set of pearly whites, but it alters his eyes. They change shape, get smaller, and absolutely sparkle. Even when wearing a mask, which is common in these times, he cannot hide his pleasure in something. His expressive eyes give it away. They are as clear as a five-year-old on Christmas morning. When he feels amused or happy, emotion radiates through those eyes.

It seems like every time I am around him, I notice something new. Whether it's the small mole on his cheek, the recently discovered clef in his chin, or the way he flashes a sideways type of grin. There is always more to observe and take in.

He walks with confidence, talks with confidence, and behaves with confidence—almost cocky. But not quite. He's more calm, quiet, and reserved. However, there is a nervous energy in his movements that I can't put my finger on. A seriousness that is understood, even when he is joking. The more comfortable we become with each other, the more I get to see that playful side of him, and it is pretty adorable. Add the exotic accent to his physical attributes, and it is enough to make any girl swoon. He personifies sex appeal.

Fair-minded, goal-oriented, and good-hearted. If it stopped there, I probably would not be writing about him. I have met many men with great looks and kind attitudes. I am about to drop a line that makes me nervous to even write. But, here goes; he is different. Yeah, I said what I said. Something about him is special.

It isn't what he wears, but how he wears it. Whether he is in a suit and tie or jeans and t-shirt, he emits style and class. I cannot explain it. God spared no expense with this one, on all counts. The most important qualities I haven't even touched on.

Adham is genuine. If he doesn't agree with something, he says so. Sometimes comes across as condescending, but always real. Intelligent, of course. He can hold a conversation about anything, but it is his willingness to learn and evaluate other ways to look at and think about things that is impressive. No judgment, just a thirst to know more so that he can develop his own fact-based opinion. Even then, there is no force in his expressing said opinion. No matter how much he believes it to be true.

I have watched him in many different settings. Even submerged in a group of people he doesn't know; he is always taking everything around him into account. Remembering small details that others would not even notice. Listening, learning, and appreciating. He seems to pay attention to everything. Maybe that's it? There doesn't seem to be a game in his living style; it's more like someone standing on the outside looking in and absorbing all that they can. Watching him while he watches his surroundings is similar to eavesdropping on someone while they observe a play or opera unfold. I enjoy it immensely. I can see his brain devouring and utilizing or sizing up literally everything he is viewing. I am always curious as to what he will mention later.

His care for others is sincere. Not just family or friends, but it seems that every person who is part of the human race has a place card with him.

He is a doctor by profession, a surgeon to be more specific, and he once told me that he would rather teach students to perform surgery than actually perform them himself. When I asked him why, he said it is where he could do the most good for the world, passing on that knowledge and preparing numerous surgeons to save more lives. I have never met anyone like this. He represents fairness, justice, and, above all, giving everyone the benefit of the doubt. Whole heartedly.

What is odd is that even having the qualities I just mentioned, he is not a soft or weak person. Quite the opposite. Strong, steady, and considerate. He has integrity. Unmatched character, and he is a gentleman. His personality is complicated, understated, and elegant. I will say again; he appears to be a different breed than I've come into contact with.

For months, our relationship remained at a comfortable and even tempo. Clear and unquestioned. Calm and sure. Perfect. His boyish charm always kept me amused and entertained. It does still.

After Christmas, I returned to Cairo, and he treated me to an evening on a sailboat on the Nile. It was a simple gesture, and it was a much-needed escape from my life of recollection and written words at the time. I will never forget that evening for several reasons. The first being the night itself as the sun set on the city. The reflection on the water is stuff Hollywood movies are made of, in the romantic sense. It was picturesque.

He was leaning back against the side of the boat, the hazy light of the remaining sun behind him, giving everything an orange, pinkish glow that I will always associate with Egypt. It was the first time I saw him at complete ease. The effect it had on me was quite the opposite.

I was entranced as I listened to him relay some trivial information. He had his head cocked to the side, and I caught his eyes, just for a brief second. His exterior softened somehow, and he almost appeared shy or vulnerable. I have honestly never wanted to touch someone more in my life than I did at that moment. I became nervous and confused. Flight mode kicked in for me. I would have swum back to shore if that is what it took to get me somewhere other than in front of him and away from his gaze.

Later in my room at the hostel, I lay awake trying to analyze my feelings and how they seemed to have changed in an instant. My thoughts wondered and settled on Chase for a bit, and it dawned on me that at that precise moment my memories of him and his part in my past didn't bother me for some reason. It didn't hurt any longer, and I wasn't quite sure when that change had taken place.

As relieved as I was by that fact, I still had enough wits to realize it had taken somewhere in the range of thirty years to get to that point. The thought of feeling that way again would take me the rest of my life to get past. I made up my mind that night. I would not allow myself to give into whatever emotion this was. Ever. But I wasn't ready to give him up either. It seemed foolish to me to lose a friend over a fleeting crush.

Time has continued to move forward here in Egypt and has been filled with so much work and traveling in and around the country; it has gone by rather quickly. One of the few constants has been our friendship. Which has seemed to flourish more due to the fact we never really know if we will see each other again. Time spent together is always enjoyed to the full extent.

We are just as different as we are alike. He levels out my soft and somewhat sentimental side. He gives me much-needed balance.

With each passing year, I have become more and more hyperactive; I push against my inclination to become easily excitable. Excessively so. When I am around him, I calm down naturally. Without even trying, he somehow manages to quiet my inner storm.

Finally, after months of texting, short coffee meetings, and phone calls, we made plans to meet at my place in Sharm El Sheikh. He had accepted a job in England and was leaving the country. I urged him to take a few days and spend them by the sea before he left, and he agreed.

Being an Islamic country, dating is prohibited. Although we were not and are not dating in the true sense of the word, it was tricky. It doesn't just go against the Muslim faith; it is also illegal. Any private contact between an unmarried couple is forbidden and therefore risky.

He stayed in the hotel next to my complex. We spent the day in the Bedouin tent and relaxed with my friends. After the sun went down and it was considered safe, we snuck him up the backstair well to my flat. I felt like a sixteen-year-old girl hiding a boy from my parents. Still makes me giggle.

Sitting in my place watching a really awful American movie side-by-side on my couch seemed like it would be the highlight of our time together. Like so many other times in my life, I was wrong. This time, happily so.

Have you ever played a scenario in your head so many times that it feels as if it has already taken place? I had envisioned that kiss a million times in the months leading up to it. Usually, my fantasies are better in my mind; not this time. That kiss was not nervous, uncomfortable, or new. It was natural and familiar. Passionate and aggressive, with a hint of softness. I would have been pleased beyond belief to stay in his arms engaged in that kiss indefinitely. It was a new comfort zone.

I resisted the hell out of the next foreseeable step in the evolution of our relationship. I realize now that I was scared. Not of the actual act of getting physical with him, but the apprehension was more of a way for me to ensure my heart wouldn't become involved. Walls were still up, and I had complete intention to keep it that way. If his kiss felt like home, what would his body feel like?

I could literally write a whole novel based solely on those two days. I really could. A damn good one. Instead, with flush cheeks, I will summarize in the most pleasing manner I can manage.

There seems to be a lack of a better word to call the act. Sex or copulation just will not do. They just seem too scientific for me. There was no science in our union. So, I will refer to it as making love. Even though this term is generally reserved for people who are in faction *love*, we are not. The term is just fitting. In our way, we were indeed expressing love. The need for immediate gratification and love. The line was not blurred, and it still isn't. Those days were the closest thing I have had to a one-night stand, and I feel no remorse or guilt whatsoever. If giving in to lust (again, for lack of a better word) makes me a bad person, then so be it. I'll take the hit. I don't care. It was worth it.

While kissing him, the world melted away. My mind was only on the pleasure of feeling his lips on mine. His taste. The look in his eyes. Both playful and intense. Tender and aggressive. He is a constant contradiction. A paradox in all he says and displays. He coaxes something out of me that I thought was no longer possible. Desire and hope. He represents comfort and joy. Food for my body, soul, and mind.

His kiss combined with his earthy scent was intoxicating. My heart was pounding so hard, it felt as if it would escape through the bones of my rib cage. As if it was stuttering its way through doing its job to circulate my blood. It didn't take long before he scooped me up in his arms much like you would a child and carried me to my bedroom. I lost all common sense and resistance. I wanted to be merged with him; I yearned for it.

The hours that followed were unhurried and explorative. A slow, methodical expedition. Passionate yes, but also lighthearted. Easy. Being with him set my heart at ease.

In all of my experience, sex has always been about the end result. The final goal of orgasm. Trying to arrive at that outcome in the most direct and mutually favorable way. I do not think until that night I knew it could be any other way. Maybe it has something to do with the fact I knew that the end result was absolute. No questions about if it was going to happen; the unknown was *when*.

It became so soul-engrossing to just be there in the moment. Each minute stretching out to the next. Craving a repeat of the last moment spent, but needing the next one equally as much. A glorious loop of excitement and adrenaline-induced pleasure. I have never felt so submerged and lost in another person.

If I could have stopped time, I would have. I've always loved any kind of new knowledge, especially when it is obtained unexpectedly. The surprise was in the way it *felt* new; previously unknown. Experiencing him for those few hours of my life was something I wouldn't trade for anything. The way he felt, the way he made me feel, is ingrained in me. Making love to him just made sense, in a logical way as well as the physical one.

All walls were down, all bets were off. The rest of the world didn't exist.

Afterward, I felt strange. Dizzy. Shaky. Probably hormone-induced. Oxytocin is a sweet natural drug. I am sure there was tons of it surging through my body. Whatever the culprit, I was so damn content. Per usual for me, sleep would not come. Even lying in his arms. I laid on my side and watched him doze, taking note of all the little things I wanted to remember. Mental snapshots that I still recall and hold dear. I remember missing him already, though he was still beside me. There is something so pure and unadulterated about that.

Thinking back to then, the memory I seem to recollect the most is surprisingly not sexual in nature.

We were on my couch; I was lying down with my legs in his lap. His hands were on my thighs, and we were laughing about something. I don't remember exactly what was so funny, only that he was calling me a cliché. The smile he was wearing could have lit up New York City. So much familiarity in the simple act of relaxing and resting my legs on him. I truly miss the safe feeling of that. It's so rare for me to let my guard down and feel so comfortable.

I didn't need him; I wanted him. There was not one small bit of using one another for validation. We are two strong and honest souls who are lucky enough to have met and who get to periodically share space with each other. And luckier still to have willingly given a piece of ourselves to the other.

I don't feel the need to question his intent, and he, in turn, doesn't question mine.

It always gives me so much relief to put into words what I see as important. More in this chapter than some previously. It has not escaped my attention that what I have described is what inspires romance novels and love songs. Having this to write about and to file away in my good history makes my smile a little wider, my singing a bit louder, and my frame of mind brighter.

It is astounding the difference a few hours with one person at the right time can make. Never underestimate the power of being able to get completely lost in a moment, and never undervalue the person that made it possible.

After two days with me, he was gone. His future was calling. He has now relocated to England, and we still talk often. Mutual fondness and respect are our foundation, and it is beautiful.

What he has awakened in me does not make me feel lonely, obsessed, or worried. When I do think of him, I get a warm flush, and I smile to myself.

For once in my life, I am happy with just this. It holds so much more value to me. I am in no rush to label us. No hurry to claim him or be claimed. The lesson here is that I don't need to slap a useless, overused label on us. I do not know what we had; I only know what I feel: satisfaction. It is my hope that, above all else, we will always remain friends.

I am not afraid. To either love him or lose him. I don't know if it was intentional, but he has made himself a safe haven for me. I will never take that for granted. Real human connection is important, even if fleeting, and so very rare. The time frame of how long I have it is irrelevant. I am learning to stop looking forward in matters of the heart. The past and future can only exist in my head. I will live and enjoy what I have each day.

Life is an endless balancing act of holding on and letting go. In one way or another, we are constantly having to let go of something or someone. I am learning to let go with gratitude and grace.

Was it fate or serendipity?

I don't know.

I only know that some people wait their whole lives to feel content and satisfied. I am blessed. I received both from a stranger that I met, of all places, on a random midnight bus in Egypt.

CHAPTER 32

Two years. Two years focused on getting better. Two years of working non-stop and trying with everything in me to get out of the mess I had created. Two years of calming my soul, working through pain, and keeping my inner demons at bay.

I had a successful business I loved, work I enjoyed, and the silver lining started to show itself around the cloud. It took one day for all of it to come unraveled and for my hard work to be destroyed. One goddamned day.

I was working late one evening and had forgotten a tool at my business partner's shop. I had a job that needed to be finished before morning for a furniture show. I got into my truck and went to get it. I had a taillight out and got stopped. No big deal, right? Wrong.

Because I lived in a small town and I had a drug conviction, the officer that pulled me over asked if he could search my truck. Of course. I had nothing to hide.

Without hesitation, I allowed him to so that I could continue to the shop, get my tool, and get back home.

Under my truck seat and in the open, he recovered an old syringe. I was in complete shock. That had been a brief part of my past, yes. A long-since dead part. I still to this day have no idea how it could have gotten there. There are many possibilities.

At times, I hired addicts to help with my business. They were the cheapest hired-help around. Occasionally, they used my truck to move furniture or run errands. Maybe it was one of theirs? Maybe it had been there a really long time and had worked its way out from a hiding spot somewhere in the seat? It just didn't make sense. I'd recently asked a police officer friend of mine to go over my truck with a fine-toothed comb to make sure no one had left anything in my vehicle. Could he have missed something like that? I do not know.

All I do know is that I went to jail that night. My truck got impounded, and within twenty-four hours I lost my home, my business associate, my freedom, and mostly, my credibility. It was the end of everything I had worked so hard for.

After that incident, my probation officer started to question everything. Even refusing to document fifteen hours of my community service because she didn't recognize the signature on my card. Time that I had indeed spent and would have almost completed my hours. My probation was revoked, and I was picked up a second time and put in jail. Twice in one week. Each time I had to spend every bit of money I had to bond out.

I had nothing left to give. I just didn't care anymore. No matter what I did, I was rewarded with suspicion and misfortune, and I was completely done. Being surrounded by drug addicts and choosing to remain sober was so very hard, but I did it, and none of it mattered anymore. So, I legitimately just stopped trying. I felt so defeated. The situation finally got the better of me.

And then it happened.

While standing in line at a grocery store, I found my eyes drawn to a new issue of a mainstream music magazine.

On the cover was someone from my past that I hadn't thought of in years: Jack.

Remember the young man I mentioned at the beginning of my story? My brother's friend Jack that I met in my living room at fourteen years old? I told you he would come back into my story.

After buying the magazine and taking it home, I started to consider him a bit. One night, while taking a break from working in my shop, I messaged him.

He had gone out into the world and had become quite famous. As a member of a very popular rock band, he had achieved much success, and although he hadn't continued as part of the original band that had earned him his fame, he was still a musician with numerous solo projects and accomplishments to his name. So much so that I honestly did not expect him to message me back. Famous people don't actually check their own messages, right? But he did, and he answered me back immediately.

After catching up a bit on a short phone call, I developed an idea in my head. A dream really, but it was a dream that would take shape rather quickly in the following months. That few minute conversation put ideas in my mind that I couldn't get rid of—the possibility of a new beginning.

He had settled on an island in the South Pacific. The little bit that he told me about it made me envious. I was jealous of the second chance at peace he had acquired. If he could do it, why couldn't I?

For a couple of months, I continued to work and do what was necessary to stay out of jail until my court appearance. I knew that when I went to court, a lengthy jail term would be in my future. One that this time, I didn't deserve. There was no way around it.

I made a decision and just went with my own gut. I had nothing left to lose.

Once I finally made the choice to leave, everything just seemed to fall into place. Within six weeks of my conversation with him, I had purchased my plane ticket. Material things just didn't seem important to me any longer. My freedom was everything and the only goal I had at the time. I sold or gave away everything in my house and stayed low-key so that I didn't raise any red flags for law enforcement. I worked hard and tucked away every cent I could.

The main obstacle being that my passport was due to expire ten days before I was set to leave the country. In order to get a new one, I would have to go apply through the local post office. Which would let people in that small town know that I had intentions of leaving. I could not do that.

As I prepared for a trip of a lifetime, I remember thinking that it would either be the best decision I'd ever made, or the worst. Either way, I knew deep in my heart that it would be an adventure that would surely help me discover myself. Possibly for the first time.

I was not going to be with Jack. But I suppose the thought of being around anyone who actually knew my brother or knew the undamaged me was a wonderful incentive. It fueled me to stay the course.

I found a travel agent in a nearby city and went to them. I paid four hundred dollars to rush my passport renewal under the pretense that I had been unaware it was about to expire and had already purchased my flight.

Usually anyone requesting a passport was put through a rather lengthy and rigorous background check that included checking for outstanding warrants, bonds, and active probations. I assumed it would be money I had thrown away in the end. I knew I would not get it, and if I did, I was quite sure it wouldn't be on time to leave the country on the day I had planned. If I had to rebook, I would have already gone to court and would be in jail.

I did it anyway, and it worked.

Three days before I was due to fly, they called me and told me to come pick up my new passport. It also happened to be the day before my court date. I literally dropped everything I was doing. I went and told my sister and mother goodbye, packed a suitcase, and picked up my passport on the way out of town.

If you don't think agoraphobia is a huge deal, think again. I was physically ill the whole time I planned my escape. Every single trip out of my house, out of my town, and anywhere unfamiliar was a nightmare. Cold sweat and anxiety. I had to give myself affirmation constantly. Pulling over frequently on any of those trips to vomit or calm down. Out of control shaking and fear.

I stopped in Dallas to spend my last day with Ellinore and Tris. That night I sat them both down and told them my plans. She was sixteen, and my heart was broken. As I am quite sure hers was as well.

I still hope that she will understand that she was worth so much more than what happened to her. She was worth more than me running off. I just didn't see another road. I only saw that if I stayed, I would have ended my suffering the only way I knew how. The way I saw it, and still see it, is that I was in a no-win situation.

After a late night sitting up with them to discuss my no-plan plans, I tried to enjoy the time I last had with them. Again, it fell short.

I was about to be a fugitive from the law, and I was kind of having an out-of-body experience. Of all times I should have considered doing drugs, it should have been then. I was a mental and emotional wreck.

That last night, I kept waiting for authorities to show up at Tris's door to take me into custody for missing my court date. I was on edge. Jumpy, jittery, and full of anxiety. It never happened. They never came. The final hours before my departure, I started to calm down a bit. I had to prepare for the next day. I was convinced that I would never make it out of the country. I felt that at some point I would get caught.

The next morning, with a very heavy heart and feeling as if I was on autopilot, Ellinore and Tris delivered me to the airport. We all stood there hugging and crying, just in front of the first security checkpoint. It was then that it hit me.

I wanted to stop and run back. I wanted to erase my past and go home with my babies. I wanted to die when I thought of leaving them. I think deep down inside I desired to be stopped by an official or be denied entry onto the plane. At that moment, I wanted to be caught. Any thought was better than the scenario of leaving them.

The events surrounding my departure from the United States are surreal. As I look back on the last few years before I made the choice to leave, I realize that without each individual horrible and heartbreaking thing, it never would have happened. To this day, I am not sure what propelled me forward. I don't know how I managed to line up all of those little steps and complete so many minute details that made that moment even possible.

On Sunday, September 16th, 2018, I said goodbye to my two youngest children and, without any problems or issues, boarded a one-way flight out of the United States of America.

While walking to that flight, I stopped, removed the rather large zip-lock storage bag full of prescription medications I'd been forced to take for so long, and dropped them into a trashcan. To start over, I needed a clear head.

I did not have trouble boarding the flight that day, or any of the multiple times since. It is as though time stopped and I ceased to exist. That me is gone. I am not her anymore; she was never me.

The flight took off to clear skies, sunny and beautiful. I spent time in Las Angeles, California, for a layover. The whole time wondering if I was going to be allowed on the international flight. I had serious doubts and thought I would be stopped before my journey even started. I boarded my Singapore flight still unbelievably nervous.

I will never, as long as I am alive, ever forget the feeling I had the moment when the pilot came over the intercom and announced, very simply,

"We are now in international airspace."

The feeling I had was complete, utter relief.

I then fell asleep. I slept more soundly than I had in years. I slept so deeply that the flight crew had to wake me up to eat three different times. I was not scared anymore. The plane carried me to freedom. The flight that saved my life. It will forever be the flight that saved my life.

I had done very little research on Indonesia. My plan was not a well-thought-out one at all. I landed in Bali late on the evening of September 18th. I had randomly chosen a small town there in the picturesque hills. It was dotted with rice paddy fields and palm trees.

I was exhausted, overwhelmed, but relieved. I went straight to bed and fell asleep. I couldn't even see my surroundings in the dark. All I knew was that I felt completely safe and very, very alone. And so, I slept. No nightmares, no interruptions, no worries. I slept like I hadn't since I was ten years old at my grandparent's house.

I woke up the next morning to the sound of lizards croaking and a beautiful young Balinese woman preparing coffee on my veranda. The air was thick with incense and flowers.

I walked out, sat down, and drank that coffee in complete peace and cried. I just cried. I don't know if I had held it in so long that I could no longer keep it in, or that my beautiful surroundings in the tropics were just too much for me, or that I finally felt safe. I only know that that cup of coffee was the absolute best cup of coffee I have ever had in my life. I had breakfast, drank my coffee, and just wept.

Observing my surroundings for the first time felt like opening a Christmas present and not wanting to play with it to preserve its newness. I just wanted to hear everything around me, smell everything, and touch all of the interesting flowers and plants. Taste the unusual fruit on my plate I had never tried before, and soak in the vibe. It was complete magic. It was so great and much better than I had ever imagined. That morning was above and beyond any expectation I had ever had about anything, ever.

I was fifty years old. I had exactly fifty dollars to my name after I paid for my room and a brand-new ten-year passport. I had a roof over my head for the next two weeks; no plans or concrete life were planned out. I had no job, no ride, no friends, or any real way to communicate. And yet, somehow, it was the first time in my adult life I felt any kind of real peace.

I often look back on that day and marvel at the fact that I, at no point, felt scared. I had no fear. An emotion that had been my constant companion since I was a child left me alone. Leaving that previously filled space empty and available for more needed emotions. Good emotions were something I'd missed out on.

I suddenly became aware of my lack of those soul-feeding feelings. I had been in survival mode for as long as I could remember. I made a deal with myself then and there that I would never allow myself to be in such a deficit of food for my heart. Never again.

Those first few weeks were pretty great. Like a dream sequence that kept going on and on. After so long of my life running me, I didn't know what to do with myself. No schedule, no boss, no appointment to keep or people to take care of. Nobody to answer to. Whew! Just, wow. I was having to learn to live on my own and for myself. Without a doubt, the most difficult thing I have had to tackle. Taking back my own life.

I realize now that I actually fed on taking care of others. Doing for people. Acts of service were not only the way I expressed love but also how I got self-worth.

For me, if I did something that didn't affect someone else or didn't get verbal praise or a paycheck, then it went unnoticed and was therefore valueless. The only way I knew how to function or live was for someone else in one way or another. I had always been someone's daughter, sister, wife, or mother. My children had been the driving force behind every bad job or relationship I'd ever had and kept too long. My poor children carried the weight of my happiness and failures as well as success in every single thing I'd done since the age of seventeen. I never understood the responsibility I placed on them all of those years.

I stayed in unhealthy relationships for the financial ability to meet their needs, or so that someone would be home with them while I worked long hours. I kept one or more miserable, dead-end jobs so that I could provide for them. Not their fault; definitely mine. Definitely wrong on so many levels. I realize now that they really just needed me home more, or at the lease, not so damn miserable when I was.

Those initial days in Bali were filled with so much sleep. Food, music, learning, praying, doubting, anxiety, and hope—all at once. On top of the fact, I had stopped all medications, cold turkey.

That was a particularly difficult time in my life. The physical withdrawal was hell, but I survived. I realized that many of the mental obstacles I was having to overcome were effects of the medicine I'd been on. What I assumed were idiosyncrasies were really direct side effects of prescription narcotics. Narcotics that I'd been on since my late twenties. The agoraphobia and lethargy left me, and I slowly started to get my own mental and physical traits back. I gradually started coming out of the fog.

I got healthier and happier. With so much trash in my head from the past, it still amazes me that I didn't find the nearest cliff and jump to my death. I tried to only focus on succeeding and experiencing all of the new and wonderful things around me.

One week turned into a month, then two, then a year, and so on. I saved my own life by making those choices. The same way I'd broken my own heart so many times before, I was making the choice to repair myself. I did it with commitment and intent.

And so, I truly started to build a new life.

CHAPTER 33

I spent some time with Jack, but I spent most of my time traveling between multiple islands in Bali.

I met some amazing people and worked on developing new habits. I started to feel a true sense of self, but I still couldn't seem to plant my feet or commit to anything permanent. I felt restless. The compulsive urge to be busy is a difficult habit to break.

Regulating feelings after I had allowed medications to do that particular task for so long was challenging. My mind seemed to be in a constant state of repair.

Being busy all of the time is a trauma response; I know that now. I just did not want to slow down and think of all I had left behind in the States. Good and bad. Honestly, I was incapable.

Nervous energy and guilt still plagued me no matter where I was or what I was doing. It would take a very long time to get to a point that I wasn't looking over my shoulder. I was always on high alert when it came to protecting my newfound freedom and peace.

After four months exploring local destinations, I figured, why not just go a little further? I left Indonesia and embarked on a once in a lifetime travel journey. I set my sights on Southeast Asia that started in Vietnam.

I landed in Hanoi alone and a bit uneasy. It is an extremely busy metropolis stretched out as far as the eye can see. Highrise after Highrise. It seemed cold and sterile after living in Bali, but I was determined to give it a chance.

Again, I had no real plan. I just woke up each day, reviewed my options, and made a choice.

The thing I remember most about Hanoi is the smell. It always smelled of food. Shops line every street, and in the morning, large copper cauldrons filled with dumplings, soup, noodles, and rice portage are ready and waiting from the moment the sun rises. The smell laces the air all day, every day. It smells of onion, garlic, liver, and fish.

Walking down dirty, wet alleyways and little hidden streets. All laden with stray cats and dogs who feast on the scraps that are thrown just outside of doorways, solely for that purpose. Daily adventure.

It was surreal observing Vietnamese men or women dressed in traditional attire to include pointed straw hats tied under their chin, wide legged pants, shirts with large sleeves buttoned up to their neck, and their feet exposed in their sandals or flip-flops. All of them sturdy and strong, often carrying the common bamboo pole that ran across the back of their neck and across both shoulders. A basket dangling on either side containing fish or vegetables intended for sale or delivery to one of the many shop owners.

Clouds of steam coming from the restaurants and eateries hover and make your eyes burn and your mouth water. It is the everlasting visual representation in my mind of those days in the city.

Every few feet there is a place to sit down at a small plastic table and eat your breakfast, sometimes shared with a few others who are enjoying their breakfast as well. In between are the most amazing coffee shops.

Vietnamese are serious about their coffee, and so there is always a crowd and so many choices. Ranging from regular American coffee to espresso to the countries favorite traditional drip coffee, the options are endless.

Every day, I went to eat my morning meal of noodles in a thick chicken broth, usually accompanied by a steam roll filled with minced chicken or pork. Then I found a coffee shop to sit with the locals and watch the beginning of the day unfold. It was a literal feast for all of my senses. I still recall the sights and scent as if it was only yesterday.

The people are generous and accommodating. They work hard and play equally as hard. They seem to have an urgency while performing both.

Smiles are not as easy to come forth, but when they give into them, they are genuine. There was never a moment when one was annoyed at my presence, and in fact, every single national I met went out of their way to show me kindness.

They are a curious group and have no qualms about voicing their curiosity. Every single Vietnamese man and woman are filled with such pride for their country, especially their local cuisine. I was constantly being offered food. They truly love to share, and their hospitality has no limits. It seemed that I never stopped eating.

Although a bit crude in mannerism in the way they accomplish certain tasks, I found them exceptional and beautiful. I quickly developed a sincere affection for them.

I toured Vietnam for two months. Taking in the sights of Da Nang, Hoi Ann, Saigon (Ho Chi Man), Bah Nah Hill, and all of the little towns and countryside in between. I met and befriended a lovely family there that I became quite close with, and we still stay in contact. I even went back to see them a year later.

From Vietnam, I crossed over into Cambodia.

Oh, Cambodia! The Cambodian vibe is one-of-a-kind, and I will carry that country in my heart the rest of my life. It is unequivocally one of my all-time favorites.

I started in Kaoh Tansey (Rabbit Island). I spent a month just lying on the white sand beach. My hut was a few feet from the ocean and invited rest and reflection.

Electricity was only used on the island a few hours a day, so many of the things that would normally consume anyone's time were not an option. Phones were put away, and the sun, water, animals, children, and food were enjoyed to an extent I don't think would have been possible in any other surroundings. That island is a dream.

I could walk the entire perimeter in a little over two hours, and I did frequently. Only one side was inhabited. The one along the shoreline facing the mainland of Cambodia; it faced the town of Kemp.

The island boasted three beautiful deserted beaches. I arose early, had my host make my lunch, and took off for the day to explore. Crystal clear water that went on forever. All meals served were basically fresh food caught from the waters around the island. The bottom of the ocean is filled with starfish ranging in color and size, the largest being as big as a small car tire. At night, the algae along the rocks and coral glow. It gave the appearance that someone had broken a glow stick and left the fluorescent liquid all over everything in its wake.

Little lean-to were set up along the beach for massages, and I made sure to get one almost every day. I relaxed into a version of me that I didn't know was possible.

I started waking up early, having my coffee, and not even considering my phone or social media. I read, I ate, I swam and snorkeled. I began to be alive. What I didn't realize then is that I was learning how to live in the moment.

The local Buddhist monks used the island for their holiday retreats. As a result, I often found myself in the midst of a group of robed holy men. The conversation and shared opinions of those cherished days will never be far from my thoughts. It has forever changed the way I perceive and interact with the world around me.

Cambodian monks are the most kind, gentle, and conscientious group of people I have ever had the pleasure of spending time with. Possessing so much social curiosity. Epitome of love and compassion;   representation   of enlightenment.

They possess a calm strength I could never get enough of, and while there, I fed off of their energy. Some days I did nothing else but spend the day within a group of them, floating in the ocean on inner tubes, on the beach, or in a circle just having whatever conversation their broken English could provide; sometimes sharing a meal.

They are amazing humans who sparked a curiosity in me that I still possess. I wanted their knowledge on all things. Especially concerning meditation and anything that would help me acquire the sense of peace that seemed to radiate from them. They never tired of passing on what they knew to my hungry and inquisitive mind. To my new friends, no question was a negative one.

One of my favorite memories of my time there is one I still fondly recall almost daily.

Along the whole shoreline, down one side of the island were primitive huts. These were the ones tourists and visitors, as well as the island natives, stayed. Just in front of those were a line of gazebos. Made from bamboo and topped with palms. Spaced evenly, every few feet, they gave the island the look of a simpler time long forgotten.

No steal or manufactured materials in sight. A few feet off of the ground, each one was equipped with a hammock on all four sides. They were enticing and charming.

So many hours of my life were spent in those hammocks, swaying back and forth, my book or a pina colada in hand, while a breeze rolled over the top of the water and brought in the moist, salty air.

I watched the sun rise and set under the protective leaves of the palmed canopies, just enjoying the sound of the waves. Often times I ate my meals in them. Islanders laid their children down for naps in them, and at nightfall, some even secured a mosquito net around one and slept in them. They were perfect.

One day, I woke up to hammering and went out to see the islanders who owned my village erecting a new one. I enjoyed my coffee while observing a lone man diligently hand-cutting each plank and beam for the floor of the structure.

As the day progressed, I noticed that other inhabitants of the island randomly showed up to help. Periodically, he was joined by a couple of men who would just slip into helping him. There was no conversation or requests for their help; they just knew it needed to be done and came on their own to lend support. Men of all ages randomly walked up and, without comment, fell in beside him with diligent, considerate work.

By the end of the second day, there were four men. By the third day, folks had roamed in and out of the project until it was completed.

As they worked, women from the island brought their children and watched them. They made food and drink and fed them. As soon as the last palm leaf was placed across the top, everyone who had taken part in the construction gathered and grilled fish and ate. They all ate together and had beer. A kind of impromptu celebration of the task being completed.

What made that situation unique is that there was never a barter or conversation pertaining to the fact he even needed extra hands. They didn't ask or agree on any payment. They all seemed to just know what came next. He didn't have to.

These people did it willingly and without hidden motive or expectation. It is as if they felt it was a duty to their fellow man, and they did it with love and diligence. I still find it so amazing.

I spent the new year on that island. Fireworks could be seen from the mainland, and the explosions reflecting over the water were spectacular. It was the one day that there were many guests from all over the world. To include Russians, Chinese, and Koreans. I was always the only American. It is still baffling to me as to why Americans rarely choose to travel that part of the world, while I consider those places to be some of the most beautiful destinations I have ever seen. I am quite sure that not many places compare.

That island was in South Cambodia. After I left, I traveled north. I went on to see Kampot, Siem Reap, Phnom Pen, and any place in between I could manage.

I spent two days exploring ancient ruins in Angkor Wat, and I still, to this day, cannot recall anything more impressive. In Cambodia, I learned to use my voice *and* my silence. The things I saw there have left a lifelong impact on me. Those are poor people with the most serving and caring hearts.

I became more aware of the need in our world for kindness and genuine camaraderie. I became someone I didn't know I could be—trusting.

I met another American there, and we traveled together for a while.

When a person sets out into the world alone for any length of time, they learn some pretty valuable things. The first being the ability to acknowledge fellow humans and appreciate them rather quickly. The game tends to get lost, and sincerity becomes vital. Friendships are formed so quickly and wholeheartedly. We, as travelers, never know how long we will be a part of each other's lives. Getting to know each other becomes direct and without the normal fear or apprehension. No time is wasted.

It is imperative. These relationships formed along the way. We teach each other what we have learned. Where to go, how to get there, what sights are worth seeing, what not to eat, and the social etiquette or acceptable way of doing things in each country.

Sometimes, if we are lucky, we meet other travelers who are headed the same way, and we travel together for a while. We part ways when one of the groups has a different plan or their holiday has ended.

Of course, mine was never-ending, so I was the one going on ahead without them. The people I met while traveling those months created some of the best memories of my life.

After Cambodia, I went on into Laos. Laos is saturated with customs, ancient temples, recreation, and waterfalls. It is, without a doubt, the most untouched country I have been to date. Rugged terrain and the most gorgeous cliff sides, lakes, and waterfalls I have ever had the pleasure of seeing. The Mekong River runs alongside and through it, making it easy to get from one place to the other. Overnight canoes and fishing boats are common, and it is a lazy excursion to get on one of them and wind in and out of the mountains, staying in fishing villages along the way.

The Buddhist monasteries are a common part of the overall culture, vibe, and scenery and dot the hillsides and valleys.

Every morning at 4:30 am, local monks lined up down the main street of every city or town and came in a procession to collect alms. We all stood and handed them their rice or porridge, and they in turn prayed and blessed each one of us. It was magical indeed.

I made my way to Phonsavan, walked through the famous Plane of Jars, and spent a few days taking in the mountain air and enjoying the French architecture. Then on to Luang Prabang, Vang Vieng. Each place was warm and inviting. The people are not used to visitors, especially American ones, so it was a different experience than any I had had before.

I zip-lined through jungles, tubed through caves, swam in fluorescent blue waterfalls, bathed elephants, and ate strange cuisine. I consider this the calming-down period of my traveling. In a country such as Laos, there aren't any major tourist attractions in the true sense of the word.

It is a country that is more suited to the taste of someone on a spiritual self-discovery journey, and I was. If a person couldn't see the inspiring beauty around them or longed for a more mainstream adventure, I can see where the novelty of Laos would be lost to them. Fortunately, I was ready for the experience and relished every single second of the crumbling ancient temples and untouched landscape. It was truly an eye-opening experience for me.

It taught me that all of the extras we work for and surround ourselves with, we really do not need. It is wasted time to invest in material objects. These were by far some of the happiest people I have ever met, and they literally owned nothing of what the world would consider great value. They placed value on things that I had come to take for granted.

A trip like this one should change anyone's perspective. Their simple lives revolve around the essential things, such as family, health, and God.

The rest just seemed to be extra, and so they are the most appreciative and loving people I have ever encountered. It truly set my mind on a new path, one of inner self-discovery. Becoming less focused on material things and more about my mark as a human.

Even now, I must keep reminding myself that illegal does not mean immoral. It allows me to ease up on my guilt enough to create the person I am meant to be. A happy one, a loving one, a better one.

From Laos, I took a boat into Thailand. I spent weeks taking trains through that remarkable country. I set my sights on Pai, to include a Hmung long-neck village I knew was close to the town.

It is set deep down in a valley surrounded by rolling hills. My pace had slowed down; I was more adventurous and less prone to fear and anxiety. The food was delicious, the people warm and friendly, and the scenery was some of the most beautiful I have ever laid eyes on. It was a stark change from the two previous untouristed countries, but oh, so beautiful.

While traveling by motorbike up a steep mountain on my way to Pai from Chang Mai, I had an accident and had to hang out long enough to heal before I could continue my journey. Pai was the perfect place to do so. It was as if I had been dropped off in a village from a century ago. I learned yoga and meditation techniques. Meditation has had a huge impact on my life.

When I left Pai, I went to Siam (Bangkok) and caught a flight home to Bali. But I didn't stay. After two months, I continued my travels. I went to a few more continents and then eventually back to Bali for six months. The longest frame of time I had sat in one place since leaving the United States.

I settled in a small town up in the hill country called Ubud.

One day, as I finished up my meal in a small cafe, temple was starting. Hindu is the main religion in that region of Indonesia. The streets were full of men and women dressed in their temple attire. Consisting of colorful lace galabias for the women and traditional shorter skirts for the men, with their signature short cotton head wrap.

I observed a procession of Balinese women holding their containers of food in ornate gold pots. The women transport the larger ones on top of their heads, which is common for the culture. The children were dressed to attend as well. As I watched them, it started to rain.

Everyone I saw that day, including the children, looked the same way. The corners or their mouths turned up slightly. When I smiled, they smiled back, bowed or nodded. They greeted each other,

"Hello brother."

The air was pungent with incense, that made small clouds along the path. Add the smell from the street food vendors and the rain, and it was truly one of a kind; Unforgettable.

I remember as I walked to my apartment, I realized that I'd been smiling all day. I was calm. I was not waiting for the next thing in my life. The next purchase, the next engagement, or the next man. I didn't have the feeling of waiting on anything. I was simply left with a wonderful sense of belonging and gratitude. I felt saturated in love and peace.

People often ask me what it is like to travel these places alone.

I will answer by saying that I go to each country with no expectations. I go humble and respectful. I get welcomed into each new culture after a while. In retrospect, I can actually pinpoint the moment I became accepted into each one.

For instance, while in Cambodia, I was on the island for many weeks. Somewhere around the fifth week, the family on the island brought me some of their dinner and invited me to a birthday party that evening. That was the moment I was accepted into their circle. It is truly one of the most amazing feelings.

At that point, we were all just human beings sharing a meal. Learning and loving each other. It is one of the single most gratifying feelings I have ever had.

It is not just a meal; it is human mingling of our souls. You don't need to talk. You just understand, appreciate, and validate one another.

When I left the island, the matriarch of the family grabbed my face, and with both of us crying, she said to me in broken English,

"You are good; you can come live with our family on our island, and we will build you a bungalow in the jungle. Please come back."

Then she kissed both my cheeks. A truly beautiful, heartfelt moment that will live with me forever.

Another question I get asked is how I can afford my travel.

I get a very small early retirement check monthly. When I need to, I write content or edit for an online company. Somehow, I just make it work.

I travel to the cheapest countries and have stayed in some fairly questionable hotels, hostels, and homestays. I have used equally scary modes of transportation, such as local buses, trains, and tuk-tuks. On two occasions, I've been robbed. Once at a money exchange in Hanoi, the other by a fellow travel companion in Laos. I have had dengue fever and COVID-19, and several medical and dental procedures. There were a few times that I ran out of money and stayed with farmers to help them plant or harvest rice. Taking care of animals or children in exchange for my food and lodging.

These have been character-building experiences for me, and I'm not embarrassed or ashamed for any of it. I've enjoyed each interaction and the possibilities they've allowed me. I have restored faith in people. I somehow feel connected again to the human race. It has been worth every risk and the occasional adverse experience.

Each moment of each day I see as an opportunity to better myself and release some of the pain and damage I've held onto for way too long. It has given me a sense of direction, even though I never know which direction I'm going. I can't completely explain it. It seems that once the leash was taken off of me, everything became an adventure. Even daily mundane things are exciting to me. The chance to learn and to grow is never ending now, and not tainted with past failures.

A person's brain is their own. They're born with it and all of its imperfect emotional and psychological make-up. It is the hand you have been dealt. You can do all of the right stuff, to include all of the things that are supposed to keep it healthy and functioning properly, but at the end of the day, you're still left with the deficiencies you are prone to have. Simply put, you are still going to have to battle who you are. There is no way around it; it's just the way it is. An almost daily fight with who you want to be, the way you want to think or feel, versus the way you *actually* do.

You can look at that as an obstacle, or you can look at it like a challenge. Either way, you must look at it.

Just be sure to remember that other people's opinions should never mar or change your opinion of yourself. It isn't your onus to please the people you are surrounded by. It is, however, detrimental to come to an understanding and decide realistically what you expect from yourself.

My realistic expectations for myself started in Southeast Asia. This has been a journey of self-love and personal discovery, reflection, and tolerance. The lessons have been a slow, deliberate unlearning of all the unhealthy ways I had learned to cope and survive. The amazing people I've met along the way have healed me. The way people should. I was just unaware of the process and how it was meant to work.

We heal by love. Whether that is by strangers or family and friends, it doesn't matter. As long as compassion is given and returned and love is felt, it can truly transform you.

Sometimes unknown humans are the best source; I am living, breathing proof of this fact.

In February 2020, after six months of being in one place, I left Bali for Egypt. I was restless and in search of an adventure. I got way more than I had ever hoped or dreamed.

CHAPTER 34
Rerouting

I have been in Egypt for one year and two months.

It feels like home; I feel connected to the people and the country as a whole. Yet, I know in my heart it is time to move forward. It seems that I have much time to make up for.

I will be moving to London in just a few short weeks. Leaving the only source of comfort and security I have had in several years. I have truly, without a doubt, discovered my inner strength and peace in Egypt, and it will be difficult and emotional to leave. But I know I must. Getting too comfortable would alter the future I'm working towards.

I am convinced that each time a person chooses the safe route, they lose a little bit of their life and what it should be. With each adventure passed up ending in a pile of regret and unlived moments. All because of the fear of the unknown. I choose not to be that person any longer. So, I must go.

Almost three years ago, I made up my mind to leave the United States. I've been traveling ever since. Many countries, beautiful experiences.

Indonesia, Vietnam, Cambodia, Laos, Thailand, Denmark, South Korea, Malaysia, Singapore, UK, and Egypt. If I include long layovers, I have been to and through many more. My goal was ten countries in three years; I did that in less than two.

I'm asked often if I have a favorite, and truthfully, I do not. However, the ones I have the fondest memories of tend to be the countries that made me the most uncomfortable in my growth as a human.

I have spent most of the last year grounded because of the global pandemic. I have had to put my travel plans on hiatus. As places start to open up, I will continue my explorations. I will continue appreciating this planet, as well as learning from and loving the people who inhabit it. Just me, my laptop, and my backpack.

I go into these countries as a guest. I come into their nation as a visitor. A traveler. Their politics and beliefs are none of my business. So, I mind my own.

Every place I've been has been humane to each other and very accepting of my western ways and questions. I have at no point felt in danger or disrespected, and in fact, I've felt much safer in my travels than in my own country.

With each new place, I do a bit of research and go in knowing what is expected of me. This gives me the ability to loosen up later if I need to on certain things. I go in to submerge myself in the culture, not to stand out as a tourist.

I have completely different experiences than people on a short holiday. I very rarely stay in touristy spots or go with tour groups and generally choose to stay away from those areas and travel alone. My travel habits are financially necessary and methodical.

I don't judge. I do not feel American ways are better. I've never been of the opinion that a whole culture of people is bad because of the actions of some. In turn, they don't assume the worst of me from what they have heard or news they receive. I assure you, there is evil everywhere.

I am American. Even with my past, I'm proud of my home state of Texas. I am proud of my relationship with God, as I see and feel him, and as my soul and understanding allow me to. I thank the universe that I was raised in an unbiased atmosphere that encouraged me to seek the truth and understanding of my own personal God. I am not and will never be so vain as to believe that we are the only folks on the planet to have figured it all out. We are all humans sharing a planet who have each killed in the past using belief in our perception of God as an excuse.

We are going the wrong way. We are here to love, help, and understand one another.

I know there are countries that appear to be barbaric; I've not traveled those. So, until I experience firsthand how those people behave, I'll not comment on it.

I will say that I've spent most of my time in Asia, where Muslims, Hindus, Buddhists, and Christians, along with many other belief systems, live side by side in happy harmony. I have many Muslim friends, men and women. The marriages are similar to Christians. The main difference being that they drop to their knees five times a day to pray to *one* God, and they don't throw pork on the grill at the weekend barbecue.

I am not afraid of differences. I will not be afraid of other humans or other cultures. I welcome the new knowledge and the opportunity to learn, love, and grow.

I wouldn't trade these years for anything in the world. I am not in any way the same person I was when I started this journey. I'm not scared of the unknown anymore.

I'm not waiting for something or someone to make me feel happy; I have found that in myself. I've learned to graciously let go of things and people who are not meant for me.

And finally, I do not always have nightmares when I close my eyes for sleep. I am slowly forgiving myself and others, and it is making my soul lighter. I just keep putting one foot in front of the other every day. I try to love as hard as I can, and seek to understand all things that have made me who I am and brought me to this point in my life.

Remember Leo's speech in the movie Titanic? The one about having air in his lungs and being happy living and loving and appreciating everything he had from one day to the next? I understand that fully and completely now.

We are all part of the same family, put here to love and support each other. All cultures and walks of life deserve your time and attention long enough to try and understand them. It's all about learning selflessness, empathy, sympathy, and love. These are the only things that matter, carry any weight in this life, or follow you after. There is nothing more valuable. Not in day-to-day life while you are living, or in your memory after you're gone. So that—my friends—is where all my energy is going.

It doesn't matter if you're in Kampot, Cambodia, or Dallas, Texas. You can run all over every continent and to every edge of this beautiful planet, but you absolutely cannot outrun yourself. No matter which country you find yourself in. So, I had to make a choice.

I promised myself a year into this journey to focus on my personal growth and become the person I needed to be. I am content and amazed at the process that brought me here. I will never stop investing.

Last year, I made up my mind to write a book. As I write these final words, I'm reminded that it's come about because of the work I have done on my self-awareness. love, and tenacity. I will never give up. I am worth it; life is worth it.

I'm happy; no one has the key to that happiness but me. No one's approval is needed. I am proof of that. I don't need anyone for validation; neither do you. Sometimes singularly is the only way to find yourself and achieve your goals. If you can't find someone that matches your vibe, it's perfectly okay to walk alone. It's more than okay.

I will not settle for anything less than what I deserve. Finally.

Ignore negative people, and do what you need to. Stay true to yourself. Have faith. Have hope. Don't ever give up. Do not settle. Stay sweet and compassionate. Love unconditionally. Give back with money as well as deeds. Live a life you are proud of. Be strong. Be brave. Be loving.

Mostly, learn to recognize the small things and appreciate them. Life isn't always fair, but that doesn't mean that you don't need to be.

Learn to forgive. Learn to forgive yourself. Love everyone with all you have. Live through the experience no matter how hard it is, and love yourself enough to let go.

Believe me, you are worth loving. You deserve happiness, and so do I.

EPILOGUE

I arrived for the second time in the United Kingdom two weeks ago. I already miss Egypt, but I'm lucky enough to have a piece of that country right here with me.

As I sit across the room from Adham in his small flat watching him nap, my mind is trying to make sense of the last few years.

I'm overwhelmed with memories and all that has happened in such a short period of time. The unique and sometimes erratic circumstances that have brought me here. How am I even the same person I was when I left the United States? What is the defining difference that enables me to sit in front of this window, watch the rain, and feel peace and hope? So much needs to be relayed in these last words, and I'm battling to get my thoughts in some kind of collective order.

Immediate thoughts go to what is in front of me. This man happened to cross my path at the exact time I needed him to. Do I love him? Yeah, I guess I do. Am I in love with him? I don't know, and I'm in no hurry to be certain.

There is so much more to explore, and it will take time. I will let this unfold slowly and enjoy every single second of the process. That is my gift to myself after all of these years of rushing through life. I will allow myself the luxury of just being a part of something with no known outcome. Attachment is something I can't afford in the type of life I've created for myself. I am learning. I will take things as they come. Good and bad; it's life.

I am no longer of the opinion that love is somehow a free fall into bliss. I now believe that it is a carefully orchestrated and controlled event. One that we can manipulate or quit at any time. Love is an intentional endeavor between two people who are absolutely sure that they want it.

They invest in one another equally and with earnest for the want of a common outcome. And it's when that endeavor ceases to be conducive to our emotional or mental well-being that one should consider walking away. It makes the whole process a bit sweeter to let go of preconceived notions. Knowledge comes from experience, and this one time, I have no desire to rush it.

As lovely as our relationship is, I have to be realistic. Adham is young and will eventually want a wife and children. It's no secret that what we have is temporary. We both understand and accept that. It doesn't mean the feeling of care is not forever, but the relationship we now have cannot be.

We are happy apart and share joy when together. He is not my reason for my new-found contentment, but rather a part of the whole collective picture. I'm not dependent on him, nor is he to me. This is genuine care and amity, and it is eye-opening and beautiful.

When it comes to the realization someone is not going to be a lifelong part of my story, I have a choice. I can either run away to save myself the inevitable pain, or I can draw closer to them to enjoy every second. I have decided to draw closer. It has proven to be a worthy endeavor.

Success in a relationship is not counted in how long a person is a part of my life, but instead, how well love was expressed. Together, we seem to be good at the sharing and expressive part. Pressure would only lessen its value, and that would be waste.

No matter what happens, I've made the choice to keep involving myself in this, and in the end, I will accept consequences. As long as I'm able to give and receive love, I am living.

Things move in and out of a person's life so damn quickly. We all have to decide daily what to let go of and what to keep. What we hang onto has significant consequences with what and when it's replaced. The outcome is always up to each of us and our choices.

I should have whiplash from all of the plot twists in my life. Adjusting and learning healthy ways to deal with those have been the most difficult lessons for me.

I have learned more in the last three years about who I am and what makes me happy than I have in all of the years previous combined. I will not deviate from what I know to be fact. I will not accept anything that doesn't feed my soul and mind. In any aspect. This has become the key to my healing and happiness. This is what gives me hope.

Thinking back to the lovers I've had; I am of the opinion that each one was worth it. I have no regrets for any of them, to include my three husbands. Even if I consider the damage they caused.

I still speak with a few of the leading men in my life. I have absolutely not one ounce of space in my heart for anger, resentment, or blame. In reviewing them now in my mind, they each had some wonderful qualities. I tend to focus on those.

Although some memories are naturally filled with pain, I won't let that dominate my overall opinion of the men I chose to give parts of myself to or share my life with. I hope that each one is living a happy, healthy, and worthwhile life. Especially Conor. He couldn't help his illness, and that must be its own kind of hell. His heart is a good one, and he deserves some peace and love.

Everyone has their own battles. I am not one to judge or try to figure out the motives in anyone's decisions. It's all in the past.

What I can focus on is what each one gave me. Each one loved me in the way they were capable of. I am sure of that. Every single person I have had contact with, or shared time with, has made me who I am. Not just the men.

I can eat with chopsticks because my mother used to take me to eat Chinese food as a treat when I was a kid, and she taught me how. I enjoy wine because my second husband introduced me to it. I like a certain perfume because my best friend bought it for me when I was twenty. I cut my salad into little pieces and eat it with a spoon, because of Adham, and I bake cookies on foil because Nina taught me that particular life hack when I was seven.

I'm a writer because my 6th grade teacher encouraged me to write. I like some music and movies because my children or others I loved, loved them first. I am made up of the influence that every single person I've ever cared for has given me. Even the ones who weren't permanent, and it's a beautiful testament to the impact others have on us as we journey through life.

We absorb, learn, and become from other souls. Each person I've had in my life has added to who I am. They have molded me, guided me, taught me, and developed me. For that, I will always be grateful.

Few people from my past are left in my life.

The ones that have stayed, I appreciate.

I hear from my cousin Misty quite often, and occasionally, my mom and sister. Lacy is doing well and now gives her time and energy to God and charity work for addicts and the less fortunate. I talk with Scott on occasion, and a few of my cousins on my mom's side reach out to me on social media. Periodically I catch up with my childhood friend Jack, and I still speak with Marsha a few times a year. I can't dwell on the ones I no longer have a connection with.

The most difficult part of the last few years has been missing my children. They are all adults now, and each one has their own opinion on whether I was a good mother or not. Depending on their mood, what day it is, and which one you choose to ask.

They are all productive members of society, and I am lucky in that each one of them is a good person with a good heart. They are all strong and loving. If I were to judge my parenting skills based on that fact alone, I would say I was successful. I am pleased. I speak with them all by video chat or phone call; some more than others. All except for Dean. He's chosen to stay away from me these years, and as heartbreaking as that still is, all I can do is understand and respect his decision.

I've come to the conclusion that no mother is ever worthy enough or ready to have children. No matter how prepared they believe themselves to be. Our parents are still trying to get over their parent's failures, just like their parents before them. Young minds don't take into account the fact that they are just living and learning along with us. Most of it is new to both parties.

I think the same goes for my mom and me; we grew up together in many ways. I didn't know how to be a daughter any more than she knew how to be my mother.

We don't speak as often as we should since I left. I wish that she was a more prevalent part of my life so that I could tell her that I forgave her for what she didn't know and that I am grateful for what she did. She deserves sincere thanks for the fact her effort and love were always there. I hope my daughter and sons can and will forgive me for my shortcomings someday. I am hopeful that they will eventually understand.

This is life. Joyous, painful, mundane, exciting, meaningful, frivolous, new and old. Both exhausting and renewing. Real life includes failures and triumphs, love and loss without reason, and crippling pain and humiliation. It's fast. This life goes by so fast. It is weeded with regret, hate, animosity, confusion, and jealousy at times; it is all just part of being human.

Choose love. Choose to forgive yourself and others. By making that choice every day, you are choosing to live. By actively choosing this, you are becoming brave. More than that, you're choosing to be a part of the energy and compassion that will be passed on to our future generations in this cycle on this Earth and beyond. For that, you *must show up every day*. Empathy and sympathy are everything. Karma is real, whether you believe it or not. It is real and has a specific job in our lives. Karma's pain is what it takes to get the knowledge we need to stop the cycle.

Feel the pain. Wipe your face, and get through it. The sun will come out again. You will find your peace again. It is a privilege to be a part of this process. No matter what road you're on.

Three years ago, I was a wreck. I was sad, exhausted, stuck in the endless set-up for failure legal system, and I had zero hope for any kind of mental, physical, or emotional recovery from trauma or addiction. I was on a litany of prescription medications, and all I could think about was taking all of them at once so I didn't have to wake up and feel loss or pain any longer.

I worked constantly and still couldn't pay my bills. I lived in a town that never gave me a chance to prove myself or gave me credit for the steps I'd taken to turn my life around and stay out of the system. I was done.

All of that changed when I decided I had nothing to lose and left.

It hasn't been all puppy dogs, magic moments, and rainbows. It's been hard, lonely, and sometimes impossible to see a future past the pain, loss, betrayal, and resentment.

I am now almost fifty-three years old. I've been clean of pharmaceutical medications for the last three of those. I have a job writing that I love, and a few friends I've met on this road of rediscovery that I completely trust. I work out; I have turned to holistic medicine. Meditation and being alone bring me peace.

I still have a long way to go, but I see a happy future for myself for the first time since 1993. I'm grateful. I have been given a second chance to become a happier, more loving, empathetic, and healthier me.

If someone wants rid of something as badly as I did, they must do whatever they need to do to save themselves. If you want it enough, you have to make it happen. No one else is going to save you. Your family deserves you the way you are supposed to be. Happy, healthy, and alive. If you don't do it for yourself, do it for them. Before you run out of time.

From my experience, advice is stupid. Mainly because what works for one person doesn't necessarily work for the other. Someone needs to be open enough to receive advice and then apply it to their own life. Which is often unrealistic.

I've found that advice from someone who has screwed up more in their lives to somehow hold more truth than from someone who hasn't. That said, there are a few key things I have learned that I do feel the need to pass on. We won't call it advice, but rather a few words of wisdom.

Don't listen to someone's words. Instead, pay attention to the look in their eyes when you first see them. Initially, the fleeting look someone has in their eyes will say exactly how they feel about you. How they perceive you. You must look quickly before their natural instinct to hide behind a mask of mediocrity takes over. The eyes are indeed the window into the soul; they cannot lie. Sometimes actions and words do.

Is there light in their eyes or joy upon seeing you? Are they receiving you in all of your glory or sometimes not so favorable self? Are you in the habit of reciprocating?

The way we give ourselves out each day, the exchange, is the most important. Work on that skill. Receiving someone's attention and listening, even when you have nothing to gain. Especially when they aren't your crush or they can't do anything for you.

Do they feel safe? As a friend, as a lover, as your child or sibling. If not, you're failing. You are inadvertently contributing to their failure too. The thing people need the most to feel valid is to be heard. We all need to be seen, heard, and when possible, understood. Being mindful and present in the moment is encouragement in itself. Sometimes it doesn't matter why a person is hurting; it only matters that they are.

When you aren't around, when you're gone from this planet, this is the only thing people will recall. Did they feel loved by you? Could they feel safe enough to love you? Was it an even exchange? If this is the case, every second of every day we should strive to hold up our end of this bargain. The human exchange. Nothing in this life defines us more than our ability to give and receive love.

Make a point in your life to live with intent. Intention is what it takes to make dreams come true and keep the demons at bay. Relax and enjoy this journey; but don't ever get so relaxed you're lazy about it. It takes energy and focus to create a life you can be proud of. Let things flow, but do not, under any circumstances, let your life run you. Always explore all options and possible outcomes to make an informed decision, do the work, and then trust and let it go. Rest.

When things get really bad, always remember not to make permanent decisions based on a temporary circumstance.

One of the quotes that's gotten me through the last few years is simple:

"Cry standing up."

Meaning: Things are always going to get bad in one way or another; it's just a part of life on Earth. Pain is inevitable. Sometimes it's a direct consequence of your actions; sometimes you are just the casualty in someone else's war. Either way, it's okay to hurt. It is okay to cry; it is okay to have a meltdown or whatever the pain brings. But do it *standing*. That way, after it's over, you can continue your walk. Keep walking forward. Keep moving in a forward direction. Never let it get you completely down. Feel it, acknowledge it, and process it; just do not *live* in it. Don't let it become so much a part of you that it changes your mindset and keeps you from seeing a better future.

I'm not sure where I will be in a year, who I will be surrounded by, or even what country I'll call home. I have seven years left on my passport to figure it out. As much as my over-thinking mind wants to dwell on the fact that I have no concrete plans for my own future, I have accepted the fact that there is no way I can possibly have all of the answers right now. All I can do is continue healing, try to become the best version of myself that I can, and always live each day with gratitude that I have this opportunity. The rest will work itself out.

It's taken me all of these years to learn to live each day as it comes. For the first time in my life, I'm living for myself. I will live and enjoy each moment. I will live in the now. I get to choose who I allow into my life and who I will share myself with. The past is something I can finally put to rest.

Everyone can decide on their own if I am a bad or good person. Whatever conclusion you or anyone draws from my story, won't affect me. This is my journey; it's my path and my mistakes, no one else's.

I will live it in my own truth, with newfound peace and appreciation. I finally like me. That fact alone has made all of this worth it.

After all, I am just a soul living a human experience. We all are.

***

(cue the ending credits music)
THE IS ME *from the movie*
THE GREATEST SHOWMAN.

Acknowledgments:

This manuscript was truly a five-year cathartic purge.

Special thanks to the staff at SHARKS BAY UMBI DIVING RESORT in Sharm El Sheikh Egypt. Who started out as strangers, and ended as extended family. This Author will forever be grateful for your kindness and patience in answering my endless questions. To Krisi Morua for your diligence in reading each chapter as I finished and your never-ending faith in me, thank you. For the London group: David Ratajczak, Ania Kowalewska, Gosia Malgorzata, Andre Fomiciovas and Niko. For their unwavering support and input, thank you. To Ase Kolsboe Lejbolle; without your love and friendship I wouldn't have finished this work. To Marianna Coppola, Laura Coppola, and Mariam. To Hala Ahmed, Osama, Omar, Bebo, Laila, Misty Engfer, Riyaz Delilkhan, Tracey Farris, Scott Binkley, Trish Carr-Buchanan, David A., Johnatan Capalera, Lee and Kimberly

McGovern, Enrique Gomez, Rafiq Kiswani, Omar from Aussie, Capt. Abdelrhman, and Giang Tien and her beautiful Vietnamese family; For more friendship and love than could have ever been expected, THANK YOU. And finally, to Sharon Harrison, the first person to read the book. Without your encouragement it is doubtful it would exist. And for my mom. I love you.

Look for these other titles

from Jamie Lee Carrie

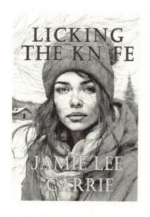

Made in the USA
Coppell, TX
06 January 2025

42354878R20270